NO VILLAIN NEED BE

NO VILLAIN NEED BE

Vardis Fisher

1936

THE CAXTON PRINTERS, LTD.
Caldwell, Idaho
and
DOUBLEDAY, DORAN & COMPANY, INC.
Garden City, New York

PRINTED AT THE *Country Life Press*, GARDEN CITY, N. Y., U. S. A.

FIRST EDITION

To

DON LEWIS

'Tis morning: but no morning can restore
What we have forfeited. I see no sin:
The wrong is mixed. In tragic life, God wot,
No villain need be! Passions spin the plot:
We are betrayed by what is false within.

GEORGE MEREDITH

PART ONE

MAY 24, 1914

He had been turning corners, seeking a long road that would climb the sky. The old dread was with him, it would go with him; but he would conquer it. He would fight all his life to conquer it. And here, where none could see, he fell to his knees and made a vow. He made a vow to himself. "I promise myself," he said, "that I'll conquer fear. I'll fight and fight until I can laugh, too, and be glad. I will, I will, so help me, God!"

NELOA was dead. Vridar had seen her lying very queenly and still in a white gown; had knelt by her, whispering her name, and had kissed her cold eyelids and cheeks and hands; and had filled his pockets with her lovely hair. He had seen her enter a blazing furnace and had heard the iron door close. But he did not believe that she was dead. All this, he reasoned, his mind delirious and his world broken, had been a bitter jest. She and Mertyl had plotted this awful nightmare to chasten him and she was alive somewhere and she would come to him again. Deep within him, like a heart deep within its flesh and beating there in agonized expectancy, was this belief: with him when he walked the streets, uncertain of where he was or of what he did; and with him when he slept, drugged with veronal, and dreamed.

And when, in lucid moments, he knew she was dead, he turned despairingly to some power, some certainty, that might support him in this crisis. There was only one. Like Carlyle he had worshiped heroes: the great men of the past who had suffered and fought and won: not the Cromwells who murdered for the Lord; not the Napoleons and Cæsars of earth. His devotion had been given to quiet men of great courage and incorruptible minds: to Socrates and Spinoza, to Shelley and Keats. And in this crisis, with nothing fixed in its own unalterable goodness, and with no philosophy, no idealism, that did not betray, he wondered if there was any-where on earth a person, a thing, a demonstrable fact, that was worth a spirit's martyrdom. There was no such person among his friends. For Dennis Altrock spiritual suffering was a meaningless term in the rhetoric of nonsense. Jake Arlow, the Jew, was closer in comradeship; but he was afraid of depth and intensity, and all his days were witty cynicisms hung against time. Mertyl was lost behind a sardonic leer that hid his pain.

If, Vridar reflected darkly, some person could place a hand on his shoulder and say, For twenty-nine years you have fought against odds but you will win. . . . You have tried to be generous and clean but all your ideals have betrayed you. You have gone in headstrong zeal from blunder to blunder like the fools of all ages whose hearts have ruled their minds. And now you are face to face with that agony which has been suffered by all the great creators of the past; of which Tolstoy wrote to Rolland: that purgatory of the soul through which Shelley passed, and Rossetti, and Meredith, and Carlyle. Go ahead now and make your fight. . . . But there was none to speak to him, and in these days he had no faith in himself. He would flee to Washington Park and hide there alone and write of himself in scathing abuse. . . .

> *All that I am, all that I've ever been,*
> *Is the sickly bridegroom of despair and sin. . . .*

And then with relief, with strange and peaceful quiet, he would plot his own death. He would put himself out of a world in which only the brave had a right to live. This thought was with him when, on the second day, he received the urn: a small thing of copper with bone dust on the lid. He held it to him and kissed it and his mouth was white with bone dust. This was Neloa, this small can of bone; this and the hair he had taken when she lay in the white gown; and nothing else remained. Of her vibrant womanhood, of all that he had known and loved, there was nothing anywhere save these and a little smoke in the sky.

And this thought was with him when his mother came for the children. She met him, white and trembling, her eyes asking one question.

"Son——?"

"Yes."

"I want to see where she lived."

And Vridar went with her and his sons and came to the back yard. They entered the yard and came to the silent and gloomy windows, with shades drawn; and Vridar's younger son, a lad of three, looked up at Prudence and said, "My mama doesn't live here any more." Vridar swung as if a knife had been driven to his heart and went away and hid. . . .

And the same thought had been with him when three days ago he and Mertyl had gone to meet Athene. They met her in Washington Park and for a long moment Vridar looked at her. And then:

"She's dead, Athene. She killed herself." He stared at her searchingly. If Athene had shown joy or any hint of triumph he would have walked out of her life. But Athene turned as white as death and she trembled as if he had struck her. She came to him very slowly and looked up at him and he saw intolerable anguish in her white mouth.

The same thought was with him in all hours, awake or asleep; and after Prudence had gone home, taking the children with her, Vridar went with Athene to the park. It was here in many a while that they had talked of courage and achievement and of what together they must do; but he hated the place now. He hated Athene and himself and everything on earth—everything but the urn that lay under the pillow where he slept. He was smoking cigarettes now. In this evening among trees hung with autumn loneliness he smoked one package and another; and he said:

"Athene, if I have been a coward I must kill myself."

"That would be cowardly. No matter what you have been, what mistakes you have made, you cannot do that."

"There is nothing else to do."

"There is everything. There are your sons. We must take care of them."

"But I can't go on without faith."

"Have you forgotten the poems of William Ellery Leonard?"

Vridar now thought of them. He had seen them a year ago in an edition privately printed and he and Athene had read them together. He remembered:

She opened . . . with a vision on her face,
And hands uplifted to immortal things,
And past me flew . . . upon her toilet case
An emptied glass with foam in awful rings. . . .

And he remembered, too:

We dare not think too long on those who died,
While still so many yet must come to birth.

"Yes," he said at last, "I remember. But he had friends with faith in him. We have none—none but Jake."

"It is enough if we have faith in ourselves."

"Faith in me, Athene? I'm a cowardly son-of-a-bitch."

"Vridar! It's cowardly to talk that way."

He bowed his head, his world swimming.

"Someone," he said. "If I had someone to see me for what I am. Someone to see me for what I am. Then I'd know what to do. Then I'd know if I'm only a coward and a fool. . . ." And in this hour, with his mind searching desperately, with his mind darkly wondering whether he would use poison or a gun, he thought of Thurman, the chairman of his department: that small man with the ageless face and the magnificent eyes.

"I know!" he cried, rising. Athene sprang up and grasped his arm.

"Vridar, please!"

"I know! I'll go to Thurman! I'll let Thurman be my judge!"

"Vridar, please try to be calm. We must think." She tried to draw him to the bench but Vridar shook her off and stood before her, trembling and white.

"I'll tell him everything, Athene! If he condemns me, then I'll know what to do!"

"Vridar, no. This is our problem."

"I'm going to Thurman!"

"Vridar, please don't! We must fight this thing out alone. We——"

"I'm going to Thurman," he said.

And with Athene crying after him he went swiftly through the park. When he reached the Midway he waited for Athene and she came running to him.

"Vridar, please! Let's talk it over first."

"No!"

"Vridar——"

"I'm going to Thurman and nothing can stop me!"

He grasped her arm and together they crossed the Midway and went south on a street. They came to the front door, and Vridar stood by it for a long moment with his whole body shaking. Then he pressed the bell. The housekeeper ushered them in, and they stood in a large room with books everywhere; and after a moment Thurman entered, his brilliant eyes an interrogation. "I'd like to see you," Vridar said, and Thurman waved them to chairs, and for a long moment there was silence.

"Professor Thurman, we're in trouble and you're the only person——" He broke off and looked at Athene. "Besides that," he said, "we think you ought to know."

Thurman's face was sympathetic. "Yes," he said. "How can I help you?"

Vridar hesitated again, feeling that his tragedy, his loss, when measured against the infinite sum of human heartache, was unimportant. Millions had come to such grief as this. Millions had suffered and died and had been forgotten; and in the eternal and changeless record of striving and defeat not even a footnote remained. In every year thousands killed themselves, and their only obituary was the sensational distortions of a tabloid.

"I don't want to weary you," Vridar said at last, "with
the story of my blundering life. I just wanted to tell you
that my wife has killed herself. Whose fault it is, I don't
know, we don't know. Athene and I tried to act with honesty and courage. And now—— Well, that's all. And we
don't know—I mean——"

"Now," said Thurman, "you reproach yourselves."

"This is what I mean," Vridar went on desperately. "If
the fault was mine I'm willing to take my punishment. But
I don't know what my punishment should be or what I
should do and so I came here. You're older and wiser. I
mean—I mean you can judge me. I'm not afraid. If——"

"I rather imagine," said Thurman, speaking quietly, "that
you are making too much of the matter. Very probably no
one is to blame. To reproach yourselves now for what is
done is rather futile and absurd, isn't it?" Thurman lit a
cigarette and when he spoke again his voice was throaty with
tobacco smoke. "What," he said, "are your plans?"

"To get out of Chicago first. I can't stay here."

"Very well. And then?"

"I don't know. I—I don't know."

"And Miss Marvell," said Thurman, looking at Athene,
"is going with you?"

"Yes." For a long moment shrewd gray eyes studied
Athene. "I don't know," said Vridar, again speaking desperately, "whether I should ever marry again. I mean
whether I should live alone. No one is ever happy with me."

Thurman smiled. "I don't imagine," he said, "that you're
the kind who can live alone. Some men can and some cannot. I think you cannot." Vridar pondered this summary
and did not speak. And Thurman said: "I have always been
rather dubious of marriage. For a few it seems to be all
right. For most persons it seems to lead to misunderstand-
ing and heartache. But I don't think you can live alone."

"I don't know," Vridar said.

And now Thurman rose and the gesture, Vridar knew,

dismissed him: not because this man was bored but because there was nothing more to be said. He came to the door with them and his good-by handclasp was that of a friend.

"Keep your courage," he said, "and your sense of irony. And write and tell me how you get along."

"Thanks," Vridar said, "and—and good-by."

They went down the street in silence and came to a bench.

"I love him," Vridar said. "He's a great man."

"Yes," said Athene, "and a great friend."

"Imagine how the pure in heart would have kicked us from their doors. I mean the believers in God. . . . Athene, what are we to do?"

"Go on. Be worthy of his confidence and—and worthy of—Neloa."

"Yes," he said; and he bowed to her lap and kissed her hands.

And for a little while in Vridar's life the faith of Thurman was like the presence of a strong friend. In this night he slept again, drugged with veronal; and on the next day he and Athene left this city for Baltimore. He was writing to Neloa now and out of anguish he poured the rimed and self-pitying unreason of his heart. His sonnets were terrifying in their violence; and when one was finished he would take it to Athene to learn if it had worth; and under her criticism he would sink to abject wretchedness. Because most of this that he wrote was not poetry: it was the dark madness of atonement, the effort of a stricken soul to purge itself. All day he wrote while journeying, and all night. He heaped upon himself bitter and unpitying abuse or he blasphemed God. Only once in this journey did he achieve clarity or make words say what was in his heart:

> If I have been a coward, let this be
> The curse upon me: make my path of stone

Where no life grows and none has ever grown,
And waterways lie empty to the sea.
And give me nothing good to call my own,
No friend, no pride, no faith. Abandon me
To an impotent vassalage of memory,
Unloved and unremembered and alone.

And after I am dead, leave me to rot
Where I have fallen; and let no one mark
The hair of Neloa within my hand.
Let no one curious find the lonely spot
And see my eyes and try to understand
The face of Neloa in the sightless dark.

Trembling in the emotion out of which these lines had come, he gave them to Athene.

"Is it any good?" He waited; and she read the sonnet again and again. She looked at him with grief bright in her eyes. "Is it?" he said.

"It's better than your others."

"You mean it's no good?"

"No, I don't mean that. The last three lines are good. The rest of it is neither good nor bad. The seventh line of the octave is weak. The eighth seems faintly to echo Scott."

"I'll never be a great writer," he said in despair. "I'll never be worth a hoot in hell."

"You will be a great writer some day. But, my dear, you can't write a great sonnet in ten minutes." Athene read again. "The first four lines of your octave are good. In the sextet the third line rather destroys the power of the last line. . . ." She turned suddenly and there were tears in her eyes. "Vridar, how can you expect me to be a critic of such a poem!"

And in Baltimore, after they had settled in two small rooms, Vridar spent hours in every day, in every night, trying to put into words the delirious heartache that was driv-

ing him mad. In two months he wrote to Neloa a hundred
and forty-seven poems and nearly all of them rang from end
to end with the desolation of his soul. But now and then in
a quieter mood he achieved something that Athene found
good.

> *You are dead now: but a short while ago*
> *Fell the year's roses, too,*
> *Deep around you, even as lovely,*
> *Neloa, as you.*

> *Things like me remain, ugly for living,*
> *While death uncloses*
> *To gather its choice of all that is most lovely:*
> *You and the roses.*

Or now and then, leaving a nightmare of sleep, he would
sit in darkness by a window and stare at the loneliness of
earth. In these hours his pain was hushed and there came to
him the faintly ironic intimations that were his only anchor
and strength. He would think of the millions of human
beings, striving like himself, blundering in one way and another as he had blundered; and he would be chastened for a
little while by a sense of fellowship; and he would see more
clearly the dark and ironic pattern of his life. And he would
write:

> *I can forgive the fraudulent ideal*
> *That has betrayed us: all the vulgar waste*
> *Of hope and prayer, for irony has erased*
> *Their unimportance and time now will heal.*
> *I see that we and life are but a reel*
> *Of obscene cinema wherein is traced*
> *Our small pathetic pilgrimage, debased*
> *By faith in gods that have no power to feel.*

But that you should go silent and alone
Down into death with scorn upon your brow,
Doubting I loved you and your love of me,
And leaving no way for love to reach you now:
This will I not forgive until I see
The last god gibbeted upon his throne!

II

●

DURING these weeks he was not aware that he ate or slept and he was hardly aware of Athene. Leaving his bed at daylight he would sit at his typewriter and work in furious haste until exhausted; and then he would walk the streets. He would go into the city and stand on a corner and gaze at the throngs of people, searching for Neloa's face; because he could not realize in spite of all his effort that she was dead. Somewhere, he would think, she lives and waits. Somewhere, sometime, I will find her. And he would enter buildings and hunt through department stores; go up and down the long streets, missing none; and stare at every window where he saw a face. Twice he thought he saw her and his blood leapt in bewildering rush and choked him; and once he thought he heard her call his name.

A river flowed through this city and close by his rooms it was spanned by a high bridge. It was more than a hundred feet from where he stood to a shoulder of rock below, and this rock he gazed at so often and so long that he knew every mark of it as he knew his own face. He visualized again and again every moment of his death and every emotion: of his standing poised on the side of the bridge, and of his plunge down, judged unerringly to bring him headfirst to the stone; and of what he would look like when persons found him there. This picture became so vividly real that, upon looking below, he could almost see his crushed body and blood on the rock. He could see the white faces of Athene and Mertyl; his stricken parents hurrying eastward to claim him; and his sons as orphans in a friendless world. And then he would shrink back, despising this wish to kill himself. He would stand here, thinking of thousands in every year who went deliberately to their death; the tens of thousands who wanted to and did not; and of himself formerly when he thought little of these tragic persons, noting only that this one and that, of strange name and strange dwelling place, had gone to their graves. He wondered about them now: their long struggle against odds, their heartache, their swift end; and the way he and millions had read about them and turned to another page, forgetting them in the moment the page was turned. For human life, after all, was a wearisome commonplace, and no one could be long interested in another's heartbreak and death.

If I were to kill myself, he thought, looking down at the stone, there would be a short notice in the Baltimore papers. A hundred thousand persons would read:

MAN PLUNGES FROM CHARLES STREET BRIDGE

Early this morning a Baltimore and Ohio switchman found on the river rocks a man who had leapt to his death from the bridge above. He has been identified as Vridar Hunter, until recently a graduate student in Midwestern University. His parents are in Idaho where Hunter was born. He has a brother in this city and a common law wife whose name is Athene Marvell. Both are mystified by the rash act. He seemed in good spirits when he set out at noon. . . . His parents have been notified and the body now rests in the Homeland Home for the Dead. . . .

Yes: a hundred thousand persons would read and yawn and turn the page. A husband, stirring his coffee, might say:

"Mary, just how many damned fools have jumped off that bridge anyhow?" And Mary, looking thoughtful, and wondering if Jimmie was washing his ears, would answer:

"Quite a few, it seems to me. We're always reading about them."

And in another home:

"It's just as well a lot of these persons kill themselves. The world is a lot better off without them."

"That's quite a jump, isn't it?"

"Damned if it isn't. He must have hit with an awful bang. . . ."

And so, in one home and another, the end of his pilgrimage would be summarized. Athene would sink in grief but in a few years she would find love again; Mertyl for a little while would be very grave and cynical; his parents would settle to a fixed and aching soberness of thought; and his sons would grow up in ignorance of both parents, saying, "We did not know them very well." And that was all. And if that is all, he thought, why shouldn't I do it? and he would look around him to see if anyone watched.

One person did watch him but Vridar stood here in every day for a month before he became aware. It was only little by little that the constant presence of this policeman drew his attention and aroused his suspicion; whereupon, believing that he was spied on, he studied the man until his belief became a certainty. He was annoyed and he went to the officer and spoke.

"You watch me here on this bridge. Tell me why."

"What do you mean?"

"Just what I say. Why do you watch me when I come to this bridge?"

For a long moment the officer studied him.

"Why," he asked, "do you come here?"

"To look at the river. Is there anything strange in that?"

"There might be. Why do you spend so much time looking at the river?"

"Because I have nothing else to do. . . . But you haven't answered me."

"I know why you come here."

"Why?"

"Because you're planning to kill yourself."

"I—how—how did you know?"

"I haven't been a policeman thirty years for nothing."

"But I—— Tell me: do I act strange?"

"You act so I know what you're up to."

"And you don't want me to? Why should you care?"

"Oh, mebbe I don't. But I thought if I stopped you, you might change your mind. They usually do."

Vridar never came to this bridge again. He still felt impelled to self-destruction but now, rejecting the river rock, he went into the country, thinking of trains. On the edge of the city was a railroad track, hidden by a jungle of forest, and he often went to it and sat on a pile of ties. On an evening in November he heard a locomotive approaching and he rose, shaking from head to feet, and sat close by the rail. When the train draws near, he thought, I can fall over the rail and in a moment I'll be dead. . . . When the engine came again into sight around a curve he reached down and clutched a handful of gravel and rubbed it sharply into the flesh of his palm. The engineer saw him now and warned him with blasts of steam and the brakeman leaned from the cab and roared. But Vridar did not move. He could hear steel roaring upon steel under the impact of brakes and he could feel the wind driven by the engine; and in this moment, with death close upon him, he heard Neloa call his name. He leapt aside and the locomotive struck him and spun him down the embankment; and when, a moment later, he sat up, he saw three men leaning from the black cab and staring at him. Neloa's voice was still ringing in his ears and he got to his feet and searched for her, running into jungle growth and calling her name. He lost himself in a thicket and threshed wildly, with despair goading him to frenzy; found his way out and ran to a clearing and listened, with blood roaring in his ears; and ran again. He was still running when he heard his name called. He stopped to listen but his heart was so loud that he could hear only its sound. And then he looked around him and saw Athene.

She was standing on a hillside not far away. She came

toward him and he stared at her, his senses swimming darkly; and as she drew near he could barely see her. He looked around him, confused, wondering about Neloa. Again and again she spoke his name before he realized that she was speaking or knew that her face was very white.

"Vridar, don't you know me?" She came close to him and looked at his eyes. "Vridar!"

He sank to earth, trying to understand that it was not Neloa who had called. Athene sat at his feet.

"It—it was you," he said.

"Yes." For a long moment he gazed at the earth and Athene studied his strange eyes. "Vridar, let's go home."

"You followed me out here," he said, still trying to understand.

"I follow you all the time." She moved close and put an arm around him. "Vridar, I can't stand it! You're driving me insane!" He gazed at her, wondering about this. "You're not being honest with me," she said.

"I know it," he said, speaking the words as if they were part of a ritual. "Yes, I know it."

"You came out here to kill yourself. I know you did."

"Yes, I did."

"Vridar, you're not being fair! If you die I want to die with you!" Her voice was frenzied. She began to weep. She lay to the earth and hid her face and he could hear her grief. He stared at her and then around him at the hills. For many minutes Athene wept and Vridar did not move; and then Athene sat up and shook her wet hair back. She grasped Vridar and shook him and her voice was hysterical with anguish. "Vridar, shake out of it! Look at me!" He looked at her. She got to her feet and tried to drag him after her. He rose and she faced him and he was aware of her hands trembling on his arms. She led him and they went down a path and came to the city; and still leading him as if he were a child she entered a trolley and they rode home. They got off near the bridge and crossed it and on the way

over Athene spoke to the policeman and he spoke and smiled.
Vridar saw the smile but he did not understand. They came
to their rooms and with wild hands Athene undressed him
and he did not protest. She led him to the bathroom and
pushed him into the tub and she turned steaming water on
until he sat in it to his waist. She massaged him, her hands
moving in furious power over his flesh; and little by little
he came to himself and realized where he was and what she
did. He rose from the hot water, loudly protesting, but
Athene with strength that amazed him shoved him to a bed
and rubbed him vigorously with a rough towel.

"I'm all right," he said at last. "Athene, please."

Athene went to pieces now. While Vridar put his clothes
on, she sat in a chair, shaking terribly and moaning. He was
appalled by the white anguish of her face.

"Darling," he said, kneeling at her feet, "I'm all right.
I know everything now."

Athene was so wild in her stare and in the way she shook
that he was frightened and he laid her on the bed and lay
by her, speaking to her gently. For a little while she would
stop shaking and lie rigid and he would think she was all
right; but then she would try to sit up and the agony in her
voice would unnerve him.

It was hours later and they were both quiet.

"Vridar, you must promise me something."

"All right, dear."

"If you decide to kill yourself you must tell me."

"But I'll not. I'll never do that."

"But today?"

"I don't know about today. I don't think I would
have."

"But you were right on the track!"

"Well," he said wearily, "I don't know. I can't remember what I did."

"After this there's only one thing we can do."

"What is that?"

"When you leave the house I'll go with you."

"All right, if you want to."

"But I can't follow you. I can't keep up. I almost lost you today. And I'm sick of that. Vridar, I can't go on like that."

"I know."

"And you promise me?"

"Yes."

"What do you promise?"

"That if I decide to kill myself I'll tell you. But I won't, Athene. It would be cowardly."

"But you're not in your right mind, Vridar. Do you realize that half the time you don't know what you're doing?"

"I guess I realize." He looked at her. "Athene, you ought to leave me. Why let me spoil your life?"

"Now you're talking nonsense!" She came over and sat on his lap. "Vridar, you can be an awful fool. You told me you were a fighter."

"I am," he said.

"All right, then let's fight out of this."

He was silent for a long moment.

"We will," he said.

III

●

VRIDAR rose at daylight and began a long poem to Neloa, using the stanza form of Meredith's "Love in the Valley." He wrote during the early morning and forenoon and while he was staring in rage at a bad line he heard voices. He realized, then, that he had been hearing voices for a long time. . . .

Deep breathes the summer; on the haze the blue-wings,
Silver-spots and orange-tips hang like lucent gauze;
Stridulous the locust; shy behind a serviceberry
Sits the silvered ground squirrel with breakfast in its paws.
Dust-choked lies the long road, hill to hill-top cable;
Swift skips the chipmunk, loud shrieks the loon;
Through the seas of sunlight flashes scarlet tanager;
In the western sky there hangs the memory of a moon. . . .

He was pondering the last line, wondering how he could put into words the ghostly unreality of a crescent in bright sunlight, when the voices came to him again, low and insistent. And he knew now that his mind had recorded in a strange way a part of what the voices had said. They had been talking of him. He went to a chair close by a wall and listened. . . .

"You have to understand," Mertyl was saying, "that a person can be insane and still know what he's doing. He has been insane ever since Neloa died. But I don't think he'll kill himself. I wouldn't worry about that. If you understood him better——"

"I do understand him."

"No you don't. For years he has had a crazy wish to reform the world. He would die to make the world better, except that he wouldn't make it a damned bit better. But

he doesn't know that. Has he ever told you about his childhood?"

"Quite a lot, yes."

"Then you ought to understand what's driving him.
We had much the same childhood. I've become a philosopher and he has become a poet. You write poetry, too. Do
you know why a person writes poetry?"

"I probably wouldn't agree with you."

"Of course you wouldn't. A person writes poetry because he feels guilty and inferior."

"I don't agree."

"I knew you wouldn't. You're another idealist. And
that's what makes it so funny: two idealists together and
instead of helping one another you drive each other to what
you call sonnets. It's tragic, I guess, but it seems only
pretty damned funny to me. . . . But I wouldn't worry
so much. Keep a level head until he comes to himself. It
might take only another month or two, it might take a year.
Try to keep his mind off himself. I'll tell you what I think."

"Yes?"

"I think it would be wise to trot him around and make
him see people. We should take him to shows, picnics,
parties. The worst thing he can do is to sit at that typewriter all day and pound out his dirges. Maybe I could get
him to go to the university with me. Do you know Becky
Hammond?"

"No, I guess not."

"She would be good for him. Let's take him over tonight. . . ."

Vridar returned swiftly to his machine and when Athene
came to him he pretended to be lost in his stanzas. He was
remembering what had been said; trying to think about it;
wondering if it was true. Earlier he had heard, and remembered now: "Don't be so hard on his stuff. Even if it is
bad, praise it. . . ." He thought of this statement as Athene
bent close to read his lines.

When the world of twilight lays its fields of darkness,
Heaping blue on mountainsides, dusk upon the hills;
When a splendid wind rolls against the heated sunset . . .

"You needn't speak," he said, rising. "It's bad. Everything I write is bad."

"Not everything, dear. Not by any means."

He looked at her and smiled. It was the first time he
had smiled since Neloa's death.

"As a critic, Athene, you have a hell of a hard job. It's
hard to praise what has no worth."

"But you've written some fine things. You have some
good lines in this."

"Nonsense. I'm only an imitator. I read Meredith and
write like Meredith. I read Robinson and write like Robinson——"

"And now and then you write like yourself."

"For instance?"

Athene got a pile of manuscript and sat on the floor
and told him to sit by her. He sat by her, wondering what
Mertyl's cynical mind was deliberating now.

"This."

"Read it," he said. "But don't read it if it's a damned
imitation."

"It isn't. It's you."

"All right."

Too well I know, my dear, that you are dead:
I saw you lying rigid with the brown
Of poison on your throat where it ran down;
I saw you later, silent, white and bled.
And once again I saw you, still the same,
When with your hand in mine I made a vow;
And then the furnace closed, and even now
I hear the wild red hunger of the flame.

In what brief while I learned how beauty slips
To death and darkness, and by what strange way.
Last week my pulse within your heart; now only
An urn of ashes, hushed, and one more lonely.
A week ago I kissed your flesh; today
I raise my head with dust upon my lips!

Athene faltered and turned away. Her eyes filled with tears and she rose and left the room.

And in this evening Vridar went with Mertyl and Athene to visit Becky Hammond. He had seen her once, years ago: a tall and lanky woman with a small and childlike face; a woman whose husband had gone mad and killed himself; a woman who gave way to frenzies and did strange things. When they entered her apartment Mertyl went to her and spoke in a low voice and Becky came over and gave Vridar a warm handclasp and was presented to Athene. She sat on a chair and stretched her long legs and smiled. She and Mertyl talked, and their talk, Vridar knew, was intended to cheer him; but he ignored most of it for another sonnet was busy in his mind. At last Becky said:

"Vridar, you take life too damned seriously. Look at me. I've been through hell and high water—and very high water, I assure you—but I still grin. Life is a big joke. Res est sacra miser. You're fast becoming a saint, man. Shake out of it and take a whack at the world."

Vridar gave her a faint smile. He was annoyed. Her words had scattered his wits and a line he had been shaping was lost. He said:

"Why try to be happy if you aren't? You're merely trying to deceive yourself."

"To hell with happiness. I sleep well. Now and then some man kisses me. . . . Vridar, you need a hobby."

"He has one," Mertyl said. "His hobby is to reform the world."

"No, a small hobby: bug collecting or stamps or first editions or translating. It's fun to translate. Yesterday I did one of Sudermann's stories. I'm studying Russian. I want to be a deep-sea diver. . . ."

But Vridar did not hear. He was busy again with his line and Becky reached over and kicked him.

"Leap out of that melancholy. How about a drink?" She turned to Athene. "You drink?"

"I never have but I will."

Becky rose and stretched her tall body and yawned. She returned from the kitchen with four brimming glasses and Vridar gulped his cocktail and felt more wretched. Becky talked of a prize poem by a Baltimore youth. It was called hot days have been in Montana or something of the sort and had been awarded a prize by the *Nation;* and Becky read it and Vridar thought it was the worst stuff he had ever heard.

"It's swell," said Becky. "Alia tentanda via est. The old verse forms are worn out. . . ."

They drank again and still again and Becky's tongue was loosed. She was assistant to a famous psychiatrist here and she told of patients who came to Dr. Zwing: of a woman with a tic in her left eyelid who was thought guilty of winking at men and was driven frantic; of a man who declared it to be his religious duty to murder his wife; and of another man who thought he was God. But the funniest case of all, said Becky, was that of a middle-aged spinster haunted by fear of a burglar under her bed.

"She goes out every evening and stays until after midnight. She gives burglars every chance in the world to get under her bed but they never do and the disappointment is killing her. If she could catch John Barrymore there she'd be frightened to a handful of liquid ecstasy. Her name is Hannah Border. There are thousands of Hannah Borders

in the world. Poor dear things. Now this Hannah does
thus—— Vridar, some more drink?"

"No thanks."

"Hannah does thus. She comes to her front door and
listens. Very softly she opens the door and tiptoes to a
closet which she had built for burglars to hide in. Softly,
oh very softly, she peeks into the closet and stirs the
clothes—— Vridar, you need some more drink."

"Not now."

"Hannah stirs the clothes. The swishing of the dresses
makes her almost swoon. Once she did enjoy a great big
swoon, and when she came to, the window was open and
she heard a man clattering across Baltimore. She ran out and
chased him with a broom but he misunderstood the symbolism of the broom and got away. . . .

"Yes, there are thousands of Hannahs. Every woman is
one, really. Am I right, Miss Marvell?"

"I doubt it. And please call me Athene."

"Very well. That's a lovely name." Pale blue eyes studied
Athene, and thin lips smiled. "But you're wrong. Nothing
so thrills a woman as the thought that she is pursued by a
man. I'm not ashamed of it myself. I might as well be
ashamed of my thumbs. I like to go walking after midnight
and if I see a man coming I fairly throb. If he were to leap
across the distance and grab me I'd die right in his arms.
That's a woman's heritage. Why deny it? You mean you
never feel that way?"

Athene turned in her chair. She was distressed.

"I suppose there's a little truth in it."

"A mountain. And since I've stopped dodging myself,
I begin to see that life is what it is. Vridar," she said,
turning to him, "that's what you should do."

"What?" he said. He was writing a sextet.

"Stop dodging yourself. Be man, all plumb healthy male.
Then you'd see a lot you never saw before."

"You mean a lot of women?"

"I wish I were a man," said Becky. "It must be more fun to pursue than to be pursued. Isn't it, Mertyl?"

"I find it quite satisfying," he said.

And on the next evening they took Vridar to the house where Mertyl lived. For his room and board Mertyl had become guardian of a lunatic who, in his violent moods, was determined to slay his wife. Other students had undertaken this guardianship and had fled.

"What is wrong with him?" asked Athene.

"Oh, a lot of things. Jealousy, ideas of persecution, feelings of impotence. He thinks his wife has lovers and she's too scared to eat her meals."

"Why doesn't she put him in an institution?"

"Pride. They used to belong to society. They still do in a way. She thinks he'll get well and then they'll play bridge again. Sometimes," said Mertyl, "he chases me. Once he chased me all over the house with a knife. I thought I was a goner. But I talked him out of it. He is also obsessed with suicide. Last summer he jumped out of a window and broke his leg. But he's a great fellow. I think Vreed will like him."

"You think I'll like him? Why?"

"Because you're a lot alike."

"The hell! How do you mean?"

"You'll see. This bird writes poetry, too."

When they entered the house, fashionably vulgar in its excesses, Vridar saw a man by a reading lamp. He looked up from a book and scowled. A woman came forward to meet them: a timid colorless person with a fixed alarm in her eyes.

"You can go now," Mertyl said. "He'll be all right."

The woman withdrew.

"Mr. Cortland," said Mertyl, "I want you to meet my brother. . . . And his wife." Cortland rose and bowed stiffly, his morbid gaze on Athene. "We'll leave you two," Mertyl said. "Mr. Cortland is a great lover of books. You

ought to have a fine talk." And Mertyl and Athene left
the room.

"Have a cigar?" asked Cortland, his manner glacial.

"No thanks."

"A cigarette?"

"If you please."

The two men smoked and looked at one another. Cortland's stare was that of a man with only one thought awake
and burning: a dark and murderous suspicion with a vision
of his wife at its core.

"Where did *he* go?" Cortland asked. He was looking
at the door through which Mertyl had passed.

"You mean my brother?" asked Vridar, knowing well
what the man had meant. "Oh, he's with my wife."

"*Your* wife?"

"Yes. What you reading there?"

"Where is *my* wife?" asked Cortland, his gaze still on
the door.

"She's in her room."

Cortland now fixed his strange gaze on Vridar.

"You're lying to me," he said.

"I'm not. Mertyl!" A door opened and Mertyl looked
in. "Isn't Mrs. Cortland in her room?"

"Yes. Why?"

"Mr. Cortland wanted to know."

Mertyl came over and stared at Cortland, hands on his
hips. Cortland shrank from him and looked whipped. His
lips twitched and Mertyl grinned.

"Listen, Cortland, I brought a man to talk poetry with
you." And then: "Your wife is tired. She has gone to bed."

"Yes," said Cortland, nodding his head and staring at
Mertyl. "Yes, I understand."

"Cortland is a poet," said Mertyl, turning to Vridar.
"You might like to see some of his poetry."

"Of course," Vridar said.

Mertyl left the room. Vridar saw hatred and terror in

the man's eyes now and he saw his hands trembling on his knees. "You like poetry," Vridar said quietly. "What poets do you read?" But Cortland did not hear. He was looking at the doorway through which Mertyl had passed. He was listening, with his mind tortured, his whole body awake. It is true, Vridar reflected: we are much alike. A little more, a very little, and I could have been lost as he is lost now.

Most of this night Vridar lay awake, thinking of Cortland, reading in the man's gestures, in his mad heartbreak, the parallels of his own dark years; and when morning came he did not write at all.

"I feel," he said, "like a man coming out of ether. Were you ever under ether?"

"No."

"It's an ungodly nightmare of dream and waking. Awareness is around you like sheets of flame but you're still drugged against it, as if only certain parts of you were coming to life. You feel pain and there is awful memory of pain. There are flashes of wild meaning and then a night of blackness that buries you; and you know you are fighting in it and trying to understand where you are. It's like coming out of a nightmare. And that's the way I feel now. I'm coming awake but I can't awaken." He looked at her, his eyes clouded. "I wish something would wake me up," he said.

The experience that did more than anything else to awaken him came two days later. Mertyl had been over and had left some of his notebooks. Vridar was looking through them when he came to Mertyl's journal; and he was surprised, never having known that Mertyl kept a record of his thoughts; and he turned the pages and read.

September 14. We are on the train to Baltimore. Vridar is writing sonnets to Neloa. He writes one and then another.

This is his method of atonement but he does not know it. He is insane. There is no question about that. I must do what I can to save him but I haven't decided what is best to do. . . .

September 19. I don't know what to think of Athene. She is not the sort of woman he should be living with. She is too much like him, with a strong tendency to insanity herself. She is doing her best and she has wonderful patience but her best doesn't amount to much. I talked with her yesterday but she is another idealist and doesn't understand. These idealists bore me to death. The history of religion is full of their hysterias. . . .

September 29. Vreed is getting worse. He spends all his time thinking of Neloa and suicide and unless I do something he will kill himself. All martyrdom is self-pity and he is bent on being a martyr. If an outraged world would burn him at the stake he would die happy, believing he was taking his place with all the other fakes of history. And he would be. I feel great sympathy for him. I also want to kick his sentimental pants. If he would only see life as it is and himself as he is. . . .

October 12. Vreed is moving steadily to suicide and I must do something quick. He will kill himself without knowing that he is killing himself. That's your poet for you! His death will be another great poem! As I see the matter neither he nor Neloa was to blame. Puritanism is to blame for making such sickly idealists of men. He's as self-pitying as Jesus was and is taking the same road to martyrdom. If Athene were only a hard-headed realist. If I only knew what to do for both of them. . . .

Vridar read these statements again and again. He closed the journal and paced the room and when Athene came to him he pushed her away.

"Don't," he said. "Let me think." He got his hat and went to the door and when Athene seized his arm he flung her hand off. "Please! I'm all right."

"Vridar, if you go out I'm going with you."

"No. I tell you I'm all right."

"You're feeling desperate again."

"I'm not. Look at me." He grinned. "What is today? November——?"

"—the twenty-third."

"All right: September, October, November: almost three months and for the first time in those three months you see Y again. You remember Y?"

"Vridar, where are you going?"

"You remember Y? For three months you've seen nothing but X, that self-pitying and bellyaching idealist and poet. Athene, I'm all right. I'm coming to myself. I want to go off alone and think."

"And I want to go with you."

"No. I must be alone. I'll be all right."

"But I could go with you and you could be alone. I'd just be somewhere near."

"No. You think I might kill myself. Nonsense. All that is past. I'm done with all that, now and forever. I'll be home by dark."

"Vridar, please."

He took her in his arms and she trembled. He looked at the tears in her eyes.

"Athene, can't you tell I'm all right? Must I fetch an aphorism to prove that Y is again in control? All right:

> "Here's Vridar Hunter, pitiable fraud,
> Who entered a partnership with God;
> Searched for himself on the cross eternal,
> And found himself in his brother's journal."

"What journal do you mean?"

"There. I don't know whether Mert left it deliberately. It doesn't matter. You might read it while I'm gone." He went to the street and looked up to the window and saw Athene there. "X and Y," he said, "are going off to have a friendly talk. Please don't worry. This afternoon I'll call you and report how X fares."

"Vridar, please come back a moment."

"Why?"

"I want to kiss you."

He went up the stairs and Athene came to him. She clung to him, weeping.

"I know what you mean," he said. "You want to give me a farewell kiss. But, darling, this is not farewell. This is an end and a beginning. You'll see."

IV

●

HE LEFT the city and went to a wooded hillside and sat where he could smell water and trees and look at the sky. The sky became the background of his life, and memory passed in review there his bewildered pilgrimage from infancy to his thirtieth year: of that hour, the first in memory, when his father threshed him for not counting; of that time when he sat frightened and furious on the photographer's high stool; and of that night, three years later, when his aunt Agnes terrified him with threats of the Devil and the Holy Ghost. These were the only memories of his first six years and they were all memories of terror. By that time, he reflected, I was afraid of life, and my journey now becomes a journey of fear. I went next to the Antelope country. . . .

Lost in the panorama, trying to see it as a coherent pattern, he recalled the dramatic events of his childhood and youth; and they came to him as pictures, each with its sound and smell: of a sheep with its head thrown back and its throat butchered, and the gurgling and smell of blood; an enraged father, grasping a cat by its heels and crushing it around a post: the sudden squawk, and the furry smell of it, lying in the yard; the scenes, many of them, in the corrals: the stench of burning hair and hide, the agonized bawling, the knife and the blood, and the organs thrown to the flies; the horns, tufted with hair at their base, with a round hole in them, full of marrow and bone dust and blood; nights under downpour, with water and mud falling to his bed, with the smell of elk hides and deer hides, and the wet smell of water filling the room; the trails in jungle-land, lying through marsh and bog, and the smell of stagnant water, of kinnikinic and birch, and of bedded grass where wild things had lain; the smell of fir trees in a storm and

34

the smell of the river in spring floods, and of the pelts of wolves and wildcats, spiked to the walls of the house; the smell of chickens with their feathers soaked, huddled in a basket by the stove; of cows with steaming hides; of his father with udder filth on his hands; the velvety feeling of rose petals, the hard brave texture of bark, the thrust of briar and thorn; the cool liquid feeling of water and the round smoothness of a deer's thigh-bone; the feeling of heavy quilts under nightmare; the taste of gilia petals, of wheat chewed to gum, the flavor of oats in oatmeal; the taste of wild strawberry and gooseberry and currant, of aspen bark and yarrow and wild graperoot, brewed into a tonic; of dead leaves in autumn, of rock salt placed for the cattle to lick, and the smooth saucers where their tongues had been; the taste of old tobacco quids; the jungle taste of venison and mallard duck and brown bear; of mountain trout, frying in bacon grease; of sour milk standing in vats; of curd and cheese; the sound of river waters and night winds, of wolves and the loon, of calves bawling and of chickens at dawn; of a mountain lion, screaming somewhere in pitch dark, and of a horse screaming, goaded by turpentine, and of a rabbit screaming, overtaken by a dog; the sight of chickens, hopping madly with their heads off; of a hog running wildly with two bullets in its head and with frantic men chasing it, each with an ax; the muffled sound of blows on its skull; the sound of woodchucks and squirrels, rats and mice, caught in traps; the sickening smell of mice, the sound of flies droning in yellow sunlight, the feeling of a young bluebird, wounded and dying in his hands. . . .

Such was memory of life from his sixth to his tenth year. Its only meaning was terror and pain: the wild movement of the living, the hushed composure of the dead. Four years: and in those four years I can recall no moment of tenderness and peace; no hour when I wanted to sing; no day not roofed with desolation. It was a pioneer life: raw and brutal and earnest; unpitying and hard. It was life that has been known by countless thousands in all ages and in all zones; but I was a terrified weakling, and all the beauty and peace that must have been there, I missed. Dread came to be the core of things, the beating heart of all that was; until I was afraid even of sunlight, even of myself. And then . . .

Smell of cedar on a gray butte, of sand and gravel under a hot sun, of outdoor privies; sound of Agnes and Borg, lost in amorous embrace; the feeling of chalk and books and blackboard; vision of school bullies, waiting at the bridge; the sound of Borg, neighing like a stallion, slapping his buttocks; the smell of red ants, swarming on a mound, and of Easter eggs and their paint; and a picture of Neloa: a slender child with long black hair and dark eyes and red cheeks: first memory of tenderness. . . .

I loved her, even then, with all the love I had power to feel; for until then I'd had nothing to love. I worshiped her, as in the years that followed; and now. She became a symbol for me of all that was lovely and good: my testaments; my church and prayer and passion. For eleven years I had been scared out of my wits; and hunger within me had grown to be violence; loneliness to be nightmare: and she became all things, my bread and deity, all loveliness and all hope. She and books were the only image and the only idol in my heart: in a world that had proved friendless and evil, an embodiment of all virtues; until she was no longer girl or woman but the center of heaven and the heart of God. All that I imagined I was not, all that I wanted to be, she was; and I married her and worshiped her and drove her to her death. I was mad with unreason; but even now I do not see clearly what I did; or why. . . .

For a long while he sat in thought. He strove to summarize again.

Twenty-one years had led me to see life as a brutal and terrifying struggle, with little good in it, and with the good

never triumphant: a world in which beauty was a meaningless gesture, in which peace was death. But what is beauty
and what is its purpose? . . . I was an idealist; but what
is idealism, out of what does it come? . . . Mine seems to
have come from fear, disgust, guilt, loneliness; I tried to
escape from life into a monastery of high principles; I lost
all touch with the real. Out of hunger I had made one thing
of Neloa; but she was a woman; and my struggle was
between the two: living year in and year out with the first,
denying the second; believing I'd been a fool. I was set
on a life of honesty and truth, but what is honesty and
what is truth? Ideals led me to the tragic: what were they
and where did I get them and what was their value?

He left the hillside and sought a telephone and called
Athene.

"Athene? . . . Yes, I'm all right. I'm thinking. Don't
worry about me at all. Never waste time worrying about
me. . . . No: I'm out here on a hill: a lovely spot. I'm
trying to think. . . . Not much. It is all very dark. What
isn't? . . . Yes, I promise—and please stop worrying! . . ."

He returned to the hill and drew pencil and paper and
made notes.

What are my ideals? Honesty—but what the hell do I
understand honesty to mean? Courage—and what is courage? Of clean-mindedness: but what is obscenity and what
is not and who decided the matter? Of good taste: bosh.

I was born like everyone else without notions of good
and evil, right and wrong. Where did I get those notions?
I was an animal, an organism; so were my parents; their
parents; back to the beginning. I was trained; they were
trained: but where did the training come from? I accepted
certain ideals, grew up with them: I never asked if they were
good. I really never thought about them. . . .

Now I'm a man with ideals; which means convictions;
which means prejudices; which means I'm a fool.

See Vridar out there making notes
With their addenda of morgues and motes;
Adds his ideals, reflects a little,
And finds that he has two jots, one tittle. . . .

He looked up and saw a man watching him. The man came up the hill and looked at him and said:

"What are you doing here?"

"Trying to think. Is that all right?"

"Don't you know you're on private land?"

"I didn't know it. I can move."

The man looked around him. "What are you doing? An artist? Sketching?"

"Oh no. Merely trying to think."

The man spread a coat and sat on it. Calm gray eyes studied Vridar; and the man said:

"What are you trying to think about?"

"Myself."

"Oh, the hell you are. Haven't you anything better to think about?"

"Perhaps. But today that is my subject."

The eyes studied him curiously. "Why are you thinking about yourself?" Vridar read the man's thought and grinned.

"You think I'm a lunatic. Well, I am. If a man thinks about himself you think he's crazy. Do you ever think about yourself?"

"Do I what? Damn it, man, I think you are crazy."

"All right. But I'm not dangerous." Vridar drew a cigarette. He smoked and looked at the man. He said: "Tell me: are you an idealist?"

"My God, no!"

"I'll tell you what I've been thinking. Now here I am, a person; you're another; and we have ideals, convictions. But where did we get them? Are they worth anything? Are yours worth anything to you?"

"My what?"

"Your ideals."

"I don't have any." The man drew a silver case and took a cigarette.

"Of course you have. You believe in right and wrong. Don't you?"

"Well, yes, I suppose. But I don't worry my head about them."

"Do you believe in God?"

"That's a personal question."

"All questions are. What do you believe in?"

"Nothing much. I find it satisfying just to live."

"But you can't live without opinions. Or do you?"

"Where do you come from?"

"Idaho."

"You're a long way from home. Working here?"

"Some."

"What do you do?"

"Write—or try to."

"The hell." The gray eyes studied him again. The mouth was cynical. "What sort of stuff do you write?"

"Self-pitying verse."

"Do you know Mencken's work?"

"I've read most of it."

"What do you think of it?"

"That," said Vridar, "is a personal question."

The man rose to his feet. "After this," he said, "you better find another spot. Someone will be taking a shot at you here."

"You mean some idealist? Some man of convictions?"

"I mean what I said."

The man went down the hillside and Vridar watched him vanish among trees; and for a little while he sat here, thinking of him: of his fat and sanity and his feudal air. Then he wrote:

It is unimaginative persons who are most sure of what is right and what is wrong. Well, as Montaigne says, the nursing mother of most false opinions both public and private is the too high opinion which man has of himself, and nothing is so firmly believed as what we least know.

Athene was waiting for him on the bridge. She came to him, her eyes anxious, and Vridar shrugged.

"I'm all right. I wish the hell you wouldn't worry about me."

She gave him a letter and he opened it and read: it was from Ellen Mavis, the woman Dennis Altrock had lived with in Chicago. It was hysterical and abusive. The two of them, with their infant in a baby-carriage, had set out for Mobile, with Dennis pushing the carriage. In Tennessee the Klan had set upon Dennis and thrown him into jail and Ellen had been left, as she put it, to the tigerish virtues of the town. And farther south, Dennis had received a letter from Vridar, telling of Neloa's death. "Dennis can see no one in the world but you. I said you killed your wife and he says you didn't and that I don't understand you. And now he has ditched me and is on his way to Baltimore. We quarreled bitterly and it is all your fault. You must send him back to me and you must dig into your pockets and send me some money. Money can't pay for what you've done but it can help me out of this God-forsaken nest of puritans. . . ."

"So I've made a mess of her life! My God, I suppose I'm responsible for Teapot Dome, too! . . . And she wants money."

"There's the baby," Athene said. "You'll have to send a letter and head him off."

They turned home. "What a mess, Athene! Love sets out to lick the world and ends up by pushing a baby-buggy to Mobile. Nature never does betray the heart that loves her: my God, what a stupid thing to have said! Wordsworth was right: no single volume paramount, no code; no master spirit, no determined road. But I'm waking up. I'm beginning to see."

V

FOR MORE than a week Vridar went alone in each afternoon to a hillside and strove to find logic and clarity in the confusion of his life. He had reached, he well knew, a supreme crisis; and early in December, with a pile of notes at hand, he faced Athene.

"Let's talk," he said. "I've faced through it and my mind is made up."

"Made up to what?"

"A lot of things. I know what I'm going to do but I want to talk it over." They sat by a window and for a little while he studied his notes. "For days now I've tried to understand myself. That's impossible. No person has ever understood himself. But don't you think he might if he had enough patience and courage?"

"I doubt it."

He looked at her. Her eyes were unhappy, her face colorless and tired.

"My childhood and yours we have discussed. I magnified into tragedy what for most lads would have been commonplaces. I don't know why. And you got an awful sense of inferiority because you were freckled.

"And what are we now? We're intelligent, I suppose. We're abnormally sensitive and bent on achievement. We have a lot of ideals. I find that I am abnormally sensitive to pain and ugliness and human misery—and sex. But why? Such sensitivity ought to be a virtue: it ought to lead me to sympathy and wisdom. But with me it has been a sort of vice. That much I see now if nothing else.

"We are two idealists, my dear, and we met in a great sickly mating of poetry and nobility and courage. Were our motives high and worthy? Yes, in the way such motives have always been. But what lay under the motives? What were the real things driving us? In what matters and to what extent were we evasive and what drove us into evasions? Because we were evasive and we still are. And who isn't? Well, those are a few of the matters I have in mind.

"And, darling, understand this: I'll never stoop to the cowardice of regrets and reproach. The past is done beyond all recall. Let my part of it be measured by what I do from now on. And yours by what you do. Athene," he said, searching her face, "are you not deeply sorry that we met?"

"For her, yes. But not for myself."

"But you've cut yourself off from your friends."

"All the friends I had worth having will still be my friends."

"But your relatives? Your brothers?"

"My life belongs to me and not to my brothers."

"You could leave me if you think it best. No one need know."

"That's nonsense. We must go on together."

"But let's not be sentimental. There's no reason why we must go on together if you'd rather not."

"Do you mean you'd rather not?"

"No. I want to go with you. But only if you really want to."

"Of course I want to. I've never thought of anything else."

"All right. But you may get tired of my way. I'm going to be rock and flint."

"I'm not made of butter, my dear."

"No, you're not." He looked at her for a long moment. "Well, I want to tell you what I've made up my mind to do. To try to do, anyway. All my life I've been a person lost to himself. I've been a sentimentalist. I've been a fool. I've never known what I believed or why; or why I did things; or whether I've ever done what I really wanted to do. I've been an idealist, trying to dodge myself. I've been a romantic fool, trying to dodge life. But now I'm going to be a realist: I mean I'm going to face life for exactly what it is.

"These are some things I'm forever done with. I'm done with false ideals and false gods. I'm done with self-pity and with all the books and religions and cults that appeal to self-pity. I'm done with all evasions of myself and of life. Socrates said know thyself and thousands have repeated him. But do you think any person has ever really known himself?"

"I doubt it."

"Do you think anyone has ever really wanted to?"

"Yes, I think so. I think Freud did—and some like him."

"Yes. But look at Carlyle: driven by psychic impotence to be a prophet on the mountain tops; and dying, still self-deceived. Look at Swinburne: driven into rhetoric by fear of women. Look at Byron: driven to pilgrimage by incest. Look at Swift: turned inward to volcanic furies because of disgust for defecation. Look at Nietzsche: goaded to visions of supermen because he felt himself to be a physical weakling. Look at writers everywhere: driven to romantic twaddle because they haven't the guts to face life and love it and use it. Look at me and all that I have been! Foster-child of all the emotionally castrated puritans! Spiritual heir of Jesus and Calvin and Luther, Cotton Mather and Jonathan Edwards and St. John!

"But I'm done with all that. I'm going to try to know myself for exactly what I am, and all my strength, all my courage, I'm going to bring to that job. And when I know myself I'll know everyone else."

"But," said Athene quietly, "I wonder if that is possible."

"I think it is. But it means, of course, that I can't go on in flattering self-love. It means I must destroy all pity for myself. It means I cannot have any ideology, any gospel, any shibboleth that glorifies *me* and gives to *me* more significance than I have."

"And it may mean that you'll destroy all sympathy for yourself."

"Perhaps. What of it? I can live without sympathy."

"And it may mean that you'll merely fix yourself in another kind of self-pity."

"Fine, my dear! You're using your mind now. But I've thought of that. If I'm mentally awake at every point. . . . Listen: If I run every motive to its source; discover the meaning of every impulse, every gesture, every conflict, every dream—then would I? If I study myself as a scientist studies a bug? Don't suppose that I think I can do all this in a year or two. I'm not being fooled there. But I do think I can do it. I am determined, heart and soul, to know the truth." He looked at Athene's eyes. They were dubious. "You don't think I can?"

"You're an extremist, Vridar. You swing from one extreme to another. God knows what extreme you'll swing to now."

"Well, you're not an extremist. Why aren't you?"

"I'm simply not built that way."

"Isn't life extreme? It runs from June to January. It runs to the last extremity of all: death. The golden mean of Aristotle was nothing but intellectual fence-straddling. Yes, God damn it, I am an extremist. And in this matter I'm going to the last limit."

"I don't doubt it at all," Athene said dryly. "No one who knows you could ever doubt it."

"And it doesn't appeal to you? What I propose frightens you? You don't want to share this ruthless and unpitying exploration? You don't want to lay yourself bare until you're as naked as your palm?'

She looked at him, her eyes troubled.

"My dear, I'm not the psychologist you are. I don't have that sort of mind."

"Do you want me to help you?"

"Of course."

"You want me to call you every time you dodge? You want me to drag out your motives and show them to you?"

"Of course. But what will you think of me after I am all exposed?" She smiled. "Could you love me then?"

"More. It's a cinch I won't love your evasions and shams."

"I suppose, though, in such a ruthless business I shouldn't think of love."

"If love won't stand the discoveries, then what is it worth?"

"Not much, I guess."

"Tell me: don't you feel any enthusiasm?"

"I'll have to think about it."

He rose and paced the floor and his vehemence startled her.

"I do! The thought of it shakes me clear to my feet! I know what you're thinking: you're thinking I'm about to undertake another crusade; a more devious form of atonement; a form of evasion mightier than all others. To all that I say: wait and see. I'm a fighter, Athene. I'm born of fighters and I'm not happy without a good enemy to aim at. And now I have a worthy foe: myself. All my life I've hit at the dark, with never a foe I could see. But now I have one, with me at all times; and I'm going after him with hammer and tongs."

"Isn't it," she asked, smiling faintly, "isn't it only that the Y in you is determined to slay the X? The thinker in you is determined to slay the poet."

For a long moment he stood in thought, wondering about this.

"Perhaps. I am resolved to use my intelligence. Why shouldn't I? And if the poet can't stand the scrutiny, let him perish. Yes: it will be a struggle between the two personalities in me: the poet and the thinker. All right. Let the best man win."

"But if you slay the poet, what will be left of you?"

"The mind. That's enough."

"It isn't enough. Of what use will your mind be without a heart?"

"Oh, the heart and be damned! If the heart can't stand the inquisition, let it wither! It's our emotions that betray us. Mine have betrayed me at every turn. Do you mean that the poet in a person can't survive analysis?"

"No, I certainly do not. I think the mind should direct the poet."

"Then I can't think much of some minds now directing. Anyhow, why do you say I'll kill the damned sickly poet in me?"

"For the very reason that you call it a damned sickly poet. You hate it. For years you've hated it."

"No, I don't hate it. I merely have contempt for its bellyaching, its lamentations in rime, its bloodless apostrophes to beauty and goodness and peace. I——"

"Vridar, you know what I think?"

"What?"

"That the poet in you will never survive thought. You *are* an extremist. Now you're determined to be extreme in thinking and before you're done with it you'll be nothing but a thinker. Thinkers who are nothing but thinkers are sterile."

"Well, we've never agreed on that. You distrust thought. For you it means the impotence of dialectics. I'll tell you: let me give some of the things I'm going to think about. Then judge." He looked at his notes. "Here are some at random. What is sentimentality? I've seen a lot of definitions but they're all senseless. What is idealism? What does it come from? Can it ever reconcile the heart and mind? What is the basis, what is the source, of religious mysticism? How is it related to sex? What is honesty and is it possible in group life? What is romance, what is realism? Are there vices and virtues? Why do we have so many dualisms? What are right and wrong, beauty and ugliness, truth and falsehood?

"Well, what do you think of those?"

"They're matters human beings have thought of for ages. Nobody knows what they mean."

"And you think it's impossible to find out?"

"I don't know. I just wonder where you'll end up at."

"In a lunatic asylum?" He grinned. "In the Republican party?"

"God knows."

"And here are some other matters. Why am I so violent of temper? What does the sadism in me spring from? Why do I hate filthy stories? Why do I try to write poetry? Why do I profane like a trooper? Why do I blaspheme God?

"Well, that is my program, let it lead where it will. I'm going to face myself without evasion and self-excuse; I'm going to follow every clue to its source, even if it leads to hell. I'll never seek sympathy or understanding: let none who know me condescend to forgiveness; let those understand who can. I'll never in any matter yield an inch beyond what I think is decent and right. . . .

"What I mean is this: for nearly thirty years I've been a headstrong idealist, trying to shape life to my will. I'm now going to shape my will to life. Idealists in the past have made a fetish of their loneliness. That was self-pity. Or they have left utopias to the amused scrutiny of an incredulous world. The whole history of humankind is this: a struggle to reconcile life as life is with life as we want it to be. But life may be all right as it is. Is the trouble with life or with ourselves? I think it is with ourselves. Is the world inadequate for intelligent living, or does intelligence get mixed up with emotions that corrupt it with sickly fancies and dreams? I think it does.

"Athene, look at me as I am now. I have strong convictions, as every other person has; but where did we get them? Are they worth anything? One thing I've thought out: a person is brought up to accept notions of right and wrong. And then, as the years pass, he accepts the rightness of himself, learns to love himself; thinks of himself as something intelligently conceived and grown. But—and note this—little by little and in countless ways he is self-deceived; but his habits, no matter how stupid, become dear to him; his emotional distortions become as familiar and as acceptable as his face; and his opinions, after long intercourse with unreason and prejudice, seem to be as much a part of him as his bone. And then what? Why, he has no detachment, no perspective on himself: he lives in self-love and measures all things by the standard of himself. That much I see if nothing else. That much I italicize. And such a person comes at last to believe, not only in his destiny, his goodness, his rightness; he also regards his mistakes, his misfortunes, as the result of a malign power beyond his control, and his death as a grave loss to humankind. Note that last. There you have summarized the evolution of ideals, culture, traditions: but add this: we have evolved only ideals and traditions that flatter us. Do you see the enormous implications there?"

"I can see that they wouldn't be very flattering."

"Athene, I was on the road to becoming such a person myself. What in the past have I seen with clearness? Nothing. Where have my convictions come from? The traditions of self-love. I haven't a handful of reason to support any of them. And I'm going to clean all this unreason out of me. Extremist? All right; but I'm going straight ahead to find myself and I'll never turn back. I'm going to strip my life to its foundation and build again. I'm done with the cradles and nursing-bottles and diapers of tradition. I'm done with ideas as ideas. I'm interested from now on in what and where the ideas came from.

"Well?"

"I don't see how you can do it. What you are you are
and you can't very well change that."

"No? The hell I can't. I'm a tenacious person. I have
a mind and I'm going to use it. I think I have courage:
let time tell. But you—all this doesn't appeal to you."

"It does. But I'm skeptical. If we could make it
work——"

"We'll make it work. Give us ten years and we'll do
the job."

"But, Vridar, isn't all this another way of atonement?"

"I spoke of that. Call it anything you please. If a deter-
mination to face myself without pity, without crawling and
evading, is atonement, all right. Self-evasion can be called
by an uglier name. Is it a choice between two evils? I can't
see it that way. I feel I have a worthy job ahead of me.
The world will not like my ruthless searching of human
motive? Then to hell with the world. I'll have few friends
and many enemies? The thought of enemies doesn't bother
me at all. I'll be opposed at every turn by persons full of
self-love? All right: I'm ready for opposition and a lot
of it. I've a job to do and I'm going to do it. And you
know the first part of that job?"

"I can't imagine," said Athene, looking at him uneasily.

"To return to Chicago and take my degree."

Athene rose from her chair. She came to him.

"No, Vridar. You couldn't stand it there."

"I must. I ran away from the place. I dodged it. I'm
going back."

"But you can't stand it there!"

"I must. Listen, Athene: I've set my heart to a job and
I'm going to do it. If I can't stand it, then let me break."

"And you'll break, I tell you! What will be the sense
in that?"

"I can't help it. I'm set on this with everything in me.
My decision is made and I'm going ahead."

PART TWO

AUGUST 25, 1901

And he must never listen to nasty tales or believe anything that other people might tell him; and he must believe, now and always, in the purity of womanhood and in the mercy and goodness of God. If, by any chance, boys or men whispered to him of uncleanness, he must come at once to her and report to her all that had been said. In this way he would keep his heart and mind pure; he would grow to be a strong and noble man, walking within the understanding of God. Did he understand all that she meant? "Yes maam," he said, looking darkly into the great body of life.

I

●

THEY went first to Washington, D. C., where Vridar wanted to do a thesis in the Library of Congress; and they lived in one small room close by the Capitol. The room had one gas plate, unclean bedding, and a horde of cockroaches. "But it's all we can afford," he said. "It doesn't matter. We'll eat and sleep here and that is all." And he looked from a window to the white building, set upon a hill, and from another window at the ugly bourgeois acreage that lay around him. "I should think," he said, "that Uncle Sam would clean his back yard."

They spent little time in this room. The library was a magnificent thing, with its countless records and its helpful assistants, and after being admitted to the stacks Vridar spent most of his time there. He was at the library in every morning before the doors were opened and he remained until the doors were closed, long after dark. Then he went to his room and typed his notes.

From midnight until morning he talked out of delirium and dream. He was a skeleton of a man, with sunken eyes and a white mouth. Athene prepared his meals of salads and fruits; she yielded at last to his wish to drug himself for sleep; and when she protested, declaring that he was wrecking his health, he gave always the same answer. "I have a body and it is a machine like any other machine. I have a mind to drive it. If it can't stand the strain, then let it break. . . ."

In January he was stricken with dizziness and it took him an hour to find his way from the library to his room. "I guess I need exercise," he said; and on the next evening he went down Pennsylvania Avenue to the Y.M.C.A. He came out feeling better, but after he had gone a little way through cold and sleet he shook with chills. When he entered his room he was deathly sick. In this night he was delirious and at times violent; and Athene, desperate, and ill too, worked over him until morning came.

"What is wrong with me?" he asked.

"You're sick!" She began to weep. "Vridar, let me call a doctor!"

"We have no money for doctors. I'm all right." He was ill with influenza but he did not know it. "I'm all right," he said, and he left the bed and dressed. He ate an orange and drank a glass of buttermilk. He gathered his paper and pencils.

"You're not going to the library today!"

"Of course I am. Darling, I'm all right."

"You're sick, I tell you!" She sank to a chair, her eyes angry and wet. "You're killing yourself!"

"I was chilled last night, that's all. I'm all right now."

"You don't look all right to me."

"I never did look all right. I've always looked like some kind of abortion. . . . Athene, you rest and I'll go work a bit." He went to a bathroom and scrubbed his face in cold water. He returned, hoping he had color in his cheeks. "Don't I look all right now?"

"No! You're ghastly."

He sat on the bed, wondering what to do.

"Darling, maybe I need a tonic. You rest and I'll get an herb tonic. Then I'll be all right. I won't work too hard."

He went to the library and for an hour he bent over old volumes of the London *Times* and he thought he was all right. But suddenly, without warning, he was stricken with vomiting sickness. He left the building in haste and bent over a gutter, retching in agony; and the foam on his lips was the bitterness of gall. Finding a bench he sat down, wondering about himself. Am I really sick, he asked himself, or am I pretending to be? And then he realized that he was shaking from his head to his feet. He entered the warmth of the building but felt the nausea again and returned to cold air.

And for a month he fought this sickness and went to the library, determined to drive himself to the last ounce of his strength. In every day Athene argued with him and implored. When a person was sick, she believed he ought to go to bed and rest: for her the human body was something to cherish and care for. But this was not Vridar's tradition.

"Sickness," he said, "has never put either one of my parents to bed. Nor me. They plowed right through and got well."

"Yes? And they'll pay for it in their old age."

"To hell with old age. I don't expect to live that long."

"You're ridiculous! For an intelligent man you can talk the worst nonsense I ever listened to!"

"Life, my dear, is not measured in years. It's measured in intensity. I'll live more in ten years than most persons live in eighty."

She shrugged. She looked at him, angry and helpless. And then:

"Is this a part of your notions of honesty? Is it honesty to abuse your health? I think it's another way of suicide."

"Do you?" he said, looking at her. "You think I'm dodging again?"

"That's certainly one way of looking at it."

For a long moment he was thoughtful.

"You may be right," he said at last. "Driving myself may be—well, it may be only another plan of atonement. Human evasions are subtle and dark. . . . But, God damn it, what am I to do! I won't sit around here and nurse my molecules!"

"You'll have to rest until you're well."

"How can I? I have to be in Chicago the first of April. . . . Athene, there ought to be a medicine to fix me up."

"But you won't take medicine. And you won't take it because your dad has never taken it. You won't take it because it's a sign for you of a physical weakling."

"I think you're right. You'll be a psychologist yet."

"You won't take it——"

"Now, my dear, you said it. You have a bad habit of wanting to repeat a thing after it has been admitted. As a psychologist, do you know why you do that?"

She looked at him uneasily. "Why?"

"Because you're an awful egoist—like all poets. And because——"

"Why not like all people?"

"All right, like all people. And because you feel inferior. And when you get an admission you want to repeat it and taste it again——"

"Yes, I know that. I'm ashamed of that in me. But what about the medicine?"

"I'll take it. I'll drink a barrel."

They went to drugstores and bought medicines but none of them did Vridar any good. They made him vomit; and in disgust he poured them into the toilet bowl and hurled the bottles into a rear court.

In a forenoon or in an afternoon he would rest; whereupon, feeling a little better, he would return to work. In nearly every night he was delirious and talked out of his delirium. On the next morning he would ask:

"Did I talk? What did I say?" Athene would not tell him and he would insist. "I want to know. What a man says when drunk or when delirious is what he means. Tell me: it will help me to understand."

"You talk of her. You—you seem to think she's with you and you talk to her."

"I do?" He looked at the tears in Athene's eyes. "That's cowardly of me. What do I say?"

"No, I'd rather not tell you."

"Darling, let's be sensible. I know what a hell of a mess life is for you. I know what you think and feel. But I'll fight out of this. Just give me time. So tell me, and I'll understand better what I'm fighting against."

"You probably know what you say."

"I do not. Is it reproach, affection, or what?"

"No, it is never reproach."

"Then what is it?"

"Oh ——" She turned suddenly, her movement wild. "It's—it's just despair and bitterness and—and love." And Athene rose swiftly and left the room.

Vridar lay in sickness, thinking of the matter. In every night since Neloa's death he had dreamed of her, and he had awakened full of her presence. Sometimes his sense of her was so real, so sharply the smell of her hair and clothes, the pressure of her hands, that he looked for her, or listened, expecting her to speak. And now he thought of his dreams, wondering what they meant.

A few of them had been of the past: their meetings on the Antelope Hills, when Neloa came to him in early morning through sunlight and song. But these were not the dreams that left him shaken. For again and again he had dreamed that he searched the earth and found her alive and knelt at her feet; or she came to him in an unexpected hour and smiled and said it had all been a jest; or he died and found her waiting for him in another world. All these dreams he understood: they were simple fulfillments of a deep wish. There were other dreams whose meaning was disguised in parable, and the symbolism of them he did not understand.

There was one of three nights ago. He had been in the homeland of his youth, carrying a gun; and his father was with him and they were hunting deer. They startled a herd and Vridar marked the loveliest of the does and shot her; and the wounded thing, lovely and wild in the morning, ran from hill to hill, leaving blood in her trail; and Vridar ran

after her, intending to fire again. But as he ran he was filled
with horrible realization of what he had done and he wanted
to catch the doe and heal her wound. He began to weep,
and he ran weeping over the hills; and the stricken deer vanished into a great dark canyon and was lost. He threw his
gun away and returned to his home, shaking with grief. . . .

He thought of this dream now, determined to know
what it meant. What had the doe symbolized? Something
that he loved, something that he would have given his life to
save. And as he thought of the matter, he remembered
Cowper's famous poem about himself: I was a stricken deer
that left the herd. . . . And then he knew. He knew beyond all question that the deer had been a symbol of Neloa;
and the great dark canyon was a symbol of death. He had
been an eager and thoughtless huntsman, bent on his own
pleasure, and he had slain the thing he loved. . . .

Of all his symbolic dreams, none in its allegory was more
remarkable than this one: none more simple and dramatic,
none more skillful in making art reveal what lay in his heart.
He had been trying to hide his grief but in every night he
had been building it into his dreams. And that, he thought,
is more evasion: it will never do.

He left the bed and dressed, feeling new strength. When
Athene came in he sat by her on the bed and drew her to his
arms.

"I've been figuring out my dreams," he said. "A person,
you know, reveals what he is, what he thinks, what he hides,
only in his dreams or when he is drunk. Darling, I propose
something."

"What?" she asked, looking at him with eyes red from
weeping.

"From now on to study all our dreams until we know
what they mean. It's the only way we can reach to the hidden self. And something else: I'm going to be so damned
ruthless with myself that finally all my dreams will be as
literal as two times four. We use symbolism only because

we're trying to hide something. After I've stopped dodging, my dreams will not be symbolic at all. And here's a thought: let anyone tell me his dreams and I'll tell him how honest he is with himself. . . .

"Well, shall we?"

"Study our dreams? Of course."

"Fine! Darling, we're going places."

And Vridar was so determined in this matter, so bent on making his thoughts stand nakedly, without the trappings of allegory, that in this night, for the first time in months, he did not dream of Neloa. Before sleep came he was thinking again of dreams; saying, Tonight I will dream a literal dream, with no parable in it. Some dark thought I have been hiding will manifest itself; will come out stark and clear, without disguise of any kind. . . . And a hidden thought did.

As soon as he awoke he knew that a thought had come out of the jungle of his unconscious mind and had declared itself, clearly and unmistakably, for what it was. It filled him with wonder and astonishment; for he had never known, or even vaguely suspected, that such a wish had been in his mind. After thinking of it, reaching to its sources, measuring its significance, he spoke to Athene.

"Yes?" she said.

"Listen, I had a dream. Are you awake?"

"Yes."

"Then listen. I was somewhere—the place does not seem to matter—with a negress. I was out with her, to a party or a dance; and people were staring at us; and I felt terribly ill at ease. I was ashamed. And yet I was saying to myself, Why be ashamed? You say you have no race prejudice. This part of the dream goes back, I think, to something that happened in Chicago two years ago. A white woman walked with a Negro one Sunday along Lake Michigan and a crowd followed, staring at them. I went with the crowd, wondering about the matter. At that time I said to myself, Here is a white woman out with a Negro: they are both human beings, one white, one black; but the white color, at present, is more fashionable. All these people, I could tell, resented the woman and wanted to chastise her. And I did too. But I really didn't know that I did. I had been telling myself for years that there was no race prejudice in me. Well, that part of the dream merely shows me up to myself. It would gall me to be seen with a negress. Why deny it any longer?

"But what follows is of more importance. We were next somewhere alone and she wanted me to make love to her. I stared at her mouth, each lip like a huge puffed blackness; and I thought, Lord, I can never kiss that! It made me sick to think of kissing her mouth. But in a few minutes she was so insistent, so primitive and passionate in her wish, that I resolved to kiss her. But I still felt sick. I kissed her lower lip, realizing with shame and silliness that I could never cover her whole enormous mouth with a mouth like mine. So I just kissed her lower lip, as if I were kissing the side of a house. And then——" Vridar turned and looked at Athene and smiled. "This next is the core of the dream, so let's have it. No dodging, Hunter: out with the truth. I kissed her again and it was like kissing black rubber. It was cool and leathery and I was repelled. But then, at a moment when I was ready to flee, she did something. With her mouth, I mean. She didn't use her tongue: it was the quality of her mouth: something wild, something unashamed and passionate, that stirred me. It shook me. And I kissed her again, amazed by the pleasure the kiss gave. I was shaking like a leaf—and then I woke up."

For a long moment there was silence.

"Now I'll explain it—and, God help me, let there be no sickly evasion. I've heard men say time and again that it is more pleasurable to love a negress than a white woman. Altrock said it. Gourmont says it in one of his books. Other writers have said it. Well, I was enraged by such statements —quite as good pious folk everywhere would be enraged if

I were to declare such a thing to them. My rage meant that I was afraid it might be so. It meant I resented a pleasure I dared not go and take. And you see what I've done? I've buried in my mind a wish to love a negress and learn if it's true. In my dream I was repelled. That was shame and tradition and prejudice working in me. But the kiss, after a little, I found to be wildly pleasurable. That springs from my fear that it might actually be so. . . ."

Vridar was excited now. He left the bed and dressed.

"Athene?"

"Yes?"

"You know why I woke up? Because I was still too much of a puritan to go ahead and embrace her. I was like people who buss and kiss and hug until their blood is a riot and kid themselves into thinking that it is all not an emasculated form of sexual intercourse. Kissing and intercourse, my dear, are not related. Ask fiction editors. Read popular fiction. And so I stopped where shame and good taste and puritanism say it is nice to stop. God damn! Athene, I despise myself. What sickly frauds, what erotic frauds human beings are! Athene?"

"Yes?" said Athene, smiling.

"Darling, I feel like a new man. I'm on my way. I've found a vulnerable spot in my self-defense. I'm going to do a thorough job of this. Fraud that I am! Athene, teach me to love. Teach me to be unashamed. Call me every time you see me dodging. Lay me out.

"And I see something else. I see now that the search for truth can fill a person with frenzied enthusiasm. I feel it. Another world is about to open. These sickly erotic poets, writing of buttercups and sunsets and the moon! These novelists, writing of pure women and noble men! God! They make me want to puke." He paused and looked at her. "If you ever catch me dodging, land on me. I'll land on you. Let's come decent and awake. Let's be animals so that we can be clean.

"Look. I'm over there. Vridar Hunter is over there:
with all his traditions and prejudices and absurd ideals. I'm
here: the mind, unpitying, searching. It's war to the death
between the two of us. It's going to be a grand fight. So I
have wanted to love a negress, have I? Poor fellow. Poor
stupid Vridar, ashamed to be decent. Ass, ridiculous ass!
Colossal emotional halfwit! Stinking fraud! A nice boy
with nice ideals: unselfish, disinterested, sympathetic, proud.
And what a zany!

"Athene, life does have meaning and purpose. There is
use for intelligence. I'm on my way. I'm cleaning house. I'll
never stop until all the puritan cant is out of me, the rot,
the stink. I'll be an animal again. I'll breathe clean air. I'll
love in a clean way, with my senses drunk and swimming.
Do your part——" He stopped. Athene was sitting up in
bed, staring at him. Her eyes were anxious. He looked at
her and smiled. "You're wondering if I'm delirious again. I
know. You think I'm crazy. Athene, let's do this job together. Shall we?"

"What job?" Her voice was a little strange.

"Finding ourselves. Knocking all the cant and sickliness
out of ourselves. Or don't you think we can tolerate one
another if we are honest?"

"I don't think we can if we aren't."

"All right. We can't tell where we'll end up. Right now
I had an amorous dream about a negress. Does it make any
difference?"

"It leaves me wondering about you. But that is not the
point. I want frankness."

"You'll get it. And I want you to give it. Athene, I see
a new world and vast possibilities in that world. It's magnificent." He looked around him. "Darling, let's have a
huge breakfast. Wads of bacon and fruit and coffee and
great rafts of toast!"

II

●

BUT this vision of a new world, and of a new purpose within that world, Vridar lost in the days ahead, finding it only in casual moments and not feeling it deeply then. It was a recognition in his most lucid hours: as if he were a sick man, living in a room with shades drawn, and sensing the health and brightness of a world outside. In these bleak months he completed his readings and wrote his thesis. He received in every week a cheerful and ironic letter from Jake Arlow, his Jewish friend; and he felt in all hours the patience, the quiet and uncomplaining strength, of Athene. But when his thesis was done and the journey to Chicago waited, he felt overwhelming despair. "You go first," he said to Athene, "and I'll follow on the next train. . . ." And in a night of fog and rain he saw her off and then walked the streets until dawn.

Early in the next morning he arrived in Chicago and rode a trolley to the University; and when he passed Washington Park, seeing there a spot where he had spent Sundays with Neloa, and there under trees his old trysting place with Athene, he felt sick and lost. On his ride westward there had been one fixed thought in his mind: that he must go to the dingy dark apartment where Neloa lived and see if she was there. He fought against this unreasoning possession of his senses; but after he had checked his luggage he turned swiftly to the street and came to the building and stopped. It was very quiet and very unreal: strangely familiar in every ugly brick and stone of it, yet something out of nightmare and the dark. Softly he entered the front door and stood in the musty familiar smell of the hallway; entered the basement and looked around him: but nothing was changed. There was the apparatus with which he had baled the papers; the old garbage pails; the irons with which he had shoveled coal. He went to the rear door and climbed the stairway and stood in the back yard. He looked at the rooms where they had lived, and fought against a wish to enter them, but he might as well have fought against winds and flood. He went to the door and knocked. There was no answer and gently he tried the door and opened it and went in. Other persons were living here now: the furniture, the stove, the carpets were different; but the presence of Neloa filled these two rooms. Grief was hot and desperate now in his whole being. Softly he went from one room to the other, remembering how she had sat here, how she had stood before a mirror there, with her long hair down; and how from this window she used to look at the world outside. He went to a closet where her clothes had hung and he smelled them as he had smelled them in those first days after her death. He laid his hand to a bare wall, knowing that in countless times her hands had touched it. "Neloa," he said. "Neloa, I love you. . . ."

He left the rooms and the building. He had not gone far when he met a graduate student whom he had known. Arnold Johnson was large and fat, with a plump and pimpled face that looked as if he had been massaged with oils. He breathed heavily, especially when at ease; and it had always seemed to Vridar that the sound of the man's breath gave to him a sense of opulent security against the world. He shone brightly now and slapped Vridar's back.

"Hello, you son-of-a-gun! Say, you look bad."

"Bad, hell. I'm all right."

"Where you staying?"

"Nowhere. I'm looking for a place."

"The heck. Well, I'll tell you. Let's get a place together." Vridar looked at him, wondering if it would not be wiser to live alone. "What you say?"

"Perhaps. Let's see what we'n find."

For hours he walked with this man, going from one room

to another; and during all this while Arnold talked, his empty chatter flowing like a river or a wind.

"I'm married, did you know? The swellest girl you ever did see. But she's a nurse and we can't live together. That's heck, I call it." His laugh was huge and dimpled like his flesh. "What you think of Coolidge? I wish I'd voted for LaFollette. I don't think Coolidge is so danged hot, do you? You taking your degree this spring? You got a job yet? I want to teach but my wife doesn't want to leave her nursing. I'm between Scylla and Charybdis, I call it. My wife's name is Lorraine. She calls me Alsace. But that's my honeymoon name and is just for private use. She's a witty bugger, my wife. She says, Alsace, we Metz, and just over the hill is Verdun. Pretty danged clever, I say. She said, When I Metz you, Alsace, I was Lorraine, but now I'm John's daughter and you're Johnson. You know, Shakspere was a pretty punny man but my wife is a danged lot punnier. You know Louis Untermeyer's pun? Do you?"

"I think not."

"He said the Russian Revolution was a danged poor piece of Marx-manship. But Lorraine has a dozen as good as that. She'll get a legacy in two years but she says the whole country is getting to be heir-minded. She says John Donne a heck of a good job on the man drake's root but never even mentioned how the gooses vent——"

Vridar stopped, unable to endure any more of this.

"Listen, Arnold, I plan to take my degree in two months, so I guess I'd better live alone. I'll be reading day and night."

"Sure enough. Well, if that's how you figure it. Say, man, you're as white as dough. I think you're sick."

"I'm all right."

"I want you to take luncheon with us. Lorraine——"

"After I get settled."

"Sure. That's what I meant. Lorraine——"

"I have to run along now. I have to get to work."

"Dang it, man, you sure look sick."

Vridar went to the University and asked for his mail. There was a note from Athene, giving her address, and an hour later he sat with her in Jackson Park.

"Vridar, you're sick. I knew you shouldn't come here."

"I'm all right. I'm feeling better. A quiet room and a pile of books——"

"You're not all right and it's senseless to lie about it."

"But I will be all right soon. You know, I'm going to read Voltaire and Lucian and Swift for a few days. They will set me up. . . ."

He needed a defense against himself and this city; and after getting a room near Athene's he went to the library for books. He got Lucian and Swift and Apuleius, and while he was searching the index for something else, sharp and mentally awake, he fell upon the poems of Leonard Bacon. The volume was called *Ph. D.'s* and the reading of one page convinced him that it was precisely what he sought. He went to his room, reading as he walked; and the story of the girl here, adoring her professor of Shelley, and yielding at last her dream of marriage and a home to labor under the man for a doctor's degree, was so mordantly apt, so devastating in its bitter truth, that Vridar began to laugh. The final scene in the drama choked him with mirth and tears. Because the deluded creature, after three years of labor, of devotion to petty and stupid details, chanced to pass the open door of a classroom; saw there another girl, much like what she had been three years ago, listening with wide bright eyes; and heard again the empty and rhetorical thunder of the professor's lecture. Vridar lay on his bed and howled. He roared until tears ran down his face and down his throat and then seized the book and went to find Athene.

"Here," he said, "is something you must read. You remember your instructor of Italian and how you and the other girls worshiped him with pure and sexless ardor? Your

professor of Latin with his bed-ridden wife and the parties
he gave to his girls, acting as benevolent godfather and host?
How he kissed you all good-night: a benediction with a huge
and erotic impulse behind it? But you thought he was only
a fatherly old gentleman with a white beard. Well, here is
a book for you and all the other Hunter and Bryn Mawr and
Goucher and Smith and Barnard girls. It shows how scholars
are made of virgins."

Athene took the book and read and Vridar drew a chair
close and read with her. He shouted again with sardonic
glee.

"Athene, what the hell! Haven't you any sense of the
ironic?"

"Not a great deal, I guess."

"God damn it, that story is perfect! There are hundreds of instructors like that colossal fraud. They talk of
poetry and philosophy, European travel and the stars, the
Gauguin hermitage. . . . And how the girls adore them!
What platonic throbbings plunder their wits and prepare
them for the scholarly kiss!"

Athene looked at him and smiled.

"It is true," she said. "Our professor of Italian had us
all kneeling. We thought he was romantic and adorable."

"Of course. And hiding behind a metaphor he could
have seduced any one of you."

"Not me. I was too full of Dante. But he did seduce
some of the girls. He used to ask us to his apartment to see
his library."

"And had a couch in the library. And when the girls
were weary of books they lay down and he comforted
them."

"He quoted from Gabriele d'Annunzio."

"Swell! Well, give me the book. I'm going to my room
and write."

He was overcome with wonder for human credulity and
guile and he resolved to satirize his race in a long poem. He

chose the stanza made famous by Byron and used again by Bacon.

> *Our hero wanders more than poor Ulysses*
> *From cities frescoed to the country rurals;*
> *But not in search of dragons or of misses*
> *(The first rime's by analogy with plurals);*
> *Nor does he win applause or even hisses,*
> *Nor startle wonder in the Alps and Urals:*
> *You'll learn, indeed, with pain and perturbation*
> *That he is hardly worth a peroration.*
>
> *But you may burn or lend the book, Sir: I*
> *Shall have the royalty that will be my penny;*
> *If Miss Pulitzer is your reading, why,*
> *I'll not accuse you, Sir, of much or any.*
> *There still are those who like a painted sky,*
> *And books with heroes, tall and pure and many;*
> *Though Time, the jester, I observe, disguises*
> *Oblivion nicely with awards and prizes. . . .*

During the afternoon he wrote and far into the night, forgetting his hunger and fatigue, his pain and grief and himself, with the tale flowing to his fingers almost as fast as he could pound the keys.

> *As editor I make a fair pretension,*
> *Though doubtless not so learned as Morize.*
> *A lex non scripta allows me to mention*
> *That I have gathered almost three degrees.*
> *Two I now have, and am agog with tension*
> *Because I expect anon some LL.D.'s:*
> *Coolidge, I know, has six, and Hughes a dozen,*
> *But I'm not a politician or his cousin. . . .*

He resolved to send John Doe to Mars and there have him discover a civilized creature quite unlike himself. Be-

cause of John's love of himself and the physical appearance
of himself and humankind, he would regard the Martians as
appalling monsters, with an ugliness more than hideous; and
over the implications here, over the descent of beauty to the
level of prejudice, he chuckled as he paced the room and
smoked. And when John got to Mars, he would, of course,
because of diminished gravity, leap around in alarming
fashion:

> *He crawled into a huge torpedo; took*
> *Of testimonials to last him for a week;*
> *And when men fired him into space they shook*
> *With advertising, and could barely speak.*
> *And signs—Conoco, Sir—fell into brook*
> *And scuttled away in fearful haste to seek*
> *A safer refuge in the tumbling sea*
> *(As men in wars to find democracy).*
>
> *And then: he hurdled dykes and trees and prairies*
> *With ghastly speed and wild exhilaration:*
> *His act as unaccountable as Mary's,*
> *Without the clarity of Eve's temptation.*
> *He leapt the rivers and the estuaries*
> *Like moralists who smell an assignation;*
> *And clinging to his shoulders as he went*
> *Was a vision of filmed teeth—and Pepsodent. . . .*

After writing twenty stanzas he seized them and went
to find Athene. He asked her to read them; and she did,
and smiled.

"Is it any good? It shoots through me like rockets."

"Of course. But it's the kind of satire that sizzles and
scalds. It's satanic."

"Oh well, so am I."

"It's like a series of lightning flashes, each of which re-

veals the human animal as a worm. The conclusion of each
stanza is like a lash across the face."

"Nonsense!"

"It is. Take this one." And she read:

"Their heads did not grow down beneath their shoulders
Like those of pigs and anthropophagi,
But hung above like half-suspended boulders
Somewhere between their bodies and the sky;
With vast attentive ears like leather folders,
With great bold eyes, each asking how and why:
(For my part, whether liar, thief, or bawd,
I think man is an image of his god).

"Those last two lines are awful in their truth. Can't
you be more whimsical, gentle? Do you have to leave the
reader feeling gutted?"

"I'm attacking self-love," he said. "I'm having at it with
hammer and tongs."

"You certainly are."

"I can't write whimsical irony. I smite with a broad
palm."

"Not always. Take this:

"Let that be censored. Now and then I shed
A thought or two, or feebly I surmise.
For one with suffixes accredited
To ponder on the loveliest of lies
Of all the best that has been thought and said
Between the inspiration and the prize,
Must leave some dogmas on the printed page
To flush his youth and castigate his age.

"Your couplet there is one that Pope could have been
proud of."

"But it isn't whimsical."

"Almost. It's what I mean. Or take this sly stanza:

"Nor had the woman any breasts—or drifts
Of snow, Pulitzers call them; nor of hips
More than a hint of shank; nor any shifts
Of parentheses upon the brow; nor lips
Like any crimson rosebud where it lifts
To hungry bee-tongue. (They had finger-tips;
The same I'm-hungering look upon the street;
The same biology—and they had feet.)

"But this next stanza is savage in its incest-motif. Vridar, did you have a fixation on your mother?"

"Ask me that question a year from now and I'll answer it. But now—well, how is this one?

"The men—all wiser really than the owl—
Had never heard of Tarzan: all agape
With ancientness, they had no well fed jowl,
Nor any hair upon the head or nape.
Nor had they ever—this will make you howl—
Lynched a poor Negro for a tale of rape;
Nor placed a coat for one upon the mud
Whose mind was far less royal than her blood."

"It has a fine couplet," Athene said. "The rest of it is not your best work."

"Damn it, do you expect my best all the time?"

"That," said Athene, smiling, "is what I expect."

He looked at her and shrugged. "No one makes all his lines of the same worth. No one can. Well, how is this one?

"I'm growing tired of dragging in my learning,
And so, no doubt, are you—but poets do it.
A poem, in fact, is hardly worth the burning
That hasn't much allusion running through it.

So were I ass if I were poet, spurning
The darkness that will draw the scholars to it;
And make them roar, 'By Mencken as Mencken's hero,
Here is a thesis, vitam impendere vero!' "

"No, it's too savage."
"Oh, damn it! Well, is this sweet enough?

> *"These Martians, it would seem, had come to feel*
> *The price they paid for statesmen was too high:*
> *Ten million lives and countless tons of steel,*
> *The wet red smell of glory in the sky;*
> *Leagues and speeches, covenants and repeal,*
> *And poppies redder where men went to die:*
> *A statesman is a glory, but the Christ*
> *Has cost no more of people sacrificed."*

"It makes me shudder."
"That's what I intend. The truth makes all of us shudder. All right: here's a sly one:

> *"Nor had they any culture such as ours:*
> *I now allude to that wherein the rich*
> *Are troubled by the proper size of dowers,*
> *The poor by misplaced pennies and the itch;*
> *Where some toss nightlong in their penthouse towers,*
> *And some, alas, sleep quite well in a ditch:*
> *The kind that Bismarck's fingers held, till lo,*
> *It crossed the Rhine to Tiger Clemenceau!"*

"The last two lines are splendid. The rest, my dear, is inane."
"Inane! Well, I guess. All right, I'm going back while I'm steamed up. It pours out of me, good and bad: if there's a good line in a ton—no matter, I'm getting a hell of a kick out of it. . . ."
He returned to his machine and wrote.

And not a sign—ah, rarest of paradoxes!—
Of culture's totems; nor of etiquette
Correctly corseted in opera boxes
The faintest smell or hint; nor even yet
A bon mot from the many equinoxes
Of intellectual zodiacs, when met
Artistic minds to babble in a tall
Crescendo through the march from Parsifal. . . .

He rose and paced the room, wondering with what analogue to represent the human race. In colloquial metaphor
human beings were often represented as hogs. . . . He
thought next of polygamy: that fabulous and ancient disguise of sexual avarice; that erotic greed established as an
institution of God. . . .

And next a boar whom bigamy had turned
Into a prophet married forty sows;
And all the little runts rose up and spurned
Polygamy, and swore the Law allows
One wife to each, else had the Great Pig earned
The name of traitor: why let one espouse
Two score of females when the sexes are
Divided as evenly as peace and war!

He turned next to the Ten Commandments and after he
had parodied each he stopped, exhausted, and read his lines.
He read by turn in Apuleius, in Swift, in Aristophanes, in
Lucian. Swift, after all, had written the only great satire:
he had said with unerring precision all that was to be said.
And what, Vridar wondered now, lay behind satire and the
acidulous pen: how much emotional disease, what broken
ideals and dreams, what evasion of self? I am writing this
stuff, he reflected, because my old ego is angry and sick and
frustrated. Swift hated his race but that means only that
he hated himself. He hated sham and fraud, liars and

hypocrites, half-witted moralities, cheap and theatrical ideals —and because he had found all of these in Jonathan Swift. . . .

Vridar lay in thought; and after a little while he wrote:

> *If you could see me as I am*
> *You'd slay me with an epigram.*
> *If I could see you as you are*
> *I'd wonder what you're living for.*

That, it seemed to him, said all that for hours he had been trying to say. He turned the light off and went to bed.

III

BUT he returned to satire again and again in the months ahead. It was his strength and it held him in possession of his wits. Besides a full course of study he was revising parts of his thesis, reading books in preparation for his final examinations, and memorizing dates in literary history until he knew eight hundred and sixty-three of them. One day Thurman said, "You look overworked. I hope you're taking things calmly and not reading yourself to death." "I'm trying to be philosophic," Vridar said. And he shrugged, for he was not philosophic at all. He read day and night; and sleep, when it came to him, came while he sat in a chair with a book in his hands.

"The finals," he said to Athene, "have me scared out of my pants. You know Miss Jones? She fainted in her examination last night. And Bob Wernecke looks like paste. . . ."

Everyone asked about the examination but no one knew quite what it was like. "The Inquisition," one said, "and we're the witches. It's sink or swim." Vridar knew only that a dozen learned men and women would face him across a table and question him in any field of literature or history. He read again in the Greek and the Roman periods, in the French and Italian and German; and when books became only meaningless pages he sat at his typewriter and wrote his scathing lines.

All I could see from where I stood
Was three bootleggers making good.
I turned and looked the other way
And saw three smugglers in a bay.
So with my eye I traced the line
Of Prohibition, wet and fine,
From east to west till I was come
Back to where I'd started from;

And all I saw from where I stood
Was more bootleggers making good. . . .

When the night of his examination came Vridar was
little more than skin and bone. He drank a quart of strong
tea, took fifteen grains of aspirin, and went to the Midway
and sat on a bench. He smoked cigarettes until they were
tasteless and went to look for the examiners, hoping the
more formidable ones would be sick. Thurman he did not
mind, nor Denham and Breverton: they were all men of large
sympathies and generous hearts; but he was apprehensive of
Downs, the Celtic scholar, and of John Atwater, a new
member who was, legend declared, unpitying and malicious.
And he was afraid of the visiting instructors: philologists in
fields of which he knew nothing, and historians who had
spent forty years in a small province. He was so anxious and
shaken after an hour of waiting that he ran to a café and
drank more tea: he was drunk now with tea and aspirin and
cigarettes. And when at last he stepped into Thurman's
office and saw ten scholars, all looking at him, all waiting
with questions, he sank trembling to a chair. But there was
no reason for his fright. Thurman saw it; and with quip
and jest, laughter and irrelevance, he put Vridar at ease.
When Vridar was asked, nevertheless, to read from *Beowulf,*
a poem that he almost knew by heart, he faltered and gave a
stupid translation that made him burn with shame. He
wanted to crawl out on hands and knees and knock his head
on a wall. I'm a fool, he thought desperately. Life isn't
worth such humiliation. I'll give blow for blow. . . .

Thurman asked, not factual questions, but questions
that made him think; and he liked them. He was turned
next to Downs and when he saw that man's shrewd eyes
probing him, he thought: this is where I get a lance through
me; this is where my ignorance fills the room. But he erred
again. Downs asked only one question:

"Who was Margaret of Navarre?"

"I don't know," Vridar said.

He then realized that he did know. My God: he had read of her ten years ago when a freshman in college. Vridar writhed in his chair; and Downs, showing faint surprise, turned Vridar to the colleague at his left. And Atwater did not temper scholarship with mercy: he waded in with zest. He's remembering Poe, Vridar thought: when there's a fool to be hanged, hang him. And Vridar soon realized that he liked Atwater's sharp and incisive questions: it had been the sympathy, the anxious faces, that had scattered his wits. Atwater, moreover, chose a field that Vridar knew well: Daniel Defoe and the low life of his time. . . .

"What was Defoe's station in life at birth?"

"Proletarian."

"How far did he advance socially?"

"As far as the pillory."

This thrust brought a roar from Thurman. Others laughed, too; and Atwater, flushing from end to end of his lean face, looked at Vridar for a long moment. But Vridar was all right now. His wits had returned and he was at ease.

For three hours he was questioned. These examiners were not inquisitors: they were friends. Vridar liked them. Some of them he loved. And when, finally, he was asked to leave the room, he went out reflecting that he needed more of this sort of thing: something to slap him around and wake him up. . . .

He stood in a long room now that had once been his office. It was here that he first saw Athene: at this desk he had sat, and she there by a window, when, almost two years ago, they had talked of Shelley. It all seemed very quaint and very silly now.

> *O lift me from the grass!*
> *I die! I faint! I fail!*

Yes, it was very silly: without strength or purpose: a self-pitying lover's agonized wail under moonlight. Shelley: a symbol now of ethereal purity, half man and half woman, and all saint: a sentimental nincompoop, really: a plaintive and pathetic echo of the undisciplined mind. Chaucer and Shakspere were poets for men; Donne, too, and Pope. But Shelley and Cowper and Henley were impossible asses. . . .

Thurman now entered, followed by the others, and offered his hand. He said something about magna cum laude; offered congratulations and a friendly smile. He offered some friendly advice.

"You have read too much. Forget books and do some thinking. . . ."

Vridar left the building and fled. He found Athene waiting in a park and threw himself to earth. He rolled in the deep grass and laughed.

"Darling, how funny it is! For ten years I've wanted to be a doctor of philosophy. Now I am and it means nothing. We anticipate the pleasure until in achievement there is no pleasure left. Now I want to be a great writer. There may be fun in trying, but if I ever should be a great writer there'll be no fun in the realization of it. Then I'd want to be the greatest of all writers; and, that granted, I'd want to be the greatest person on earth; and, after that, God. And if I were God I'd want to be the only god. If I were the only god I'd perish in loneliness for want of something greater to achieve. Such is human vanity. Such is the horoscope of every sensitive man of brains.

"Isn't it silly?"

"That's because you're an extremist in all things."

"Ambition is extreme. Every great man of the past has had an almost tigerish ambition. It has driven him with never a moment's peace. Isn't it so?"

"Yes, I suppose it is."

"And it's silly. We should get us a garden, an orchard, two horses and a small bunch of hens; and be reasonable and decent; and let the mad world groan through the pages of Who's Who. If we had any sense at all we would."

"My dear, I can see you doing that."

"But I haven't any reasonableness. I want to be somebody. But why the hell should I? Athene, I tell you ambition is stupid. It is neurotic and sick. Old Charley Bridwell had none. He was a philosopher. I envy him. . . ."

"Tell me about the examination."

"It was all right. I quaked and shook and fumbled. Thurman was swell. They were all swell. And do you know? I'm ashamed of these damned satires I've been writing. Human beings are all right."

"But tomorrow you'll be writing another satire."

"I suppose. I'm thinking of one now. About Commencement, I mean."

The elaborate trappings, the pompous strut and ceremony, of graduation exercises in American universities had always amused Vridar. When he took his bachelor's degree, and later when he took his master's, he had been excused, pleading sickness in the first and unavoidable absence in the second. On the second occasion he sat in the audience with Dennis Altrock and thought he would die of mirth. The president, robed in black, and looking as stiff as he would have looked had his skin been poured full of concrete, got mixed in his Latin; was prompted by a fluttering and anxious assistant; and then forgot his Latin entirely and fled into English. And Vridar wondered then, as he again wondered now, why human vanity gave itself to such silly rigmaroles of conduct. It was beyond belief: all the habiliments of orders and cults and ceremonies: the stiff and outlandish dignity of apes, some as grand goblins and kleagles, as gaudy regents of Church and State, or as professors and deans and presidents robed in medieval black and looking as solemn and unimportant as owls. It was the starched heritage of primitive folk customs: related darkly to prayer wheels and euchologies, exorcisms and cabals, golden calves and joss and seven-league boots. . . .

"Perhaps it's the buried life Matthew Arnold wrote of. For see us: a people affecting to be civilized and in our blood is the voodoo and Mumbo Jumbo and evil eye; bell, book, and candle; ouija boards and wraiths and death lights; fetishism and hocus-pocus of the Dark Ages. I can feel it in myself. Sometimes it frightens me. I can see myself with a rabbit's foot or a horseshoe; or decked out with a cardboard hood on my head; or shivering near a haunted house and yelling alleluiah; or hunting witches and lynching a Negro, or making an amulet of gnats' eyes and eagle feathers. And it makes me shudder. Of what use is intelligence against all that? Here it is: as long as we have the intellectual voodooism of commencements, it's senseless to pass anti-lynching laws."

"I hadn't thought of it that way. I imagine you're right."

"All this solemn and oracular muttering in Latin! The dead languages are a part of our modern liturgy. And I'm going to try to get out of this primitive strut. I'm terrible enough without parading around in a sepulchral gown. . . ."

He wrote to the president, asking to take his degree in absentia. He did not approve, he said, these weird and ghostly survivals of ancient darkness. There came from the president's secretary a curt little note. He would not be allowed to take his degree in absentia, even if he were in China. . . .

"That settles it. Culture wins."

For three dollars he rented a gown of black and gold and purple; and he had to pay five dollars for a hood. Long before the exercises began, some of the doctors strutted about the campus, looking like justices of a supreme court. They were self-conscious and proud. Families and friends stood in awe and watched them perform; and not in a single face did Vridar see a flicker of amusement, a hint of scorn. This was another pageant: a little more intellectual, a little less pompous, than that of a foreign ambassador riding down Pennsylvania Avenue, or laying a wreath on the tomb of Lincoln. And when Vridar appeared, decked out like a jongleur or a bishop, he felt too ridiculous for words. He looked at himself and laughed.

He met Percy Armond, a professor from Wasatch College. Percy wore a neat little mustache and walked with the dignity of an earl. While looking at Percy, Vridar remembered another Wasatch professor who, upon taking his doctorate in the autumn quarter more than a year ago, sent Christmas cards with Ph.D. after his name. He thought of the faculty rosters in university catalogs:

John Brown Doe, A.B., A.M., Ph.D. . . .

and the petty envy of those without a doctor's degree, and the condescension of those with it. . . .

"How do you feel? Pretty damned silly?"

"Silly!" said Percy. "Why should I?"

"You shouldn't. You look splendid."

"I feel splendid." And he stared, as solemn as a loon, at the folds of purple lying across his arm. "Did you buy your gown?"

"No."

"You should. You'll need it in Wasatch in the faculty parades."

"You look like an educated man," said Vridar gravely. "The world does improve. . . ."

The address to the graduates was given by M. Jusserand. For this man, an ambassador, an apostle of peace, and a scholar in more fields than one, Vridar had always felt admiration. But his admiration died in this hour. Jusserand, it is true, did not exhort the graduates to noble living, to high ideals, nor say they were the leaders of the future: he did worse than that. He pitched headlong into abuse of Germany and defense of France. His voice rang from end to end of the campus, his hands clutched air. He spoke of the United States and France as sisters, with the same ideals, the same exalted leadership among nations, the same deep and selfless wish to protect the weak and rebuke the strong. He spoke of persecuted France: the beacon of Europe, the haven of the oppressed, the foe of injustice and the friend of God. . . .

At this point Vridar could stand no more. He reached for paper and pencil and bowed to his knees; and while Jusserand talked furiously out of his beard, Vridar wrote his lines. . . .

A PATHETIC PARABLE OF PEACE

Now Xhamatoc for Kickapoo Klac
Did a honeymoon of peace devise,
Where the Rhine, a river quite as black
As any, lay sprawled upon its back
With belly to the skies.
About three miles of atmosphere
And two rainbows were fenced off here;
And a tiny kingdom of coal-mining, too,
And one young mandate, sired by a league:
But on the whole it was a splendid view:
As calm as thunder, as peaceful as intrigue.

And then that crazy treaty out there hanging
Heels down from the sky, without a speck of shame!
And Xhamatoc begins her boomeranging
With appeals to God and quite a lot of banging
In a peaceful sweet attempt to save her name.
And Kickapoo with one triumphant shout
Sticks out his tongue before she lays him out.
And then the zodiac shakes and covenants burst
As if the banging had not been the worst.

And fragments of treaties tumble down
As large as an ordinary town;
And the Little Entente then waltzed and sang
And Italy smote it with a bang.
And the Rhine, the same but for a little red,
And as calm as any boundary should be,
Gathered the League of Nations to its bed
And flowed away serenely to the sea.
And Kickapoo, with heels caught in a fleece,
First thumbed his nose and then yelled loud for peace.

And now the moral hangs in view:
The mole said pfst! the titmouse jeered;
Three times four is six times two;
And Jusserands shout into their beard.

IV

●

LEAVING Athene in Chicago to continue her studies, Vridar returned to Wasatch College. For an hour they stood on the bridge near the station, looking down at the ugly river, waiting for the train.

"We'll be lonely. We must not let it be the loneliness of despair."

"We'll work. We'll have no time to remember."

"We'll use our sense of humor. When everything else fails, we can turn to that. When you feel your heart breaking, read Swift and smile."

"But, Vridar, please don't turn into a satirist."

"I won't. But I must use it now."

"Satire is cheap."

"I know. I'll have to be an ironist until I can be something bigger." He looked at her. "Your eyes are wet, Athene. It's time to grin."

"So are yours. You grin, too."

Vridar tried to smile. He turned away to hide the sudden rush of darkness. He looked at the station clock.

"A year—twelve months—before we meet again."

"But you'll see your boys."

"Not yet. I couldn't stand it yet." He took her in his arms. She shook. "Darling, where's your irony now?"

"I'm all right. I'll—work. . . . Vridar."

"Yes?"

"You'll do nothing rash?"

"Nothing. That's all behind me now. . . ."

When he entered the train he turned to satire; and in the long journey westward, save when he slept, he sat with pen and paper and the ironic muse. It's my only strength now, he thought; it's all that saves me. And he wrote page after page, transmuting his sickness, his despair, into the sardonic line. . . .

> A pang and a groan; a gulping of pills
> And tonics and pastes; a dark wild hope;
> A clear calm voice with nothing in it
> Professionally talking of aches and ills.
> A prayer and a moan and a frantic clinging
> To a lance of light; and far bells ringing.
> Then a form bent low with a stethoscope
> And a voice that murmurs, "In another minute. . . ."

And after he arrived in Salt Lake City he never for a moment relaxed the vigil of mind over heart. It was as if he lived with a lunatic, sharply watching every move, every gesture; anticipating each waking violence; rebuking each hour of loneliness, each passionate grief. Because he knew clearly that if he once yielded to despair he would be lost. Heaped against his ironic defenses was the mad heartache of nine months, a flood of emotion that would have swept him to ruin. He felt the depth and intensity of it and was afraid. And when he felt its imminence he turned swiftly to his typewriter and leveled his grief to impotence with sarcasm and jeer.

He got a room in a house where a tall gray woman lived alone with a son who was an imbecile. This son, a man of thirty, was a dwarfed creature with very long arms. He loved gaudy things: crimson suspenders, purple ties, pink shirts and trousers, and yellow socks and shoes. In every day he was allowed to dress in his most splendid regalia and strut about the house; and the presence of him, stuttering and gesticulating and caressing his vivid colors, helped Vridar to keep his grasp on life.

"Hello there," he would say and two small stupid eyes would look at him. "You look pretty swell today." Two short thick hands would smooth the pink trousers and a thick tongue would sputter of tremendous and untold things. And after facial distortions the tongue would say:

"Gu-gu-gu-gu-gurl!"

"Girl, my eye. What would you do with a girl?"

"Gu-gu-gu-gu-gurlll!"

"I wish you had an imbecile in the house with you," Vridar wrote to Athene. "This fellow is a great tonic. All my stupendous worry and fret he reduces to nothing. When I come home, oppressed, oozing with gloom, there he is, a gorgeous spectacle of happiness, standing before a mirror and stuttering at himself. Then nothing is important and I feel a lightness that is the only strength. He keeps saying girl at me, his eyes shining with lust; and if I don't respond he flies into a great fury and wants to murder me. But if I show him a picture of a lovely girl he overflows with joy and points a shaking finger at her breast. . . ."

Vridar was teaching again but not as formerly. He still felt that teaching was noble work and he still wished to be a great teacher; but he took into the classroom now a sardonic mind and a lashing tongue. And few of his students knew what to make of him. Some sat in amazement, some in awe, and some in uneasy contempt. Only a handful understood the ironies and oblique thrusts with which he filled every lecture, or which he wrote on the outside of themes. And before long he found himself in trouble.

One day in class a girl with a soft and credulous face asked him a question. "Dr. Hunter," she said, "don't you believe Jesus was the Son of God?" Vridar looked at her and the class waited.

"Why do you ask that question? I haven't been talking of Jesus and God."

"I just wondered. I don't think you do."

Vridar wrote on the blackboard:

The proofs of the existence of a god have made many men atheists—JOUBERT.

"That," he said gravely, "is a statement that just came to me. It is irrelevant. Most likely, too, it is meaningless. Now in regard to your question: an instructor in a university supported by public taxes is not allowed to answer frankly such a question as yours. Such answers in a state school are not a part of education. But if you are interested in the matter, and not in my opinion, here are two books you might read." And he wrote on the board the titles and authors of two books: one arguing the historicity of Jesus and one denying it. He thought the matter was closed.

Two days later there came to him from a powerful business man of the city this curt note:

Professor Hunter
Wasatch College

DEAR SIR:
I am told that you devoted an hour, or period, last week or recently in your class telling, according to your view point, why Jesus is not divine. Please advise me if this is so.
Yours truly,
R. B. ENSIGN.

For most of an afternoon Vridar pondered this letter. He wrote to Athene. "Ensign can, if he wishes, put me out of here. I am now facing the problem that hundreds of liberals in American universities have faced. Shall I be honest with my students or shall I compromise? To that, now and forever with me, there can be only one answer. I did not, of course, spend an hour or even a moment declaring Jesus was not divine. But I might as well jump against a wall as to deny it. I begin to see that many instructors have been sacrificed to the stupidity and prejudices of their students. . . . The matter is serious. Tell me at once what you think I should do." And Athene wrote: "You should be as tactful as you can but you will not, of course, make any compromises. You might write Ensign and tell him what you think the purpose of a university should be. . . ."

This suggestion left Vridar in thought. What, after all, should be the purpose of an American university? For several days he gave the matter earnest thought and then he wrote to Ensign:

. . . Let me say, in the first place, that it is not my custom to declare my personal opinions in the classroom. I am not one among that enormous class of dogmatists who know where they came from, why they are here, and where they are going. Dogma may or may not be properly taught in churches but it certainly has no place in an institution of learning. I have no student who knows what I believe on any subject, save our insensitive and stupid custom of burying our dead in valuable materials, and our persecution of the Negro and the Jew. Upon the question of what I believe in regard to God, Jesus, or Mahomet, my students can do no more than to cherish unsupported convictions.

It may interest you to know what I conceive to be my purpose and my duty as a teacher: to arouse my students to an intelligent and alert interest in contemporary affairs and thought; to awaken them to the possibilities of their own minds; and to suggest to them the stupidity of believing in anything merely because it is the belief of someone else. I try to persuade them to think, not as I think, not as you or anybody else thinks, but as they must honestly think after they have examined the evidence.

I trust you can see now that what I believe in regard to anything is of no concern to my students. Of importance for them ought to be a fearless and honest inquiry into the facts and superstitions of life. To that end it is imperative that they be acquainted with everything of consequence in modern thought. And it would be a shameless perversion of my function as a teacher if I were to deny to them the sources of the knowledge they seek. When, therefore, one manifested interest in the historicity of Jesus, I gave to her the names of two books by distinguished scholars in that field. If I erred in that, then the college I serve errs in calling itself an institution of learning. . . .

He sent this letter to Ensign and a copy of it to his president. The former ignored it; the latter wrote:

I am not writing you in any sense of criticism for what you have said and done, because I do not know the nature of it and would not presume to say until I knew the facts. My tendency always is to freedom of discussion in the classroom. At the same time I am calling your attention to the law so that you will not say anything that will bring down criticism on you. . . .

This letter overwhelmed Vridar with misgivings. For days he could think of little but its implications and the ominous finger these pointed to his future. "I see my end here," he wrote to Athene. "If the constitution of the state forbids education, then in all fairness I must abide by it. That does not mean I'm going to spend all my time talking of Mother's Day and the flag and the glory of God. It does mean that I'm in a box. . . ."

He did not allude again to religion and he strove to be discreet; but he went, nevertheless, from one difficulty to another. The editor of the school's literary journal came to him one afternoon with a story. In it was *my gawd*, and this, she said, would never pass the censors.

"The author won't change it and I don't want the responsibility."

"He won't use *my gosh* instead? *My gosh* and *my God* mean, of course, the same thing. Do you think the censors are unaware that *heck* means *hell*, *geewhiz* means *Jesus*, and *gol-darn* means *God damn?*"

"I know they wouldn't approve *my gawd*."

"They probably say *gosh-dang* but wouldn't say *God-damn*."

"And they probably say bad woman for whore."

"Oh, but bad woman sounds so much nicer."

"Their indecency makes me blush. They say peculator for

thief. I imagine they call a pimp an agent provocateur. Such a good word as spit would give them chills."

"Well, what shall we do?"

"I'll publish it if some faculty member will stand behind me."

"All right. I will."

"But I want it in writing. I'll have to show your letter."

Vridar went to a machine and wrote:

DEAR MISS ARNOLD:

My Gawd is a vulgarism but surely no objection can be taken to it in a college journal. It is, in my opinion, innocuous. I cannot believe I teach in a college which is so pious and evasive as to condemn it. Use it: and if there are objections, refer the purists to me.

VRIDAR HUNTER.

And so ignorant was Vridar of the inner workings of a small college, dependent on public taxes, that he believed this matter was ended, too. For him it was quaintly silly. But it was not silly for the Committee and as soon as the story appeared they swung into action. They called Vridar before them and he found himself facing three very solemn men.

"I understand," the chairman said, "that you approved this profanity." He thrust an indignant finger at *my gawd*.

"I did."

The three educators looked at him.

"Is it your notion, Dr. Hunter, that profanity is a decent thing in a college paper?" It was the professor of science speaking. The professor of history looked fat and solemn and a little startled. The third member stared at his hands.

"Would *my gosh* have been all right?"

"I should say so, yes."

"My gosh and my God mean exactly the same thing. Do you think God is so simple as to be fooled?"

The chairman flushed.

"And whom do you have in mind by the purists?"

"The censors, of course."

For a long moment there was silence. Vridar rose to his feet.

"It's my opinion," he said, "that you can't make monks and nuns of college students. They're men and women, not boys and girls. This unctuous paternalism that you try to establish over everything they do and say will only drive them, off the campus, to do and say worse things than you ever heard of. I don't believe in legislating people into heaven. As a matter of fact, I think we have too much legislation. I have in mind this sickly law called Prohibition. Humanity is not so bad as our judges of it declare it to be. It's all right. It merely needs a chance to be decent." He went to the door. "Have you any more to say?"

"Only this, Dr. Hunter: that such matters hereafter you can properly leave to the committee appointed to take care of them. It strikes us that you are out of your field."

"Is that all?"

"That is all."

Sick with fury, sick with shame for his race, Vridar went to his room. In a little while the door was opened and the imbecile looked in.

"Come in, Bob."

"Guh—guh—gurll!" he said.

"Bob, you know what you ought to be?" Bob grinned and showed a mouthful of decayed teeth. "You ought to be a censor. You have the precise modicum of brains." And while Bob stared at a lovely girl on a calendar, Vridar wrote in his journal.

All censors, and especially those who wish to be, are persons ashamed of their own bodies. They may be sexual perverts. They may be sexually frustrated. Not so many years ago I was a person who wanted certain books suppressed, certain persons rebuked; and I wanted these because I was a sickly puritan, sickly with notions of guilt. I see it clearly now. I also see clearly that all these pious crusaders, all these self-appointed guardians of public morality, are rotten inside. I wonder how long it will be before the world realizes a truth so simple and so obvious. . . .

And to Athene: "They're licking me here. Some professors who were affable when I came don't speak to me now. But I'm discovering myself, my dear, and that is of more importance than my job."

Two days later Vridar met the president on the campus. He liked Tom Johnson: a stout florid man with small twinkling eyes, blunt manners and speech, and short thick hands.

"Well, how are things going?"

"All right, I guess." Vridar grinned. "You haven't fired me yet."

"No," said Johnson, his eyes shrewd and twinkling. "Do you have a student named Edith Sedgwick?"

"Yes. Why?"

"And you advised her not to read the Bible, did you?"

"I advised her to read it. Like most Christians she knows nothing about it."

"Do you know Ronald Martin?"

"Yes. He's one of my students."

"Not now. His father has taken him to another school."

"On account of me?"

"That's what he said. I had an awful time with him yesterday." Johnson stepped closer and spoke quietly. "When I taught sociology before coming here I taught evolution and got away with it. I said I'd present all the theories. And every student ended up by believing in evolution." The president's eyes were all twinkles now. "Your trouble, Hunter, is that you're not astute enough. You can teach anything if you know how."

"I suppose. Well, perhaps I'll learn how."

But he had in this year no power to learn how. If a student came to his office, looking earnest, speaking out of what seemed to be good faith, Vridar talked frankly with him and to the point.

"My people are Mormons," one young man said. "But I can't see it. What do you think?"

"You mean as man to man?"

"Yes. I'm all up a tree."

"Well, I was brought up in Mormonism. I can't see it now. I can't see that religion of any sort needs to be a public matter."

"I'll tell you what I think. I think Mormonism is stupid."

"Stupid? Well, it does smell a bit too much of babies and sugar beets. . . ."

And a week later Vridar was summoned to the president's office. Johnson was in a bad humor: his face was pink and mottled, his eyes did not twinkle now.

"Listen, Dr. Hunter, what is this I hear now?"

"I can't imagine."

"Have you been telling your classes that Mormonism is nothing but babies and sugar beets?"

"I have not."

"You have not? Well, Jones was just up to see me and he was raising Cain. He says you told your classes that."

"I did not. To one of my students I made a remark bearing on the subject. But in private. I had no idea he would run out and tattle."

"That's a fine thing to be saying! Babies and sugar beets! How do you expect to teach here and say such things?"

"Can't an instructor in this school ever talk frankly with a student? When they come to us are we to evade and crawl?"

"I know nothing about that. I do know you're giving me too much trouble. I have work to do. I can't spend all my time talking to furious taxpayers."

"I realize that."

"All right. Watch your tongue."

And Vridar did watch his tongue. He spent hours think-ing about his great vulgar country and its contempt for honesty and truth. Instructors in the deep South, he had been told, hardly dared say anything at all. In this Mormon empire they dared say very little. In the northeast: but Robinson, Nearing, and countless others had been dismissed. And if students came to Vridar, inviting frankness, saying they had problems they wished to talk of, he sidestepped.

"I'm sorry. In this school an instructor cannot talk candidly with a student. Oh, he may, of course, about Christmas greetings and our glorious service in the World War. I'm sorry. But you students run right out and tell your parents and your parents come up here and raise merry hell. It's too hard on the president.

"No, I'm very sorry, but I am not allowed to be frank."

"But, Dr. Hunter, I wouldn't tell. Honest."

"Perhaps not. But I'm allowed to make no exceptions. . . . What, by the way, do you wish to talk about?"

"Oh, myself—life. My parents think I'm going to the dogs. They don't understand. They're Mormons——"

"Say no more." Vridar looked at the anxious face and smiled. "I'd like to talk. I'd like to help you if I can. But —well, try to understand how it is. . . ."

But off the campus Vridar talked, and once indiscreetly, and matters came to a momentary crisis. He was asked to read a paper to a liberal club and he chose as his subject the function of education in a democracy. His small audi-ence was of men only: doctors, lawyers, merchants: and after the paper was read the discussion turned to sex. A doctor was speaking of girls who worked their way through college.

"Some of them are plain gold diggers," he said.

"That reminds me," Vridar said. "I have a student who, for a course in sociology, has made a study of prostitution in this city. He says we have a half-dozen college girls who are supporting themselves in part by prostitution."

"It doesn't surprise me," the doctor said. "I suppose such a condition prevails everywhere."

"Any gold-digging girl is a harlot," a lawyer said. "It doesn't take three dollars. A gift will do. If a man takes a girl out and buys her candy, flowers, rings, clothes, and so with his favors seduces her, then she's a harlot, isn't she?"

"Such harlots as that," said the doctor, "would be common on every campus."

"Of course. I've known them."

"Perhaps," said the doctor slyly, "you gave some flowers yourself."

"Perhaps I did. . . ."

And Vridar forgot the matter. To him a week later came a letter from the president that floored him. It asked briefly and to the point:

Did you or did you not in an address before the Delphic Club make the statement that some of the girls in Wasatch College are harlots?

In our Delphic discussion [Vridar wrote], I said that a student of mine (John Ellerton is the name) declared there are a half-dozen girls on our campus who are in part supporting themselves by prostitution. Mr. Ellerton, I understand, has made a study of whoredom in this city. I did not ask to see his evidence. I did not say that I believed his statement to be true. . . .

And from the president came this:

It seems to me very strange that a member of our faculty, with your dignity and standing, should repeat the word of an itinerant student and cast insult at the fair womanhood of this school. . . .

This statement made Vridar shout with mirth. There it was: the Nordic traditions of chivalry, the fair blossoms of purity, the mothers of men. A harlot in an American university? Unthinkable! Harlots were degraded creatures who walked the streets at midnight and hid underground. All university girls were virgins; or if not virgins they were married; and if neither virgin nor married, they still somehow belonged to the fair womanhood.

In his long and carefully deliberated answer, he made a statement that brought matters to a head.

Your position is, I understand, a most difficult one. You have to placate the outraged prejudice and stupidity of a community, and you have also to stand behind academic freedom and the integrity of your faculty. These are two positions that it is almost impossible to reconcile. . . .

And to that observation came the thunderbolt:

I have carefully noted the letter in which you accuse the president of moral cowardice.

Vridar was so distressed that he could neither eat nor sleep. He walked the streets and while walking he met a colleague. William Morton, son of an old Mormon family, was whimsical and tactful and shrewd. He stopped now and smiled.

"Vreed, what's the matter?"

"Why? Don't I look all right?"

"No. You're the most tragic-looking person I ever saw. Why are you so bitterly unhappy?"

"Hell, I'm not unhappy."

"Your face tells a story. Are you having trouble here?"

"A little. Tell me, Bill: how do you teach? Do you ever dare suggest to your students that the world is not quite perfect?"

"You take teaching too seriously. Students don't come to you to be educated. Why bother about them? Why try to make them understand that the world isn't perfect? They don't care."

"A few of them do."

"No, you're too serious. Come over to my place and have a drink."

"No thanks. I'm taking a long walk."

"Well, cheer up. Honestly, your face depresses me."

"I was born with a tragic look, Bill. It means nothing. . . ."

When he returned to his room he found on his table a letter from Athene. It was a cheerful letter, intended to be gently admonitory, but it threw him into fury; and he wrote to her his declaration of independence in the academic world.

. . . For I remember when I first entered this college as a student, with my heart out of me at the wonder of it; and how I sat in awe before my instructors; and how my hunger for honest and fearless leadership was greater than my hunger for bread. A few students come here with the credulity that I had and they find, not wisdom and courage, but meanness and envy and feuds. There's more than one kind of murder, and the worst kind, in my opinion, is to be found in our universities. But my mind is made up, now and forever: I've thought this thing out and there's only one thing to be done. I may be fired before another year is out. But what of it? Better men than I have been kicked out and greater men have starved for it. I won't be a Judas with my students. I won't be a hypocrite to get promotion here. I won't yield an inch beyond what I think is courageous and right. Of course I'll be as tactful as I can and of course I'll not make a fetish of principle. But please stop writing to me as if you regard me as a fool seeking martyrdom. If there is no place where I can teach and give sympathy and aid to those who ask it, then I'll not teach.

And recognize, my dear, that all my life I have been a self-centered and intensely egoistic person. If I want to forget myself now and be of service to those who see less clearly than I, must I be, then, a crusading fool? I don't know. This is a matter that I am trying to understand. I am aware that those who wish to assimilate themselves into service for the common welfare are likely to be persons who are deluded and evasive. History is full of examples here. I do not intend to become a self-deceived social prophet. I feel, on the other hand, that the intensely personal life, aside from all questions of social worth, may become sterile and decadent. It is a nice problem. On the one hand, there are those who enter social service as a compensatory escape from themselves: Salvation Army girls are a pathetic and obvious instance. On the other hand there are those spiritually impotent persons who try to live in a world of their own; and it is these persons who, having little or none themselves, have so much to say of a sense of humor. This kind of fatuous cynicism is now so prevalent that it is generally supposed that a sense of humor is an unwillingness to take anything seriously. Such an unwillingness is, of course, nothing but adolescence.

I am plowing myself up, and the spirit stinks with what I had buried. I am learning a little. A colleague says I am too serious: that is the customary retort of those who have compromised and are trying to remain in their self-esteem. I keep the ironic muse constantly at my side and only an hour ago while looking at my imbecile friend I thought:

> *H. G. Wells, only the other night*
> *I saw your utopia like a great ring of light. . . .*
> *But I was pretty tight.*

Laugh at yourself, my dear, and the world is glad to laugh at you, too; be serious about any matter and the world resents your rebuke to its laziness.

Love,
VRIDAR.

V

●

A S A STUDENT Vridar had seen of the academic world
only what a student sees. As an instructor five years
ago he had been without professional rank and had not sat
in the parliamentary councils. But in this year he sat behind
the closed doors in faculty meetings and he saw and heard
with increasing amazement what was done there. At first
he was curious; later, he was astonished; and after a half-
dozen solemn and incredible meetings he was lost in wonder
and scorn. He had still cherished the belief that educators
were persons of aloof disinterestedness, of dignity and taste.
It would have been absurd to think of instructors of youth
as sly and petty tyrants who fought among themselves for
privilege; who stooped to malicious thrust; or who met in
grave deliberation over a trivial matter. And now he studied
them and their doings as a record and manner of human
life: they became his library in this year; subject for endless
meditation; and another highway to discovery of himself.

The faculty met once in every two weeks. If a matter
of sober unimportance announced itself, a hundred and fifty
men and women were called into special meeting. Such a
matter fell in January. Harry Roe, a senior, had asked permission to graduate with only five and seven-tenths hours
of physical education. He had petitioned the faculty. The
president sent mimeographed announcements calling the
educators into session. The chairman of the committee on
graduation read the petition.

"You have heard the petition," said the president. "Our
rules, of course, require six hours of physical education.
Mr. Roe has only five and seven tenths. What is the
pleasure of the faculty?"

"Mr. President."

"Dr. Allerbeck."

"I just want to say to the faculty that Mr. Roe has been a student of mine in several classes. He is a very good student. It was not possible to arrange his schedule of study so he could finish his physical education requirement. I move that we grant the petition."

"It has been moved that we allow Mr. Roe to graduate with five and seven-tenths hours of physical education instead of six. Is there a second?"

"Mr. President."

"Professor Ames."

"I question the wisdom of establishing such a precedent. If we allow one student to graduate minus three tenths of an hour, another student may later wish to graduate minus a half. After a while they'll want to graduate minus any at all." Members of the faculty laughed and Ames looked around him and smiled. Finding his subject to be rich in both wisdom and humor, he pressed it further. "Then some students will want to graduate without fulfilling all the requirements in a subject more important than physical education. In physics, say, or botany. I think it would be unwise to make an exception of physical education merely because it does not happen to be of any great importance."

"Mr. President."

"Professor Becken."

"I cannot agree with Professor Ames that physical education is of small importance." Becken looked around him and a hush fell. The intellectual giants of the faculty met his gaze but the more timid professors looked away. "In my opinion," Becken went on, "it is of greater importance than any other subject. . . ."

"What does Becken teach?" Vridar asked of a colleague, sitting by him.

"Physical education."

"Oh, I see."

"Mr. President."

"Professor Ames."

"I agree with Professor Becken, of course, that physical education is of some importance. But any ambitious young man worth his salt ought to be able to get his exercise off the campus. I'd like to ask Professor Becken to explain precisely what the value to Mr. Roe will be of another three tenths of an hour swinging dumb-bells or lifting his legs up and down. I mean," said Ames, observing that Becken had stiffened, "I mean what value does exercise under a roof have over that under the sky?"

Professors grinned. Most of them liked this warfare, these feuds, between and among departments. Becken now flushed to his ears and rose to his feet; but one of his assistants spoke.

"Mr. President!"

"Dr. Saunders."

"I wish to answer the question of Professor Ames. He asks, as I understand him, if the department of physical education is not—well, unnecessary in higher education. He does not see why walking cannot take the place of exercise in a gymnasium. He fails to understand, I think. . . ."

And for an hour and a half the argument ran. The petition was granted.

By nothing in this school was Vridar more amazed than by its inexorable feuds. Many of these learned men hated one another with candor and vigor. The dean of education and the dean of sciences had long been academic enemies; and behind the one, in sympathy at least, stood most of those who taught the social sciences and the arts; and behind the other stood every physical scientist in the school. Both of these men Vridar liked. James Monson, dean of education, was a devout and quiet man, with a pink bald head and a kindly face. He was godfather and dean of all the public-school teachers of the state: a Mormon, sincere in his religious beliefs; a Republican in politics; a devoted father in his home. There was no malice in him, no spleen. William Tergaud, dean of sciences, was of another kind: stinging of wit, hot-tempered, impatient. He saw little sense in what was called art and none at all in pedagogy: for him life was scientific or it was morbid; and in this, Vridar reluctantly admitted, the man was right. Though in the school of arts himself, and called upon, as one who professed them, to defend their rights and privileges, he admitted, nevertheless, that in this faculty, as well possibly as in others, the scientists were more level-headed than their colleagues. For one erotic shyster in any department of science, there were, he began to perceive, a half-dozen or more in any department of English or foreign languages or education or art. This was so, he reflected, because scientists were less self-conscious, less neurotically sensual and ambitious.

But he did not clearly understand the bitter feuds here. At every opportunity Tergaud buried his witty harpoons in his sensitive and unmalicious foe. He missed no chance to declare what he thought of graphs and charts, intelligence tests, and all the experimental apparatus of a rival department; and when he was weary, or when his wit failed him, other scientists sprang to the attack. And one afternoon there was almost a rout. Dean Monson, dignified, soft-spoken, but as unyielding as any other, placed before the faculty the program of his department. The program called for more money; an expansion of facilities; and the coöperation of everyone in the school. After listening to Monson, professors looked at one another; shifted in their chairs; and waited. Then Albert Duncan rose to his feet. He was a professor of chemistry: aggressive, alert, and given to scathing diatribe. After an attack on pedagogy and all that it stood for, he closed with this remark:

"There are some of us who feel that in this college we have education and by that I mean science; and we have, too, something for which, at the present moment, I can think of no better term than pedagogy."

For a long moment there was silence. On the face of President Johnson there was a quiet but dangerous smile. A few professors put hands to their brows and smiled behind their hands; others affected sudden interest in the world outside; and others looked startled and uneasy and turned in their chairs. Up the pink neck and face of Monson, blood crept like dark red shadow; and slowly, wearily, as if sick of scientists and all that they stood for, he rose to his feet. But his remarks, though gently furious, were not personal. . . .

This was the most inexorable feud but it was by no means the only one. Every chairman fought for the prestige and advantage of his department. And the success of departments in this school was measured, not by scholarship, not by the learning and dignity and sympathy of the men who taught, but by the size of the enrollment. The president himself seemed to look upon small departments without favor. There was that of ancient languages: its chairman was a shy and studious man and perhaps the greatest scholar in the school. But he stammered in his speech; he was unpopular with students; and his whole department lived for years under threat of extinction. Then there was called to his aid Sidney Jones Allport: suave and gracious of manner, nimble and amusing of tongue. Students flocked to him, not for Latin or Greek, but to hear his tales of foreign travel, his anecdotes, his gently cynical summaries of life and love.

Or there was Ponsworth Johnson, most popular of all instructors here. Much of his classroom time and many hours in his office he gave to tirades against cigarettes. "I've never seen a cigarette smoker," he said, "who can climb a mountain." He was a Mormon: immaculate, righteous, and secure. . . . One of Vridar's students came to him with tears in her eyes.

"I guess I'm silly," she said, "but Professor Johnson

made us all weep. On the last day of his classes he gives
the most inspiring talk!"

"What," asked Vridar, "does he talk about?"

"Oh, lots of things. Today it was—well, about the
glory of young men and young women. He loves young
people. He understands them. Oh, he's so nice! He says
the affection of his students makes him—well, you know:
kind of woozey, just feeling full of love and all. . . . And
you know how he does?"

"No, I think not."

"On the last day, I mean. Well, when his talk is finished
he stands at the door, and we all pass out and he shakes our
hand. Gosh, it was swell, though! And he was crying, too.
Honest he was. Great big tears ran down his face. And I
just thought I'd shake to pieces. I sure do like him. He's
just like a father." She wiped her eyes and looked at Vridar.
"But you're so cynical," she said. "You just think it's a
lot of nonsense. Don't you?"

"It is very interesting," Vridar said dryly.

"It *is* interesting! And you know what? Professor Johnson's course is the best course in school. It's sure swell.
I never liked science until this year."

"You're getting, I observe, the scientific point of view."

"What? I sure am. Honest, I'm getting so everything
looks scientific to me."

"Including tears?"

"What?"

"For your next composition do me a paper on the science
of tears."

She looked at him, her blue eyes wondering.

"I'll try. I'll bet tears *are* scientific. Everything is, you
know. I mean——" She moved toward him, warm and
tearful and womanly. "Dr. Hunter, why are you so darn
cynical all the time?"

"Would you like me better if I wept?"

"Well, it would show you were human. Wouldn't it? It would show you had a big heart. . . ."

Or there was Ellen Dobram, professor of speech and dramatics and chairman of the department: dogmatic and pious and guardian of her underlings. She employed no instructor who smoked, and she looked with disfavor on one who ate pepper and drank tea. Like many chairmen of departments, she employed, when possible, only her satellites. Her specialty was culture and the Boston dialect. Long ago she had been a student in Boston and she returned to Utah with speech militantly precise; and she kept it, exaggerating the worst of its mannerisms; and she looked with fastidious scorn at those who called a tomahto a tomato. She gave public readings; and one afternoon when she impersonated Juliet, and breathed in passionate and demure love from a balcony, Vridar shook with mirth and almost fell out of his chair. When Ellen Dobram rose in faculty meetings, more intent on her pronunciation than her meaning, professors slumped in their chairs and exchanged sly winks. . . .

Or there was Brooke Ogden, professor of French and chairman of the department: a man who said, "When I was in Paris I asked myself, If a Frenchman can speak French perfectly, why can't I? And I did. I have been told that my French is more Parisian than that of Parisians themselves. . . ." Ogden was an able teacher. But like so many chairmen here, he was a small dictator in a small province. He had a new way of teaching languages and all his assistants had to teach according to his method and his textbook. He had recently brought to his department a brilliant Jew, and this Jew, having notions of his own, soon found himself in more trouble than he could take care of. And when Vridar heard that Arnstein was to be dismissed, he went to see him.

He found a very urbane, a very sensitive man with a sharply penetrating mind.

"I'm one of your colleagues. My name is Hunter."

"Will you sit?"

"Thanks. I've heard you're in trouble here. I've been in trouble, too. What's the truth in your case?"

Arnstein shrugged. A lean hand reached for a cigarette and two cynical eyes studied Vridar's face.

"Ogden teaches French by one method, I by another. Because I won't use his method I'm to be fired. That's all."

"You're to be fired?"

"And with most uncommon efficiency."

"How do you mean?"

"Do you know President Johnson?"

"Yes."

"What do you think of him?"

"I don't know. I'm trying to figure him out."

"Well, it was this way: Johnson called me in. He said, Arnstein, I'll recommend your appointment for next year if you'll give me your resignation first."

"I don't understand," Vridar said.

"Really, there's nothing to understand. If I hand him my resignation, he'll recommend my reappointment. Then nobody can say he fired me. It will be said that I resigned."

"But you're not going to do it?"

"And why not? Jews are in bad odor here. Anyway, I have no taste for academic brawls. Where I am not wanted I do not stay."

"But that's plain damned cowardice on Johnson's part."

"And are you surprised?" Arnstein's brows moved, incredulous, and his lips curled softly. "Since when has cowardice in university presidents been a matter for astonishment?"

"But I wouldn't do it. I'd fight it out."

"You," said Arnstein politely, a little coldly, "are not a Jew."

Vridar went to his room and sat in thought. Rather than stoop to such cowardice, he reflected, I'd go out and

sweep dung from the streets. This school is only a bag
of political tricks; hatreds, some vulgar and some fastidious; and plots maneuvering under the well-bred and immaculate surface. Yet these are human beings, like persons
everywhere, like me: under our superficial principles, we
are all cut to the same pattern: we all have the same vanities
and greed. It must be that our ideals have betrayed us and
made charlatans of us; or are we born depraved? I must
see. . . .

There were a few teachers in the school for whom Vridar
had affectionate admiration. There was John Boardman,
professor of physics: a militant and hardheaded scholar
whose scorn for most of his colleagues was an unwavering
brightness in his eyes. There was Abraham Haroldsen, professor of philosophy: a giant of a man who had about him
a weary astuteness, as if the political chicaneries here bored
him to death. There was Miles Rowan, professor of biology,
who ignored faculty meetings and stuck to his laboratory
and his work. These men and a few others were not everlastingly jockeying for promotion and privilege; never, so
far as Vridar knew, stooped to that underground gossip
which was a disease in this school; and never played to their
classes with clowning and faintly odorous jests. . . .

Day by day [Vridar wrote in his journal] I'm dragging
my opinions out of their mausoleums and hanging them like
rugs to a line. I'm beating the dust and moths out of them.
And after the flogging is done they are threadbare; because
of all my former convictions, scarcely a one is left. I'm
going to clean my house from cellar to attic: throw away
all this God's-in-His-heaven, sweetness-and-light, sermon-
on-the-mount stuff. Then if I can reach to enough of truth,
I'm going to furnish the house again. . . .

●

VI

Vridar did more in this year than teach his classes and meditate on his colleagues and himself. He wrote in every day and far into every night: two novels, an armful of poetry, most of it satiric; and letters to Athene which added in nine months to almost a hundred thousand words. He read two score of books. He went on Sundays into the mountains, thinking of persons and trying to see them clearly; and studying his dreams.

I was sitting in my office one morning when the door was opened and there was thrust in a masklike face with large pale eyes, blank of all meaning, and a large colorless mouth as grave as stone. The mouth announced

DIAMOND BRAND WALNUTS

and the face withdrew. This was my introduction to Maxwell Ohm, an instructor here, and as strange a blend of mordant whimsy and sober bombast as you'll ever see. I learned later that Max poked his head into every office in the building and made the same announcement; and, later still, that he had read an advertisement which said, Diamond Brand Walnuts Are Good. Tell your friends.

You have never seen my friends the Larmonds, and I think I never spoke of them. George is an overstuffed blob of a fellow with a keen mind and an insatiable love of the lewd. Maxine is awake, too: a bitterly unhappy person with a lean and pungent derision; restless eyes full of innumerable questions; and a tongue like a lash. As mismated a pair as you could find in twenty counties.

George is what is called romantic: adores his wife, believes she adores him; and goes in hard for moonlight, roses, the French soul-kiss, and Sir Walter's cloak on the mud. I'm very fond of them: they are swell persons; good solid middle-class; loyal, generous, and easy to be with. But they

almost bore me to murder. Because George, whose mind is
analytic of everything but himself and women, knows less
of women and what women want than I know of Szabadka;
and Maxine, whose ambition was to marry brains, can't see
now that they're of any particular use in a bedroom.

Two weeks ago I gave them the script of my Telv novel.
They read thirty pages and were so infuriated they threw
the poor thing (and it was so beautifully typewritten on
bond paper) to the floor and kicked it from the front porch
to the linen closet. They must have done so; because when
they thrust it back at me it was so mussed and bedraggled
that the hero, ideals awry and mouth agape, was hanging
out of it like a sawdust doll caught by its heels. My hero,
they say, is a fool, a dolt, a dud, a nincompoop, an oaf, a
churl, a vulgarian—and at this point they sank exhausted.
My heroine is a sprig of horseradish; and my theme stinks
of bad breath and phobias. I have a sentence in the book
that says: "Most persons never dare think of life below the
level of its navel, nor of love without a petticoat on," and
George abused me roundly. Why did I not say it, if say it
I must, poetically? George is a-hunger for poetry but like
so many he can't tell when his hands are full of it and his
shelves stacked. Really, though, he objected to what he
calls the "rank obscene nastiness."

There is a scene in a park in which Telv crushes a wish
to kiss Alice; places hands to her shoulders; says with that
monstrously stupid idealism which is my country's birth-
mark and my heritage: "Alice, do you know there are
thirteen babies born every minute?" The chapter ends
there. And that doesn't mean a thing to George and Maxine: they have a gnat's ear for irony; and besides being good
folk, they can't see any relationship between kissing and
babies. They were, they said, sickened, left white, doubled
over, by the obscenity. Note that.

"I like wholesome books," George said. "Good decent
books. Uplifting."

"That must mean," I said, "that you feel a vast need
of uplift. Persons who are all right, reasonably decent, sane,
honest, aren't always morbidly in search of uplifting books."

"I abhor mental nastiness," said Maxine, "and that, Vridar, is all your book is. It's a gutter-book. It's downright rotten. . . ."

And then—honestly, Athene, this is what happened. It is almost incredible. Then I stayed to dinner and one of George's inlaws came in. At dinner he twitted George and spoke of his huge and philosophic contentment; said:

"Every bone in his body is restful, at peace."

"Every bone except one," said George.

And the three of them roared with glee. I ask: can you beat it?

I'd like to know how human beings of intelligence can live in such lush and overgrown moral stupidity; why those —and this without exception has been my experience—who howl so at what they call obscenity in books have such leprously erotic minds. It's not because they are humorless, is it? Is it because they have no perspective on themselves? Or is it merely this: that tradition has shaped us to expect from books, from art, what we have learned we cannot expect from ourselves? Is it only that human beings demand a vicarious glorification of themselves and their race in books and know deeply that their own minds are rotten, their own hearts unclean?

That must be a good part of it. Now take George: he howled like a Comstock at my serious effort to show a sickly idealist and why he is sickly, and yet every time he sees me he has some stinking privy filth that he must tell. And he tells it with such relish, with such lewd twinkling of his eyes, with such lustful licking of his mouth. Refer this matter to the pure: it is beyond my simple mind.

I've finished Amy Lowell's *Keats* and it shook me clear to the floor. Great and heroic and tragic poet. His renouncing of Fanny, his going to Rome to die, his patience in dying: a splendid record that reaffirms our faith in humankind. It almost made me weep; but I said, Hunter, weeping is either a childlike response to frustration or self-pity. Then I stood up and took a swat at the wall—and if Amy had been there I would have taken a swat at her. For she threshes mightily in the records, trying to prove that Keats did not have syphilis; as if it matters to anyone but spinsters.

Reading of Tschaikowsky has given me strength, too. Turning on his deathbed to men around him: "Gentlemen, I'm afraid I'm an unconscionable time a-dying." I've been reading of Liszt, Grieg, Wagner, Beethoven: all of them were as mad as hatters. In their lives, and in the lives of so many others, I find parallels of my own: the same pitiable weakness when a fist was needed; the same furious temper, violent extremes, morbid interest in sex, shame, guilt.

At the Delphic Club an M.D. gave a review of a recent book: *Post Mortem,* by another M.D. It is an attempt to give certain great men of the past a medicinal once-over and explain their stupendous follies. Ivan the Terrible and Schopenhauer, he says, were syphilitic; Henry VIII's splurge in wives was induced by the fact that Anne had syphilis. Luther's hallucinations came from diseased ears and all Protestant sects stem from an ear that was not what ears should be.

I know the poetry I'm sending you isn't much good. The other day I was thinking of human hypocrisy and I worked up such a gargantuan fury that I did a sonnet to Shelley with this sextet:

> *Shelley was honest: him they gave the rot*
> *Of moral righteousness that hid beneath*
> *Its platitudes its stinking sexual cancer.*
> *Shelley ignored, but this would be my answer:*
> *I'd reach into their hearts and throw its snot*
> *Like maggots gutted in their pious teeth.*

It is awful, isn't it? It came out of me sizzling. I showed it to Max and he thinks it is swell. "But then," says he, with a solemn leer, "I've always liked snotty things." After it was done I said, Hunter, why so furious? What the hell do you care about abuse of Shelley? Are you not rather identifying yourself with the gentleman? And then I lar-ruped myself with great gusto and stole away, abashed, to meditate on Bob, the imbecile.

The muse kicked me out of a sound sleep last night and bothered me with this trivia:

A RADIO ANNOUNCER GOES TO HEAVEN

A lunch of snow-white milk and honey;
A small weird sense of feeling funny;
An astonished look at his old wife who
Lived forty years after he was through;
And a stroll to learn if the aches and ills
Of heaven are relieved by Phooier's Pills.

The angels are looking a bit rococo
And filling their tanks with Standard's Conoco.
One plays a harp, one chants a ditty,
And one young girl looks gol-darn pretty.
He sees an enemy whom once he jeered,
And Moses not far off, combing his beard.

To life, he thinks, it's a hell of a sequel.
To make all the angels exactly equal.
It's heaven all right, but where are the Packards?
Where are the billboards and posters and placards?
And he says to the Lord, "If I had my way
We'd develop this country and make it pay."

He looks around for he has not seen
A sign of Lux or of Listerine.
No Crazy Crystals or MJB,
No Maxwell House, no Lipton's Tea.
No Lucky Strikes and no girl with a pose
Amorous and ready within its clothes.

He seeks God out and he says, "Great Sir,
We need some testimonials, some whirr!
I know a man for a thousand dollars
Will speak right up for Arrow collars!
I mean, Sir, it is rather surprising
You don't do a damned bit of advertising!"

My dear, do not let your dreams worry you so much. Just what they mean I cannot say: they sound like birth phantasies. But if you cannot be calm and reasonable in trying to understand them, then ignore them. If you keep on you'll be fancying yourself a homosexual next, or a downright Messalina.

My own dreams I am still trying to probe to their source. Their symbolism often evades me but now and then I catch a horrific intimation, another truth. Last night I had a most distressing one: I dreamed of intimacy with another woman, without pleasure, with a suffocating sense of shame. I knew at once what it meant. It means *I hope* I do not wish intimacy with any woman but you, yet doubt; and the fact that I dream of the matter shows that I do. But tyrannical scruples lay me out and all feeling is taken away. It proves what I wish, and renders the wish impotent with what I want. I am slowly coming visible to my scrutiny and am seeing more and more the difference between the animal I am, and the monster of virtues which, like everyone else, I have pretended to be.

My novel came back yesterday. This publisher says, "We found much in it to interest us but there seems to be no place for it on our already overcrowded lists." If their lists were overcrowded, why did they bother to read it? Publishers must think all authors are very simple fellows. Their way of dismissing us with a sprig of holly is beyond all reckoning.

Did I tell you I have an answer from Monckton? He says, "My eyes unluckily are in such condition that it is impossible for me to read your script." It serves me right. Why the hell should I expect a busy critic to look over my stuff? But he needn't have lied about it. He should have said, "My dear fellow, thousands of young upstarts like you ask me to read their scripts. Is it impossible for you to understand that I have my own work to do?"

Today the novel came back again. "We enjoyed the actual writing but frankly we did not enjoy the theme." That makes six publishers who have said no. Every rejection leaves me feeling a bit sick and flogged; but I say,

Hunter, you are a vain and ambitious fellow and because publishers prefer sunshine novelists, you fly into a fearful dudgeon. If you want to be published, then write something simple and sweet. You can't expect readers to like you if you sit down in your pigheaded way and tell the truth about things. Evasion of truth, Hunter, is your country's major industry, and has been yours too, my fine fellow, until recently. And then I run off a hundred lines of irony and feel better. Query: is irony another, a more profound, kind of self-pity? Damned if I don't believe it is.

The other novel is spreading itself over the pages and the hero is putting me out of my wits. He gets out of hand and goes rampant from scene to scene until I want to murder him. In one hour he has my sympathy; in the next I try to kick him out of the book; for a more tireless and impetuous fool never harassed an author. But the book has meat and bone in it and enough truth to make it unpopular.

I heard about President Johnson an astonishing thing today. Max is writing an article for the *American Mercury*, and Johnson, hearing of the matter, called him in. "He was very sweet," Max says. "He put an arm to my shoulder and almost asked me to dinner. He's afraid I'm going to write about him. He gave me a rapturous metaphorical kiss and said how brilliant I am." But I can hardly blame Johnson. I see now that he has a hell of a job in this bigoted community of zion.

Had dinner again with the Larmonds. Said they: "Vridar, you're an awful egotist. You think you're a genius but you're only a dinky instructor in a dinky school. Vridar," said they, "you bore us." I was annoyed. I said to myself, Hunter, they called you an egotist and you don't like it. You don't like frankness. If they had said, Vridar, you're a great man: some day you will shake the earth and throw the sun out of its orbit, how I would have thrown my chest up and strutted. But no. Let me be fair with myself. You say now that I'm bent on self-discovery I'll make myself out to be an awful monster without any good qualities at all. I'll try not to, my dear. I realize there are no monsters anywhere except the images of self-love.

The Larmonds tried to razz me, of course, because they're afraid I see through their shams. A mole could do that. We were playing cards. Said Maxine, with the weary hauteur of a duchess who feels imminent bellyache:

"George, dear, will you get my coat?"

Her coat was lying on the sofa almost within her reach. George dear hopped up as if he were about to be knighted and got the coat and draped it around her, murmuring meanwhile of love and pneumonia and chills. With a patrician shrug she settled to her cards. She then saw that I was amused and she turned upon me a broadside of caustic summary. And after that, suddenly, with her most charming laugh:

"Vridar, don't you think he's a dear?"

"I think," I said, "he's an intolerable ass."

And then the deluge. They both fired at me and I drew all my muskets and fired back. I said:

"George, don't you know anything at all about women? Don't you know they have only contempt for these cavaliers who lay cloaks in the mud?"

Zounds and furies, said George, and Maxine tried to destroy me with a stare. But they are very unhappy. They have sense enough to suspect that all is not honey in their relationship. They yielded a point and asked for more punishment.

"What do I think you should have done? With a woman like Maxine? To make her love for you frantic and clinging? You should have said, 'Mon amie, get your own God-damned coat.' She would have adored you then, at least for half an hour. As it is now you're not a lover or even a husband: you're a big eager houseboy who packs roses home and quotes Eddie Guest. One of these days Maxine will be gone and you'll be whistling for her. She'll hike out and get a man who will almost break her neck and throw her into bed; and after that she'll scrub floors for him and be happy. As likely as not, she will sing songs. . . ."

And were they furious! I waited until they hurled all their thunderbolts; and then:

"Women, George, who like men always gentle, considerate, kind, serviceable, are women who haven't an ounce of passion in them. What they need is a maid and a butler. But the women you like, the women I like, are women who want hell to break now and then. I mean, of course, that they want to feel that a man is more than a domesticated tomcat."

George protested. He said Maxine was seraphically happy; adored him. Here was a marriage like that of Pickford and Fairbanks: perfect, indissoluble, headed for heaven. But Maxine, taking her woe by the horns, and speaking out of frankness that amazed him, said:

"No, darling, Vridar is right. You really *don't* understand much about women."

"I don't?" asked George, staggered.

"You don't. I would have liked you better if you had told me to get my coat. You wait on me too much. Of course," she said, again with her charming laugh, "I like to be waited on. But I don't want you to be just a factotum."

George sat in prodigious amazement. I left him, looking as if someone had kicked out of him everything but the astonishment and the fat. You will say I should have kept my nose out. But I am very fond of these two. They are splendid persons but their marriage is headed for a reef because they are tied hand and foot with a lot of half-witted traditions. Maxine has a mind that is remarkably keen if she would use it. So has George: but he is standing in his own light and can't see around his face.

Here are two intelligent persons dodging themselves with the alacrity of a theist harmonizing the gospels. Things between them must come to a crisis; and it is George, the blind oaf, who will suffer then. Maxine wants a man who will break her to her knees and then lift her gently and kiss her; arms that will tremble with both tenderness and dynamite; a mind that will annihilate her feeble sophistries as fast as she invents them. But George now is only a big boy for whom love is romantic, with a languishing Juliet in a balcony, and a Romeo muttering his platitudes among the fig leaves.

And the more I see of them and others the more I do meditate on women and what women want. There are tens of thousands of women who are, of course, emotionally half-dead, and some who are wholly so: with the fervor of a sloth and the imagination of a yak. For them man is a household article, a functionary of bed and board. These are the women who are running this country now, because this country does breathe and moan under a petticoat. And what is wrong with this horde of half-females? Is it a sense of sin and guilt? Is it constipation? Or is their biology just wearing out? Or are they left frigid by blundering obtuse lovers? All of these, I dare say, and more.

You have said, Athene, that you don't like any sadism at all in men. Darling, you are a liar. Here is the truth about you: you have, like every ambitious woman, a huge ego and you resent anything that makes it look ineffectual. You have come to feel, therefore, that the mastery of the male is an unreasonable advantage. You remember Edna Millay's sonnet in which the woman is caustic about the under-position? There you have it. I suggest that you come to yourself in this matter.

Max Ohm is weird in his sense of the diabolic: a man wholly lost in mummery who is never himself: a solemnly sardonic mask. In almost every morning now he thrusts his mordant limestone face into my office and makes an announcement. Yesterday it was:

> *Did God tell her ere she went*
> *She had borne a president?*
> *Did God ever let her see*
> *Little Calvin's destiny?*

These lines, I am told, are from Edgar Guest's epitasis to Coolidge. Last fall Max ran a whole series on Red Grange. His first:

GRANGE IS CARRIED TWO MILES BY STUDENTS

On the next day:

GRANGE'S FOOTBALL JERSEY IS TO BE FRAMED

A week later:

GRANGE IS NOMINATED TO CONGRESS

The fourth:

GRANGE IS OFFERED $120,000 A YEAR

The fifth:

GRANGE IS PRESENTED TO COOLIDGE

> *Will Jehovah let him see*
> *Little Calvin's destiny?*

And finally the crushing announcement:

> This completes your course of five lec-
> tures in contemporary American history.

All these announcements he made into every office along the hall. He is a superb actor. In his own way he is summarizing the cultural and intellectual level of the United States. Note these which he delivered last month:

> Bruce Barton says Jesus was the founder of modern business.

> The Metropolitan Insurance Company declares that Moses was one of the greatest salesman and real-estate promoters that ever lived.

> Gloria Swanson has married the Marquis de la Falaise de la Corduroy.

Only this last week he gave what he called his snapshot course in American æsthetics. I was reading themes when he opened the door and gave his first "lecture."

> Often a bridesmaid but never a bride.

On the next morning I was expecting him but his face when it appeared was as grave and expressionless as a slab of granite.

Poor Edna's case was really a pathetic one.

He gave ten "lectures" in the field of American æsthetics but I recall at this moment only one other:

I think he's quoting from Shelley.

He is so appallingly apt and pungent in everything he says that he tickles me to death. Imagine the happy thought of summarizing American æsthetics with ten stupid and vulgar blurbs from popular advertising. And he is about right at that: such is, alas, our æsthetic level. His principal anathema seems to be Kilmer's silly poem on a tree. He has made his own parody of it, not too clever, the last two lines of which read:

> Nature can make a Dewey or Royce
> But only God could make a Joyce.

And my office, I repeat, is not the only one into which he delivers his Hudibrastic javelins. He is, declares Max solemnly, educating all his colleagues. The more sedate ones, whose culture has run somewhat to fat, think Max is crazy; others dismiss him as a schoolboy and a nuisance; and still others shake their learned heads and return to the matrices of textbooks. Only one of them seems to understand the sharp and plantigrade earthiness of his commentaries: his solemn gibbeting of the excreta of dullness. This one is a woman: tall, dark, Indian-looking; with a repressed laugh which, if she ever lets it go, will end up in a good purgative fit of cussing.

And Max, of course, also finds himself in trouble here. How could such a thrusting mind avoid it in this monastery? Last year, Donnaugh, then chairman, called him to the carpet; and the matter as told to me by Max, without even a hint of a smile, runs like this.

"He called me to his office and I sensed at once that another gutted empire had been laid on his lap. 'Ohm,' he said, 'I hear unfavorable things of you.' I looked boyish and well fed. I twiddled one thumb and kept the other in readiness for twiddling: and he prestidigitated: 'I am told that you said the president of the Mormon church thinks he's a little tin god.'

" 'I did not,' I said. I looked at him with uttermost frankness. 'I positively did not.'

" 'The reports declare you did. I have a dozen students who declare you did.'

" 'That I did what?'

" 'Called the president of the Mormons a little tin god.'

" 'But I did not,' I said, twiddling furiously. 'I deny the allegations and demand a jury trial.'

" 'You deny it?'

" 'I do. I rebuke it as unscholarly and unscientific.' The man looked at me and tried to think of something else to say. Like Miniver Cheevy he thought and thought and thought. And then:

" 'Ohm, you mean to tell me there's no truth in these reports?'

" 'I do. I oppugn them.'

" 'You what?'

" 'I oppugn them. I'm oppugning right now.' He sat down, his forehead bursting with dew; and his misery was so extreme and his mind so out of order that I took pity. I took pity and threw it at him and it was like a halo around his head; and when I looked out I saw a star in the east and three wise men walking across the campus. 'I declare on my honor that I did not say what you have said it was said I said.'

" 'Then what *did* you say?'

" 'I said the president of the Mormon church thinks he's a litle tin Jesus.' "

And that is Max Ohm for you. He sends stuff to Mencken's Americana; he writes parodies of the Congressional Record; he writes love poems that would make you shriek. And in the classroom he must be for his students an incredible sphinx. My students, also his, bring me the tales. Max will stop right in the middle of a lecture and groan as if in pain and then walk to a window and strike an attitude there, his chin in a palm, his gaze on the outside world; and he will stand there as if carved for fifteen or twenty minutes, with every student staring in amazement. Or he will simulate sudden and volcanic fury and suddenly smite his desk and demand in a high squeaky voice:

> I wonder if the Sphinx
> Has found out what he thinks?

And then he will stride out and vanish, leaving his students thrilled in every capillary. His students adore him. He gives them more in an hour than some of these dull horses give them in a year: something like flame that arouses them and sends them to fresh wonder.

Am glad you like the hat-rack article in the *Mercury*. It has raised a great storm here. I thought it a superb piece of irony and assigned it to my students. The librarian hid the magazine and now I'm in trouble again. Imagine a harlot of one Christian sect taking her patrons into the cemetery of another! A more unerring and potent commentary on the utter folly of organized religion it would be impossible to find.

The more I think of the matter, the more I believe that love, save as a sexual thing, or as maternal and paternal, is too recent and superficial to be a powerful shaping agent for good. Like communism it must wait on education and knowledge. For our fundamental drives we must use the ancient impulses and direct them; and such a one is hate. I am serious. Hate seems to be a negative thing but that is only because we have assumed all hatred is bad. It can be the most positive thing in life.

Publishers are amusing fellows—almost as amusing as authors. The novel has returned again with praise and thanks; and there seems to be something on the publisher's conscience. He writes: "Do not suppose that we never publish books that will not sell." As examples he gives E. L. Grant Watson's *The Contracting Circle*, saying: "A far finer book than *A Passage to India* but so subtle in its treatment that it could have no sale." But note: Watson published at least five books before this one. He gives

Niven's *Justice of the Peace*, "A book that has been hailed on both sides of the Atlantic as one of the great books of this century but which because of its ruggedness could not possibly sell." Note: Niven had already published at least six novels and the edition the publisher talks about *is a reprint*, and it now carries two prefaces, one by the ubiquitous Morley and one by Walpole! He gives Updegraff's *Dancers in the Wind*: "One of the most whimsical and charming books it has been my pleasure to read in a long time. But we knew this book would have no sale." Note: Updegraff had already published at least four books. . . . I got Niven's hailed-on-both-sides-of-the-Atlantic masterpiece but I couldn't plow through the first chapter. If this is a great book I ought to be thinning beets.

Why should publishers be so transparent and silly? They need not try to give me a gentle metaphorical spanking. They need only say, To hell with your book. We don't want it. But of course they have hearts and they know how many desperate and vain authors are dying to see their names in print. This publisher might have explained, though, why, if hellbent on publishing books that won't sell, he dropped Hemingway as if the man were a hot iron.

Spring is here and I feel the old gypsy stir and smell the open roads. Soon we shall meet and we shall not be what we were a year ago. I'm still a colossal noddy but I'm making progress. The question of sentimentality I have settled: in art, in life, in love, it is nothing but self-pity; and why so simple a truth escaped those who have written all around the matter I cannot understand. Self-pity is also what Ruskin calls pathetic fallacy. Self-pity is the heart and blood and backbone of popular fiction, of belief in personal immortality, and of the country we live in. It is the impelling urge that sends literary expatriates wailing to Paris. It rests at the core of most persons' opinions of themselves.

You once asked me a question and I said I would answer it within a year. I try to now. I never had an incestuous fixation on my mother: she was not a sexual symbol for me: she was too stern and unemotional and always too busy.

I do not remember ever having been kissed by her or taken
to her lap. But she was, on the contrary, a symbol for me
of protection, refuge: an anchor. Freud errs in the enormous emphasis he places on the incest motif. Countless
men are hopelessly attached to their mothers and in many
a case there is an incestuous element; but usually, I think,
the relationship is only one in which the son remains forever in adolescence and his mother remains for him as a
symbol of protection against the buffetings of life. That,
rather than incest, is the source of all these banal self-
pitying popular songs about motherhood, as well as the
feminization of the earth and the sun.

And is it not tragic the way human beings are self-
deceived and become emotionally lost? I look around me
now with eyes coming awake, and I read, and I perceive
that the overwhelming majority of persons today are still
in their emotional childhood. No wonder they fly into the
face of Freud. They are hiding a problem of some kind,
precisely as I was, years ago, when I hated him. If we have
so many young men who wish to marry a woman like their
mother, it is because they are afraid to leave the symbol
of mother and go out into life; and the girls who wish to
marry a man like their dad are chiefly, I should guess, girls
with masculine strivings who are ashamed to be women.
Their fathers have become for them a symbol of masculin-
ity; and when they marry a man they try to dominate him,
because that's the nearest they can come at being men.

And all that is obvious to anyone who has the courage
to think. My next point goes deeper: thousands of persons
today "admit" all this about themselves but their admissions are intellectual only. More: these persons, being neurotic, take pride in the admissions; fancy themselves as
heirs of truth; make a cult of the thing and so pretend
to be sophisticated; and really admit nothing at all. *They
don't realize that an intellectual admission is one thing, an
emotional recognition quite another*. And this explains
something that has long confused me: I have observed in
persons the habit of saying of another, He is slow to learn;
all these matters are common knowledge. I was confused

because I thought I saw in the person making such a statement a woeful ignorance of what he was saying: I mean that everywhere we have intellectual admissions: they are easy and quite in fashion. I see almost nowhere an *emotional realization* of what the admissions mean. That is what I must come to: then I shall not belong to this glib group who glibly accept certain Freudian premises and at the same time betray with fury, expressions of disgust, anger, scorn, pity, that very sickness within themselves which they so glibly admit as being general in others.

When an author like Dickens or Hardy broods in vast and tearful grief over his characters, it means nothing in the world but a vast and tearful pity for himself. He projects himself into the bedeviled pilgrims and invites the sympathy of the reader—and gets it, because the reader weeps, not for the characters but for himself as projected into the characters: an abused and misunderstood and (yes, indeed) very splendid person. There you have it. And this truth of self-pity and self-love, and all the sentimentality it spawns in art and in human relationships, is one truth, certainly, that anyone must discover and *understand* before he can see at all clearly or move with courage. The extent of it is appalling to think of: it reaches into nearly all poetry, into all philosophy and religion; and it is the god and holy ghost of that nebulous and lachrymose empire called romance.

I am reaching to some truth and my enthusiasm grows. I look with increasing favor upon myself as the chief laboratory subject. I'll be glad when we're together and can plot the destruction of ourselves as angels, and the understanding of ourselves as animals: a woman and a man.

VII

●

TO VRIDAR'S office in the spring of this year came many girls from his classes. Some of them wanted advice and a few of them sought the meaning of the scathing aphorisms which he scattered through his lectures; and all of them, he realized, wanted much more than they asked for. There was Sylvia Ashley.

"If you don't mind," she said, "I'd like to have you explain some things."

"If I can."

Sylvia laid a notebook on her knees.

"You say a lot of things I don't understand." She studied her notes. "I wonder what you meant by this."

"Read it."

"When people are angry they say what they mean; and then, of course, they are sorry they mean what they say."

"I see nothing to explain in that."

"But I don't understand it. It troubles me. And the other day you said, If you can't be right, be righteous."

"Well?"

"But righteous people are right, aren't they?"

"You think so?"

"I've always thought so. I've been taught to be righteous. I looked both words up. The dictionary says right comes from the Anglo-Saxon r-i-h-t which meant straight, not crooked. And righteous comes from that and the word w-i-s which meant wise. So righteous means both straight and wise." She looked at him soberly and Vridar restrained a smile. "It seems to me," she said, "that it would be nice to be righteous. But I don't think you think so."

"What else do you have there that troubles you?"

"Well, this: You said there are bad people and good people, and the bad people feel sorry for the good people and the good people feel sorry for themselves. Did you mean anything by that?"

"I think I must have."

"Then what did you mean?"

"You believe there are bad people and good people, don't you?"

"Of course I do. There are."

"You and I are both good people, aren't we?"

She looked at him, a little startled.

"Well, yes. I suppose we are."

"And who are the bad people?"

"The bad people?" She was a little annoyed. "You know who they are. Why do you ask me?"

"I don't know. I'd like to."

"You don't think all persons are alike, do you?"

"Yes, in the way that monkeys are. Some make more noise, some are more cunning, and some, of course, are more intelligent."

"Oh, but there are a lot of differences."

"Yes. Some are fatter. Some have false teeth. Some murder and some only want to."

"Now you're talking the way you do in class."

"But I'm serious. Your notion that you're a good person is merely a notion that flatters your vanity. It has no meaning aside from that."

"But you don't think a murderer is a good person?"

"He may be. Some have been. There are all kinds of murder, you know. We punish the lone murderer and build monuments to those who murder as a group. But it is all murder."

"You have very funny ideas. And a———?"

"Thief? Harlot?"

"Yes."

"Some harlots are very fine women. I've known at least one who was. The trouble, Miss Ashley, is this: we have traditional notions of what a good person is, or a bad one.

We have traditional notions of what is virtue, what is vice. And here are you and I, and millions, taking these traditions and living by them, and believing in them as we believe in our clothes and our mush. And what are they doing to us? Well, quite clearly they lead us into wars; they fill our asylums, our jails; they drive thousands to suicide; they place nearly all of us in unhappy and blundering lives. Now does it not seem to you that there may be something wrong, something false, about notions that produce so much tragedy and waste? Don't you think it would be intelligent to examine them and try to see where they come from and why we stick to them?"

"You are very radical," she said.

"Does the word radical frighten you? Jesus was so radical they hanged him. Cows are not radical, are they?"

"No," she said, smiling, "cows aren't."

"Now imagine a more intelligent cow. She says to the herd: as long as we go about on four legs, eating grass, and moving between a pasture and a corral, we'll always be cows. Let's learn to stand up; clean off the lice and dirt; and see, at least, if there aren't better pastures somewhere. And some day, says this cow, getting to her hind legs and looking around her, we may even learn to fly. And all the other cows are horrified. They say this cow is radical. They slice her up into beef and ship her back to Mr. Swift."

"But even if she learned to fly she'd still be a cow."

"Oh, but she'd have another name then. We don't call ourselves monkeys, do we?"

Sylvia looked at him and burst into merry laughter.

"You're very funny. I don't think you mean a thing you say."

"You mean you think the present pasture is best."

"But I like to hear you talk. . . . May I come again?"

"Certainly, any time you please."

Many of these students came, it seemed to Vridar, because they were weary of their parents and all that their

parents stood for. Most of them were the daughters of
Mormons; and an ideology of babies and beets and zion, of
apostles and priesthoods, of prohibitions against coffee and
pepper, whisky and tobacco, tea and coca-cola, they found a
little unimaginative and dull. But they also came because
they were women, seeking love. They were not aware of this
and he was left to meditate on the ways in which human
beings, driven by an ancient impulse, disguised or buried
their motives and pretended they were interested in un-
related matters. Traditions of shame, attempts to lift themselves from the animal level, had made them dishonest. And
so it was, too, that these girls, self-deceived like persons
everywhere, were not attracted, as tradition declared they
should be, to the pious and gentle instructors. They sought
those in whom they felt dynamite and the devil. They
sought that earthy and animal surface of life at which emotions were frank and unashamed and vital. They were
alarmed by the unorthodox, in ideas and in ways of living,
but they intuitively recognized in it the only vigor and the
only strength.

There was Patricia Arnon: daughter of an old Mormon
family and one of the most brilliant students in the college:
a lovely girl with sad eyes and a bitter mouth. She came into
Vridar's office and sat close by his desk and fixed on him a
most disturbing scrutiny.

"What," he asked, "can I do for you?"

"A lot—if you will."

He met her gaze and was startled. He looked away.

"What do you mean?"

For a long moment her dark and unhappy eyes studied
him.

"Do I embarrass you?" she asked.

"Not at all. In a little while, I imagine, you'll say what
you came to say."

"It wouldn't surprise me at all." Again there was silence.
And then: "Dr. Hunter, I could, if I chose, come here and

talk as the other girls talk who come here. Of life, I mean, and art. Of all the respectable res gestae of men and mice. I am sorry, but I have studied Latin. What these other girls don't dare say, I dare. Will you listen?"

"I am listening."

"I have a secret. I think you guessed it long ago. You've noted my confusion in class and you have known its meaning."

"I have not. Noted your confusion, I mean."

"Are you going to meet frankness with evasions?"

"No——"

"Nothing in the classroom misses you."

"Well, I have noted your confusion. I've not understood it."

"I think you're lying. You know that I'm in love with you."

Vridar rose to his feet in astonishment. He went to a window and looked out and then he came back and looked at Patricia.

"Your irony," he said, "is dreadful."

"My irony?" She flushed. "I never expected this from you. Such a cheap retort."

"I'm sorry. It was cheap. I'm very sorry."

"Why did you make it?"

"I thought you were jesting."

"You did not. You still meet frankness with evasion."

For a long moment he sat in thought.

"It's true," he said at last. "I'm being mean and ridiculous. All right: I'll be as frank as you are. But to explain why I made that retort would be to tell a long tale. It may be enough to say that when a very young man I suffered under the crushing conviction that girls did not find me attractive. I have no good reason any longer to believe that, but old notions stay with us and betray us to stupidity. And I was not sure, really, that you did not come here to jest."

"You are still dubious. Is a woman in love with a man a phenomenon?"

"Hardly. Though it may depend on what you mean by love."

"I mean physical love. There is no other kind. I mean I came here, frankly and unashamed, to offer myself to you. I did not expect to be taken. I merely hoped I should be." Vridar stared at her. Such a candid and forthright person he had not seen in a long while. "I felt," she went on, "that you would understand. You are not a pious moralist who does all his seducing in the dark. I believe you are a man for whom sex is a decent daylight thing. Am I wrong?"

"Intellectually I am such a man. Emotionally I am still threshing."

"This, Vridar," she said, dropping all formalities, "is the only life I shall ever have. I am twenty-two. I am hungry for love. But the only men I want love with are men who have outgrown their adolescence and their filthy stories. I mean men awake, clean, decent. I don't mean men who worship their mothers and sleep with whores. I am frank about it and, believe me, I am not ashamed.

"I have had one lover and the experience is distressing to remember. He was a blushing guilty fool. He knew nothing and he'll never know anything. Most men are still fraternity boys when they reach forty. All they know of love is what a bull knows. . . . I do not embarrass you?"

"Not a bit. I like your frankness."

"And don't imagine that I am proposing marriage. I thought perhaps you are hungry, too; that we see alike in these matters; that we could be friends. But if you don't want me——"

"I am sorry. I have—well, call her a mistress."

"I did not know that. Is she here?"

"No, in Chicago."

"Well," said Patricia with a wry smile, "that settles it.

But tell me: are you always going to be a monk when she's so far away?"

"I—I don't know. I can't give an honest answer to that. I know only that I wish to be decent with her."

"Would she care?"

"I suppose. Women do, don't they?—and men."

"Yes, I suppose. I suppose I should. It's our vanity." She rose and smiled and offered her hand. "Well, more ado about nothing. We resume our former relations of instructor and student. You are Dr. Hunter and I am Miss Arnon to you, sir." The smile left her face and she gazed at him with eyes darkly luminous. She went to the door. "Credula res amor est," she said, and let herself out.

And there was Wilma Reagan. She came one night to Vridar's room, bringing with her a short story, declaring she wanted criticism. This excuse was so palpably silly that she threw the story to the carpet and stood on it.

"To hell with the story," she said. "I came to talk."

"About what?"

"Life and love and fiddlesticks. You know they're going to kick me out of this school? Honest. I'm a bad egg." She sank to a chair and took a cigarette. "I'm going to tell you the story of my life and misdeeds, and you, my dear doctor, must listen."

"All right: shoot."

"I am twenty; father dead; mother lives in St. George— and, man, you should see the dragons down there! Well, a good Mormon family—so good that for sixteen years I never tasted pepper. Then—then I found I liked pepper, and men, too. Odd that I should. Young girls are not supposed to like men. They do—but don't tell anybody. And so I looked all around St. George and found the best man there and for a month we were happy. Then I was sent to college. Am working for my board and room: a big Mormon family:

Nevens is the name. Mrs. Nevens thinks I'm bad and won't let me go out and says I lie a streak. I do lie. And now they're going to throw me out."

"Why?"

"Because I'm bad. I'm an animal. I love and smoke and I like loud long laughter. I follow crazy impulses—such as coming to your room tonight."

She smoked and looked at him. Wilma Reagan was not a lovely girl: she was large and ungainly, with small shrewd eyes and a wide mouth. She leaned forward now and smiled.

"The stories about me are exaggerated into great fables. I do like to be kissed and loved. I like fun. But I'm a straight-A student. Shakspere is all right but he doesn't fire my blood. Besides, he's dead. . . . Will you help me?"

"How can I?"

"Do you have any faith in me?"

"Plenty."

"Then call Mrs. Nevens and tell her you're my guardian or something. You'll know what to say."

"I'll do my best."

Wilma stayed here until almost midnight, talking of many things: her alert and cynical mind reducing them all to laughter and jest. She was, as Vridar had known for months, the kind of unmoral person that is called psychopathic. She would lie and steal and whore; for in all matters, right and wrong meant less to her than the wind in the night. But she was the most brilliant student he had in composition.

And when she rose to go he saw in her eyes what had most unmistakably been there ever since she came. And she saw his faint smile.

"I know what you're thinking," she said. "I didn't come to talk. I came to crawl into your bed. But I'm glad I didn't. I need something to respect. . . ."

In the next morning he called Mrs. Nevens.

"Hello? Mrs. Nevens? This is Vridar Hunter of the

College. You have staying with you a girl named Wilma Reagan?"

"Yes. Do you know her?"

"She is one of my students. Is she giving you trouble?"

"Is she! Frankly, between us, I do not approve what she does. Her training has been very bad. She stays out late——"

"How late?"

"After midnight. She crawls through windows. For a college girl to act in such a manner——"

"What sort of men does she go with?"

"I haven't seen them. I don't want to."

"Have you taken the matter up with President Johnson?"

"I have. And I've looked into her past life. She's not the sort of student a college can be proud of. She should be dismissed."

"But she's a very brilliant student. I'll tell you: let me see what I can do to fetch her around——"

"She lies like a blue streak. She even invents tales——"

"I know. She has too much imagination."

"Call it that. I have another name for it. . . ."

Two weeks later Vridar received a letter from Patricia Arnon. It said:

MY DEAR DR. HUNTER:

I am very unhappy and am leaving school. I wonder, as you must, now and then, if physical love is worth the candle; and, if not, what anyone can put in its place. All my experience has been fragmentary and curiously unpleasant. For you the world may be only a squeezed-out lemon and for me it may eventually be only that.

I told you I have had only one lover—how many more can a lady with a conscience have?—and that he was beautifully and amazingly stupid. It is rare that we women meet men who have not forgotten that women are females, or who, discovering them to be, can be decent about it. I fully believe that every college and university needs a course in love-making for men. But such civilization will come long after you and I are forgotten dust. In our own country, meanwhile, men will be boys and the Renos will multiply.

Other girls talk with you and they want what I want; but they disguise it in questions about gerunds or Pater. It is supposed—but there is no truth in it—that women like safe tidy men who thrive on platitudes and biscuits. What we seek, in spite of our training, is flood and whirlwind—unless we seek babies and a nest for them, and at present I have no taste for either. And so I am left to meditate on the girls who troop to your office, or to the office of Max Ohm, seeking love that will be all tender fury, yet trained to seek and marry those queer and properly buttoned creatures who will be their husbands and eldest sons.

I am off tomorrow, with the wide world before me. Remember me with gentleness. Let us be friends.

Good-by,
PATRICIA.

Vridar thought of Patricia and Wilma and of himself. Their interest, it seemed to him, lay not in what he most deeply was, but in that external and bitter cynicism behind which he hid; and in this he saw intimations of another far-reaching truth. And in his journal he wrote:

The very fact that the more intelligent and sensitive and imaginative women are attracted to the ironic tongue and the furious heart declares most of our traditional notions of women to be false. It is not alone that scathing speech for them is symbolic of the powerful mind. The truth is deeper and more significant than that. It is in part, of course, a wish to be mastered and taken; and it is also a tremendous indictment of American manhood at the present time. For we are training men like dogs into being a sort of house-pet, and women, though they find pets amusing, do not find them wholly satisfying as lovers. Chivalry flatters a woman's vanity but it is pretty soupy diet for her hunger—as my good friend, Larmond, will in time learn. At its beginning and at its best it was never more than an insincere gesture; and women, I imagine, were always shrewd enough to see it for what it was. But it has grown into one of our most enormous and undefeatable institutions and in its process of growth it has steadily robbed the male of that aggressiveness and of those somewhat violent methods of wooing which were his heritage and right. He has become nothing but an overgrown and bearded boy with a bunch of simple mannerisms such as hat-lifting and bows and the placing of chairs at dinner: half eunuch and half fool.

The reasons for this seem to be many. There is first the Nordic glorification of chastity and all the unclean cults that have been born from it; and there is, closely related to it, our neurotic reverence for motherhood. Motherhood is a splendid thing and demands respect; but it does not follow that we are justified in making of it an idol and an altar, and establishing in its service carloads of mammy singers and holidays and obscurely incestuous verse. But our attitude toward motherhood is less, I think, an incestuous one than it is a perpetual mother-and-son relationship, with all the sons arrested in adolescence. And in consequence, American manhood is abdicating to impotence and stupidity; and the time may come for us, if we go on as we are going at present, when we shall have a matriarchal society, with the men as abashed and abject simpletons staked in a garden, to be used for breeding and chores, and to be locked in their kennels when not wanted.

The results of the abdication are already everywhere to be seen for one with eyes to see. Take the way women develop contempt for the mannikins they marry and to relieve their boredom as well as to find new channels for their hunger join clubs and talk endlessly of art; write verse; sit for hours in gossip; and play bridge. Or note how the bolder ones run pellmell after visiting celebrities, and especially artists; for there is a legend, founded less on fact than on fiction, that artists are unmoral devils, insatiably amorous, and aware, both by intuition and experience, of what a woman wants. These wives, I observe, often bring their husbands along, quite as they bring their vanity bag; and the poor creatures, ill at ease, and vastly uncertain of what it all means, stand back in the shadows as if they were sons or brothers; and after an evening of boredom they find their beds and sleep again. It should be noted, too, that American men, trained to revere their mothers and to marry wives who are mother-substitutes, exhaust their sexual energy in their work. They plod all day and come home with need of little save food and sleep; and many of their wives, without much to do, sit around and grow fat and amorous; build their lives into their sons; or run out, fluttering and bright-eyed, to see a visiting artist. Nearly all our fiction, in consequence, is written for them and becomes their vicarious lover. For in respect to art, if nothing else, our society is already matriarchal.

There are, of course, some lovely ironies in all this. The great lovers of the past—the Casanovas and Don Juans—have been, as likely as not, homosexuals or some other sort of pervert. Having had little taste for normal intercourse and little passion for women, they have been able to make of love what we have chosen to call an art. They have so simulated passion as to deceive the women who came to their beds; and, with their own hunger neither impulsive nor eager, and with their vanity reaching to excesses out of their emotional distortion, they have been able to refine and prolong to the last degree all their methods of titillation.

And there is this: women are, beyond all reach of exaggeration, unmoral and earthy, practical and sane; except, of course, those deluded and bewildered ones who try to take and use the stupid moralities that men have evolved. Women have no taste for, and, deeply, can see no sense in, ideologies and art, metaphysics and decalogues; because they perceive, in their wise and ancient way, that all these are quite unnecessary additions that men have heaped upon life. And here is another of those lovely ironies. Men, having got the weird notion of guilt and sin, have evolved compensatory moralities and have browbeaten women into accepting them; and women, now lost in the pathetic unclean fog of the matter, and believing earnestly that they are what they are not, are, in unconscious and terrible vengeance, placing men (with the help of the men, of course) in a condition of emotional serfdom. And this is the price that men, if they are not careful, will eventually pay for their idolatrous folly.

Neloa—and I now confess this with abject humility—was as unmoral as trees and flowers; and my blunder and her tragedy lay in the fact that I tried to force upon her a morality and an idealism for which she had no understanding and no use. Her death was a rebuke to that crusading zeal which men—and we say, of course, the *best* men!—have employed ever since they got the dark and unclean notion that they were sinners against their god. She was a pagan and her way was clean. I was a creature of cultures and distortions, mouthing my awful cant about greatness and purpose, ideals and progress. Our struggle was a struggle between a way of life which, were we to throw away our cheap and puritanic ideals, we should all wish sanely and wholesomely to follow, and a way of life which has produced our prophets and religions and bigots.

All this is rankest heresy for the pious and God-thumping American public. I am glad that at last I see it with some clarity and that I have the courage to face it and set it down. . . .

VIII

●

I T WAS late in April when Vridar met Ferdinand Thomas.
He did not like him. He tried to avoid him as formerly
he had tried to avoid Dennis Altrock. He did not like him
because this man seemed to him, on first acquaintance, to be
effusive and superficial: a lusty radical deferring to rainbows; an irrepressible boy who, with persuasion and scorn,
was bent on reforming the earth. And as Vridar listened in
silence, trying to weigh the man, he little dreamed that
Ferdinand Thomas was to become his closest friend.

Ferd was half Welsh and half Spanish. He looked like a
Spaniard and he had the impetuous mannerisms of the Latin
people. Some persons thought him handsome and some
thought him as ugly as a frog: he had a large head, curiously
misshapen, as if the skull had been flattened and a drunken
potter had reshaped it: getting no feature precisely where it
belonged: leaving a great bulge of forehead; a wide mouth
which, in a grin, ran far into either cheek; and a long nose
that reached down and almost across the short upper lip.
But in this strange disarrangement of features there was
something very pleasing and for a lot of women there was
something devilishly attractive: half satyr and half prophet,
with his dark eyes full of fire and mischief, his broad smile
as candid as sunlight.

Ferd was a radical and a crusader. He had been dismissed from four American universities and each dismissal
he looked back upon with huge smacking gusto. Zest, indeed, was his most noticeable trait: a vigorous and insatiable
love of life, of argument and a good fight, of old whisky and
adorable women. He was wholly without tact or discretion,
and for some persons here he was only a noisy vulgarian,
forever thrusting his long nose into matters that were none
of his business. His students swore by him and gave him

gifts. Nearly all of his colleagues distrusted or despised him.

The chief interest of Ferd Thomas in these months was the vanities and dishonesties and scandals of the academic world. With the patient and relentless curiosity of an Upton Sinclair he prowled in dark places, ferreting out the gossip, the records of meanness and cowardice, the pompous announcements and the strut. Of the professors here he learned more in a week than Vridar would have learned in ten years. He learned that this dignified old owl, with a wife and ten children, had tried in Boston to seduce a woman and had failed; that this stately image of a New England gentleman had sat in his office and held a girl's hand until she screamed and fainted; and that this one, in spite of religious fervor and rapt devotion to charity, had a bastard son in a far place. And these were only a few of the many which he told with such bright and mirthful earnestness, with such lusty snorts of joy and scorn, that Vridar looked at him in astonishment and said nothing at all. Ferd told of the feuds and seductions among colleagues where he had formerly taught. Nor was he content to drag from closets every naked and blushing skeleton of this school: when this job was done, he devoted himself to the city; and what he learned there, much of it legend only, but much of it supported by records in the city clerk's office and elsewhere, would have filled a book.

Now and then Vridar and Ferd spent an evening in the apartment of Max Ohm. They were very unlike, Max and Ferd, but each was a specialist in his own kind of mimicry: the one with his chalklike and solemn face, his mordant wit; the other overflowing with relish and zest.

"I'll burble," said Ferd. "You ever hear me burble? Really? Listen and I'll burble for you. . . ."

And one evening Vridar laughed at these clowns until he was sick. He lay on the floor and howled, looking now at one, now at the other; and listening to both. They were telling tales of former colleagues.

"Listen, and I'll tell you a tale of Professor John Armstrong. You ever heard of Professor Johnny Armstrong? No? I thought you had. He got him a wife. Honest to God, I'm not lying to you: that man got him a wife. You should see his wife. And they went on a honeymoon. And they honeymooned. And one night, weary of honey, Bertha —Bertha Josephine, really—said to Johnny, 'Darling, I'll turn on my stomach now.' And Johnny said—shoot me if I'm lying in this—Johnny said, 'I didn't know you had ever turned it off.' Now by God, that's the truth!" Ferd shouted as if enraged. He turned, snarling. "I tell you Bertha didn't like that! She said it was crass and gross. She said it was rowdy. She said it was homebred and homespun and just like the vulgus. And she went right out and divorced Johnny. Listen!" said Ferd, turning around with furious gestures. "I'm tired of the way you snicker at me! . . ."

And Max, looking as oafish and sleepy as an owl, softly intoned:

> *"I can't even guess what they fed honest Abe*
> *But Herbert Hoover was an Ovaltine babe."*

"And now," said Ferd, looking with affected amazement at Max, "now I'll tell you a bedtime story. Jack and Jill went up the hill. And why? That's the question. Now Jerry Dorwald was a gentleman with appetites and most of his appetites ran to co-eds. He had a wife. He had a lot of wives but he was married to only one of them. And one office; and the telephone rang. Jerry answered that telephone. I swear to God the fool did. And a sweet voice said, 'Jerry darling, I missed you last night.' And what," asked Ferd with loud anguish, with his eyes rolling, "did Jerry say? Why, he said, 'Honey, who is this?' "

"Have you ever heard of Bingham Bosworth?" asked Max, sitting up.

"Sure, I've heard of Bingham Bosworth."

"I never have. I hoped someone had heard of him. And Martha Martin: she worries me."

"I'll tell you about Martha Martin. She's a straight-A student. She is fat and round like the Republican party——"

"Lord, I'm glad," said Max. He was sitting like a mummy, with only his blue eyes faintly alive. "Tell me," he said, thrusting his neck out and looking at Ferd with sudden interest. "Are you constipated?"

"Am I? Oh, Ohm, sweet Ohm!"

"I am," said Max. "It's the great American pastime. I'm writing a cantata on the subject. Would you like to hear one of my arias?" Max went to his piano and played and sang.

"I've—tried—spinach—I've tried yeast!
Of oils Ivedrunksometwentytonsatleast!
I've—eaten—bran—stovewood—and figs!
I've ridden aFordandIvedancedjigs!
Oh, I've—dug—ditches—and—Ivepulleddowngarages;
I've tried—rubs—kicks—gruntsandmassages!
I've—stood—onmyhead—and—I've—bent—over—double
ButIstillhave—thesameoldtrouble!"

Ferd rose to his feet, his wide mouth bawling with joy; and Vridar, after staring at the grave satanic face of Max, burst with mirth and choked. Max rose and came over and looked down at him with side-splitting owlishness; and he said very softly:

"Have you tried yeast?"

And these two, Max and Ferd, who became his friends, Vridar studied as he had formerly studied books. He remembered Byron's statement that a person's mouth and not his eyes reveals what he is trying to hide. Ferd's mouth was wide and frank, with two rows of teeth visible, when he smiled, almost to his last molars; but the mouth of Max was as fixed and expressionless as concrete: the lips barely moved when he talked and they rarely smiled. And Vridar studied with patient interest not only the mouth and eyes of every person around him: he studied every mannerism and gesture, the walk, the smoking of a cigarette, the use of hands: few details, no matter how small, escaped him, and every detail was significant. A girl in his class laid her hands at her side, hiding them in the folds of her dress: they were short and chunky hands and she was ashamed of them. Another girl had bad teeth and always smiled with her lips pressed together. A third had huge ears and dressed her hair down over them in fluffy bangs. There was a professor here, no larger than a boy, who had double heels on his shoes and walked in a curious brisk manner as if stretching to the sky; another with a mole on her forehead which she hid under a curl of hair; and another who, with a tooth like a tusk in his left jaw, drew his smile queerly into his right cheek. All such matters as these he had long observed and had known the meaning of. He had learned to read in himself, and so in others, the meaning of a smile or a shrug, of a restrained laugh or sneeze, movements of hands and legs, and facial mannerisms, whether genuine or feigned. And now he reached to self-revelations less obvious than these. There was a girl who talked with him in his office and her nervous hands, directed by her unconscious mind, drew her skirt little by little above her knees; and this deep and hidden wish to undress before him made him smile. There was a shy young man who, while talking of errors in composition, scrawled vaguely phallic symbols in his notebook, wholly unaware of what he did. . . .

You can see, Vridar reflected, that persons, in respect to knowledge of themselves, fall roughly into three classes. There are those fortunate persons who are unself-conscious: they are almost never aware of themselves as something that moves darkly in a strange dark world. They laugh and talk and do things, understanding nothing of themselves, little of life. You feel at ease around them. They are happier be-

cause they think less; but they are also without exception
creatures of habit. All matters of right and wrong they
know and never revise or question and they furnish, in consequence, enthusiastic recruits to mobs and violence, to
lynchings and inquisitions. These persons are shaped entirely by dogmas; and once a Baptist, Mormon or Catholic,
a Republican or a Democrat, they most likely will remain
so. . . .

And there is that second group, most tragic of all, most
self-defeated and wretched, and most symptomatic of our
present age. These persons are self-conscious but not self-
searching and you can see them anywhere. Of these we fill
our asylums and psychopathic wards, and to some extent our
jails; for these persons, never at ease, always miserably aware
of themselves, and persecuted endlessly by their fancies, are
lost in darkness largely self-created. Out of this class, increasing daily, come most of our religious leaders, crusaders,
fanatics, artists—and many other sorts of idealists of infinite
variety and deadliness. This group, in times past, has con-
tributed most to social progress; because, when not too
deluded or misdirected, it is a mighty force for good. But
it has also, because of blundering zeal and morbid hunger
for distinction, given us our wars and many of our forms of
exploitation and all of our false gods. To this group belonged Jesus and Luther and Calvin, Dante and Milton and
Wordsworth, Napoleon and Cæsar and Woodrow Wilson.

And there is a third group, very small in number, and
still too ironic in point of view, which is both self-conscious
and self-searching. Upon the growth of this class, and upon
nothing else, rests our future and all our hope and faith.
To be self-conscious is one thing: those who become so have
nothing to do with the process but are shaped by circum-
stance and heritage. The source may be a physical deform-
ity, or a sexual distortion of one kind or another, or a sense
of guilt and shame for any number of reasons, or persecutions in childhood. Out of such unhappiness come the alert

mind and the sensitive heart. But to be self-searching is another thing: this requires tenacity and courage and the scientific attitude of mind. It requires the destruction, or at least the vigorous discipline, of vanity and self-love. It requires the recognition of self as a strange phenomenon not demonstrably related to significance or meaning or absolutes. George belongs to the first group. Maxine and Ferd and Max belong now to the second. Ferd, I think, will keep after himself until he arrives in the third. If Maxine ever becomes self-searching, she will have a mind that will cause any person to sit uneasily in her presence. . . . "And all that," he wrote to Athene, "is only the beginning. It offers enormous possibilities. I foresee a race of men and women aware of themselves and of what they are, with all subterfuges and evasions behind them; and, in consequence, of what they can hope to achieve. Such knowledge, and such knowledge alone, I believe, can save us from the prophecies of Spengler. . . ."

IX

ATHENE was appointed to an instructorship here and in June she came West. She took a small apartment near the college and Vridar lived in a single room three doors away.

"I suppose," he said, "we must be very discreet. Too many persons around us live within the oppressive limits of legal sanctions. If they learn we are lovers they'll raise an awful stink."

"Yes, of course. We'll have to be very careful."

"Should we get married?"

"No. I'd lose my job."

"Yes, you'd lose your job. But what if we get caught? We'd both lose our jobs then. All the unhappily married will be snooping around to learn what we're doing. They'll be awfully mad if they find out. Lord, they'll be in a fury! Every person, my dear, who blunders into marriage wants every other person to blunder in and suffer with him. That's the reason they howl their heads off about free love. They want it to be bought and paid for."

"Well, we'll have to be very careful."

"In public I'll almost ignore you. I'll call you Miss Marvell."

"Yes, but don't overdo your acting."

"Oh, I'll be clever. I'll take you to shows. It will be rumored that I am shyly wooing you."

"But don't be too shy."

"After a while I'll be bolder. It will be rumored we're falling in love. Then the gossips will be happy. Their eyes will shine with vicarious consummations. They'll be envious. But they'll imagine us somewhere in the future with ten kids and an apartment full of unhappiness. That will make them feel better. Athene, I used to be that way."

"What way?"

"I used to howl in rage about free love and all that. I choked up with envy and went wailing to God. I felt murderous. I banged around and threw precepts and platitudes at everybody. I would have made a swell bishop or something."

"And I would have made a good bishopess."

"If we had married years ago, wouldn't we have reformed the earth! How we would have gone after the sinners! Anthony Comstock and Carrie Nation, whanging people right into heaven. . . ."

Vridar was as discreet as he knew how to be. He spent many an evening in Athene's apartment but he always came under cover of darkness to the back door; and they drew the shades carefully; and they almost whispered their words. Now and then, if Vridar spoke too loudly, Athene would rebuke him; and he would roar:

"To hell with the puritans! What do I care?"

"Vridar, in heaven's name!"

"What do I care?" he would say, whispering now. And then aloud: "To hell with them!"

In this summer Vridar's mother came to visit him. She looked at him day by day with searching eyes; and at last, convinced of his evil ways, she spoke her mind. She wept and for half an hour Vridar listened to her grief and reproach.

"I never knew a son of mine would do such a thing! I'd never a-believed it! I'd rather be dead than see you this way!"

"What way?" he asked, a little furious.

"Living in sin! Living in lust like a common hoodlum! My God, I would never a-believed it. I've always had such dreams for you. You were always such a clean and noble boy and you had such noble ideals. And now, to see you like this! Oh, I'd rather you'd a-stuck a knife in my heart!

. . ." And she wept afresh, vanity and self-pity shaking her with great sobs.

"Listen, Mater——"

"Oh, I don't want a-listen! I'n see, can't I? I'n tell you aren't what you used to be!"

"Mater, will you listen a minute?"

"There's nothing you'n say, Son. You've broken your mother's heart. And all my life I slaved for you. I worked like a slave for my children and I trained them to be noble and good. And now—— My God, I wish you'd killed me!"

"Mater——"

"Please don't talk to me. There's nothing you'n say. I wish I was dead, that's all. I wish I was dead."

Vridar looked at her: at her wrinkled and anguished face, her wasted body, her hair turning gray.

"It's true you slaved for us. I'll never forget that. You did for us what few mothers would ever do for their children——"

"And what do I get for it? Just heartache. And I'd never a-done it if I'd known you'd come to this. Never! I wouldn't a-been a slave all my years in a lonely place. And now I wish to God I'd never been born!"

"Mater, you make it hard to be honest with you. I could have lied about it. Most sons would probably have done so——"

"You couldn't lie. You never did lie. Thank God for that."

"I could have lied," Vridar went on patiently. "But when you asked me I told you the truth. I've tried to be a son worthy of you. I am still trying. But some things we do not see alike——"

"And thank God we don't! Sin is sin, my son, and it will never be anything else."

"That is what you think. I do not believe in sin. But like all mothers you want me to go through life with every belief and prejudice you have. But I won't do it. Call me ungrateful. Say I'm going to hell. Say anything you like. I have my life to live in what seems to me the most decent way——"

"And you call this decent?" Her wet eyes were wide with scorn and amazement. "You call it decent to live in sin with a woman!"

"It is decent. We love one another. The stinking little ceremony you call marriage means nothing to us. I've seen too much of your damned marriage. Most of it is legal whoredom. If there's any sin on earth it's among you married people."

"Son, what are you saying?"

"The truth, and you don't like it. Like all good pious people everywhere you don't like it. And another thing, Mater——"

"You'n talk till doomsday, Son, and you can't change me. Sin is sin and I know it when I see it."

"Another thing. I'm your son and in a lot of ways I am like you. You're not the only one with flint and dynamite in you. You have been a magnificent mother. But you are also an indomitable person with a will of iron. So am I. Nobody can change you in a single thing you believe. All right: nobody can change me——"

"Well, all I know is I wish I was dead. I wish I was dead a thousand times rather than see you this way." She stared at him a long moment, her eyes anguished and worshipful. Then she went to his bed and lay there, moaning out of desolate grief.

Vridar sought Athene and told her what had been said. She was distressed and he knew she was weighing again the cost of the life she had chosen.

"You needn't look that way," he said, annoyed. "Don't think I'm weak with pity and doubts and regrets. It pains me to see my mother unhappy. She has been a remarkable mother and the debt I owe to her I can never pay. But the source of her grief, its prejudice, its erotic sublimation, its blind and self-pitying selfishness, I hate with everything in me. I know how she has slaved. I know what sacrifices she has made. I know how she set her heel on her pride and came among my father's people. How she suffered their lewd scorn and jest. How for twenty years she lived in loneliness in a lonely place. All that I know. But I also know that motherhood is blind and ruthless and selfish. In a lot of its motives it stinks. It is enormous in its capacity for unhappiness and ruin. Everywhere I go I see mothers who have made eunuchs of their sons. And I hate all that. I hate it in the way I hate exploitation and injustice and moral cowardice.

"So get that look out of your eyes. If my mother had had her way, I'd now be a dinky little Mormon bishop somewhere, swindling my neighbors and preaching platitudes. I do feel unhappy about it. It does grieve me to see her anguish. But there is nothing I can do about it. Mothers are that way and we can only leave them to God's pity. Don't imagine anything she can say or do will make me falter. I'm made of iron, Athene. I'm not the one stricken with doubts. It's you. You're the one wishing the hell you were out of this situation."

"I'm not."

"You are. I saw it in your eyes."

"I admit I don't have your ruthless nature. I can't be— I can't be ruthless."

"No. Not even when you know you're right."

"How can I be sure that I'm right?"

"You're afraid of public opinion, my dear. You've always been. You're afraid of the huge stupid judgment of humanity. I don't give a God damn about it. My mother represents one way of life that is the heart and core of this wretched country we live in. I represent another way. Between the two there can be no truce, no compromise. Is that ruthless? All right. But you'd make the thing Janus-faced: puritan on one side, free man on the other."

"I would not!"

"Then why all these doubts? Why this fear, this distress, every time we run into a force that is our enemy?"

"I am a fighter," said Athene impatiently. "I'm not militant like you. If I were a weakling I'd not be here now."

"Yes, I know. Well, let's fight. There's nothing worse than death ahead of us. The meek-will-inherit-the-earth-stuff is all right for those who like cemeteries. From now on I'm going to stand up and whack my enemies right in their beards."

"And who are your enemies?"

"Myself chiefly. Traditions and forces."

"You'll wear yourself out whacking things in their beards."

"That's all right. I'll wear the beards out, too. Then," he said, "I'll see the face of things."

"Vridar, what am I to do now? Your mother will hate me. I've taken another's place and she thinks I'm living in sin. And you say to fight. What has fighting to do with a matter like that?"

"Everything. You're not fighting my mother. You're fighting what she stands for. And there's the point, Athene: you don't want to fight what she stands for."

"I'll admit I like to live in peace. With persons anyway."

"There is no peace on earth. Peace is stagnant. We grow in storm and conflict."

"Yes, and wear ourselves out in conflict."

"To hell with peace. We'll find plenty of it after we're dead."

"Vridar," she said, looking at him strangely, "you're a most amazing person. Already in your life you've had enough conflict to wear a dozen persons out. And yet, here you are, lusting for battle."

"I'm a fighter, my dear. My battles have just begun."

Of Vridar's self-searching, which became day by day
more determined, he talked with Athene in every week or
two. For a week or ten days he would live in silence, thinking fiercely of himself and of the persons around him; and
then he would deliver his stormy opinions. He felt that at
last he was on a path that did not lead to a blind end and
his enthusiasm grew as he probed to his buried life. Athene
did not have his zest or his hungry wish for certainties or
his restless interest in philosophy and politics and humankind. And to her evasions, her specious reasoning out of
vanity, her pride and self-love, he gave no peace.

"Teach me," she said. "I want to grow. But pretty soon
you'll have me stripped to my bones."

"Both of us. We'll be two splendid skeletons."

"But I'm not a completely selfish animal."

"Of course you are. So am I. So is everyone."

"You don't believe in disinterested conduct?"

"No, nor in ghosts and magic."

"But I feel——"

"To hell with what you feel. What do you think?"

"I think there is disinterested conduct."

"An example."

"Well, take a person who gives a building to a university——"

"And has his name on a tablet above the door."

"But suppose he gives anonymously."

"All right. Then he has some sense of irony. His vanity
chooses a more hidden and devious method. Athene, the
word vanity is offensive for you. It shouldn't be. All is
vanity: true. A long time ago human beings got ideals and
saw they were exploiting one another and were ashamed.
They invented the myth of unselfishness and behind it they
have hidden enough exploitation and cowardice to fill a universe."

"And you really think we are all utterly selfish?"

"Of course. But I no longer find selfishness abhorrent. Some kinds seem more decent than others. That's all. They may not be a damned bit more decent. This man makes a fortune and buys a yacht. This other builds a cathedral. But we all act within our self-esteem. . . ."

And again:

"Athene, what a filthy thing humanity has made of love. On the one hand we have those who delight in smut. On the other hand we have purists and snoops and censors. I used to be one of these dunghill crusaders. Oh, I was a clean lad with a laundered and starched mind. I was a guardian of morals and how I loved myself! I ranted against obscene books; nakedness; free love; kissing in public—and smiled at God. And how He must have despised me. And you?"

"Oh yes, I was a good clean girl."

"But one group is just as bad as the other. In varying degrees we are all guilty. But I'm going to get all this erotic snot out of me. I'm going to be able to use these terrible four-letter Anglo-Saxon words without feeling the blood burn in my pious hide. I'm going to understand that they are clean and splendid words. And more than that: love for me—and I mean good lusty physical love—is going to be as natural as food and drink. Before long now I'll not be peeking around to see if God is watching me. I'll sail right in with all my hair standing on end——"

"Now you're being ridiculous!"

"No, just an ape. And are you with me?"

"Of course. Women, my dear, are naturally franker in those matters. We'd be decent if you men would let us."

"I know it."

"You made me feel more ashamed than I'd ever felt."

"I don't doubt it. Well, I had a fine training. I loved storks. Once, when very young, I looked at a doll and reflected with pleasure that it was sexless. Darling, I should have been Adam. If Eve had whispered in my ear I'd have complained to God."

"Oh no. You always liked that sort of whispering. And I know something else."

"You're insulting me."

"You've never really been ashamed of sex. You've been ashamed because you weren't ashamed enough."

He looked at her and pondered the statement. "You look like a sweet simple girl," he said, "but you do have a mind."

"If you hadn't kept one eye open all the time, where would you be now?"

"A Mormon missionary."

"Another John Calvin."

"Sure. Well, let's be serious."

"No. You're most serious when you're clowning."

"I'm serious now. Life is real, life is earnest—but that is not what I mean. And how should I presume? I thought once when I read the Bible that Moses should be sued for libel. And that is not what I mean, either. Men who dote on married life aren't much to kiss their wife. Is that it? Or perhaps: marriage gets a man melancholy and listless but he sure picks up when he grabs him a mistress. Or do I mean——"

"You mean you're crazy. Do you think you'll ever be anything else?"

And again:

"Darling," he said, making a face, "I have impulses to rape."

"Indeed. What man hasn't?"

"You think they all have?"

"I think women aren't interested in those who haven't."

"You are using your mind, aren't you? Well, we men are like roosters. I remember what my mother once said of hens. Hens, she said, are like women: they run like hell but

when overtaken they yield and look happy about it. Are
you like a hen?"

"An educated hen. I choose my roosters."

"And what a rooster you got in me! Well, here's my
point. The truth about human beings seems terrible when
you first face it. After you've lived with it a while it doesn't
seem terrible at all. You begin to respect humanity more,
not less. And after all the admissions are made I imagine a
person could be a friend of himself."

"That's the best thing you've said in weeks. You have
a philosophy of life there."

"I'm working toward it."

"And after he has become his own friend, then he might
also be the friend of others."

"Exactly."

"My dear, that is something to build on."

"But think of all the admissions that have to be made.
Until then we are bottled up in darkness. Now I admit impulses to rape: that means that, aware of them, I'll always
restrain them. And so with impulses to murder or steal or
anything else. Darling, here's an important point: do you
know why I have always been so sadistic?"

"You're an extremist in all things."

"But this extreme. Abnormal sadism is caused by fear
of impotence or doubt of one's manhood or sexual distortion. Now note the comedy there. I was a timid quaking
lad, afraid of girls. I didn't think they found me attractive.
What did I do? Just what thousands do. In fact, what
didn't I do! I developed a compensatory admiration for
strong and brutal men. I shrank from all forms of brutality
because I was attracted to it, just as puritans shrink from
what they call sin because it allures them. In the same way
a lot of men won't drink whisky because they're afraid to
find out about themselves. Well, I didn't feel potent and
lusty enough to be two-fisted. I turned away from life.
When I met you I was head over heels in the nonsense of

Plato. I was an ardent pacifist. And these ardent pacifists—
how the truth would knock the wind out of them!

"And that isn't all of it. Lord, no. I had that magnificent emotional stupidity which so many persons admire. I
was earnest. I believed in brotherhood and equality and
virtuous women. It is incredible. I believed in virtuous
women because I didn't feel I'd ever be sleeping with any of
them and I wanted them to stay virtuous. All married men
who feel they must be faithful to their wives want all unmarried women to be virgins. You see? And I believed that
a lily is more pure and unimpassioned than a rose. Honest.
I was a specialist in such evasive symbols.

"And here is still another aspect of the pure and holy
matter. I read a review of a novel the other day. The critic,
a man, said the hero was a nincompoop. He couldn't understand why the heroine loved him. He meant, of course, that
women should love men like himself. Then I read a review
by a woman. She said the heroine was a fool. She did not see
how the hero could be attracted to her. She meant, of
course, that she herself is the sort of woman men should
love. There you have it. Now I used to read novels and
think the hero was an ass: the boob in *Tess*, for instance.
Which meant that he was not like what I thought I was.
Which meant that I was sweetly in love with myself. What
a man! Vridar Hunter: how noble in reason! How infinite
in faculty! In form and moving how express and admirable!
In action how like an angel! In apprehension how like a god!
The beauty of the world, the paragon of animals! I am
overcome by my splendor," Vridar said, and mopped his
brow. "I read Walt Whitman: he was swell. He deified himself and mankind. He apostrophized mightily through a
thousand pages, proclaiming the self-pity of Walt Whitman.
And how this self-pitying country loved him! How it likes
any protagonist in a novel that is a vision of its sickly notions of itself! That's the secret of your best seller.

"Darling, what a man I was. How like an angel as I

went tearing around in my crusades. How infinite in faculty when I failed to see that the only obscenity is in a person's mind. And the whole beauty of the world in that part of me showing above my clothes. How vigorous—like a bowl of meringue! How noble in reason—when he figured out that men in books were detestable if not like his sweet opinion of himself!

"Well, there are admissions for you. Seeing my way to them has not been easy. But I feel better. I feel less unclean."

Athene was smiling at him. She said:

"And are you going on forever, dragging admissions like black cats out of a sack?"

"As many cats as I can get hold of. My dear, I've worn myself out trying to think I'm a swell fellow. Really, I'm not the center of the universe. But you think you are."

"Oh, do I?"

"Sure. You sit there and it seems to you that the universe is equidistant from you at all points. And when you move you take the center with you. Are you never ashamed for yanking it around that way?"

Athene broke into laughter.

"But, Vridar," she said, "you are still very sadistic."

"Apes are. You ever watch them? And you were attracted to me chiefly because of my sadism. Yet note the comedy there. I talked of Plato and poetry and ideals and all the while you thought you loved me."

"I loved you for those, too. They were the gentleness."

"The sadism masquerading."

"Vridar, did you really love me then?"

"I respected your mind and integrity. I felt tenderness. Does that add up to love?"

"It adds up to something that satisfies."

Vridar went over and sat at her feet.

"Athene, don't you feel any enthusiasm for this search for a little truth?"

"More than I did."

"Do my harangues distress you?"

"Less and less."

"Will you love me after I'm stripped down to what I am?"

"It will be my weakness if I don't."

"There won't be much to love. Just a handful of appetites. A hunger for certainties. A lonely ape without any hair on its chest."

"Why in the past have you alluded so much to that matter? I mean your caustic thrusts at men with hairy chests."

"You shouldn't have to ask that. Because, of course, hair for me was another sign of virility."

"My dear, you have enough virility. If you had more you would drive me crazy."

"But you'd like it better if a little more hair grew on it."

"I've never been obsessed with hair."

"Well," he said, "I'm getting along. I've grown more in the last year than in the other thirty. But I had already done some thinking. I was ripe for an explosion and I'm blowing all over the map. I've been a fool. I shall be less and less one. I'm getting so I can read a person as easily as a book. So long as it isn't a book by Kant. And right here we're in a gorgeous clinic. Wait until you see some of the specimens I'm studying now. . . ."

X

●

TO THIS college came a young instructor named Carlyle
Orcutt, and his wife Elsa. They were to become Vridar's
friends but in this year they exhausted his patience and excited his scorn. Carlyle was a small slender person with
somewhat foppish mannerisms. He was twenty-three but
he looked no more than seventeen and in his emotional im-
maturity he was no more; but he had traveled a lot and
had read a great number of books. The persons he had seen,
the foods he had eaten and the liquors he had drunk, made
the exotic patterns of his talk. He liked to remember that
he had seen Hemingway and other expatriates; to talk, with
a gently patronizing air, of London, Paris, and Rome.

It was abroad that he met Elsa Vlomberg, a German-
Irish girl. Elsa spoke French like a native and had taught
French two years in Nice. There had been a whirlwind
courtship, an elopement, and a vague astonishment thereafter. They were two young sophisticates, the first Vridar
had ever seen: they addressed one another by their surnames,
devoted themselves to strange foods and cocktails, looked
with weariness at this smug Mormon city, and played bridge.
And against his will Vridar yielded to their tutoring and
learned to play this game.

He learned much more than that. In one evening and another they filled him with amusement or pity or rage. With
sly words, with artful innuendo, they rebuked his blunders,
summarized his rural heritage, and smiled behind their cards.
Now and then he seethed like a cauldron within but in these
first months he never let his fury out. Not for some time
did he see the irony of the situation, or himself as one who
grew angry because what they said was true.

When he blundered in his playing—and his blunders were
stupid and many—Elsa declared in her brightly malicious

way, "They're walking the streets of London, Orcutt." This oblique summary made Vridar sputter with wrath. And when Vridar and Athene lost, as they always did, Carlyle's glee was huge and gloating. He would add the figures eagerly, as if he had vanquished a kingdom; and he would say:

"We made a dollar on that. That is, if we were playing for money."

This last statement was always so definite a summary of Vridar as an impecunious hill-billy that he would say to Athene later, "Did you ever see bad taste so implacable and mountainous?"

"Never. I don't understand why you go around with them."

"I want to understand them. Besides, I'm an ass to get furious. I want to get at the reasons there."

Often they came to Athene's apartment, and now and then Ferd came, too. Ferd, unlike Vridar, was not a person who restrained his scorn, or who, deliberately affecting obtuseness, invited persons to show their souls. He despised the Orcutts and after looking at them with amazement he tried to crush them.

"In the name of God," he roared, "cut out all this damned posing! The fact that you've been to Europe doesn't mean you've talked with the Sphinx. Where," he asked, addressing Carlyle, "do you get this eyether and nyether stuff? You're not in England. Or does this Salt Lake Valley look like Sussex to you? And you," he said to Elsa. "One of these days I'll give you the psychology of a sophisticate and you'll curl up in a closet and moan. . . ."

During these assaults Vridar sat with his searching stare on the Orcutts. Carlyle would redden with anger and stride about, or he would puff his cigarette and blow smoke through his nostrils, or he would turn his mouth outward in a ripe red pucker. His eyes would flicker with spite. And Elsa, more inscrutable, more alert and intuitive in her perceptions, would reveal only by her eyes what was in her mind. She had lovely eyes which, in moments of serenity, looked almost blue; but when annoyed they were dark gray and shadowed and full of deep quiet hatred. It was in these moments that Vridar felt pity. They are only children, he reflected. They will grow up. . . .

"You think you're a great smoker," Ferd said scornfully. He was speaking to Carlyle. "You're like any old grandmother who doesn't inhale. . . ."

And in other whiles Vridar watched them closely, waiting for the unpremeditated gestures that would betray their thoughts; and the gestures came. When Elsa reached for a cigarette he saw her hand tremble; a sudden brief quivering, almost a spasm, in her lips; and something haunted and desolate in her eyes. In Carlyle's one-syllable cough or in the wrinkling of his nose or in his sharp intake of breath followed by a narrowing of his eyes he read the grammar of his emotion. And though Vridar, in times that were many, had suffered anguish under the malicious jibes of these two, he felt, when listening to Ferd's bludgeoning scorn, a deep sympathy. And this sympathy grew and affection came with it. For he was learning to understand; to reach to the darkest and most hidden motives; to see the meaning of envy and scorn and malice, distrust and spite. And he was learning tolerance.

"The Frenchman was right," he said to Athene. "When we understand, we realize there is nothing to forgive."

But the Orcutts, nevertheless, demanded more of patience, of restraint and pity, than had ever been demanded of him or was ever to be again. Carlyle jeered at Vridar's wish to be a writer. "Are you still scribbling your journalism?" And again: "I suppose it's your great ambition to write a best-seller." And again: "Don't you realize that a writer has to live first? Have you ever been east of Utah?" And one evening his malice was more than Vridar could stand. He let his fury out.

Among the students here was a lean and ungainly youth of twenty with a brilliant and sardonic mind. His mother was a Jewess, his father was Irish, and his name was Moses McGuire. Everyone called him Mac. Never had Vridar known any but himself so full of cynical bitterness, of hatreds and conflicts, as this youth. Never had he known one who could talk in such scathing epigram or reach more unerringly to the real motives behind human pretense and sham. Mac despised the smug and pious life of this college —a wedlock of gentile steers and Mormon heifers, he called it; and he regarded himself in all hours, in all moods, with implacable loathing. Vridar liked this youth and understood him. "When you feel the devil and despair upon you," he said, "come to my room and we'll talk." And Mac came often and did all the talking, pacing the room like a specter of Satan; and he talked in such magnificent rhetoric, in such pungent aphorism and diatribe, that Vridar sat in astonishment and said nothing at all.

Mac had been reading Freud and he was trying to understand himself. His obsessions infuriated him. When he walked the streets he was impelled to count all the squares in the pavement; to measure his long strides to the lines in the walk; and to count windows and doors and trees, the number of persons who passed him, and the peaks in the mountains roundabout. He cultivated and became a master of the sardonic gesture. One afternoon he wanted cigarettes and Vridar went with him into a drugstore. Mac strode to the counter and fixed his cynical gaze on a quart of carbolic acid. For a full minute he looked at this bottle and the druggist looked at him and waited. When the druggist asked, "Do you wish something?" Mac ignored him. Then he swung with theatrical suddenness and looked at the druggist, his whole face a bitter sneer; and that man, as if set back on his heels, withdrew step by step, with anger flushing him.

"Cigarettes," said Mac, "and an ounce of carbolic acid."

When he was on the street again, he set the bottle of acid on the concrete and ground it under his heel. "I have a suicide obsession," he said. "I have to crush it." And he laughed. His laughter was a harsh cawing, mirthless and bitter.

One evening when Vridar was sitting in his room, trimming the lines of an ironic sonnet, Mac strode in. He remained until after midnight, talking out of furious derisions and laughing his terrible laugh.

"Hunter, what is the trouble with me? Is it because I am half Jew and half Irish? That insuperable ass, Ludwig Lewisohn, would say so. Is it because I play pinochle and smoke a pipe? Is it because the Bible and the Koran don't mix in theological porridge? Your good friends, the saints of Zion and Deseret, would say so. Is it because my chest is thin and hairless? Or am I afraid of my mother?

"When I was a small lad I used to run out and play. I capered and twit-twitted. Imagine me out in the back yard with a bevy, flock, swarm, drove, herd, covey, litter, farrow —what is the right word?—of little girls, twit-twitting. And then my mother would come to the door and yell at me: a voice like a fog-siren, a bosom like a mattress doubled over. And I was paralyzed. Even yet I shudder when the awful maternal wail of her voice streaks through memory like the cry of a female ape falling out of a tree. And she would take me in and moan over me and kiss my erotic little cheeks; and I put my erotic little hands up to her breast: mother and son, the Virgin and the cherub. How pure our love was, Hunter! What sweet and innocent ecstasies when I straddled her leg and teeter-tottered in aphrodisiacal ups and downs. What wonders of holiness when she kissed my innocent little mouth and cooed in seraphic purity of her lamb and sweetheart. And my old man, Hunter: where was he? Out in the three-leaf clover, seducing the blondes."

Mac laughed. Never in his life had Vridar heard such laughter as this.

"There's a law of compensation according to Emerson, that frigid deacon of orchotomy; and because my old man whored with Rabelaisian relish, I take a maid for a moonlight walk and am deserted to the sagebrush and owls. Lovely women stoop to folly but my name is McGuire. And I'm left to walk home under a nameless star and my mother holds my trembling palms until I fall asleep. After midnight she tiptoes to my room to learn if I'm sleeping well. And there I lie, snoring at the ceiling, with my dreams full of virgins.

"Hunter, what is wrong with me? Why when I take a girl out does she draw me to her lap and reach down to see if my diaper is clean? I've thought my way around Freud and back again but he hasn't explained what Yorick never dreamed of." He stopped and fixed on Vridar a bitter sneer. "You sane persons scald me like acid. You meander through life like a cow, munching your platitudes and belching your cud; and what you don't know is precisely everything there is to learn. You halfbacks of the academic world! You with your six times five and your morning tabloid and your bowl of oatmeal! What do you know, Hunter, except Frank Crane and Elbert Hubbard and Mark Sullivan?"

Vridar looked at the bitter face and smiled. "There's a row of books," he said. "Talk to them and get it out of you."

Long and loose and lean, Mac strode to the books.

"Aristotle and Beerbohm, Huysmans and Cabell. . . . Why don't you have Adam Smith, too? Have you heard of Bruce Barton? There's a guy you could pal around with: Bruce and Vridar, two intellectual concubines of Jesus.

"Well, Hunter, what is wrong with me? Is it paranoia or is it dementia præcox? Paresis or anorexia? Algolagnia or claustrophobia? Or is it euphoria? You know damned well, Hunter, it isn't euphoria. It's algolagnia." And Mac's laugh came in sunken violence from his thin chest. "I'll tell you. I need a blackboard and charts and a camera to make you understand. It's masturbation, Hunter. There's the cat and what a cat! But why in the name of all the eucharistic dervishes should I bother about that? Have you read the recent investigations of the subject? You haven't, of course. They're not to be found in McIntyre's column or in the platitudes of Coolidge.

"Listen. A recent study of ten thousand M.A. and Ph.D. women in Germany discovered that ninety-four per cent of them were guilty. The percentage of men is higher. In other words, Hunter, over ninety per cent of your civilized world is a masturbating world. At one time or another it has indulged in that lonesome little pleasure called self-abuse. And I can see them everywhere. This faculty is lousy with them. I sit in a classroom and they're all around me. I'm talking," he said, with a sudden devilish leer, "to one now. But anything as common as textbooks and sneezes does not explain me. But what else?

"Seriously, Hunter: tell me. Was it the tyranny of my mother? Is it because I once saw a little maid without clothes on? In God's name, what is it?" And he sank to a chair, shuddering with self-loathing, his sallow face twitching with anguish.

And there was Michael Rowe, son of a great surgeon. Mike was also one of the most brilliant students in this school; and, like Moses McGuire, he was bored with the pettifogging evasions of his instructors, with their refusal to give a frank answer to a frank question. Mike imagined himself to be fascinated by ugliness. Of a girl he would say, "She's so damned ugly she fascinates me. I follow her around just to meditate on her amazing disproportions." He was fascinated, too, by offensive odors, and by all kinds of acrid or bitter flavors. "I was sitting by a girl in class today and the smell of her fascinated me. She smelled like a mixture of heliotrope and stinkhorn and sweat." And again: "Have you ever smelled Professor Biddle? She has the most gorgeous and well-bred stink about her. I could just sit and smell her for hours and meditate on her epithelial membrane. . . ."

Mike wrote an essay for the school's journal. In it he said:

Our St. Georges of the academic middle ages know less than nothing of what goes on around them. They doubtless remember that they spooned when youngsters and closed their eyes on the succulent kiss. That was all very well: it led to babies eventually and helped to support the patent medicine industry. It was through some such ecstatic maneuvering that I am where I am.

But in the school there is, in my humble opinion, an excess of amatory erotica and a most noticeable dearth of the best of what has been said and thought. In automobiles around our campus, fair maids, after enduring a lecture on life is real and life is earnest, and handsome gentlemen, after peering at a bacillus acidophilus in a blob of milk, do retire to the closed sedans and draw the shades. And there they do suck tongues and exchange spit. . . .

From end to end of the college, after this essay appeared, there was consternation and rage. Instructors spoke of the matter to their classes and rebuked the author; and the committee on censorship swung into action. Mike was called to apologize for his "immoral and obscene writing" and for an hour behind closed doors he faced the inquisitors. Then he rose and helped himself to a cigarette and yawned. "You witch doctors," he said, "bore me." And he walked out, leaving three professors speechless with amazement.

The committee demanded the expulsion of Michael Rowe. Vridar heard of the matter and entered the case. He went to the president's office and found Johnson in a dark and scowling mood.

"I came," Vridar said, "to see about Mike Rowe."

"What about him? I'm tired of his insolence."

"Was he insolent with you?"

"He has been nothing else. He said, I'll bet you I'm kicked out of here. I told him I was not a betting man. All right, he said, I won't raise you." And Johnson stared at Vridar with his face twitching.

"I know he is insolent but his insolence is only an adolescent gesture. He's a very brilliant student. I think it would be a mistake to expel him."

"What would you do?"

"Ignore him."

"What did you think of that essay? I'm told he handed it to you in your advanced course in composition. I'm told you gave an A to it."

"I did. It was an A paper."

"Do you think that's the sort of thing college students should be writing?"

"Why not? It's true."

"What do you mean by true?"

"I mean our students do enter automobiles and draw the shades and neck. It's a part of our college life. Why shouldn't it be written of?"

"But don't you think it was pretty vulgar?"

"Perhaps no more vulgar than kissing. Some students do suck tongues, you know. Some of them do, like savages, exchange saliva. A reading in ethnology shows it to be an old custom."

For a long moment the president looked at Vridar. "And you think we shouldn't dismiss him?"

"I think if we expel a student as intelligent as Mike Rowe we admit our failure. One Mike Rowe is worth a hundred of these dull fraternity boys whose wickedness is underground. I think, too, that Mike is insolent and up to tricks because he knows we're evading truth in this school. Do you deny that?"

"That is not the point of our discussion."

"But it really is the point. If this college were what a

college should be, the Mike Rowes would give us no trouble. They'd respect us. As it is now they have contempt for the whole lot of us."

"Well," said the president impatiently, "I'll see. I'll consider the matter."

In this evening Mike came to Vridar's room. He stretched in a chair and yawned and lit a cigarette.

"They're not going to expel me," he said.

"That's good."

"It's bad, if you ask me. I'll never amount to anything if I stick around here."

"That's a youthful point of view. You'll outgrow it."

"You don't get me. I wasn't kicked out because my father is a powerful man. If I had belonged to the hoi-polloi——"

"That's not true. President Johnson is a pretty good president. He has a tough job here. Imagine yourself in his place. Imagine yourself with religious bigots trooping into your office every day and raising hell. Imagine yourself with all the fraternal orders of the city telling you what to do. Imagine yourself with a stupid and reactionary legislature."

"Well, I suppose you may be right. But there's no education here. This school is always two decades behind its time."

"You'll grow up, Mike. You'll be a writer some day."

"I'm a scientist. I observe men and bugs." He opened the door and passed out but after a moment he thrust his head in. "I should have used the word saliva," he said.

XI

●

IN THIS YEAR Vridar and Athene went to week-end
parties. They were song-and-cocktail parties and Athene
had little relish for them; but for Vridar, absorbed in studying other persons and himself, they were revelations of
what he sought. When hilarious with brandy or gin, some
persons, he had learned, were themselves, with most of their
attitudes stripped away. Others, more hopelessly lost in
posturing and sham, came to an ambivalent deadlock and
sank to a morose and melancholic stupor. There was Mac:
early in the evening he would sing old ballads and leer at
women; but later, having drunk so much that his impulses
rose to confound him, he withdrew into silence and looked
out of bitter scorn. Carlyle smoked one cigarette after
another and sulked and watched his wife with morbidly
jealous eyes. An actress from a stock company whom Max
Ohm brought now and then lay on the floor and shrieked
and tried to kick out of her clothes. Ferd was all song and
clowning but his nonsense for the most part was indirect
and unwinking gestures at women. And Vridar, half-drunk,
and studying his emotions, perceived clearly that the erotic
impulse was most lively of all in his blood and mind.

Their intoxicants were sold to them by a strange half-
blind man who was known as Utah's official bootlegger.
He made peach brandy by the barrel. "Next to sugar
beets," Vridar heard a man say, "Jason Tooms is Utah's
greatest industry. I don't know what the peach growers
would do without him. . . ." This man, a state official,
gave to Vridar and Ferd their letter of introduction. It
said:

DEAR JASON:
These men are college professors. They are all right.
Sell them anything they want. . . .

It was in one of these evenings that Carlyle Orcutt drew Vridar aside. Carlyle's eyes were unhappy and furtive and malicious.

"How," he asked, "are your boy friends?"

Vridar looked at him, wondering what he meant.

"My boy friends. What do you mean?"

"I mean your boy friends, Mac and Mike."

"Oh, Mac and Mike. They're all right," said Vridar, looking at the cunning eyes.

"I suppose you have some grand times in your room."

"Listen——" And then Vridar understood. He turned away in pity and in the next evening he spoke of the matter to Athene.

"Imagine his insolence! I tell you I'm not going to mince matters from now on. I'm going to give these Orcutts the dressing down of their lives."

"It will do no good. If you get furious, Carlyle will be convinced."

"Convinced of what?"

"That you are a homosexual."

"What of it? Am I to worry because malice strikes like an adder?"

"I'd ignore him."

"I won't. And do you know why he asked that question?"

"I could make a guess.'"

A week later after an evening of bridge Vridar resolved to speak. The malice of both Carlyle and Elsa had been unusually alert. Their insinuations had been more daring, their spleen more vengeful. And Vridar, with impatience growing to fury, pushed his chair back and spoke.

"Listen," he said. "For months I've been trying to be your friend. I've ignored your insults and abuse and all your God-damned stinking little ways. But I'm done with that. If you can't be frank and decent in friendship, then we'll not be friends." He stared at them and they looked at one another. "Does either of you know," he asked, "what the source of malice is?"

"Orcutt, he says we're malicious. Fancy that."

"You're the two most malicious persons I've ever seen. If all the malice were squeezed out of you you'd be no bigger than walnuts."

"Malice," said Carlyle, "is not mental alertness."

"Oh. So you're mentally alert, are you?"

"Much more than you are."

"You've been to Europe, have you? You've sipped chartreuse. You've smelled the streets of Rome. And all that in your mind adds to mental alertness. Carlyle, you know no more about life than a frog knows about Jesus. You——"

"Here it is," said Elsa. She had got a dictionary; and in her strange voice, both tremulous and barbed, she read from it. "Malice, from malus, meaning evil. 1. Enmity of heart; malevolence; a malignant design of evil. 2. Law. State of mind shown by intent to commit an unlawful act. Orcutt, have you been meditating on unlawful acts? Do you mean," she asked of Vridar, "that my husband, my little Carlyle, has been plotting unlawful acts? Orcutt, for shame! And me trusting you!" She looked at Vridar, swiftly, her eyes bright; and her acting was so superb that Vridar smiled in spite of himself. "Synonyms. The book says ill will, spite, grudge, malignity, rancor, virulence, venom. Orcutt, do you have all them things? You bad boy! And the book says see resentment."

Vridar shrugged. Athene was right: he might as well try to move mountains as to invite Carlyle and Elsa to an open frank moment.

"R-e," said Elsa. "R-e-m, r-e-n, r-e-p. Requiescat. Maybe," she said, glancing at Vridar, "that is what you meant. R-e-s, r-e-s-e-r: here: r-e-s-e-n-t-m-e-n-t. A feeling

of indignant displeasure because of something regarded as a
wrong, insult. That," she said, glancing again at Vridar,
"seems to be what you feel. Synonyms: anger, choler, displeasure, indignation, enmity, hatred, ill will, animosity,
dudgeon—that's a slick word—malice, spite, grudge, rancor,
malignity, pique. A deep dudgeon, this nice book says,
means a ruffled temper. Orcutt, he's in a deep dudgeon.
Or in a high dudgeon: the book says he might be in a high
dudgeon. . . ."

Carlyle was smiling faintly and wrinkling his nose.

"Well, the book says malice, active or malignant ill will.
Spite is mean or petty malice." She closed the book and
looked at Vridar, her eyes narrowing. "You're in a deep
high dudgeon," she said.

Vridar rose and turned to Athene.

"Come on, let's go."

Outside, walking homeward, Athene said:

"I told you it would do no good."

"Don't worry. It did plenty."

"I don't see how."

"Wait. You will."

Two weeks passed. Then the Orcutts came to Athene's
apartment and Vridar was called over. He sat where he
could study their faces, but during this evening he did not
speak. It was Elsa who talked: she was chastened, and so
was Carlyle, and Vridar felt friendliness for both of them.
Carlyle moved about nervously, and Elsa's hands trembled
when she lifted the cigarette to her mouth. She did not
allude to the evening of two weeks ago. She was still an
actress, only half visible behind her mask. For two hours
she talked of herself and of Carlyle, gently castigating
both. . . .

"My chin is nothing," she said, and she drew deeply
from her cigarette. "I've always hated myself for having
no chin. Carlyle has no chin, too. If we ever have a child

it will be chinless." Her voice caught a little and her eyes were darkly unhappy. "Orcutt, could you stand a chinless son?"

"What?" His eyes were unhappy too.

And Vridar wanted to say:

"Forget about it. It doesn't matter. Let's be friends. . . ."

And after they had said good-night like two rebuked children and had gone, self-conscious and unhappy, down the street, Vridar turned to Athene. He felt as if he had made a mountain of nothing. For within him now, and to become, as the years passed, the most alert and active force of his life, was the power to project himself into the life of another and understand its grief and conflicts and pain. This in him was already so active, so in possession of his senses, that the persons in his novels were as vividly alive for him as anyone in flesh and blood. He thought of them and peopled the earth with them; for between their world and his world, in point of actual being, there was no difference at all. During this evening he had lived Elsa's shame and Carlyle's, their fumbling effort toward peace, as deeply and fully as he would have lived them had they been his own.

"It all makes me feel pretty mean," he said. "I have no quarrel with anyone. I have no enemy except myself."

"They were pathetic," Athene said. "Elsa was trying so hard to be honest and frank."

"Yes. Well, they're all right. There's an honest and decent person in everyone under the pretenses and sham. Strip the obscene mask away and there he is: a bewildered child in a dark and bewildered world. All of us."

"But they're both choked with malice and envy. Why, I wonder. We are nobody to be envious of."

"I don't know why. They've both had unhappy sexual experiences, I guess. They are both adolescent. But they'll grow up. They have keen minds. They have generous

hearts. . . . And you don't know why they're envious of
me?"

"I don't. You don't seem to me to be an enviable
person."

"I'm not. But I seem to be. Mac throws his daggers
into me. A lot of persons do. It's because I seem to be a
very smug and serene person just because I choose to be
inscrutable. They don't know what a nightmare my life
has been. They don't know what a hell it still is. And so,
supposing that my skin is thick, they lay into me. I do not
flinch—at least they do not see me flinch. So they have at
me again. Full of distrust and doubts and bitterness, they
want to reduce me to their level of anguish. They don't
know I'm already below it."

"But there's more than that to it. They're afraid of
your mind."

"You wouldn't flatter me, would you?"

"That's an unworthy retort. People are afraid of you.
You look right through them just the way you look through
me. Vridar, don't you know that your stare can be a terrible thing?"

"I suppose. I don't intend it to be."

"It's when you're absorbed in studying a person's motives. You forget yourself and sit there looking at a person,
with a thousand thoughts in your eyes."

"I'll have to stop that," he said.

"No. But realize why persons fling jibes at you. I've
flung them myself."

"I know it."

"When you look at me until I feel naked, then I want
to undress you and make you feel naked, too. That's
human nature."

"Yes, it's human nature. Well, I won't get furious with
them again. Nor with anyone. I'll be their friends, let them
say what they will. They'll grow up after a while and be
ashamed of their meanness."

"But why do you feel you must be everybody's friend?"

"Why shouldn't I? When we love ourselves less we love other people more. Or is love too strong a word?"

"It depends on what you want it to mean."

"Sympathy and tolerance: those are enough. Anyway, my dear, I've been a self-centered person much too long. I'm weary of it."

"You won't be less self-centered. You'll merely have a larger periphery."

"Thanks. You are right and you put it very aptly."

"And as you have pointed out the person most preoccupied with self is the artist——"

"Except some in asylums."

"——and if your periphery becomes too large you'll lack intensity in art. So just how large is it to be?"

"Athene, you're beginning to use your noodle."

"Under your tutoring," she said, and smiled. "Answer my question."

"Well, I don't know. But I do know this: any person who finds other persons disgusting or contemptible is a person still so full of self-love that he is pathetic. Art of value surely must push its periphery beyond that. Now take me. I was angered by the Orcutts because I still think too much of myself. I should be grateful to them. With their malice they have led me to a sharper vision of myself. I still have too much vanity. I want praise and I get leering derisions. I want to be so damned stupid that I can't see that the derisions are of more worth than the praise. It's time, my dear, that I understood more and condemned less." He gave Athene a wry smile. "I'm a little weary," he said, "of admiring myself."

"But aren't you likely to push that periphery so far that you'll get out of focus? That's what happens, you know, when the artist rides off, as Stephen Leacock would say, in all directions at once. Look at Marcel Proust. He was positively sick with self-love."

"Yes, look at him. In his huge volume he never once dug to the real important truth about himself."

"But some regard him as the greatest of modern novelists."

"That means nothing to me."

"It should. It means this, that the whole source of his greatness was a morbid and self-centered interest. That has been true of a lot of writers."

"All right. All right, then, I'll write a book about myself and then I'll shove the periphery out. How's that? After I'm done with this sickly Vridar chap——"

"You'll write about some other sickly Vridar chaps."

"Perhaps. The world is full of them. But, Athene, look here: are you telling me that I must forever live within my prejudices and self-love and write within them?"

"Unless you destroy them. You've said so yourself."

"All right, I'll destroy them. I'm doing so. Here's one that is on its way out now. Some books I used to love, some I used to detest. I mean books with flesh and mind. All right: I loved some because they flattered me, made me think my life had meaning. I detested some because they outraged my prejudices and my self-esteem. So it is with everyone. But don't tell me that I'll get out of focus if I destroy such a half-witted part of me. Or take another matter. We all like persons who deprecate themselves. Why? Because their self-deprecation exalts us by comparison. A pretty irony, that! When the Orcutts came tonight, subdued, rebuked, I felt very friendly toward them. And then I thought, Vridar, my fine lad, watch your step. And while Elsa talked I sat there and listened and thought of this new revelation of me. Imagine it! I felt as friendly as hell merely because they were castigating themselves. My-my! I began to feel that I had been right, they wrong. I tell you, God damn it, our self-love is awful! Instead of feeling friendly I should have felt ashamed. My ego for the moment had conquered. For the moment they were abject and how I flowered in self-esteem!

"Athene, to hell with all that. If I'm a person of strength, I should admire strength, even when it slaps me in the face."

"But, my dear, if a person has been wrong, shouldn't he feel apologetic?"

"Wrong? Who's to say he was wrong or right?"

"Well, as I see it, you're trying to get yourself to the point where you'll have no convictions. Then you'll be a dead center."

"No. I merely don't want convictions that rest on vanity. And tell me this while I think of it: have you ever thought there might be any homosexuality in me?"

"No. It's too silly to think of."

"I had no sexual experiences with boys. My whole erotic life was fixed on girls. They shook me like bugles——"

"You're on the wrong track," said Athene impatiently.

"All right. But I'm still too damned erotic."

"All artists are. Haven't you said a thousand times that's one big reason why they are artists?"

"Yes, and it's true. I'll tell you why I'm too erotic. In adolescence my body gave me pleasure and no outside agency was necessary. Then what? I developed an abnormal love of myself. I was a tiny pleasurable world of my own. See how simple it was? And then? Why, I developed a sense of guilt and shame. And then? Life disgusted me. I fancied I could improve it if I had a chance. And then? I became a zealous idealist. There's the evolution of the artist for you. And how the truth would make most of them sizzle! A lot of them, of course, don't spring from so common a thing as masturbation. Some are homosexuals: Walt Whitman. Some—— But the source of art is not, my dear, a decent subject." Vridar grimaced and lit a cigarette. He smoked and stared at Athene.

"Take you, my dear. Mind if I talk of you?"

"Go ahead."

"When you were a child, lecherous men fondled you. They stroked you and you liked it. And because your body gave pleasure to you and to them you got the notion that it was a pretty magnificent temple. You learned to love it. You fixed the center of the universe in it. And that, with variations, is the story of all of us."

"But art is more than an erotic phantasy. You can't tell me it isn't."

"Yes, there's more to it. But what?"

"Well, we are creative by nature."

"Some do not seem to be. Well, I'm saying only that among the great artists, sexual distortion of some kind has been the big urge. But let's not talk about it any more tonight. Let's not be serious any longer."

"But I'm still worried," said Athene, smiling, "about your periphery."

"Well, let's have a huge cocktail. That's the best thing in the world for pushing a periphery out. . . ."

XII

●

AT THE END of this year and of his second in this school Ferd was dismissed. With tireless and stormy eloquence he had opposed military training and he had been guilty, with Vridar and another, of spending an hour with Scott Nearing when that hunted man came like a thief in the night to this city. This was the third college from which Ferd had been dismissed for preaching peace.

"And it's time you learned," Vridar said, "that you can't preach peace in an American university and hold your job."

"Don't I know it!" he cried, snorting with scorn. "But I believe in peace. Honest, I'm a queer fellow. Murder distresses me."

"And what are you going to do now?"

"Oh, I have another job. Didn't I tell you? They don't want me here but they've given me swell recommendations to other schools. . . ."

And Ferd went to another college and with unabated zest he devoted himself to the unearthing of cowardice and the exposing of frauds. Twice in every week he wrote to Vridar, telling of what he had learned.

. . . I must tell you about Professor Leonard Ayres. I won't sleep unless I tell you about Dr. Leonard Ayres. He is deaf. He packs around a great ear apparatus. He loves bawdy tales. His ears come forward like a staghound's when he smells a succulent bit of stink. But you have to shout at him. And so his colleague and friend, Professor Arnold Hoag, takes him up to the roof. As eager as a librarian on the trail of a naughty book, he hikes up the stairs and the ladder and through the roof door; and Hoag follows; and Ayres adjusts his apparatus and Hoag shouts into it. He shouts little obscene tid-bits into it and Ayres smiles all over as if Cleopatra were caressing him. And when he comes down he sits at his desk for an hour, remembering, tasting; smiling all over with a big buttered sexy smile. But Ayres is a magnificent moralist in this school. He says Shakspere should be expurgated. He says Chaucer had a nasty mind. He says *Erik Dorn* is an obscene book. . . .

. . . I must tell you about Professor Adam Brown. He's very humorless and nice and looks at you so earnestly that you want to sing Christmas carols. He teaches the modern novel. Most modern novels, he says, are pretty bad. And he means bad. To make it clear to you: he means immoral. He was reading some French novel in which a man rapes a woman. That set him to thinking—as a scientist, I mean; as a student of the improbable and imponderable. He decided the Frenchman was a liar. He decided to learn if it is possible for a man to rape a woman. If I'm lying in this, may the robins build a nest in my skull. But don't think that Adam experimented with a student. No: with his wife. He said to her—and imagine with what scientific seriousness—that he wanted to see if he could rape her. He wanted her to resist with everything she had, including the vacuum cleaner and the portrait of Daniel Webster. And what happened? Don't laugh at this. Don't doubt it. I heard Brown tell it and two others heard him. He chased his wife all over that house; he seized her; she screamed and fought. They turned tables over, frightened all their kids into the next county, and their neighbors into the cellar. And when the battle was done, there lay Professor Adam Brown on the floor, exhausted, undone, and not able to waggle a finger; and there stood Mrs. Brown, with half her clothes off, with her virtue intact. "And," said Adam Brown, looking at us with humorlessness that would have split you wide open, "I know that French author is dealing with improbable situations. Art should concern itself only with the probable. . . ."

After leaving Wasatch College, Ferd wrote and published some articles about a dozen of his colleagues. One morning Vridar saw an office door open and saw a furious man throw a magazine into the hall. It was one of Ferd's former colleagues throwing the portrait of himself to the janitor: the same man who, a week ago, had hurled *Elmer Gantry* through a window. Nor was Ferd content to write these scornful and scathing portraits. He also wrote an article for a liberal weekly and it was sent by the editors to President Johnson. Hearing of the matter, Vridar wrote for a copy of the article, and it came to him, together with the president's reply. It was the reply that held Vridar's attention; it was the most evasive document he had ever seen. And while Vridar was deliberating it, there came to him from the editors a request for his opinion of the matter.

"What should I do?" Vridar asked Athene.

"It's hard to tell."

"It seems to me there's only one thing I can do. This is not a matter that applies only to this school. It's not a matter that applies only to American education. It's a choice between orthodoxy and liberalism. It's a choice between the puritanism that persecuted Dreiser and that wish for decency and courage which his revolt symbolized. There is only one choice to be made."

"Yes, only one. But it will mean the end of you here."

"I know it. But is that important?"

"Not in comparison with the other."

"All right. Then I'll speak out."

Vridar spent an evening and most of a night writing to the editors. He wrote and destroyed and wrote again. And at last he said:

What I say here is significant for me less in its bearing upon this school than in its implications of weakness in our educational system and in our national life. But first I wish to correct the president in a few of his statements.

What he says of the training and success of Ferdinand Thomas as a teacher is, in my opinion, beneath the dignity of his position. The president must know that it takes more than a Master's or Doctor's degree to make a good teacher and he should not forget that many of his present faculty were trained in this school when it was hardly, if at all, more than a Mormon institution. To point out, therefore, that Thomas is a graduate of a denominational college seems to me graceless and beside the point. The president says that a Master's degree or a year of graduate work is demanded of instructors here but there are several now teaching here who have neither. All this, as well as the president's statement that Thomas was a poor teacher, is nothing but a cheap attempt to justify his action. Of all the teachers I know, Thomas has power more than any other to fill his students with enthusiasm and to awaken their minds; and it is significant that when an eminent Mormon tried to persuade his students to sign a statement that his teachings were subversive, they refused and reported the matter to him.

The president says that Thomas asked for a leave of absence and was denied because a leave obligates the College to reappoint. This too is an evasion. I left here in 1921 with a leave and when I asked to return the following year I was told that my leave had been a formality only. The president says that the "turnover in the faculty the last six years is about as low as it possibly could be, and only for better salaries." I can give you the names and addresses of several who left because the college would not reappoint them. The president declares that men "of all views are allowed to go on in their work unmolested and affiliate themselves with local groups" and that he has no control over his faculty "religiously, politically, economically, or ethically." Both statements are false. No man could keep his job here if he were to tell of the travesty of justice in Massachusetts, our cowardly interference in Nicaragua and elsewhere, the real truth of Prohibition in this city, or a thousand other facts which students in the interest of wholesome government ought to know. It is true, nevertheless, that the president himself is a liberal and would, I believe, staff his school with persons of integrity and courage if he were not restrained by the ultra-patriotic groups which endow the school with their patronage.

And that, after all, is the only significant thing in this whole matter. Let me admit that two years ago I was very bitter toward the cowardice of such schools as the one I'm now in and that I read with lusty approval those scathing attacks in magazines on our universities and the persons who teach in them. But my bitterness was adolescent bitterness. Since then I have thought of the matter and I perceive now, as you must, that education in a democracy, supported by public taxes, and directed by boards of business men, must defer in all important and vital matters to the prejudices and superstitions of the community it is supposed to serve. It is futile, then, and it is stupid, to deplore want of education in a country in which there is no demand for it, or to abuse professors and presidents because they do not do what, within the system, they have no power to do. Our unendowed universities and colleges are, it is true, staffed for the most part by men and women who have neither imagination nor courage. But they are, nevertheless, precisely the sort of teachers that democracy demands and the only kind it will tolerate.

Our president here has written you an evasive letter, but there is nothing surprising in that. He is, I venture, the best president by far that this school has ever had, and he would do many things that this community will not allow him to do. We have here a very difficult community. We have religious feuds, bitter and of long standing, and he is at the mercy of prejudiced demagogues. He has written you, I observe, about a thousand words of mild abuse of me, and in not a single instance has he told the truth. He has given you the gossip of persons of the city. But what of that? I perceive at last that he is not my enemy, nor are my enemies to be found among these timid and quaking souls who teach here. My enemy and the enemy of Ferdinand Thomas is that stinking and neurotic Calvinism which is the god and holy ghost of our country; which has so nearly strangled it and us that art is almost dead among us, and joy is an obscene thing, and asylums and jails are filled to overflowing with the evidence of our cowardice and shame. This college is one of its paid instruments.

To publish an article about it, exposing its meanness, would be about as sensible as to try to cure a man of syphilis by pointing a derisive finger at his disease. . . .

Vridar sent a copy of this letter to President Johnson. "He'll call me to his office," he said to Athene, "and we'll have a merry time." But when he was summoned two days later, he found not an angry but a chastened man. The president stared at him, his mouth twitching, his eyes unhappily amused. And suddenly in his abrupt way he spoke:

"Dr. Hunter, I've always admired you for two things. One is your frankness. The other is your ability to get things done."

"Thank you. You're a pretty frank person yourself."

"Sit down. I want to talk with you." Vridar drew a chair and sat. "About Ferdinand Thomas," the president said. "I think you overrate him. In my opinion he has only a very average mind. In my opinion, to be frank, he is not above the average of our college graduates here."

"I don't agree at all."

"Why don't you?"

"Because I know him better than you do. In my opinion he is more intelligent than most of your faculty here. Beyond all question he has more integrity."

"I think you're wrong. I don't think he could get a doctor's degree in any good school."

"And I think he can and I think he will. I think he'll make you eat your words before he's done with it."

For a long moment the president stared at Vridar.

"We'll wait and see," he said.

"All right, we'll wait and see."

"Did you approve that article he wrote?"

"It was too exuberant. But in nearly all respects it told the truth."

"Did you think it ought to be published?"

"No. I said I didn't in my letter. In the last two years

I've read a dozen articles which have excoriated our universities and those who teach in them. I think such abuse is futile. It is superficial."

"I'd like," said the president a little bitterly, "to have some of my critics tell me how I can do more than I'm doing. They give ex cathedra judgments. They write of academic utopias——"

"I know it. But just the same, if I may say so, there's no valid reason why you should evade the charges. If I were in your position I'd admit them. I'd say, Now look here: This college is supported by religious bigots and patriotic fanatics. They don't want the truth taught. They want the prejudice and superstition within which they live. If they don't get what they want the legislature will withdraw all appropriations. As president my hands are tied and I can do no more than administer——"

"Yes," said the president, a little impatiently.

"Because," Vridar went on, "the only school in a democracy that can be worth anything is the endowed school. And I've been wondering," he said, "if you'd not like to have me resign."

"I've never asked you to."

"I know it."

"I've always stood behind you, haven't I?"

"When it came to the showdown, yes. You've listened to a lot of stupid gossip."

"Gossip, yes! I have to. When enraged taxpayers come to my office I have to listen."

"I know. Well, I think it would be best if I got out. I'm a liberal and there's no tolerance in this school for liberals."

"You don't have to leave," the president said. "Understand that."

"But I see no point in remaining. I'm opposed by nearly every powerful Mormon of the city." Vridar rose. "But I want you to know that I appreciate the way you've stood behind me. But with only one member of the Board of Directors supporting me, it is clear that the time is coming when I shall have to go."

A week later Vridar met Roger Merwyn on the campus: a tall handsome man, suave and self-assured: another Flammonde with news of nations in his talk, with that in his manner which tradition owes to more than fifty years. Merwyn, with tact, with shrewd and self-seeking alertness, was playing the game: he had been promoted twice in three years and it was rumored that he would be the next president. He now drew Vridar aside and asked: "How you getting along?"

"So-so. I haven't been fired."

"But you're not selling yourself."

"Well, maybe I'm not for sale."

Merwyn's smile was a little pitying. "In this world, Hunter, a man has to sell himself—in a university or anywhere else."

"Just what do you mean by selling myself?"

"This. Here you are, a well-trained man. You've received no promotions. You're on no committees. You've made powerful enemies. But you spent a lot of time and money getting your training and now you have something the world wants to buy and will pay for. You've got to let the world know what it is you have to sell. You have to present yourself in the market in the most attractive way you can ——"

"As if I were a toothpaste or a toilet paper?"

"As if," said Merwyn impatiently, "you were a trained man ready to fill a big job. As, in fact, you are. But competition is strong. I've been watching you: in your first year you had four courses in literature and one in composition. Now you have three in composition. You know what that means?"

"Of course. It means my chairman dislikes me and is trying to force me out."

"And it's your fault. You haven't played the game."

"And just how should I have played the game?"

"Make friends and choose your friends wisely. You haven't done that. Your friends are all rebels: Ohm and Orcutt and the radicals in the Delphic Club. The Unitarian minister. You have to establish yourself in the good-will of the community: give talks to the women's clubs; identify yourself with some church; keep yourself before the public. And, frankly, you ought to cultivate a charming manner."

"You mean I should talk prettily of beauty and progress; pull wires; wear a gracious smile——"

"I mean you should do what you must do." Merwyn shrugged. "There's no use jumping against a stone wall. The truth—it may not be pleasant but it's the truth—is this: men who get ahead in the world are men who take advantage of other men's blunders. And, when necessary, they keep their mouths shut. But look at you: you had to let everyone know that you sympathized with Sacco and Vanzetti. Well, so did I, but I didn't shout it from the housetops. You had to go down and see Scott Nearing: you ought to have known better. You just defeat your own ends."

"When we see injustice are we to keep our mouths shut?"

"It does no good to open them. You merely invite ill-will."

"You mean we're to have no convictions?"

"I mean," said Merwyn curtly, "that we all have to live. We have families. Moral indignation is fine but it doesn't butter our bread."

"But the human spirit doesn't live on butter."

"I mean," Merwyn went on patiently, "that you might have become chairman of your department. I was pulling for you. But now you're out. Ward doesn't like you and he'll never rest until he puts you out of here."

"Listen, Merwyn: when I'm an old man I don't want

to have to look back over forty years of little dishonesties and plotting and empty smiles. I don't want to build a middle-class home upon other men's blunders. More than that: when I was a freshman in this college I wanted leadership. I didn't get it. And for my ignorance I paid an awful price. Now, because I want to try to give leadership to other young men, young women——"

"Your first consideration should be for yourself. It's all right to help others if you also help yourself at the same time. But you haven't helped yourself by getting friendly with the Unitarian minister: do you know that man makes beer in his home? And Ferdinand Thomas, opposing military training: you didn't have to run around with him. You can't preach peace and keep your job here. You didn't have to mention Margaret Sanger in your classes, did you? You didn't have to put *Marriage and Morals* on your reading lists. You didn't have to say you believed in Mooney's innocence. You didn't have to come to the defense of such students as Mike Rowe. No, Hunter, all those were unnecessary blunders. They have cost you your job."

"I know it. Well, thanks for your interest."

Vridar crossed the campus, thinking of Anson Ward, chairman of his department. Ward was playing the game. He had been chosen as a man who could whip his staff into obedience and avoid scandalous outbursts: a strange mixture of self-pitying paternalism and pig-headed tyranny. It was an ironic girl named Agnes Millburn who told Vridar of the first.

"He thinks I love poetry but for me it is only a lot of nonsense that scans very well. He knows it by the yard. By the foot, should I say? And he hovers over his emotion and drones pentameters at me until my head swims. He likes tender love-poems: not erotic stuff: he never comes within a mile of that. What kind do I mean?"

"Metrical euphemisms?"

"No, what Mac McGuire calls the metaphysical orgasms. And what a hypocrite I am. I go into his office and sit and he talks to me in a deep fatherly voice as if I were his daughter, and every point he makes he supports with half a mile of perfectly metrical platitudes. And I pretend I like it. If it's Shakspere, I like Shakspere. If it's Milton, I like Milton. I'm shameless. . . . Do you like Ward?"

"Yes, but not his reactionary ways."

Ward was more than a gentle and poetic godfather. Within his department he was a dictator: a deep-voiced and almost tearful Machiavelli who deceived, with his gentleness, all but the most alert. When he called his staff together he talked quietly, almost sadly; but far down in his resonant voice or shadowed in his watchful eyes was the threat of an implacable will.

"Well, darling, I've just talked with Merwyn. I'm on my way out."

"Haven't you known that? And why in the world, Vridar, did you ever come back to this Mormon college?"

"Oh, I thought I could be a liberalizing force."

"And you've made it more hopeless."

"Yes, it seems that way. Well, our sun has set in zion. . . ."

XIII

●

THIS was in March. Vridar had been here three years, and besides teaching his classes he had written six novels and three volumes of ironic verse. After sending a novel to a dozen publishers he would lay it aside. Formerly, every rejection of a manuscript had left him sunk in despair, but as he went ahead, searching himself and others, and perceiving more clearly with each passing week that writing, too, was a form of vanity, he saw himself as an indefatigable ego, demanding the suffrage of readers.

"If publishers don't want my stuff, that's their business. To hell with authorship anyway. If I ever grow up I'll stop this feverish scribbling and live more happily for being obscure."

"Darling, I can see you doing that."

"I would if I had any sense."

"Then you'll never have any."

"What's wrong with my junk? Isn't it full enough of self-pity and heroines? Does it whack too many prejudices on their simian tails?"

And then, in April, there came a letter accepting his sixth novel and he burst in on Athene with such clamor that she thought he was pulling the house down. She sprang to her feet in amazement and fright.

"Now what is wrong?"

"I've landed a book!"

"No. You're spoofing again."

"Honest. See how I puff and swell. See me strut. . . ."

Athene took the letter and read it.

"Well, they seem very enthusiastic. The best thing of its kind in ten years. They compare it with Willa Cather's best."

"By the way, I ought to run over and see Willa. Is she

in town, I wonder?" He seized the letter and read it again.
"Kiss me!" he shouted. He jerked Athene to him and kissed
her. "Is the kiss any different?"

"It tastes a little of Who's Who."

"Smell me." He sniffed of a sleeve. "The Hall of Fame
odor. I knew it. Now compose yourself and I'll address the
universe." He sank to a chair and grinned. "Isn't it funny?
I'm funny. The whole world is mad. Here I am: I've placed
a book and a sense of vast importance storms my blood and
rocks my mind. I begin to fancy myself as a great fellow.
Almost," he said softly, "a master mind like Will Durant.
Remember? He was on our Master Minds series last fall and
gave us a round-trip ticket to pessimism. But note: only
yesterday I went around in a funk, feeling snubbed, as if I
were a planet that astronomers ignored. And now behold
the change: I have very personal relations with destiny. I
am about to add to the confusion of libraries and the happiness of the manufacturers of paper and ink. Pretty soon now
I'll be giving a testimonial to cigarettes or soap. Next I'll
dress like a monkey, starched and stiff, and give a lecture
on the relation of art to beauty. And finally, all decked out
for the Ironic Jester, with a bald head and false teeth and a
pitiful little refuge of fame, I'll retire quietly under a mouthful of dust. Is it not a pretty legend? My dear, I may write
and have published a dozen books and some weary critic
may say of me—— Well, the critic will say:

"A word is necessary at this point to dismiss the elaborate
pretensions of Vridar Hunter. A morbid and psychopathic
upstart from the wastelands of Idaho, he managed, with
dogged and humorless zeal, to get a part of that desolate
and rocky empire into his dreary tomes. Beauty and love and
tenderness and peace he had no taste for; for his personality,
supported within by a grim and fleshless skeleton of Calvinism, he padded and fattened with all the distortions and
horrors he had ever read of; and the result, quite clearly,
was something that did not justify the ways of God to man,

or even, less importantly, justify the ways of man to God. . . .

Listen: I have three more sonnets for that volume. Implore me to read them. Say, Darling, read those magnificent poems you wrote. Say, You colossal genius, you vain and simian nitwit, read those lines that will be heard around the world —I mean around the room."

"All right," said Athene, smiling, "I implore. But you don't read your stuff well."

"There you go! A crack like that when I'm ready to clarify the imponderables."

"You'd better let me read them."

"Nonsense. I'm an author. Don't authors hike around the country and read their stuff? Don't they stand on a rostrum and throw handfuls of Olympus at the audience? Didn't Amy Lowell plant herself like a boulder and declare that her polyphonic harmonies were millennial? No: you must be humble when a great man reads his metrics. Sit with your eyes popping out and think, What a great man he is! What a splendid fool! Are you ready?"

"I'll try not to yawn."

"These are three pretty little sonnets that sum me up as my friend Roger Merwyn would have me be. I wrote them after that talk with him."

"Well, read them and stop your clowning."

"Do you know why I clown?"

"Read your sonnets."

> *"I'm tranquil now and I am circumspect,*
> *For I've achieved the attitudes of those*
> *Whose gestures are immaculate, correct,*
> *And whose deportment is an austere pose.*
> *The savage in me never thumbs its nose*
> *At such hypocrisies as make the art*
> *Of being civilized; and culture flows*
> *In endless disenchantment round my heart.*

Ruin and death may hide behind the task
Of keeping honesty safely underground.
But I'm polite—and that's enough to ask;
I speak—and there is nothing to astound.
I smile—and friends approve my gracious mask.
I laugh—and they are pleased with empty sound.

"Do you want to make any criticism at this point?"
"No, read the others."
"Does my voice carry overtones of glory?"
"Read the others before I get up and whang you."

"I teach the cheap morality that lends
Its uses to distrust and war and hate;
That makes of flatterers our dearest friends;
And sycophants of men who educate.
That dwarfs religion to the foul estate
Of casuists and fools, and apprehends
A skulking vengeful god to lie in wait
For us and potter with our tragic ends.

Ah, beautiful are these: the child that grows
To be a deacon or a doctrinaire;
And Elbert Hubbard's sweet arpeggios
Of rhetoric; and all the earnest prayer
That breathes throughout The Man Nobody Knows. . . .
Upon my desk are Lucian and Voltaire! . . ."

PART THREE

SUMMER, 1910

The Idea would come, gently insinuating, voluptuously soft and warm; it would grow in his heart, like a lovely fragrant weed, until the small garden of his better life was choked and overrun; and then it would flower upward, pushing its alluring foliage into his mind, sinking caressing roots into his heart. It twined tendrils round his nerves, laid its heavy loamy odor on his breath, and ran down into his hands. . . . It made a suffocating solitude of earth, a passionless yellow waste of the sky.

I

●

VRIDAR had spent three years in Salt Lake City and these years he had crowded full. In addition to his writing and his teaching, he had spent many hours in reflection, usually in the quiet after midnight; and he had come to see himself, in some respects at least, for what he was: an animal with deep and primitive hungers, with ideals that drew their sanction from unreason, and with prejudices and attitudes nowhere supported by facts. He had been an intensely egoistic and self-pitying person, and these qualities, he now perceived, were darkly but unmistakably related to the whole blundering upsurge of humanity toward goals. It was the person driven by sensitive self-love, and profoundly disgusted with himself and with life, who conceived of unattainable ideals and moved in his restless and fevered pilgrimage to unattainable ends. If not an earnest and humorless zealot, he was ironic and cynical and negative: the one still striving without perspective, the other arrested in unhappy scorn: but both reached back, in ways and by origins still shifting and uncertain, to that primitive wayfaring tribe that left the jungle convinced of sin. It evolved thereupon, as a huge and compensatory gesture, its metaphysic of unselfishness and justice and peace, and the innate goodness of humankind; and missing somehow at that point, in that crucial era, its road and its destiny, and taking to its heart a false and bitter judgment of itself, it fixed its direction upon sterile negations and abjured its birthright. And so it had been, in the whole historical record of its dark and devious journeying, a race lost to itself and to ecstasy and joy, supporting its distortions with myth and legend and tradition, evolving whole systems of specious reasoning in support of false premises, and betrayed at every turn by false ideals that led to the inevitable and

unpitying logic of death and chaos. In its obstinate intercourse with unreason, in its weird taboos placed against
its clean and vigorous appetites, and in the dark and terrible
deities of repression and self-denial were to be found the
origins of every modern dilemma, of every colossal self-
betrayal, heaping persecution and death upon the negative
altars. Nor was there any evidence today that a deluded
humanity, on a false path, and lost among the distortions
that blunders had multiplied, was sufficiently rebuked by its
stupidities to try to see its way to a fresh start. Behind
it lay kingdoms that had risen and perished. Behind it lay
an almost unbroken record of persecution and war and
death. Its asylums and jails numbered thousands. Its stark
tragedies, headlined in newspapers around the world, had
about them such a repetitious casualness that they were
almost obscene. There were prophets of ruin, prophets
of new orders; but they all talked within the periphery
of those traditions and dogmas which had brought the
entire civilized world to the brink of collapse. There was
no voice—and if so, where?—that spoke from beyond that
periphery to the tumult and violence within. There was
no perspective that reached out of the neurosis to solid
ground. Everywhere there was still talk of beauty and
peace, of ideals and leadership: of all the old concepts that
were rapidly perishing in their own meaninglessness: the ver-
biage of misunderstood and wholly undirected hungers: the
salvation of a thing in terms of its own neurotic sickness
and its superficial and undisciplined visions. There were social experiments in which patterns were shifted and nothing
changed. There was talk of new things and nothing was
achieved, and nothing intended, save a disguise of something
old. The whole social structure was sick under its own delusions and despair, with those of most courage and strength
turning, like frantic aides in a hospital, to the succoring of
the hopelessly weak and diseased. And as the sickness multiplied and became more acute, neurotic optimists multiplied

also: art swung desperately to its romantic evasions: crusaders for decency thundered over the stricken landscape: cynicism flourished in cults, sophistication became a meretricious national flavor, and expatriates sent up adolescent plaints from far places: and all these were symptoms of intellectual bankruptcy and spiritual ruin. . . .

For three years he had been searching himself. He had faced many truths which most persons denied with that wrathful disgust which declared their guilt. And not only that: he had come to see that an unevasive view of himself, without all the spurious and traditional virtues, was less difficult to admire, to respect, than that former view to which he had clung. In his view now there was nothing terrifying, nothing mean: on the contrary there was something elemental, something with integrity and strength. He was an animal; a rather preposterous creature in clothes, hiding his nakedness as if it were a thing to be ashamed of; with intimations, but intimations only, of intelligence and reason; with emotions, primordial and deep. They were vigorous clean emotions that could be put to clean and vigorous use. Within a social order they had to be disciplined and controlled. But they were the blood and heart of everything profound and vital and good and they gave to the mind the only strength and meaning it could have. Restrictions had to be placed on appetite. Except on gluttony, he reflected, looking down at Manhattan. The more privileged still gorged their bellies; and the women, losing those curves which ravished the thoughts of men, poisoned themselves to destroy their fat. Except avarice, too: this hunger was approved and glorified. The meanest of the hungers were most respected and granted the most license; while physical love, the deepest and most constant source of beauty and religion and art, was degraded to whoredom. . . .

His progress during these years he had measured by his dreams. Four years ago they had all been allegories, each

cunningly hiding what lay in his mind and heart; but now
they were as literal as his hands. His wishes no longer employed themselves in fabulous disguise. Some of them astonished him a little. He came to see that his unconscious mind
was, in comparison with that which stood within the
circumference of awareness and meaning, the only significant part of him. It had depth and spaciousness, as if
worlds were buried there, not only contemporary but
ancient; and his conscious mind was only a shadow, only
a distortion, of the unremembered record. It was superficial
and not a little pathetic. Below it was the wide dark reach
of all that he was and had been, lying to the farthest
boundaries of time; and the more vividly he sensed this
almost ageless heritage, the more he thought about it, trying
to draw it into consciousness and form. For here, written
by his emotions and recorded by his mind, was more than
a summary of thirty-two sentient years. There was the
strange and haunting intimation of himself as something
more than man, and as something infinitely less: of primeval
fellowship with darkness and terror, with superstition and
impetuous unreason: a sense of the jungle and the lost dank
smell of it; of the first troubled beginnings of mind and
thought. And dreams again and again restored him to one
level and another, far back in his ancient pilgrimage: now
losing him in a wilderness in which his muscular self alone
had meaning and use; now delivering him to the deep and
eternal hungers: of love, of food, of struggle; or now
making of him a desperate thing, choked with terror, hunting his way over a friendless earth. Or he was thrown back
to savagery and sat in a black night, bowed in idolatrous
worship to a fire, reading in its flame the soul of earth;
or dancing round and round it in the first frenzied beginnings of religious fear, his fetishes standing like sentinels
in a dark and dangerous world; or yelling in mad and
bedevilled gibberish against his enemies, as, in plain fact, he
had often yelled as a man. He had clowned so much during

these years that he had not only convulsed Athene with
laughter; he had also nearly frightened her out of her wits.
After hours of reflection and study he had yielded to emotional excesses, with all his senses threshing in blind violence
toward delivery and catharsis. His outpouring of meaningless syllables, his wild harangues in words that were to be
found in no dictionaries, his contortions of body and face:
all these, Athene had said, were lunacy pure and simple, no
matter how picturesque. They made her laugh or shudder,
and again and again they had made him shudder, too: as if
he had come to a brink and had looked into a mad void.
For often in these emotional storms he touched something
so vivid and elemental that the power of it, the deep and
unreflective logic of it, amazed him and restored him to the
sterile calm of thought. Then he would stand quietly,
trying to capture and hold this ancient and unutterable
meaning: as if, fighting blindly among the superficial and
civilized externals, he had uncovered something so vitally
alive that it admitted of no definition. And all this he
understood. He knew now that the spontaneous clown was
a person torn by inner conflict and driven to confession:
that was part of it, and in contemporary literature it had recorded itself in some naïvely pathetic and wholly unintelligible disguises. The fact that these writers were taken with
such earnest seriousness by so many suggested how wide-
spread was this impulse to confession and catharsis, and
how buried these lives. . . . But there was another aspect,
too, in himself and possibly in the others: a revolt against
the enervating patterns of culture and a wish to strike deep
into an ancient strength. . . .

Nor was it only in these emotional orgies that he touched
the profound. When he moved, like the persons around
him, in the feebly civilized patterns of restraint, herding
the dead ends of emotion into the tautology of speech or
into the vacuous smile, or into the small and spiritually
unnourishing details of eating and lecturing and going to

bed, he felt less than half alive; and the persons around
him seemed so stiff and formalized as to be weirdly unreal.
When he sat at his machine to write, then the emasculated
attitudes fell away and there opened to his emotions, and
obscurely to his memory, the vast expanse out of which
he had come; but his groping for words left it too long
on the threshold and it fled. It came again in intimations
and again was gone and the pages of his prose and verse
held less than its shadow and suggested only at his most
desperate effort its passion and reach. And it was then,
disappointed and cheated, that he would seek Athene and
astound her with such antics as she had never dreamed of.
It was then that the full meaning of himself rolled in upon
him, like a deeper darkness out of darkness; and all his
emotions fought out of their prison and came, in a sharp
and terrible instant, to a magnificent integration; and he
was delivered to that kind of peace that only love, of all
civilized hungers, had power to deliver him. Then, and then
only, did he strip all traditions and evasions aside and stand
for a moment, stark and honest, for what he was. "And all
this," he had said to Athene, "is not insanity. In a way
it is the final dying convulsions, born out of a tortured
childhood. But it is much more. It is an attempt to spill
all my emotions to sunlight and air and growth. It is an
effort to strike through these deadly civilized attitudes,
this emotional castration that is like a blight upon my
country. It is in part a tremendous effort at regression
to a more primitive and vital level; but that also is what
war is. That also, if my guess is right, is what Germany
is headed for. It is, too, the final bitter conflict in me
between X and Y, Shelley and Machiavelli. And yet that
is not true. There is no such thing really as a conflict between two personalities: the Jekyll and Hyde story is nonsense. No: it is this: all of us are born to and face the
superficial and empty thing that we call civilized life, with
all our hungers reduced to a well-bred gesture, with our

heritage lying dark and tragic and impotent under our fear.
At our backs, and pressing eternally, is the profoundly
emotional and hungry thing that we are; the vital and vivid
savage; millions of centuries, with all their voodooism,
exorcisms, chants, witchcraft, demons, totems, heliolatry,
conjuring, magic, ghosts. That is what we are under our
powdered skins: as profound as the sea, as ancient as the
night. And today, as I see it, we have one problem and one
only: that struggle between our enormous and vivid heritage, the eternal and pressing night at our backs, and our
cowardly and evasive pottering around with that heritage.
All our social problems are but aspects of that lone struggle.
All our asylums are filled with it. All our hypocrites are
made by it. And all our paradoxes: wars in the name of
God, murder in the name of justice, persecutions in the
name of peace. For I am, my dear, a darkly endowed animal
that yells and curses, makes love, tries to seize property, and
slobbers its food. But I'm also a magnificent beast, and you,
and everyone. Our endowment is a magnificent thing. I'll
never again doubt that. . . .

"No, darling, I am not mad. Try to understand that at
last I am coming home to sanity and peace."

He remembered his words now. He had these reflections
while standing in the Woolworth tower, looking down.
Upon leaving the tower he went to Athene's room.

"This city is a grand thing," he said. "It seems to be the
greatest psychopathic ward on earth. I see walking textbooks everywhere. It will be my fault if I do not learn a
lot here. . . ."

●

II

A WEEK later he stood in the Woolworth tower again. Below him, transfixed in violence, lay a sea of roof and cornice and spire, abutments and smokestacks, abysses and gorges and ledges, as if a sky of brick and steel had fallen. Among the crags of iron and stone were the streets, lying in fog and smoke like the sunken backs of ruin. Trolleys like green toys disappeared into caverns; elevated trains like huge iron reptiles crawled headless and tailless along their darkened gorge; and human beings everywhere, absurdly small and nervous, moved in the shadows without looking up.

Vridar looked into the east. To his left now were three mammoth bridges, swung over East River on ropes of steel. Beyond lay Brooklyn, another rigid chaos enveloped in smoke: a great smudge full of dirty walls and blackened towers. He looked into the south and before him now lay the harbor, with the Statue of Liberty standing desolately unclean in cold fog. Tugs and barges plowed furrows through a gray sea. A passenger boat was bearing upon Ellis Island which lay like a pile of shadow on the harbor's breast. He moved again and before him lay Jersey City, another blur of pinnacles and blind walls. Above it the sun was a burning disk in smoke piled upon the skyline. In the foreground was a long and ragged wharfage of piers and docks, with a few boats lying in; and fronting it was another on the opposite shore; and between the two lay the turbid and solemn Hudson, deep and heavy and darkly green. . . .

> *One by one the gods have gone to rest:*
> *Cybele of mountains, Ceres of the plow;*
> *Eos and Zephyrus and Melpomene,*
> *And Cronos of the Islands of the Blest:*
> *Not one of them is on Olympus now. . . .*

Close by a young man and a young woman were spitting, the one competing with the other. "See," said the man, "how far I can spit." The girl laughed happily and leaned against him. Then she spit in turn and wiped her mouth with the back of a gloved hand. Another man thrust a coin into a fixed telescope and peered through. "I can't see a damned bit farther," he complained to no one. "This thing is a fake." And he peered into the slot where his coin had vanished. "If I could spit on a bald head," said the man with the girl, "I'll bet it would sting like a hornet. Hell, I bet he would jump. See how far up we are." "Only think," said the girl. "Only think what man has done. With just his hands." "If I was to jump off," asked the man, "how long would it take me to hit?" He leaned over as if to see. "You know, in Japan they jump into a crater. Thousands of them. Why is it when I get on a high place I want to jump?" He stared at the girl, his mind wondering about himself.

Vridar moved again and looked northward over the blurred city. In his ears was the deep and troubled sound of the acres of an iron sea. In his nostrils was the searching pungence of ocean wind, carrying a little of the clean depth of lost isles; but in the wake of the breeze came the breath and sweat of the city's millions. Upon the streets below, for one not accustomed to it, the smell was like that of seaweed and pond water, of unventilated bedrooms and old bones. In the streets by the docks, or in Greenwich Village or Harlem or the East Side, was a smell like that of foul swimming pools.

He left the tower and entered Wall Street, a deep and narrow canyon of gray. At its head stood Trinity Church and once in every year it spilled Christmas chimes against the walls of stone. Perhaps here was the symbol he sought: the epitome and the trademark of the United States. Entering an underground corridor he rode home. The Beethoven Academy of Music was another symbol: a correspondence school that tutored in harp and violin and steel guitar. Its instructor of violin was a Russian immigrant with an overwhelming beard; and he didn't know, Vridar had been told, a violin from a 'cello. The professor of harp was a mythical name on the letterheads.

The Village was another symbol. Once it had suffered the glory of æsthetics and pose but now it was a smoky depression of decaying roofs and crumbling walls. It had a few dens and speakeasies surviving under quaintly silly names: there was Romany Marie's, a rendezvous for artists overcome by posturing; and here, two evenings ago, Vridar had seen a writer of sad and deluded genius, sitting among Chinese lanterns, sucking tea through a reed a yard long, and clutching his hair over a prostrate muse. Here was synthetic art at its greatest reach of impotence. What remained of the Village now wisely hid underground.

Vridar sat by the one small window of his room and looked through. A wrecking gang across the street had shattered an old building into a pile of ruin and the stink of it was unbearable. New York City, many visitors had said, was a thing of magnificent beauty; and so its skyline was, in an obscure and indefinite way, when looked at from far out. "You won't like New York," Mertyl had said. "But if you stay here two years it will get you. It's like opium and an aphrodisiac pulsing in stone. . . ."

Vridar left his room and walked along Sixth Avenue. Overhead an elevated thundered upon its iron path and shook a mist of grit to the street. In a newsstand an aged woman was huddled in rags, her face like wrinkled cowhide, her hands like claws. Up and down the sidewalk paced an unclean fellow, with a placard on his back, advertising halfsoles. A legless beggar looked like a man sitting in stone to his crotch.

At the entrance to a subway was another creature, foul and old, sitting with pencils in her lap and a few pennies.

Her upper lip was long and yellow and full of unremembered details. And Vridar saw, on glancing back, that one withered leg came like a root from the folds of her dress. He dropped a nickel into a slot and swung an iron turnstile. He went down a stairway of stone and stood on a stone platform, waiting for an iron train. He shouldered his way in and was wedged between a large soughing Jew and an old woman with pouches under her eyes. A little way off was a young girl, her mouth scarlet, and over her stood a tall youth, amorously intent. Another man, hanging from a strap, was gently insinuating his leg between the legs of a girl who sat before him. Down low, among the wedged hips and bellies, Vridar saw the sober eyes of a child. He grinned but the lad only looked up at his mother and again at Vridar. Vridar turned a little to watch the man who had invaded with his leg.

A New York psychologist had declared, but not in print, that subway riding was the largest and most covert sexual perversion to be found anywhere. But it was not perversion at all. Hundreds of men, crowded into these savage journeys, hugged tight against women and moved a little this way, a little that, as the train rocked and shuddered: hips against hips, bellies against backs: the roar of the train or jazz: underground rides or dancing in dark cabarets: Bergson's élan vital or Freud's libido: the large and multiple fabric of euphemism, gathered round like a cloak: small overtures to copulation, all cunningly disguised in innocuous symbols, in erotic witchcraft: the final overwhelming summary of puritanism and its age. If this man were naked, and this girl, men everywhere would rise in fury and pitch him into darkness; but with nainsook between, chemisette and brassière. . . .

And clothes were curious symbols, too. Like nuptials, like bedrooms and pillows, they were a staple of jest: nightgowns and pajamas and garters, and above each the warning

of proverb and fable; human emotions cabined by scruples
and spinning their hysteria; pleasure as the harlequin of the
Scandals and Follies, or leering from the tabloids, or con-
triving dark innuendo behind cotton and serge. Pleasure as
a manic depressive, asylumed in Manhattan.

He left the train and followed a stream of humanity to
light and air. He turned east and flowed with the crowd, his
feet lost in a current of feet, his identity muffed in a void
of sound: men carrying large stomachs, with fat overhang-
ing their collars; women entombed and panting; girls with
complexions fighting against smoke and paint. "Short skirts,"
said Mac McGuire, "show how crooked the world is." He
went south and passed the glittering Chrysler tower; came
to a dark street that smelled of rain dripping from hen-
roosts, of rubber scalded against stone; another corner
turned, a murmuring as of far seas, a smell as of wet rags;
another, and a low dark street dying upon the air. But a city
of glorious skylines and cathedrals, of picturesque docks
and blue palisades, of Fifth Avenue and Broadway. If Manhattan could stand up, with its feet in Battery Park, it
would have Harlem from shoulder to shoulder across its
heart. The Great White Way would be somewhere between
its navel and its knees. Yes: for the United States contrived
its ironies with impeccable taste: Trinity looked into Wall
Street, and Ellis Island lay almost within the shadow of the
Goddess of Liberty. . . .

Vridar walked for hours, trying to catch the spirit of this
city: it rolled in upon his senses and overwhelmed him and
he wanted to rise above it and look down. He was striving
to catch its meaning in an epigram: was it, like Baudelaire's
life, an oasis of horror in a desert of ennui? or Caliban philos-
ophizing from a bed of stone? or only a mechanical monster,
made of all the knots and elbows of earth? He thought of
Frost's poem on the brook; he remembered and paraphrased
Auslander:

This city is dead.
Everything that you can say
Has been quite definitely said.

And he remembered: And the gods were not ignorant that such a monster was maturing and that some day he would bring evil upon men. . . . But there was no evil here or anywhere: it was only a vulgar and stupendous microcosm that summarized an age. Countrysides were ravaged and drawn into suburbs; wooded hills were buried under concrete and brick; streams once clear became open sewers. State lines roundabout existed only on maps. And millions, like himself, lived in the heart of all this and heard its sound while they slept; and others, living on a margin, commuted day by day into its loins; and others withdrew year by year like people retreating before a flood. . . .

And in still another way he thought of this city: it was a great symphony of consonants, without overtones or range: a convulsed asylum of dissonance. All its favorite trademarks and shibboleths were cacophonous: tabloid and subway and dock, frigidaire and macadamized, bridge and girder, skyscraper and progress. In contrast stood all the liquid loveliness of a world now ancient and dead: dell and hill and melody, sunlight and flowers and peace. And in time there would be here, an architect had said, a city of twenty millions: multiplied towers, and subways under subways; underground caverns electrified; sidewalks in tier on tier. And in this mighty sarcophagus of steel, psychiatrists, no doubt, would multiply, too, and begin, after a while, to analyze one another. He remembered great men of the past who had hated cities but he did not share their hatred: this was a thing to understand and not to abuse. In Central Park he sat on a bench and strove to summarize what he felt.

Our ribs are now the ribs of steel,
Our flesh is flesh of iron and stone;

We stir like mortar when we feel,
We feel the rivets in our bone.
The roar of industry, the whine
Has shaped us, and has shaped our art;
We feel the girder in our spine,
We feel the motor in our heart. . . .

But this, he reflected, would never do: it was the plaint
of those who ranted against mechanized existence and spiritual martyrdom. It was the wail of those who sought a
quiet refuge and cherished their self-pitying despair. He had
long ago accepted the scientific method and the scientific
approach to life and he had repudiated the sickly apostro-
phizings of spiritual weaklings. But the laboratories and this
city he could not, in these weeks, reconcile. There was no
meditation, no ironic detachment in this mad and delirious
place: it made him think, on the contrary, of Lesbians in
midnight shows, shaking, as some poet had said, their implacable thighs; dealers in seafood, selling gin in codfish
packages; bootleggers still wearing Hoover buttons; children
erotically playing and wondering about love; the wells of
loneliness and what Maisie knew. Textbooks of cases, of
obsessions and phobias. . . .

Oh, my dear Sir Harry Orbid,
You are morbid, you are morbid. . . .

Millions of persons working like slaves, eating and sleeping
and breeding: those and nothing else; millions riding these
subways with rarely a happy face, a bright and vital face,
among them; millions fumbling through the vulgar details
of a meaningless life. And there were visitors, groomed and
smug and well fed, who talked of beauty and slept in clean
rooms high above the smoke. There were columnists who
slept above the smoke and wrote of the glory and romance
of Forty-second Street and spent their winters in Florida

or Nice. But this was not a city of witty irrelevance or of posturing and psychopathic poets or of bloodless æsthetes or of the pathetic negativism of sophistication. It was a dark and terrible city of slaves; and under their feet, around them, overhead, was this mighty copulation of steel and stone. This was the United States of America, summarized and delivered to an island: his country and his age. . . .

III

●

IN UTAH there had been a few Jews in Vridar's classes
and they had all been intelligent and alert; and he had
said, "Give me Jews and nothing but Jews and I can teach.
These smug unawakened Christians wear me out." And now,
in the university where he taught he found himself facing
Jews, with a few Italians, a Swede or an Irishman, an Ar-
menian or a Turk. He felt upon entering the classroom that
here were students, eager and awake and ready for the truth.
But he learned too that most of them were cynical, skeptical,
and very malicious. He had been teaching youth from the
countryside and small towns: orthodox groups with the
dogmas of their parents: Mormons who believed they were
the latter-day saints of earth and that the Salt Lake Valley
was the zion of a chosen people. Now he faced heretics and
scoffers.

And in every day here, during his first weeks, he was
amazed by the difference between what he had left and what
he had found. That both student bodies could be American,
living under the same flag and in the same year, he could
hardly believe. In Utah he had never dared to approach truth
or had found himself in trouble when he did; and here he
dared not evade it. If he hesitated, a challenge was flung.
If he tried to soften, or if, reflecting that these minds were
immature, he sidetracked bold questions, a derisive voice
tripped him and a scornful class shouted with glee. And two
months passed before he realized, before he dared believe,
that he could go to the heart of matters and lay every
problem open to its core. There was academic freedom here.
There was a bold and eager intelligence that demanded facts
and nothing else.

But there was much more than hunger for certainties.
The wakefulness was neurotic and morbid, the dubiety was

cynical and stark. These students were like this city: fever-ish with eagerness, vast and blundering in their reach and dreams. And sometimes Vridar felt when looking at them that they were less animals than machines: they were loud and vulgar, as if competing with the din around them; and they moved as if, wound up, they had an excess of energy and nothing on which to spend it. In the hallways and in the streets they poured in confusion and babble, drawing to the surface and overflowing. Utah, or any countryside from coast to coast, was sluggish with tradition and the changeless; but New York City was the vanguard, the tides, rolling upon the headlands and shores.

And for weeks Vridar was lost in wonder and study. These Jews, he observed, were bold in their love-making: they pawed the girls, backed them against walls and thrust against them, seized their hair and jerked their heads back and kissed them. But these erotic gestures were morbid in their violence. These students were erupting with emotion as if the clamors of the city had driven all their hungers to the surface; as if they felt orgiastic, even when sitting in class. One evening a woman about thirty years old came in and sat in the front row. She looked at Vridar while he talked and on a sheet of paper she recorded the curious symbols of her mind. When the class was ended she gave the paper to Vridar.

"I do this kind of thing all the time," she said. "It's meaningless. Why do I do it?"

"I'll look it over," he said.

He was surprised by what the paper told him. At a casual glance these scrawls were meaningless. A closer scru-tiny showed them to be phallic symbols, the genitals of both sexes. Vridar took them to his brother who taught psy-chology.

"I want these," Mertyl said. "They're the best example of unconscious drawing I've ever seen."

"I have others from other students."

"I don't doubt it. They're common here."

In the same class a lovely Jewess sat alone at one side of the room. One evening she startled Vridar by saying:

"Dr. Hunter, tell me this: why do all the men of this class sit on one side of the room and all the girls on the other?"

"Well," said Vridar, "you had better ask the men. Why do you sit over there alone?"

"I don't know. I don't want to." And after a moment she added: "What is wrong with the men in this class?" Vridar stared at her and then laughed. "You think it's funny?" she said. "You have a strange sense of humor."

Almost no day passed without some revelation of this kind. In another class Vridar read a composition and was talking of it when a Jewess stopped him.

"You know," she said, "what I think is the matter with you?"

"With me? Is something wrong with me?"

"Yes. You're a puritan."

Vridar was flabbergasted. He stared at her and felt blood hot in his cheeks.

"Oh," he said, "you think I'm a puritan." And in a quietly amused voice came the answer:

"Aren't you?"

Both of these girls in the weeks that followed came to Vridar's office. They wanted to talk only of the erotic and themselves and he was distressed, not knowing what to do with them. The first of them, whose name was Rose, even followed him to the street and said she was going to his room.

"To my room? What for?"

"Nothing the world would disapprove. Just to make faces at you. Tell me: couldn't I do some typing? I'm a swell typist."

"No, thanks. I do all my own typing."

"Then I'll make your bed."

"My bed, thank you, is made."

"Then you can pretend you're Socrates and I'll listen."

"Here's your subway. Beat it."

He tried to dismiss her but this girl faced him at every turn. She grasped his arm. She mocked him.

"Is your time so priceless you can't give me an hour of talk?"

"Why are you such a fool?" he asked impatiently. "You know what you want."

"I want you to talk. You are so very aloof and wise."

"You're being very ridiculous."

"Listen, tell me this. I was at a party the other night and I was drinking and suddenly I went wild. I ran to the bathroom and locked myself in. I kicked around in there and broke everything. I yelled. And when the men came to the door do you know what I did?"

"I can't imagine."

"I tore my brassière off and threw it out to them. Now why did I do that?"

Vridar went up the street and she followed him. She put herself before him and walked backward, her eyes and smile mocking him.

"Why," she asked, "did I do that?"

He came to the building where he lived and drew a key. He unlocked the door and stepped inside. Rose tried to follow but he locked the door against her and went up the stairs, feeling very absurd, feeling that life was very absurd.

The other girl, Moxa Cahan, did not try to go to Vridar's room. She asked him to hers and when he said no she came more frequently to his office. This girl, unlike Rose, was shy of manner but no less bold of thought. She was fair-skinned and flaxen-haired and looked like a Swede. Her laugh was low and gurgling and full of amusement for herself.

"Shall I tell you," she asked one afternoon, "a story that will make you laugh?"

"I'm very busy. I'd rather you'd tell it to some other instructor."

"Don't be mean. I want to tell it to you."

"All right. Be brief."

"Well, it's this: I'm afraid of men. They paralyze me. And so I've done a very funny thing."

"Yes. What is it?"

"There's a nice boy I know. He's only seventeen but he's grown. And now——"

"Yes, and now?"

"I'm living with him. We're in a big room and each of us has a bed. He's on one side of the room, I'm on the other. I made him promise——"

"Go on with your story."

"I made him promise to leave me alone until I tell him. Don't laugh. It is nothing to laugh at."

"And how long have you lived that way?"

"A month."

"And does he behave himself?"

"Yes. Oh, he's afraid, too. He never bothers me at all."

For a long moment Vridar looked at her.

"So that," he said, "is the reason you called me a puritan."

One day Vridar turned to a colleague who had been here many years.

"Is this city," he asked, "nothing but a huge aphrodisiac? Do these students think of nothing but sex?"

Jack Farlane yawned and made a face. Jack was a poet, and an excellent poet too, within the fastidious pasture he had fenced off for his muse. He was a sardonic person with enough defenses against life to fill a catalog: he turned everything into jest and epigram, and laughter that was empty of everything but pain.

"What else," he said, "is worth thinking of?"

"Seriously, though. A lot of these Jewesses are hell-bent on seducing a gentile. That's because of a feeling of racial inferiority."

"Have they been chasing you down corridors?"

"You teach a course in the romantic poets——"

"Don't hold that against me. I can't help it if Shelley was romantic."

"—and the girls come in here and pile on your desk six deep. They do everything but take your clothes off."

"My clothes are sewed on."

"Do you know Brownell's statement? This young generation is not emancipated. It is merely unbuttoned."

Jack rose gravely.

"Just absent-mindedness," he said. "I forgot what I was going to do."

Another instructor said to Vridar:

"This department is lousy with men who seduce their students." And he told of one who had been dismissed a year ago. This man had used a "technique" common to those in college faculties who made seduction one of their major interests. He talked of poetry and metaphysics and art, of the illimitable wonder of life and the universe, having learned, like many another, that these subjects excited girls to platonic raptures. He invited a girl to his apartment to see his curios; whereupon, putting her at ease, he gently enthroned her by the fireplace. He set her in a great chair and draped her with a Turkish shawl; took off her shoes and put on her feet a pair of Persian sandals; gave her a long Chinese cigarette holder and put in it an Egyptian cigarette; urged her softly to sip cointreau from a delicate chalice; and burned incense. Then he sat at her feet, robed like a mandarin, and talked gravely of beauty. After a while he gently undressed her and fetched Japanese pajamas and threw over her feet a fur-lined pelisse.

"He seduced as many as four girls in one week," said this solemn young man, his eyes sharp with envy and disapproval.

But Vridar was not interested in tales of lecherous conquest. He had seen seducers in college faculties and knew their ways and their hearts: an unnatural childhood had led them to an ego-identification with sex and they made sexual conquest a measure of manhood. Vridar was interested in what some of his colleagues called the loud insolence of these Jews. In the middle of a lecture one afternoon he was stopped by a voice that said, "I don't think you know what you're talking about." At first such sudden pronouncements left him at the end of his wits. They annoyed and offended him. But after a while he tried wise-cracking; and he was surprised to learn that these students, with impartial candor, were ready to jeer the vanquished and applaud the victor. He observed, too, that his sly witticisms which in Utah had made his students yawn were here seized upon with enormous relish. These Jews liked sharp intellectual skirmishes. They liked the aphorism that summarized in acid.

And all this, Vridar came to see, was a part of their heritage. When he asked Mertyl what the psychology of the Jew was, Mertyl said: "They have no ego-identification with country or land or home." That was it. Having been kicked around for centuries as if Asia were a stadium and they a football, they were mentally and emotionally awake as no other people were anywhere. Their wits had been sharpened but their emotions had been left anchorless: they had no flag, no country, and only an amorphous and scattered tradition. They had a profound sense of insecurity and a nomadic and disintegrating integrity. Having no strong ego-identifications, they did not sulk when set upon and defeated, as was the custom of the persons Vridar had known: they took their blows as education, and learned from every blow they received. They wanted to be, not gentiles, as many persons declared: they wanted to identify themselves with those symbols of permanence which gave to gentiles a sense of racial and religious and social integrity. And all this opened to Vridar another revelation of the human mind and heart.

It forced him to revise or abolish some notions which he still cherished. He himself had always been what is called a modest person. Though militant and aggressive at heart, he had never pushed himself forward, having been thoroughly instructed by his mother that boldness was vulgar and ill-bred: self-deprecation, on the contrary, had been one of his most patient and painstaking gestures. He had learned long ago that nothing so annoys most persons as aggressiveness: there had come to be, in fact, the typical American rebuke: "How you love yourself!" He had learned to despise hogs of all kinds: the table-hog who takes to his own use the best of the food; the love-hog who pushes with ruthless ardor into all the embraces available; and the property-hog who lays hands on everything he can seize. Recoiling from these, he had gone to another extreme: he had practiced self-denial until it had almost become a religion; he had always believed that it was better to give than to take, better to listen than to be heard. Self-effacement, standing sick and demure in the shadows, had been his law of life.

He now looked at the matter to see if he had been a simpleton of still another kind; and he saw, and wondered why he had not seen before, that modesty, so smiled upon in the Christian world, was only another evasion. The person who most admired self-effacement was the person, quite precisely, who felt most insecure, who was most afraid of life. He disliked aggressive persons because they made him feel impotent and futile. He liked the retiring and self-deprecating gesture because it made him feel more impregnable within that small and shoddy fortress of scruples which he had built for himself.

And so it was that human beings spoke of insolence, of smugness, of conceit: meaning only that these traits when militant and poised made them feel inadequate to face the grim and relentless struggle to survive. For human beings were determined to recognize no virtue in excess of what they discovered in themselves and when such excess declared itself they rebuked it and tried to make of it a vice. So they had come to the sophistry that beauty is only skin-deep; that the meek are more generous of heart; that the unpropertied are more favored of God. They wanted the more important human endowments to be hidden, like sex, underground; and in all these matters, including the erotic, they despised and fought with persecution and scorn any evidence that another was more richly endowed, or more in possession of pleasure, than they. And the person who retorted, "You certainly love yourself, don't you?" also made admissions which, if he understood their deep and self-evasive implications, would dye his cheeks with shame.

This, then, was the reason Jews had been persecuted: they were, or had come to be, the most aggressive and militant race on earth. For the self-pitying and self-effacing gentile they were insolent. And while thinking of the matter, Vridar remembered a story told of James Joyce. When Joyce was introduced to Yeats, legend declared, he said, "We have met too late. You are too old to be influenced by me." And commentators by the score had jumped on the statement with both feet and had cried, "Ah-ha! What astounding conceit!" Unashamed candor was still too much for weaklings.

"And how funny," Vridar said to Athene. "I came here and these Jews knocked me over. They sickened me with what I chose to regard as their unmitigated cockiness. Where was their modesty? Alas! Their good taste? Alack! With what patient cowardice we deceive ourselves on a thousand fronts. What magnificently stinking confusions we are lost in. . . .

"Then I sat down to think my way through the matter. I grasp a handful of my cherished notions and emerge from thought with my hands closing on emptiness. Darling, I've

always been such a modest person. I knew that people liked
me better when I didn't stick my rump up. But the human
animal is naturally a loud-thumping creature and in self-
effacement he develops neurosis and withers and wilts. And
how these Jews hung me up by my heels! Take those girls:
they wanted to lie with me and they made the matter as
plain as words could make it. And I caught myself thinking, You're not a very modest wench. I was still too in-
decent to meet candor with candor or to realize that only
frankness can be clean."

"But, my dear," Athene said, "you miss something. In
the erotic gesture of the female there is also subtlety, finesse
—call it what you will. The male demands it. He prefers
it."

"But isn't that only a more egregious aspect of vanity?
He merely insists on being the aggressor. And if in some
matters we find it wise to modify our heritage, would it not
also be wise to allow the female to be more overt and less
devious?"

"But would you not find her less alluring? Can we escape
our biology? Does not the woman's demure retreating whet
desire?"

"I suppose. But are we men everlastingly to reproach
her if, despairing of our boldness, she becomes more direct?
For centuries now we have hurled derisive epithets at such
women. We have called them strumpets and bawds. The
bondage of women today is erotic, not economic. We men,
it seems to me, demand too damned many privileges in this
game of love. When we are hungry we pursue; when we're
not in the mood for amorous chase we want women to sit
back in demure chastity and wait. Some of them get tired
of waiting——"

"Well, I'll have to think of the matter. Another thing:
can't there be an excess of chest-thumping? It can be
neurotic. At least, you have said so."

"Yes, it can be. A lot of persons make a big noise to

hide their fear. A lot of them affect an aggressiveness they don't feel. Some of these are driven to excesses and we call such an excess paranoia. But my point is this: because of our timidity and evasion we've come to look with favor on the person who deprecates himself. If a person says, I'm nobody, I don't amount to a snort in a wind, how we warm to him. I mean, of course," said Vridar, smiling, "how we warm to ourselves. And I mean, too, that Jews have been persecuted because gentiles have been afraid of their energy and brains. I don't mean they're more intelligent, but they certainly do use more of what they have. I mean we still persecute them because our intelligence is still the serf of a self-pitying puritanism. That is what I meant."

"Well, I think I can agree with all that."

"All right. Let's go out and find a drink of gin."

IV

●

FERD and his wife, the Orcutts, and Moses McGuire had come to New York City. About twice in every week Mac burst into Vridar's room to unload a cargo of cynicism or to heap abuse on artists and logicians. He strode in one morning when Vridar was busy on a chapter of his eighth novel.

"I come," he said, leering, "with a stipend from the national fund for worthy artists. What are you writing now? The great American novel, an elegy to Brooklyn Bridge, or a letter to your mother?" He unloaded a pile of books from a chair. He sat and stretched his long legs and turned upon Vridar a loose and bitter sneer. "Listen, Hunter, why don't you write Christmas greetings or birthday jingles or valentine legends? Do you want a plot for a best-seller? I'll give you one for a drink of gin. . . . Where's your gin?"

"There in the bathroom."

Mac went into the bathroom and drank and came out. "All right: take a modern young couple and have them go in for free love. They will experiment and if their body odors are compatible they will live together. Then precept by precept they will grow apart. Their challenge of holy tradition will toss them up to three hundred pages of tears and blunders and then, moonlight by roses, they will learn that their contempt for marriage was only an adolescent gesture. They will discover that marriage is beautiful and sweet and your heroine will kiss her wedding ring and your hero will shake with intimations of rapture. That book will sell. It will make a million unhappily married people feel better and jewelers will recommend the book to their friends.

"Or here's another: Interview fifty married women and learn how they were proposed to. Call it Consolations for

Old Maids. Lord, what royalties I can see in that." Mac lit
a cigarette. His hands trembled. "Hunter," he said, "you
get more complacent all the time. You take life in great
gulps, with interludes of sleep and digestion and fornication.
When I look at you I know that life is profoundly meaningless."

"When you give up cynicism," Vridar said wearily,
"you're going to be out of a job."

"Listen to the oracle rumble! Hunter, when you try
to think you make me feel as if I were watching an elephant
try to fly."

Vridar turned and looked at the bitter face. "Listen,
Mac, why don't you make an effort to grow up? Are you
going through life on a handful of feeble aphorisms?"

"Feeble? Because you can't understand them? To tell
the truth, Hunter, I'm more profound when asleep than
you are at your most agonized zenith. My aphorisms distress
you? Oscar Wilde distressed people, too. Now here: a
pessimist thinks all women are bad; an optimist hopes they
are. Now there's a thought that goes over your head like
an aëroplane. You sit around here with these tail snarls
from your spavined pegasus and imagine you have Mount
Olympus in your pockets. And have you read what the
critics have said of your dull and shameless book? Keats
was dead at twenty-five, Shelley at twenty-nine. Congreve
at your age threw his pen away. Marlowe at less than your
age had written his mighty line. Scores have been alive and
famous at an age when you were reading Zane Grey." Mac
paused, grunting with contempt. His eyes glittered with
spite. "Hunter, there is no difference between an evangel-
ist and a patriot of art. Both leap like jackasses out of
repression and bray. Did you ever observe that a woman poet
never writes or writes badly after she marries? Find a soft
chair and rest that placid hinder of yours and meditate on
that." Mac paced the room now, measuring his strides, and
stopping now and then as if to find his footprint. His pale

mouth sagged, his grunts were scornful. "You have," he declared suddenly, "the pathetic American notion that anything that has studied grammar can write a book. You belong to the tribe of Von Tischendorf. . . ."

Vridar slipped a paper into his machine and wrote.

I hear him talking of the two-by-four,
I feel him search the comma of a line;
He tastes æsthetics and with superfine
Despair he strides dithyrambic round the floor. . . .

"The muse embraces him!" Mac cried, and he stooped, with hands on knees, to leer at Vridar. "My God, the golden complex flows into rime!"

Thinks: Glaube dem Leben . . . and then: Damn the
    whore!
And makes an aphorism of the Nine;
À la fin de la guerre, le déluge, yours and mine!—
And adds to life one semicolon more. . . .

"There you sit," said Mac, "declaring in your solemnly avuncular manner that this is that and that is this. I regard you, Hunter, as an incredibly impeccable platitude. You have the obtuse and triumphant perfection of a cartwheel. You grieve because no Theocritus rises to sing of barns and cows and hencoops, and the magnificent lewdness of this city never penetrates the mortar and concrete of your skull. Lord Christ, what a picture you make, sitting there scribbling like any spinster with all your wits arranged and marked like merchandise in a Woolworth store. . . ."

Thus he, the sophisticate of an iron age,
Turns syllables to overflow his purse.
Approved by the obscene casual tutelage
Of youthful follies, all his lines rehearse
Their proper length until they fill a page
And die in some anthology of verse.

Vridar rose and handed the sonnet to Mac. "If you keep on," he said, "you will be indistinguishable from these pathetic New York eunuchs who call themselves sophisticates. There is a poem for you. And now run along: you've worn me out."

Mac read the sonnet, murmuring derisions.

"I'll be back," he said. "I'll get under that thick skin of yours before I'm done. I'll make you sob like an old maid reading *Ulysses*."

"All right, but run along now."

After Mac had gone, Vridar lay on his bed and closed his eyes. He saw all the lush wealth of a countryside: meadows aglow, fields of grain upon which a breeze was a dimpled journey, hills like banks of blue fog; clouds like heaped masses of dandelion bloom; a sky aflame from sunset to zenith. He saw fragrant roads with their miles lying upon distance; fronded ponds and alfalfa depths and the drip of orchards. . . . A week ago he had said to a group of students from this great city: "Suppose you have a day to spend where and as you please: write a composition telling what you would do." And not one of them went in fancy to Europe or the South Seas or the Orient. No: more than eighty per cent of them declared they would go into the country and lie on the earth under a fragrant tree and dream. They wanted to find old log bridges, sunken, overgrown with moss, under which water gurgled along banks of amaranth and cress. The air under such bridges was sweet with hidden growing and odorous decay. For an old bridge, one said, sunk in a meadow or lost in an upland pasture of clover, was a lovely work of art: aged and mellowed with its own quiet being, with golden rust upon the spike-heads and moss upon every scar of the ax. And roads, said another, were lovely things: they disappeared into thickets of dog rose or popple and scattered trails through undergrowth: mallow and galium and goldenrod, gaillardia and cinque-foil. . . .

Vridar went to a window and looked out. He always felt depressed and a little sick after listening to Mac's spiritual impotence. Mac should not have come to this city: it was opium that kept his sensibilities at intense white heat. It was all that Vridar could do to support this vision of blackened towers, of dwarfed trees fighting against smoke, of patches of dirty grass. One of his colleagues would stand by a window and look at a few stunted trees and exclaim: "How bee-utiful this morning! It makes one realize that life *is* good!" And Vridar would look at the fat round-bellied smugness of the man and reflect that persons who deeply felt the beauty of life almost never spoke of it.

And now Vridar looked at a leather bag that had been with him for four years. He had never opened it and he doubted that he ever would; for within, quiet and dark, were Neloa's letters, her cookbook and locks of her hair and a copper urn. It was something always with him that he never spoke of, even to Athene. And he wondered now if his heartache were self-pity only or if in it there were not something larger and more splendid than grief, as in his love and Neloa's there had been something that still lived above their misunderstandings and loss. He remembered Leonard:

> *Did I not know*
> *The use of crêpe, the etiquette of woe?—*
> *Yes; but I'd business more severe than that:*
> *Knowing how hungrily Death leered for me,*
> *I seized on life wherever it might be. . . .*

And he turned now to letters that had come from persons who had read his novel. One of them said:

> . . . I have withdrawn into isolation so complete that I now have no contacts with life (I am a bachelor) except in books. I feel that the way I have chosen is cowardly and your story makes me wonder if you have not found some positive faith the nature of which you will, if I do not presume, suggest to me. . . .

And Vridar wrote:

. . . I am trying to discover myself in terms of human fellowship. I have been romantic and evasive: I mean the absorption of self by small and intense and self-pitying interests. I find it increasingly difficult to hate anyone or anything because hatred is fear and I am no longer afraid. It will not follow, I think, that I shall end up by loving all things; for many persons, like many trees, or many of anything else, are so distorted by cheap ideals and evasions that they give to ugliness the only meaning the word can have. Such distortions I cannot love but I do try to understand. Anatole France declared we need irony and pity. I think understanding and sympathy without the irony will do. But how far we miss these today our humanists or any other of our cults declare by the rancor and bad temper of their preachments. . . .

The other letters were abusive. A woman said, "Your novel is the most brutal thing I've ever seen. I wonder what sort of inhuman monster you can be. . . ." Some critics, too, had declared Vridar's novel to be brutal, and their statements left him pondering the word and what it could reasonably mean. There were amusing paradoxes here. The human animal, he reflected, is the only animal that kills for the love of killing: we call that sport. The actual and commonplace conditions of a man struggling to survive are called brutal. Most persons seem unable to understand the raw animalism of one who must cut through all decencies in order to live at all, or to realize that they would do so under the same ruthless demands. But many, secure and privileged, expect persons to defer to civilized amenities when the only matter at hand is enough bread to eat and a place to sleep. Such expectancy must argue incredibly callow souls. . . .

And there were Vridar's friends.

"How's the big brute?" Ferd asked. "Did you know you are brutal?" And Elsa said:

"Vridar, for shame. You're downright cruel. Why don't you write of pleasant things?"

"I'm a fine member of society. Brutal me!"

"I shuddered and shivered like a ditheist," said Mae Dwon. "My God, how my bones shook!"

"I'm writing another such book now," Vridar said. "How's to read a scene?"

"Sure," said Ferd. He stooped and scowled and added softly: "Read your stuff." And Vridar fetched a manuscript and read.

"This is a farm scene. It goes like this. Hang the bird from its feet from a cord or shackle with the breast toward the killer. The head of the bird is then grasped by placing the thumb and forefinger of the left hand between the eye and the ear on each side of the skull. An ordinary sharp knife, preferably with a blade about two and a half inches long and one fourth of an inch wide, is then inserted through the mouth in such a way that the point is just back of the skull and toward the left of the killer. The killer now presses down with the point of the knife and draws it slightly forward and across the base of the skull to the right. Ordinarily if this cut is carefully done the jugular veins will be severed and a stream of blood will follow immediately out of the mouth. When the killer sees that this stream of blood is flowing nicely, he then debrains the bird. Debraining is done by inserting the point of the knife through the groove in the roof of the mouth and then forcing it backward on a line midway between the eyes and the ears. After the knife has been inserted far enough to reach the brain, it is twisted slightly. If it has been placed correctly the bird flops and usually makes a distinctive quack. This serves to loosen the feathers and the next operation is their quick removal. If you do not sever the veins at the first cut, try again——"

"Stop!" Mae cried. "My God, man, you made that up!"

"Is that worse than anything in my last book?"

"It's cold-blooded. Honest, Vridar, a person has to be degenerate to write such stuff. Don't mind my frankness."

"Nonsense. You mean only a degenerate could kill in such a manner?"

"I do."

"Do you mean all turkey-raisers are degenerates?"

"Turkey-raisers, my eye. I've known farmers. They weren't like that and they weren't like the monsters in your book."

"What I've just read," said Vridar, "is from the Pocatello Cold Storage Company. It is called How to Dress Turkeys. You like turkey, don't you? And they taste better, you know, if killed in this slow and meditative way."

"It's the only way to kill a turkey," said Carlyle. "It spoils the meat to cut their heads off."

"That settles me," Mae said. "I'll never eat turkey again."

Vridar looked at Athene who was sitting back in shadow and smiling. He winked.

"Send that to your critics," said Ferd. "Have it served up with their next Thanksgiving plate."

"But they don't kill except for fun."

"You sickly Americans," said Ferd, scowling around him and affecting rage. "The tiger kills the antelope, the spider eats the fly, and you eat the turkey. You boil lobsters alive to add to the flavor. You sentimentalists!" He struck an attitude and looked furious. "Your ignorance," he said, "fills the room like bad air. Don't you know that the person who howls most about brutality is the one who feels the deepest compulsions toward it? Don't you know the one who howls most about sexy stories is the one who wants to sneak off and fornicate? The torturer and the zealot always fill the same skin. You," he said, turning to Mae, "are the monster. You big sickly pile of womanhood! You stuff your great belly with turkey. Do you know Robinson's poem about the butcher? Never mind: you wouldn't understand it." And then, with gestures so preposterous that everyone smiled, Ferd minced across the room and seized a bottle of gin. He drank and turned round and round, looking at one and another. "I don't understand," he said, "why I associate with children." And then: "Ohhh, let us sing as the birdies sing! Tweet—tweet-tweet—tweet-tweet. . . ."

Moses McGuire had not spoken in this evening. He now grunted and stretched his long legs and drew his mouth into its loose and habitual sneer.

"You persons all remind me," he said, "of a bunch of shoddy dilettantes out of Picasso. Out of l'École de Paris: Montmartre ambassadors from Bohemia at their most gorgeous reach of imbecility. You should have played around with Van Gogh and Gauguin——"

"Mac has been sitting there," said Mac, "thinking all that up."

"Imagine," said Mac, "what Van Gogh would have done with you: precisely nothing. You are all substance without flame. But you," he said to Elsa, "are all flame without substance: he could have made a nice blob of surrealism out of you. What frauds you are," he said, taking a cigarette. "Bors Emmet is right. Art has become a eunuch with homosexual tendencies. Its cheap little illusions, its feverish inbreeding: the infantilism of Modigliani and Stein——"

"I suppose," said Mae, "you're repeating Bors Emmet word for word. You're as big a thief as Oscar Wilde."

"You," said Mac, leering at her, "are the most implacable pox I've ever laid eyes on. You and your true-confession stories: your huge uterine gestures at romance: Mae Dwon, the Sappho of Manhattan, writing your verses for Christmas cards!"

"Shut up," said Ferd. "We didn't come here to listen to your psychopathic murmurings. We came," he said, using a gin bottle as a baton, "to sing as the birdies sing. Come on now, everyone. . . ."

V

●

$\overline{\hspace{2cm}}$

A T WEEK-END parties in Salt Lake City and here Vridar
had been surprised, while searching himself and others,
by alcoholic revelations. He had found himself wooing other
women, and this, he argued, could mean only that he was
still erotically evasive. Wooing another woman was all right
but it was not all right if a man did it only when full of
brandy or gin. And in reflecting on this matter, it seemed
to him that he could not expect to *reason* himself out of
emotional difficulties. He would have to act.

"So I'm going West this summer," he said to Athene,
"and face myself out in this. I'll not be another D. H.
Lawrence, trying desperately in one book after another to
arrive at a decent copulation."

"There's more to it," said Athene. "It's the artist in
you."

"Oh, to hell with that. I'm not hiding behind flattering
notions. The world thinks artists are just boys who won't
grow up. They are just unmoral fellows with great relish
for lovely experiences. Plain asses, in fact, and I'm one of
them."

"Artists do have greater zest. It's not strange that
they run to women."

"It's not a matter of zest. It's a matter of something
buried that they won't face. Darling, the full and frank
story of any artist's life would make the world howl."

"It would howl all right—but not with joy."

"Do you care if I go?"

"Of course I care. But that's not the point. Your life
is your own."

And Vridar went with Ferd to Salt Lake City and he
wasted no time. There was Kate Marbury who liked to talk

of Jeffers and Verlaine and Rimbaud. She was the daughter of a wealthy merchant and lived alone in a great house and she told Vridar of two lovers she had had: both fools, she said. "One of them cried like a child." There was Virginia Holt, a former student, who had said years ago, "If I don't seduce Vridar Hunter before I die, I'm no lady." Virginia was tall and queenly, with eyes of sultry blue and a strange mirthless laugh. The only lover she had had, she said, weeping quietly, was her father. . . . There was Harriet March who affected droll wit and talked French. "Quelque prix qu'il en puisse coûter?" And as Vridar went from one to another, he knew that he was releasing himself from his old psychic impotence of fear, but he was aware too that something remained. And one night at a party he met Jean Standish.

He was sitting back in shadow, watching a dozen men and women make a caricature of passion, when he saw a girl looking at him with a veiled and attentive stare. She had black hair, and eyes of a lustrous and inscrutable brown, and an impudent mouth. He felt a sudden shock of recognition but he had never seen this girl before. He turned away, wondering about her, and then he went over and sat near her.

"Let's dance," he said. They danced. "You remind me of someone," he said. "I can't imagine whom."

"Do I?"

"What is your name?"

"Jean Standish."

"Mormon?"

"No. I'm from Arizona."

"Here alone?"

"Yes."

"Let's go."

They went to her home and sat in her parlor and Vridar looked at her. He was profoundly moved and he was trying to understand why. The smell of her hair and clothes, her

way of looking at him, of using her hands—all these he had
known before. She was betrothed to a man in California
whom she did not like. She was twenty-four.

Vridar rose to his feet, feeling very absurd, and moved
around the room. What, he wondered, had taken possession
of him now?—for here he was, shaking like a man in fever,
with his heart beating up in his throat. He wanted to take
this girl in his arms. He felt with annoying irrelevance that
she had been in his arms before. He wanted to kneel at her
feet and put both arms around her and talk of God alone
knew what utter nonsense. And this wish grew with the
silence and he fought against it; he said within, I must take
my hat and get out of here. . . .

"Why did you leave the party and come with me?" he
said.

"I don't know. I've been wondering why."

"Do you want to go back?"

"No."

He looked at her hair and eyes and mouth. He went over
and sat by her and took one of her hands. She moved toward
him and he kissed her and held her against him.

"What is wrong with us?" he asked, his voice annoyed.
"This is just like a silly scene out of Harry Kemp's autobiography." He stared at her and asked again: "Why are we
such fools?" She did not speak and he rose and paced the
room. "I think I should go. In fact, I know it. Do you
live alone in this place?"

"Yes," she said and took a cigarette. He went over and
held a match.

"Why don't you tell me to go?"

"I don't want you to go."

Her eyes, her way of speaking, were something darkly
and deeply out of his past. He wanted to laugh but he could
not even smile. He sank to a chair and stared like a woe-
begone oaf at his hands; and when he looked up after a long

moment Jean was gazing at him with eyes that sent something wild and unreasoned through his blood.

"Are you married?" she asked.

He hesitated. "Yes," he said.

"I was afraid you would be."

"Are you ready to go East?" Ferd asked one morning.

"No."

"No? Damn it, you look pretty queer to me."

"I feel queer."

"Are you falling in love with Jean?"

"God knows."

Vridar spent his days and his evenings and now and then his nights with Jean Standish. He struggled with tireless patience to understand this mad and heartbreaking infatuation for a strange woman. Nor was the infatuation his alone. They ate together and walked into the country or up the canyons to the east.

"Let's go," Jean would say, "before we wake up. Darling, let's go to the other side of the earth."

"No. That would be silly."

"But we love."

"We're just out of our wits."

"We loved from the first. We needn't try to understand it. These things don't fit into words."

"Nor into reason. We are two fools, Jean. How long would we go on this way?"

"Forever."

"I know better than that."

They were walking down a street and she stopped by a jeweler's window. "Darling, look: all the rings. But I suppose I'll never wear a wedding ring now. You'll leave me and I'll never marry."

"That's more nonsense."

"Do you love your wife?"

"Of course I love my wife."

"And me too. Darling, you should have been a Mormon."

"Let's not talk about it."

And one morning in Jean's apartment Vridar was washing her hair. He made a suds, wondering all the while about himself: summarizing himself as the most incurable dolt in the world; wishing he had never come West. He let her hair down and Jean reached up and drew his head to her and kissed his mouth. "Darling, I'm going to love to have you wash my hair." He took her hair in his hands and shook it loose and it fell in a great blackness down her back. In this moment something struck into him like a knife. He stepped back and looked at her hair; and wonder and revelation gathered to the moment; and then the whole meaning came to him like a blow. He cried aloud and went to a chair and fell upon it and clutched his face in his hands.

And twenty-four hours later, still amazed, he sat by a coach window and stared at the desolation of Wyoming. He was remembering Jean as he had seen her last in the station: a brave girl who looked up at him and smiled and said, "I knew it couldn't last. Darling, I knew. Sometime, before you have forgotten, write and tell me what it all meant for both of us. . . ." Of what it had meant for him he was thinking now. He was still thinking of it when he sat with Athene in their apartment in New York and poured a cocktail and lit a cigarette.

"Well," he said, "I've seen my way through the biggest emotional jam of my life. The girls and their names, and what we said and did, are of no importance now. At first the impotence held me. I smashed it little by little and hour by hour. I have cleaned out of me my shameful guiltiness about sex: what my terrible early years did to me in that respect I have undone.

"Well, I had to do it. You know that. I couldn't conquer shame by thinking about it. I had to do something. It did no good to tell myself that what I did in adolescence nearly everyone has done. You can't change a fixed emotional attitude by thinking about it. It is silly to do nothing but think about it. People go crazy doing that." Vridar glanced at her luminous wet eyes. He shrugged. "The portrait of the artist as a young man," he said. "Well, you think I am making excuses. You think I'm dodging as I used to."

"I don't know," Athene said.

"I'm not. It was my problem and I had to face it. Damned if I'll go on forever, dogged by shame and fear. And to hell with what anyone says about me. I'm going to be honest with myself. Shame is the bastard of all emotions and I'm going to root it out of me. That's why I did what I did. Well, don't you think I should?—conquer shame, I mean?"

"Yes," Athene said.

"All right. And listen, my dear. As long as my attitude toward women is shamed, impotent, I can't be decent toward you. That's the way I see it. There can't be any decent love between us until my love transcends the tyranny of physical possession. That tyranny grows out of feelings of inferiority and shame, guilt and fear. Fear of women, shame for what I did years ago. I'm sick of it. Great God, I won't be a jealous idiot all my life! I was false to her by being what the world would call faithful. I'm going to be faithful to you, and to do that, I must first be what the world would call false. That's the way I saw it. I remember your statement that when there is no jealousy there is also little intensity: you're right. But jealousy with me has been an absurd extreme. I've broken it. I've broken that damned absurd impotence which is one of the curses of modern life. The world is so stupid in this respect that it regards fidelity in love as the absence of physical contact. It's all right for these husbands and wives to have their erotic fancies, wishes, dreams; but they must stay out of other beds. On the one hand you have the puritans with their minds full of smut. On the other you have these sophisticated people who fornicate around with a passionless smirking zeal that is ghastly to think of.

"Well, there's the story. I may be an ass but I don't lie to my wife."

"I wouldn't live with you if you did."

"Oh, I could be a clever liar. My dear, I could be one of the slickest liars on earth. But my kind of vanity won't tolerate lying."

"Vridar, you haven't told me everything yet."

"I know. Well, the rest of it is a story of evasion." He smoked his cigarette and looked at her. "I met a woman," he said. "Let's call her Mary. I became infatuated with her. The spirit of irony left me, all detachment, all reason, and I was a fool again. I was with her day and night. I was mad. And one morning—I was washing her hair—thinking of myself, her, you—and wondering. Then, suddenly, it came to me. I saw what I was doing. This girl, this Mary, was a substitute——"

"For Neloa?"

"Yes." He went over and sat at her feet. She laid hands on his hair. "Athene, I've been weak——"

"And strong. You could not face yourself in all these matters without great strength."

"And you knew? You've known all these years that I was still seeking—her?"

"Yes, I've known. I've been a kind of mother to five years of grief."

"But in Baltimore I said I'd fight out of it. Never for a minute, I think, have I ceased to fight."

"And I have been waiting."

"I know. And with what patience. The world would not understand that."

"The world would say I'm very stupid."

"Athene, Mertyl is right: Freud's theories are absurdly narrow. Mertyl is right in this: nearly every sensitive and imaginative person today established in childhood an ego-identification with sex. That was my trouble, yours, and practically of all the persons we know. That's why the world is madly preoccupied with sex today. It's not a matter of incestuous wishes: that's only a small aspect of it. It's hardly even a matter of complexes.

"Darling, take me. When a child I was driven to *think* of sex a thousand times more than any child should ever think of it. I came to think of myself as sexually inadequate. See? So then what? Why, like so many, I came to feel deeply that I could prove my manhood, my self-respect, only by seducing a lot of women. I buried that wish: it outraged my self-esteem. And there was my struggle. There is the struggle of millions. Now I'm no longer burying it. Now I see that sex became for me a symbol of monstrous importance. And Freud, in arguing that the drive is incestuous, is off the track: incest is only an aspect of it. The drive is simply that shame which forces children to think of their bodies and to make of sex the chief ego-symbol of their young lives.

"And what is the cure? Mertyl, I think, is right again. Make the sex-obsessed person *think* sex, *act* sex, until he breaks that morbid fixation on it. Then, with his energy released, his mind freed, he can live a decent life. If he doesn't break it, he will become a censor or a crusader or a writer of weird sublimations—such as the ordinary popular love story; or he'll be an inveterate reader of love stories: some sort of awful fraud. Well, I've dragged the whole thing out into the open and I'm looking at it and breaking it. For it is slavery, this obsessive preoccupation with sex which is the most striking thing about the Christian world.

"Athene, shall we be married?"

"Well," said Athene, turning uneasily, "if——"

"If I don't mind? It doesn't matter. Marriage means nothing to me. But if you think you'll feel better about it——"

"It might save me some persecutions."

"All right. Let's do it now."

VI

●

HAVING caught himself in another evasion, Vridar wondered in how many other matters he was still self-deceived. "I'm destroying old habits," he said, "but am I getting fixed in new ones?" Ferd declared he was. Some of Vridar's habits, he said, were taking on the holiness of ritual. One was his patient brushing and massaging of his thinning hair. Ever since Neloa's death he had been going bald and a little gray and these signs of age and decrepitude worried him. Into his dying scalp he had rubbed a half-dozen remedies; he had bought a headgear and had sat patiently under its burning rays; and he had explored into the literature on baldness. Dr. Sabouraud, having found only one bald eunuch in a hundred and forty-seven, related baldness to sexual precocity.

"Where," Vridar asked of Ferd, "does that let you off?"

"Never mind me. Your Sabouraud guy is probably bald himself. He has worked out a theory that flatters himself."

Dr. Muller declared *soul emotion* to be the cause. Nessler believed in hair migration.

"And there may be some truth in that. Every time I lose a handful on my skull I get a single solitary sprout on my chest."

"How many do you have now?"

"Nine and a seedling. But I had none until I started to go bald."

Engelbach related baldness to the endocrine glands, Goodman to nervous shock, McLeod to the wearing of hats, and Nagler said it began in childhood.

"McLeod," Vridar said, "must be loved by the hat manufacturers."

He also investigated hair preparations. There were, he learned, several hundred cures and tonics on the market.

Lucky Tiger, favorite of all, had arsenic in it, but was advertised, nevertheless, in a thousand newspapers, and barbers bought it by the barrel. And there were hundreds of shops that devoted themselves to the bald head, male and female, and his vanity led him one day into a glittering establishment. He saw so many men here with hairless heads and the guilty manner of schoolboys, and so many lovely girls hired to massage their skulls, that he looked in amazement and went away. "To hell with hair," he said to Athene. "I can't be bothered. Eventually the whole human race will be bald and æsthetes will look back in astonishment to that time when hair on a skull was regarded as a thing of beauty. . . ."

Vridar also pottered around with his bridge plate of four false teeth. From time to time the plate hurt his gum and he would tinker with it, using whatever tools he could find. Ferd came upon him one morning when he was engrossed and busy: he had a file, a hammer and chisel, and a pair of pliers. He was filing and twisting and shaping; and Ferd, after watching him a moment, stretched out in a chair and howled with joy.

"Have your fun," Vridar said, grinning at him. "It won't be so damned funny when those chunks of bone in your mouth begin to loosen and drop out. Shall I tell you something that will make you happy?"

"Do—if you can make me any happier than I am now."

"I went to dinner the other night with Denham. He's a critic, you know, who was one of my professors in Chicago. He brought a girl with him and we had a great spread in a snooty place on Forty-fourth Street. And right in the middle of the dinner, when I was chewing bravely on a succulent chunk of something, Denham asked me a question and I could only sit there as if I'd been hit on the head. For this damned piece of bridgework had got stuck in my food and lifted out of place. I couldn't get it back in place and I couldn't speak. Don't tell me I should have swallowed it. Denham must have thought I was an awful fool."

Ferd got to his feet, bursting with joy.

"Well, what did you do?"

"Oh, I fetched a big napkin up to my face and got the hunk of teeth into it and slyly freighted it to my pocket."

"And you sat there eating with your teeth in your pocket?"

"With four of them certainly."

"And did you ever answer the question?"

"Hell no. I just acted pretty silly. Could I have said five minutes later, I'm ready to answer your question now? Denham's attitude changed toward me then and there. He wanted to get away. I guess he thought I was rude: we never know, my friend, what lies behind so many matters in life. Wars have been started over such misunderstood trifles as a man's teeth out of place. But his eagerness to get away might have been a sudden erotic interest in his girl. I hoped it was that. . . ."

And Ferd also whooped with glee over Vridar's experimenting with foods. "When," Vridar said, "is concern about health neurotic, when is unconcern stupid? I don't know. I do know that I see constipated people everywhere I look."

"Very well," said Ferd. "But when I'm buried my body won't be full of psyllium seed."

Habits, it seemed to Vridar, were the most inexorable enemy of human thought and growth. What habits, he asked, am I forming now?—and he searched himself for the fixed attitude, the inflexible rule. It seemed to him that he was falling into the week-end ritual of the gin party.

He had seen many persons drunk and drunkenness had taught him many things. He had learned that pious persons who, when sober, detested profanity, often cursed, when drunk, everything under the sun. He had learned that persons who, ashamed of sex, grew indignant over nakedness or frank books or unmarried love, became, when drunk, starved animals who wooed with frantic ardor anything that looked like a woman or a man. He had learned enough to fill volumes and formerly he had often been astonished but nothing that human beings did or had power to do astonished him now. He was glad for drunkenness, too, because instead of putting him in disgust with himself or others it had led him to a fuller and franker fellowship. In a few cases, and superficially in many, drunkenness was a tyrant and not an instrument; but in most cases it was only an attempt to break out of the prison built by shame. Now and then a person, not having learned that drunkenness was catharsis, debauched himself repeatedly and blunted his senses and his awareness: he missed in it the spiritual values and the underground road to emotional health. And now and then one, ashamed of his excesses, tried to urge others to drink. It was these persons who annoyed Athene. "They want me to get drunk," she said, "to see if I won't let some fellow seduce me. The motive there is their own sense of shame. . . ."

And Vridar saw that, with exceptions, drunkenness was, in plain fact, quite the most wholesome thing in the neurotic and morbid civilization around him. Under the calm surface from coast to coast, this country of his was a seething neurotic mass and out of its buried and distorted life sprang cults and charlatans and pious frauds. Sensitive and intelligent persons knew that something was tragically wrong with them: they resented the suffocating clutch of scruples and precepts and all the negative taboos laid against their heritage and its fulfillment. It was not, as simpletons believed, that they wished to debauch themselves: on the contrary, they wished to achieve catharsis at any cost and to become clean again. And so they rose in secret and underground revolt, undirected and lost to darkness, with no leaders of courage and vision to stand forth and say, These people are all right and all this debauchery under Prohibition is nothing but their protest against an assumption of their degradation. You have here a nation being crucified by the negative and shameful doctrines of sexual cowards and the nation is in revolt. A few of these persons, wiser than the others, are using gin as an instrument of catharsis; the rest of them, unable to understand what they seek, are being driven deeper into shame. . . .

And this vast phenomenon of a nation driven into cellars and urged to feel vicious made Vridar smile. Now and then the blundering cowardice of it filled him with wrath. He had been called a pessimist and a cynic, but he had more faith in humanity, it seemed to him, than was to be found in any moralist anywhere. To hell with all these prohibitions and decalogues and laws: he would take them away and give human beings a chance to be decent. This conviction under which his nation rested—that it was depraved and vicious—was a monstrous lie. Two-by-four saints, ashamed to think of their bodies, ashamed of love, were legislating the country into complete negativism.

"How long," he asked Athene, "must we be governed by these repressed cowards who try to legislate us into heaven? How long before we shall learn that our lawmakers are the most distorted persons among us? Now we have a negative attitude toward love and joy. Now all our laws are don'ts, all our religions, and practically all our culture. What we need today is some great affirmations. But look: a man can't woo a woman without feeling guilty about it. He acts like a fool and looks like a fool. We can't reach to the profound wonder of sexual rapture without feeling that God has fixed His face in a puritan scowl. We are no longer decent in anything. We can't even try a man for murder without making a national vulgarism of the trial. If the man is found guilty, editors profess a deep and sadistic pleasure, too stupid to realize that their pleasure is orgiastic. We can't read advertisements without reading perjury. We can't listen to the radio without hearing the insincere and ingratiating whine of some bought hireling.

"Darling, the only obscenity, I see now, and the only way we can profane life, is to be afraid of joy. Give us some affirmations that will fill the sky. Give us a sense of joy that will sing instead of being an incestuous crooning. Great God, why can't we laugh and be decent and unafraid! . . ."

And it was with deep gratitude for what gin had done for him and for many of his friends that Vridar sat in these parties and saw the pious pretense go momentarily to its death. Not all of these persons were making of alcohol an instrument of courage and strength. Not all of them would fight out of their distortions: two of them, he believed, would go insane—and they did. Others would struggle to slough their vicious training but would yield at last to the pose of the humanist or the æsthete or would withdraw into the sick mysticism of the Church. Others, more determined, would rise in one triumphant alcoholic hour and another, feeling with increasing certainty their stature, their depth, and that buried integrity of character and fellowship which prohibitions had not destroyed. These, in looking back, would see in gin parties the final throes of adolescence, the last desperate effort to be reasonable and clean. They would realize, too, that the country of their birth and home was a nation of adolescents, self-deceived and self-betrayed, and lost in the stern and sterile attitudes of cowardice and shame. Instead of fighting all this from the inside, or withdrawing into a monastic cult, they would rise above and beyond it and see in clearer perspective out of what it had come. Out of this vision of understanding and sympathy, and out of this alone, could a new leadership be forged and a new path taken. . . .

But this lay in the future. In the present hour there was no sign of leadership: there was only increasing confusion and a sick effort to save a sick culture. And Vridar watched with growing sympathy and interest the tragic betrayal of his nation and his age.

VII

●

THEY were in the apartment of Mae Dwon. Mae was a
large woman with a large strong face and small hungry
eyes that were almost green. She was a hack who wrote and
sold Christmas greetings, limericks, paragraphs for philate-
lists, and true-confession stories. On one side of the desk
where she wrote was a photograph of Anthony Comstock,
on the other a photograph of Voltaire. "I adore," she said,
"the ironic juxtapositions. And allow me to present Miss
Jane Rinks."

A tall thin girl blushed.

"How are you?" she asked in a timid quaver. She gave
a strange upward jerk to her yellow head.

"Jane," said Mae, "has just come to the big-big city.
And sit down, my dear. You look a hell of a lot better sitting down."

Jane flushed. There was anger in the pale blue eyes that
looked at Mae; there was hatred in the way she caught her
breath. She sank to a chair and her lean hands were busy
with nothing in her lap.

Mae fetched tall green glasses. "I call this Hoover cocktail," she said. "It's a noble experiment. . . . Like it?"

"It's not bad."

"It has inspired thirty-six Christmas greetings, two
stories on furnishing a kitchen, three on wallpaper for bedrooms, six Easter carols, eleven doll tales, and a limerick.
Forgive Jane: she doesn't drink. But deep in her virgin heart
she loves Cain because he was more able." Jane stared at
her fingers. They were long and bony and had white nails.
"I've imagined Jane in six different amorous situations,"
Mae went on, "and I've sold every one of them. . . . Wait,
genius is poking me."

Mae ran to her machine to type. Vridar sipped his cock-

tail and watched her. Like Moses McGuire, she was lost in
the bog of psychology, referring to it all her longings and
dreams. Before her everywhere went a derisive finger. And
this Jane, at whom he looked next, was a timid shadow of
a woman: too unlovely for love, too frigidly thin for passion,
she would build her life into romantic reverie within a structure of shame. . . .

"Well, read it."

> "There is a young virgin named Rinks,
>   And she thinks and she thinks and she thinks;
>   And all that she knows
>   Is the desert that blows
> Its sand in the face of the Sphinx."

"Very fine," Vridar said, "but also very unpitying."

"That," said Mae, "is the story of my life. I could add a
comma, an exclamation, an adverb. But that's the big tale.
You know Housman's line? We lay hands on our hearts
when we think. That's me. Mechanism has reduced my soul
to protoplasm. And what behaviorism has made of my mind
I refuse to tell. Once upon a time—but really, I presume."

"Go on."

"Once upon a time I was going to be a social service
worker. My body: it did not make men think of love. No
Leander ever swam a Hellespont to look for me. And the
only man—he's a Jew, and when he looks at me I feel as
naked as a peeled banana. There! I fell flat on a phallic
symbol: my unconscious mind does trip me up. But to the
devil with it. Tell me: is your book selling?"

"It didn't sell."

"Well, you have, my dear, a gift of yearnings and de-
spairs too greatly noble for this iron age. As one besides
Huxley might tell you. But I write better stuff than any-

thing you've heard. Nobody knows it. And I doubt it. May I read something?"

"Of course."

"Strain your mind, Jane dear. This is not a Sunday-school maxim.

> *"For people grow and shut the door*
> *That opened on the Hebrides,*
> *And like strange aliens from the seas*
> *Their youth and hope are washed ashore.*
>
> *They get urbanity with doubt;*
> *They mellow—which may mean that sand*
> *Has filled the footprints down the strand*
> *Where youthful feet once ventured out.*
>
> *And these with glory in arrears*
> *May smile at those who dare the waves,*
> *And meditate upon their graves*
> *While wisdom murmurs in their ears.*
>
> *Ah, they have wise sepulchral airs:*
> *They say, Grow old along with me:*
> *These phantoms marching to the sea*
> *Who scatter proverbs in their prayers."*

"It's swell," Vridar said. "Isn't it, Athene?"

"It's a nice epigram."

"I wanted the last two lines to summarize—well, these wise head-nodding old people: elles ne comprenaient guère ce qu'on disait!"

Others came now: the Orcutts, Ferd and his wife Milli-cent, Mertyl and his wife, Mac, Larry Hopkins, and Wanda Jewett. They marched in and filled the room and in a few

moments they were all dropping witticisms over their cocktails. Vridar sat back in a corner with Athene and studied
them. All of these persons, like himself, like persons everywhere, wanted to strut upon the stage and excite admiration
and envy. Each had his act, or several little acts, that
fetched applause. Carlyle had two acts and both were very
amusing: he could walk like a lifeless automaton of wood or
he could affect most horrifying idiocy. Larry Hopkins, with
a doctor's degree in psychology, was the most obtuse person
Vridar had ever known. The formulas in textbooks he knew
by heart but of psychology he knew nothing at all. It was
a custom of his to get a room overlooking an apartment in
which girls lived and to spy on them with glasses. Now and
then he went into a kind of trance and fell out of his chair.
Larry at thirty-three was a virgin and his stock-in-trade was
sexual vulgarities. He laughed a great deal: a humorless
stifled giggling that flushed his fat round face.

Elsa sneezed. If in the same evening she sneezed twice,
Carlyle had to kiss her hand. She waited now, her face
puckered, and another sneeze came. She thrust her hand
out.

"Here, dearie, kiss my hand."

"Kiss your own hand. You're closer to it."

"Oh, you beast. Aren't you going to kiss your darling's
hand?"

Carlyle wrinkled his nose and looked at her with charming derision. He went over and kicked her shin.

"You old bitch," he said. "I'll hit you so damned hard
you won't know whether you're a wife or a concubine."

"You're a brute," said Elsa. "Dearie, I sneezed twice.
They were big loud sneezes. Here now, kiss your lady's
hand."

Carlyle looked around him, wrinkling his nose and pretending to be in disgust. He bowed to her hand and kissed
it. "The old bitch," he said, gesturing with his cigarette.
"I've nearly worn her hand out. Hey!" he cried, and

he thumped her on her skull. "You sneeze too damned much. . . ."

Wanda Jewett was singing.

> *"My father sells snow to the snowbirds,*
> *My mother makes synthetic gin;*
> *My sister makes love for a living:*
> *My Gawd, how the money rolls in. . . ."*

Wanda had a lovely doll-like face and shrewd eyes. She was by her own confession one "of the ineradicable virgins." One evening she had asked: "Don't men get a complex on blood or something? I can't stand the thought." Like Larry, like most of the persons here, Wanda loved what an American poet had called smubtleties. When listening to tales of love, she seemed to withdraw into an eager virginal guiltiness. Her eyes shone, and in the rise and fall of her bosom Vridar observed her deep and excited interest. . . .

Another person now entered. Vridar had heard of Telv Ethlec but had never seen him before. He was now introduced to a man in his late twenties: Irish obviously: a mop of black hair, dark unhappy eyes, and a thin sensitive mouth. . . . Telv was now talking with Mae. He was excited. His words were ringing.

"You say these men like Frank Hill who hate this dirty industrial age are exceptions. All right. It's the exceptions among men who make history. You don't think——"

"But I don't give a damn about history. Telv, you're out of tune."

"That's another middle-class sophistry. Jesus was out of tune——"

"Oh, to hell with Jesus!"

"Progress has been a matter of getting out of tune——"

"And to hell with progress. You're an insufferable egoist. You have no tolerance——"

"Tolerance," said Telv, "has never found a chronicler. You're a coward, Mae. Once you'd rather be a pagan suckled in a creed outworn. Now it's Okay, America! All you Judases kissing your Christ for a piece of silver. . . ."

Vridar turned to Athene. She was smiling at the clowning of Ferd and Carlyle.

"Athene."

"Yes?"

"You remember X? He's over there declaiming. Listen."

"You make me sick!" Mae was crying. "Honest to Cotton Mather, you do. You make me feel as if I'd eaten beetles. Why don't you become a minister and spread your gospel from a pulpit?"

Telv shrugged. "You meet argument with wisecracks. The truth plows you up."

"It's not the way I want to be plowed."

"Or you meet argument with vulgarity. You're middle class: fat, vulgar, greedy, and stupid."

Mae went to him, dimpling. "Kiss me, prophet."

"You're a fool."

Telv was looking at her. Vridar could not see his eyes now but he saw him shrug and reach for a cocktail. And he thought of the cautious little spider, advancing to love and trembling with fear; and of his ravenous lover who sometimes ate him before the caress was done; and of scarabs and geotrupes, mating and murdering. Among all carnivora, sex was largely a matter of insult and slaughter. He could see the fury in Mae's eyes. He smiled and thought of carabes, digging up slugs and boiling the luckless creatures in saliva; of the sphex wasp, burrowing in the viscera of crickets and eating them alive; of the Alpine analote, coupling with a male sprawled on his back and at the same time eating from the torn belly of another male, held in her claws. Of human morality Fabre must have had curious thoughts: the male mantis, emptied of blood by his polyandrous ogress and eaten limb by limb. In human mating there were weird intimations of the lowlier customs; for love-making, when natural, was a rather savage prelude; and a man in mating felt a wish to destroy, a woman to be destroyed. . . .

"Do you recognize X?"

"Yes."

"He wants to love Mae but is afraid. His fear he calls ideals. Funny, isn't it?"

"Pathetic, I'd say."

Mac was now telling of a group of New Yorkers with whom he had spent an evening.

"She said, Do you accept Adler or Jung or Freud? Another said, Have I Korssakow's psychosis? Another, Have I fantastic melancholia, fragmentation of psyche, imbalance of personality, or clonic spasm? This Ethlec guy," he said, swinging, "has gynophobia. And Choy Rolfe, do you know her?"

"No," said Mae. "Of course we don't."

"You should. A legacy has allowed her to indulge her taste in disease. She's had everything. She had astraphobia, but when it was explained to her that all animals fear thunder and lightning, she threw that away and got another. She developed a vendetta mania. She wrote abusive letters to famous simpletons and nearly died of fury when no answers came. Then she stumbled into nymphomania. In the Metropolitan she suddenly laid hold of a marble man and almost jerked him off his roost. And thus she goes, staggering through to a tombstone. She breathes implications. She sleeps with an armful of postulates. She yawns guesses at the infinite. Hunter, have you read Krutch's *Modern Temper?*"

"Yes."

"Is love in as bad a mess as he says it is? What's the matter with that guy?" He turned to Mertyl. "Is there any formula in your assortment that fits him?"

"I have a dozen that fit you like a glove."

"Yeah?" He squared off and leered at Mertyl. "Listen

while I summarize all you know." Mac drew his lean cheeks
down until dewlaps lay under his jaws and his mouth was a
straight and merciless line. Everyone in the room looked at
him, aware that Moses McGuire was getting ready for one
of his mightiest gestures. He looked around him with narrowed eyes. "I shall now give you," he said, "a summary
of civilized life. Life for you, for me, for all the obscene
apes who dream and fornicate, is an anarchy of diminutives,
obsessed by haste; meaningless scintilla spun into philosophic
motes; mannikins of etiquette, measuring the proper yard-
age of gesture; rags of goaded sound; tumultuous iotas of
the senseless, dragged out of incoherence and fenced around
with a syllogism; the shavings of delusion and lunacy;
labyrinths of nervous fidgetings, asylums of errata and corri-
genda, blots and flaws; encyclopedias of misprint, visions
scuttling to the minims of phantasmic goals; myopia and
cataract, lippitude from squinting through lenses; morals
herded on a delirious sea of mumpsimus; the agonized mi-
nutiæ of aimless journeying, the windfalls of scientific muttering, the snarls and tabloids of gutted destinies; love
ravished by logic and fables glowing in the stone towers;
words with fat bellies piled upon the tedium of sermon
and prayer; the dust of precepts on pulpit and nave, and
the lonely temple with its ceramic Christ. And more: ideals
harelipped and clubfooted and hunchbacked, the smug fatu-
ities of mitred precisians, and love, licensed to breed. There
you have all that Krutch tried to say and all that historians
of the future will ever be able to say of our age. There you
have humanity whittled down to its size. Let the little fat
wise boys have their smug intellectual dimples. Let the
lean and erotic and cynical boys whore around with theories
instead of women. Let the old maids murmur in virginal
terror that light is light and sweetness is sweet. They
merely heap vulgarities upon an already vulgar life."

Mac stopped and shrugged and reached for his glass. Mae
rose and went to the kitchen and Larry Hopkins was quick

to follow her. Vridar went, too. Mae was squeezing a
lemon. Larry stood by her, fat and patiently amorous.

"That son-of-a-bitch," he said. "That Mac McGuire.
He's the stupidest man I ever saw."

"Oh, darling," said Mae. "You have a mind like the inside of a cantaloupe."

VIII

●

THEY were at Mertyl's apartment. To Mertyl's parties came what Ferd declared to be the most gorgeous assortment of freaks on earth and when around them he was as happy as a boy at a circus. But they saddened Vridar. He watched them and thought of his own dark life, and of the tragic wastelands out of which these persons had come.

On the davenport sat a man named James Shard. He strummed a banjo and crooned in doleful falsetto to the mistress at his side. Shard had spent four years in an asylum and had twice tried to kill himself: the last time he drank poison in Central Park but he drank so much that he vomited. For three months he lay in a hospital. But no one seeing this man now or meeting him on the street would have supposed that his days were haunted, his nights an agony of horror and sweat. He looked cadaverous but he seemed wholly at ease.

Across the room from him sat Tony Scarvelli, small and timid. Tony was a druggist and none of his patrons ever suspected what a nightmare his life was. This man was so terrified that he never dared enter a street alone. Sight of a train threw him into a convulsion. He hired a psychiatrist to ride with him to and from his store. But when in a group of friends, as now, he laughed and sang and seemed as happy as a child.

By a window, between James and Tony, sat Shelley Ames. Shelley was a beautiful girl who had had two lovers, both of whom left her; and now she brooded in melancholy and despised herself. "Men don't find me attractive," she had said to Vridar and had smiled her bitter smile. At these parties Shelley sat in strange deep quiet, her lovely face turned away; or now and then she burst into song.

Oh, I like the land of Nieber and I like the land of Nar,
But I love the way the men love in the land of Nicobar. . . .

Not far from Shelley was Kenneth Chadwick, holding his
cocktail to the light. He had lunched with Chaplin, played
golf with Greta Garbo; vagabonded with Jim Tully and
hunted edentates in Bolivia; counted the canephoræ in the
Florentine friezes and thrown a fragment of the wall of
Jericho into the Dead Sea. He knew Montparnasse from
stem to gudgeon. For forty-eight hours he had sat in a
Chinese cangue.

"You're the most indefatigable liar," Mac said, "from
here to Washington, D. C. There aren't any Florentine
friezes. There never was a wall around Jericho. You've been
reading Halliburton."

Thereafter, when Kenneth spoke, he looked around to
learn if Mac could hear. Kenneth, like James and Tony and
Shelley, had been a patient of a famous New York psychiatrist. He was a tall handsome man but he was impotent.
"All women adore me," he said, and pursued them furiously.

Bors Emmet was a painter.

"Have you any hands?" Mac asked him gravely.

"Of course I have hands."

"Then why don't you use them? Your stuff looks to me
as if you paint with your toes."

Bors had his room hung with photographs of imbeciles,
most of them reproduced from Tredgold. Great art, he said,
no matter in what form, should recapitulate the entire past
in its representation of the present. A painting of a man
which did not suggest behind the wakeful intelligence the
eons of savagism out of which he had come and which still
made ninety-nine per cent of what he still was and of what
for a long time to come he would still be was false art. "It
is the same in fiction," he said to Vridar. "These novelists
who portray man as if he were an intelligent and godlike
animal are stupid. Most of your literary artists write as if

they were unaware of more than the last two thousand years. No wonder their stuff is superficial and silly. . . ."

Mac was turning the pages of a book. He was announcing with scornful emphasis that Swift and Baudelaire and Rousseau and Gogol and Hoffmann and Schopenhauer and Nietzsche and Tasso and Eichhorn and Palestrina and Benda and Dussek were all insane. "And Montanus, there's as queer an ape as ever lost his wits. He thought he was a grain of wheat and he wouldn't budge for fear a bird would swallow him. A canary chased him into a trunk. . . ."

And James Shard in a lost nasal voice was reading from a book called *New Backgrounds for a New Age*. "Is there not something a little tragic here? Has not something beautiful disappeared with the passing of the sweet pretenses of yesterday's adolescence? My God," said James, looking around him, "I'll say there has!" James read and Mac talked and Vridar tried to listen to both. "These young people are blinded and wearied by a maze of rules and data. . . ."

"Lloyd ate sawdust for the same reason that people eat yeast today. Is it true, as Hergesheimer has said, that all writers are caught somewhere between constipation and neurosis? And when they eat yeast I dare say they land in the big-circulation magazines. And there was Pierre Stamboul, half French and half Turk, whose trinity was handkerchiefs and garters and brassières. Let's see the hands of all those who don't want to hear about Stamboul. . . . What? No hands? . . ."

Shelley was shepherding her attitudes. When she looked at a man there was a swift weird light in her eyes, an awakening and a death that offered the secret of her. Telv was saying to Mae Dwon that fourteen thousand persons went from New York City in every year to psychopathic wards.

"God knows," said Mae, "how many don't go who are as crazy as loons. Subway stabbers, Brooklyn Bridge jumpers, bus exhibitionists. . . ."

And Mac, now leering at the frightened Tony, cried:

"Gather ye rosebuds while ye may, the equinox but once." Then, with grave irony, he declared himself to be an aglossolalist, lost in his cosmothoric sense of the donjon. "Does anyone here like Scriabin's vomits of cacophony?" And he swung to Telv and affronted him with a lecture on Jollos and Oczeret.

Choy Rolfe came from the bathroom. She was another patient of the famous Harrison Hawke. She now sat near Vridar and turned to talk to Shelley and Vridar listened to what she said. With pleasure, morbid and eager, she was telling of other patients: of a woman who washed her hands after touching any object, particularly her underwear or shoelaces; of a girl who dreamed persistently of being stabbed by her father; of a university student who fainted when left alone with a male instructor. . . . On and on she talked, eager to prove that the whole world was obsessed and mad.

"That's enough," said Shelley. "I'm as weary as a weeping willow now." She raised her well-bred eyebrows and looked suddenly at Bors Emmet.

Mac swung and clutched Mae's chin as if it were a doorknob. "Great stoof!" cried James Shard, and his laugh was a purring twitter. Shelley looked up with delicate amusement. Mac grasped Mae by her throat and shook her and Mae gave him a loud and burning slap on his sallow face. The blow left a red stain that slowly faded.

"This," Mac cried, "is some D. H. Lawrence heroine with murder in her glands! Hide the paper-weights!"

"Run along, boy. Your beard is too thin."

Mac struggled with her again and fell to the floor. He lay there, white and sick. "Women," he said, "seem in a fair way to destroy love by being frank about it." He rose and went to the bathroom. Mae looked round her and winked.

"He has," she said, "that hysterical function called a conscience. I'd feel sorry for him if the tabloids had not made all tragedy ridiculous."

And all this around him, Vridar was reflecting, was a shameful and bastard birth. Precepts and prohibitions swarmed in the moment. Synthesis perished in analysis. When Greece became conscious of itself it died; and Rome likewise. A flower, conscious of its calyx and stamen, ovule and pistil, and seeking endlessly to understand them, would degenerate into a weed. A lark, with its mind spying on its pæans and canticles, would soon croak like a raven. Civilization, it seemed, was a process of making life complex; and the function of art, surely, was to reduce it again to simple terms. But today there were writers who staggered across the literary landscape with their armfuls of incoherence; some wrote recitativo eulogiums to chaos; and some gave their moods to verbal electrolysis and scattered words over a page. Meanings were being isolated and stared into insignificance. Some poets of genius, having stripped their lives to the unimportant moments on which they stood, projected humanity against the infinite and invited contempt. Self-pity had turned them into adolescent cynics. Others, having no courage to face life, had fled into the Church and were busy glorifying the turgid emptiness of apostolic creeds. And still others, profoundly uneasy under the impulses of barbarism, set up as humanists and preached their negative doctrine of culture and restraint.

But intelligence, it seemed to him, was not a menace, as some declared it to be. It was not being used: that was all. The emotions overpowered it and threw it into an attitude. These persons here tonight were all richly endowed; but afraid to face themselves they were flying off at wild tangents and seeking to escape. If Choy Rolfe had power to admit, frankly and without shame, that when a child she was incestuous with her father; if this big impotent lout could only come to his senses and realize that he was seeking a woman like his mother; if Shelley would recognize the ways of love and the ways of men: if they could only be, in Mac's phrase, the brides and bridegrooms of life. . . .

And here was Mac: speaking of himself he had said: "I wear the cloth of the acolyte, I bow to rubric and beadroll; but I also lie with voluptuous bacchantes on velvet, and all my desires are Pompeiian reds. . . ."

Mae came over to Vridar. She turned to Athene. "You don't mind if I get friendly with your man?"

"Don't be silly."

"I have," said Mae, "a little effort, a small premature child. I wrote it after reading that poem of yours the other night." Vridar took her lines and read:

> *My life was sketched and paragraphed:*
> *A dozen verbs, a score of nouns*
> *For traveling from towns to towns;*
> *One adjective that laughed.*
>
> *Some adverbs that were pious, some*
> *That strained at leashes; one that leapt*
> *And vanished one day when I wept*
> *To hear a passing drum.*
>
> *Conjunctions principally: the ands*
> *And buts and ifs and the unlesses*
> *Connecting doubts and hopes and guesses*
> *And dying like my hands.*
>
> *With dreams transmuted into slang*
> *And love colloquial; with ears*
> *Still catching echoes of the years*
> *When nymphs and sirens sang!*

"You remember," she asked, "Mac's summary the other night? This is mine. Like it?"

"Yes. It's a good summary. It's not so diabolic as you usually are."

"I'm a woman, my dear. Under my thick hide I am all heat and tenderness. Well, thanks. I'm glad it isn't rotten."

"Show it to Athene."

Ferd was clowning now and when he clowned he captured more unerringly than any other person Vridar knew the simian heritage of man. With one stroke he put himself back to the level of apes and employed their facial contortions and their bright alert gestures. And while watching him Vridar thought of those times, years ago, when he had tried to realize fully his blood-record. In the last year he had gone frequently to the Bronx Zoo to study apes and their anatomy of love and he had learned much. And Bors Emmet was right in his statements about art and what, if it was to escape the Spenglerian prophecies, it must do. Art today was falling into meaningless patterns and much of it had come to be patterns and nothing else. The old romantic concepts that had once given to it a dubious and timid existence had been sucked empty; and the more shoddy and spurious it became, the more some persons talked about it, as if art were one thing and life another. There were Vridar's colleagues: poets and novelists and critics: their reverence for art filled him with astonishment and mirth. Their notion that art was superior to life, or in any way more than a selective and artificial aspect of it, could mean only that they had rejected life as vulgar and had enthroned themselves as its superficial critics. Spengler was right: such persons had abandoned themselves to the deadly emptiness of patterns and cults and codified criticism: they were the last feeble voices of an age that was dead. And while thinking of them and of the tremendous vitality of Emmet's artistic creed, Vridar wrote these lines, trying to catch both in summary and contrast:

> *He sits through afternoons of talk and tea.*
> *His prison makes a gracious overture*
> *From shallow chambers, and a cavalier*
> *Bows low upon his cracker; then the spoons*
> *Take up the converse and a kitten mews.*

He snores athwart the loges and the pews.
He curls in bed with stomach to his knees
As once he curled in crotches of the trees;
And one by one he counts the ironies. . . .

Beneath the sophistries of an afternoon
He smells the glamor of a jungle moon—
And then remembers how to hold a spoon.

He read his lines and then rolled them into a round hard ball: they were an echo of T. S. Eliot; and Eliot, he remembered, had once been on the right track. He had anticipated, however obscurely, the direction that art must take to save itself from the attenuated neurosis into which it had fallen. But humanism had lifted him by his conscience and restored him to evasions.

Mac was again wooing Mae. He was struggling with her like a boy of fourteen and making faces and epigrams; and while watching them Vridar thought of love-poetry of the past and of the present. Yesterday it had been the laughing red sweet mouth of wine but today it was

> *. . . let me make it plain:*
> *I deem this frenzy insufficient reason*
> *For conversation when we meet again.*

Yesterday it had been

> *. . . for thee all soft delight*
> *That shadowy thought can win,*
> *A bright torch, and a casement ope at night,*
> *To let the warm love in.*

And now:

> *My dear, our world is sick,*
> *For science now shapes it to the form*
> *Of soulless data, and from its waist*
> *God has withdrawn His arm. . . .*

Mac was brimming with ideas. He was going to write, he declared, a book about love. "All great lovers of the past, whether mythical or real, have been women. They have never believed, even the most superstitious of them, that love is sinful, and love has never led them to tragedy except when they have mated with soft-headed idealists like Telv Ethlec. The oppression of women, my friends and enemies, has been emotional, not economic. Hallucinated tutors, masquerading as lovers, have been trying for centuries to persuade women to exalt the pleasures of flesh into the sophistries of spiritual devotion. And too often they have not failed, as the wives of the unfortunate fools called artists could testify." He paused and looked around him with solemn relish. He noted the distress of James Shard and leered at him. He resumed. "But in spite of suicide as a shortcut back to common sense, as in the case of Shelley's wife, Rossetti's, Meredith's, and God knows how many more, women have never accepted the Christian notion that love is sin. And now, in a despairing effort to keep women in bondage and convinced that love is vile, men have risen like a pack of crack-brained hoodlums to denounce Freudianism. For no man ever gets an investment in his daughter unless he is too cowardly to love his wife, and no woman ever makes a little sweetheart of her son until her husband leaps up in spiritual agony and deserts her bed. The cynicism of modern women is nothing but disgust for the pious and blushing inefficiency of men. They feel they are unworthy if they cannot follow men in their rampant pilgrimage to the sexless gods——"

"Oh, to hell with you!" Ferd cried. "I've heard Vridar say all that a dozen times. It's true, you ridiculous caricature, but you never thought it out."

"Nor did I," said Vridar. "That's Cabell. All that's to be found in one of those magnificent books which his ungrateful countrymen can't understand."

"Cabell?" said Mac, nonplussed. He came over to Vridar,

his eyes derisive. "Hunter," he said, "you're ambitious.
Well, so was Cæsar. Cæsar wanted to conquer the world and
you want to get into Who's Who. You like a lot of company. And I've heard it rumored, Hunter, that you're going
to write an honest book. Now tell me why in hell you want
to write an honest book."

Vridar looked with amused eyes at this gaunt sardonic
student of Machiavelli.

"You couldn't understand. You'd distress me by your
effort."

"Listen, Hunter, don't try to be subtle. You're about
as subtle as a Rotarian eating beans." Mac turned to Ferd
who, drunk and theatrical, was intoning an old ballad. "See
your friend here," he said. "See the mighty rhonchus of
rhetoric! He's going to write an honest book!" Mac stared
at Vridar, affecting amazement, and then helped himself to
another glass of punch. "Why," he asked, "are you going
to be silly? Why should anyone write an honest book?"

Vridar sipped his gin and looked at Mac. "Because every
other kind has been written," he said.

Mac turned with a sardonic whoop. "Listen, you children of Gertrude Stein! Look at this object. He says an
honest book has never been written."

"And it hasn't," said Ferd, affecting rage. "Name one."

Mac put his feet far apart, his hands to his hips, and
narrowed his eyes. "Hunter, where did I ever get the idea
that you have intelligence? Now what do you mean by an
honest book? . . . Tell me. I'm humbled. I'm chastened.
I'm face to face with a titan. Lord God, how you will shake
librarians out of their chairs! Critics will jump out of windows and run down the streets with their pants off. Recon-
sider, Hunter, before you annihilate the world."

Vridar smiled; and Mac, overtaken by a moment of
friendliness, pulled a chair up and sat facing him.

"Honest," he said, "why do you make such threats? Do
you want to scare the world right out of its diaper? There

has never been an honest book: I'll grant that. But you can't write one."

"I know it. A long time will pass yet before a completely honest book is written. In an unfortunate moment of enthusiasm, I merely said I would try."

"But you shouldn't even try, damn it. You'll make people awfully unhappy. Take Mae: she wants to love me but thinks she ought to love you. She'll wear her bones out in that dilemma. Take Telv: an honest book would ruin him. He still believes in gnomes and menads and Stalin. He magnifies all his emotions into convulsions. Let him be. . . ."

Telv overheard this. He came over.

"Leave me out of your vulgar middle-class harangues!"

"I can't. You're like the atmosphere."

"You pathetic charlatan," said Telv, looking at Mac.

"Yes, and you pathetic disciple of Marx. What you miss, my fine lad, is that people are oppressed by what they are not or can't get. If you could learn that one fact you'd be a man instead of a wandering vengeance."

"You bore me," said Telv. "You ought to be a lobbyist in Washington."

"In the past, Ethlec, man pitched his glories on the sky. He rose above the small and unimportant planet on which he toured the universe. His gods were tenants of chaos. But today his elves are statistics——"

"Even a man as dull as you," said Telv, "ought to see that the masses are exploited. But you belong among those for whom an aphorism is more important than a man fighting for enough bread. You can see that the world is rotten. Is that a condition you approve?"

"No. I don't approve my nose, either, but I can't change it."

"You don't want to. You're selfish and stupid. Like Oscar Wilde you spend all your time trying to hide your cowardice in wit." Telv turned to Vridar. "This man," he said to Mac, "you esteem above all others. And this man is a communist whether he knows it or not."

"Bawds and trulls! Are you?"

"I haven't thought my way through the matter yet."

"There are only two classes," said Telv. "We have exploiters and exploited. You fellows can't sit on the fence forever."

"You're an Irish fool," said Mac. "What we need today is a hundred million Isadora Duncans. There wouldn't be any utopia builders like you. There wouldn't even be any H. L. Menckens." He looked around him. He had an audience again and when Mac had an audience he rose to great heights. Most of his aphorisms, it is true, he thought of in the loneliness of his room, and some of his speeches he memorized. He now addressed himself to Mae. "I ought to be in a synagogue or a monastery," he said. "I could larrup myself into the frigid ecstasy of a friar." And he drew his long face into a horrible caricature. "Or see me when I make love to Shelley there. I loose a flock of epigrams in her face. She yawns. I nail her hand and croon tenderly. She sighs. Listen: bawds and pimps and harlots, brothels and rape and incest, filth and corruption and vice and hate and politics: if civilization is a nice thing where did all those words come from? Ponder that in your slow meditative ways. To hell with Telv Ethlec and his I'm-Jesus complex. I'm going to applaud Al Jolson, glorifier of the Edipus myth; Henry Ford, patron saint of iron and tin; and all the other intellectual giants who have made *okay America* another shot that has been heard around the world."

"I invite your attention to the group here tonight. There is Bors Emmet: he eats a huge meal and grunts like a cherub while he meditates on the prognathous jaw. There's Telv Ethlec: God must yank His beard when he looks at him. There's Mae Dwon who aches about Celtic sensitivity in a Nordic world. There's James Shard who sits in mournful idiocy and asks if she will love him in

December as she does in May. There's Mertyl Hunter with
a head so full of psychological jargon that he blows Freud
all over the room when he sneezes. There's his brother, a
gargantuan imbecile who fancies himself as a bald ape writing an honest book. There's Ferd who totes around the
notion of himself as a Spanish don in the back yards of
Seville. If you idiots don't understand me, raise your hand."

Shelley raised her hand.

"Yes, dear Shelley?"

"And what, pray, are you?"

"I'm the hermaphroditic son of Eros and John Calvin.
And now, with your permission, I shall resume. A pedant
—this is for you, Professor Thomas—is a man abandoned
by intellectual curiosity to honorary degrees. Civilization—
this is for you, Shelley darling—is the putting on of clothes
so we can be ashamed of love and make it more alluring.
And love—this, Mae, is for you—is finding a babe's mouth
where the lover's used to be." Mac paused, and out of his
eyes looked the diabolic loathing of his mind.

"My dear doctor," he said, addressing Mertyl, "I've had
dreams. Interpret this one. I was sitting in a room paneled
with mirrors and lovely naked women entered and at the
far end sat an insolent monster, declaiming from a book.
As the women passed me one by one I saw that their thighs
were scaled like the side of a fish and that their eyes were
small and black. I touched their flesh and found it cold.
I pursued them and they swam in the air, smelling of seaweed, and vanished into cannon barrels." He turned to
Vridar. "I'm going over," he said, "and sit at your brother's
feet and suck the long and homely teat of wisdom. But
first, here's an epitaph I did for you:

> "Stranger, underneath your feet
> Lies a novelist, long since rotten.
> His books none now remembers: sweet
> The grass grows on a thing forgotten!"

IX

●

VRIDAR was at the apartment of Harrison Hawke, a
well-known psychiatrist. Hawke was a small dark man
with a loose sensual mouth and restless black eyes. He had
an uptown office and made a lot of money and seduced a
lot of women. He seduced all his female patients whom he
found pleasing, as well as the wives of all his friends: a cunning and capable and unscrupulous man whom most women
found irresistible. In another apartment, far out in Brooklyn, he had a wife and two children. This apartment in
Manhattan was his rendezvous. Vridar came here now and
then to study the man and to talk with him, or to reflect
on psychiatrists and their power over human destinies. Not
all psychiatrists were like this unconscionable philanderer
but many of them were; and once they got neurotic persons
in their power the luckless creatures were theirs to do with
as they pleased.

In this evening he found Hawke playing poker with a
man named Norman Mall, and with two women, a Miss
Arnstein and a Mrs. Jode. Miss Arnstein was a fat and
voluptuous Jewess with a growth of fine dark hair on her
upper lip. Mrs. Jode seemed to be an adventuress whose
obtuse husband had driven her to seek spiritual aid. Mall
was a graduate student in a university here. When Vridar
entered they were talking of scholarship. Hawke said he
believed in scholarship.

"But I don't," said Miss Arnstein. "It made me feel
stuffed."

"I've seen stuffed women before. Perhaps you mixed
love and learning."

"In Europe," said Mrs. Jode, "love doesn't pick up these
distressing increments. The women dance. The dance of
death, isn't it?"

271

"What an unexpurgated mind you have," said Hawke, smiling at her. "Did you ever have a mother?"

"Of course." They all laughed.

"Don't you think," asked Mall, turning to Vridar, "that we have naked earthworm minds? But what else is left to us?"

"I'll soon have a naked body," said Hawke, and he stripped off his shirt. "Next comes my suspenders."

Arnstein hiccoughed gently. "Pardon," she said.

"I know what I'll look like," said Hawke, grinning. "I'll look as if a typhoon had stripped my masthead away." Mrs. Jode had raised a glass to her mouth but suddenly she coughed and snickered.

"You're a psychologist," said Mall. "Tell me: did Sappho sing because she was lovely or because she had a withered leg? I've often thought of that woman. Isn't the golden complex chiefly bone?"

"I'm wondering," said Mrs. Jode, "if I'm clean. It's a cinch I'm not going to have any luck tonight."

"There's a bath right there."

Mrs. Jode lost consistently. She had removed her rings and her necklace, both shoes and stockings, and now pulled off her blouse.

"I've always wondered," said Hawke, "why the loveliest women are the best poker players."

"You comfort me," said Miss Arnstein.

Mall turned again to Vridar who was sipping a cocktail and watching them.

"Hunter, you write. Don't you agree with me that the best poetry is limericks? At least a man can understand them. Do you know Moses McGuire?"

"Of course he does. Who doesn't?"

"Have you seen his limericks?"

"Some of them," Vridar said.

"I like the one on Robinson Jeffers."

"Watch yourself," said Mrs. Jode. "I adore Jeffers."
And Mall said:

> *"Love used to be lilies and zephyrs,*
> *But now its roan stallions and heifers*
> *Make such symbols of passion*
> *That we're all out of fashion:*
> *O shame on you, Robinson Jeffers!"*

"You say you like Jeffers?" asked Arnstein, unfastening
her belt. "His poetry, not his prose. Still, he mixes the two
very well."

Hawke slyly drew an ace from his lap and raked in the
pot. "I prefer poetry," he said, "that is more Auslandish.
By the way, does anyone agree with me that no man likes
to see a woman entirely naked? . . . Hunter?"

"Your cocktail is excellent," Vridar said.

"What I wonder," said Mall, "is why we never speak
of *ascendants* of the apes. That's a thought that troubles
me." Mrs. Jode looked at him, her eyes a little scornful.
Mall sensed the scorn and went ahead. "Another thing:
why are our super-sophisticates now preferring the ancient
superstitions? Are the modern ones worn out? Some day
I expect to see Aldous Huxley writing Mother Goose rimes."

"Another quaint form of regression," said Hawke, and
looked across his cards at Arnstein's white flesh. "Like
expatriates. But after Europe has become a province of
America and Paris is only a distant New York suburb,
where will our genius go to after saying good-by to Wis-
consin?"

"But America is, really, the most civilized nation today."

Hawke looked at Mall and scowled. "If I were patriotic
I'd resent your insult. . . ."

A week later, Vridar with several others was at the
small studio apartment of Bors Emmet. He thought Em-

were coming along all right. A synthesis, you call it. But don't you know a synthesis is impossible today? We know too much and too little."

"I've been looking at Emmet's paintings——"

"You have always taken life too seriously. Human life and human tragedy have become so common they are vulgar. We'll soon be dead. God saw that He had blundered and to help us endure His mistake He gave us gin. Drink it and don't embarrass Him." Mertyl fixed his brother with a tolerant smile. "You're an incurable moralist," he said. "You used to be a socialist. You'll be a communist next. Why wear yourself out fretting over what doesn't matter? Look at me. I live so much with psychotic people that the whole world looks crazy. The trained psychologist sees lunatics everywhere. But what of it? Humanity enjoys its neurosis. It's all an attempt to draw pity and attention to itself, now that its gods are dead."

Vridar pondered the simple pungency of that statement. It was true. Mertyl, more than any other person whom he knew, had the power of clear and cogent definition. He had said: "The core of psychology is this: we identify ourselves, our ego, with things outside ourselves. War destroys those identifications and you get the post-war neurosis. That neurosis and confusion and chaos must endure until we identify ourselves with the old ideals again, or with new ones. Most of the old ones our intelligence can no longer accept. The new ones we are still seeking. . . ." And now he said:

"It is not true that I'm maladjusted now. I'm on my feet. And you and I at last are traveling the same road. . . ."

Vridar went out and walked the streets. Everywhere in this city he found cynical derisions and distrust of emotional experience. Persons had taken refuge in that intellectual evasion called a sense of humor, and they laid their hungers and dreams under its withering scrutiny. Their country, they clearly perceived, was a land of demagogues, with only now and then a George Norris or a Civil Liberties Union like a solitary sentinel in a violent landscape of special privilege and greed. And Mertyl was right: in every human being the struggle was between the self and the selfless, the individual and the racial drives; and the sane person, the person living most fully, was the one who had harmoniously integrated the two. But today the self, the individual, was the lord and tyrant of earth; and the selfless, the lifting of group above individual welfare, had almost been driven from the earth.

On a corner of Union Square a man was shouting at a crowd. "There are only two classes of people: the ones who produce and the ones who exploit their labor!" A man with a cane stood aloof and smiled. Vridar entered an arcade. Along one wall men were inserting pennies into slots and peeping at the photographs of nearly naked women: Italians grinning at what they saw, Jews staring with all their might. The men sighed when they looked up. Across the arcade a short rugged fellow was striking a bag to make a bell ring. He delivered a blow and then looked around to see if any watched. His chest was full and proud. He felt his arms and walked back and forth, waiting for spectators. Vridar went over and affected interest and the man pulled the bag down and smote it with all his power. . . .

Vridar walked the streets again and came to the glittering sign of a burlesque show. Pictures of girls were here, naked save pelvis and breasts, and men looked at them and at one another and grinned. Vridar bought a ticket and entered. A chorus of girls was dancing, and singing bawdy songs. Upon leaving the stage, one and another stopped by a box where men sat and shook their breasts and thrust their buttocks out. Vridar studied the men around him: the guilty excitement in their eyes, their shame, their lustful and sometimes slobbering delight. Now and then a man swallowed hard and nudged his neighbor; or snickered with

sudden lewd joy. . . . And now five girls were on the stage,
each in an attitude, with her hard empty eyes looking out
at the audience; and two male comedians went from
one to another, pinched thighs, and gave the love-history
of each. They walked behind Cleopatra and looked solemnly
at her rump; and then one, in excess of ecstasy, slapped the
other's face; smote him next, and spun twice around and
fell prone. . . .

Such vulgarity, to be seen from end to end of this city,
was not unlike that enjoyed by pious folk everywhere. A
friend, an instructor in a Middle-Western university, had
written to Vridar: "I swear to God this faculty is becoming
one big filthy conundrum. I pass some on for your astonished perusal." But Vridar had not been astonished: that
most university teachers were as vulgar as any, he had
learned long ago.

And in all this there was a curiously poignant fact which
most persons missed. That a country licensed vulgar shows
and at the same time tried to suppress searching portrayals
such as *Ulysses* or *Sister Carrie* or *The Well of Loneliness*
or Margaret Sanger's pamphlets was more than a foolish
paradox. The paradox itself was unimportant but its implications were as profound as life. Human beings recognized
first, in their unconscious minds, that vulgarity was compensation for that clean sexual pleasure which they missed;
and they resented, in consequence, any searching review of
its origins. It was not that anyone wanted to suppress art on
moral grounds: that was their excuse but not their reason.
They liked vulgarity and felt need of it and did not want
it exposed.

"Do you see," he asked Athene, "how dark and devious
the evasion is there? Of course, there's more to it. Another
origin of sexual vulgarity is the fact that men resent the
sexual experiences of other men. We can't help it: that's
our heritage. And, resenting, many of them compensate with
erotic legends. Take, for instance, all the envious jests about

bridal nights. The charivari is only a disguised attack on a male that has come into possession of a female.

"And you know, my dear, it is being said that puritanism in this country is dead. To that I say poof and more poof. Dreiser and the rest of them just laid the thing open. No, that isn't it: they drove it deeper underground. Poor Henry James. Wise Henry Adams. If we could only force the whole thing into the open for a year, then we'd all be done with thinking about it. But we hide it because things in hiding assume a fabulous importance.

"And how we run around the matter. Take Lewisohn: there's a man with a mind. And yet he declares with solemnity as big as a mountain that the purpose of art is to justify us to our fellow men, ourselves, our god. Imagine that. There's no need to justify ourselves to anything. If a person doesn't feel guilty, he doesn't try to. I wish Lewisohn would stop walking arm in arm with God. Do you know that he says Cabell is a romantic and a fool?"

"Well, Cabell once made you furious, too."

"I know. Yes, of course he did. He exposed me. *Beyond Life* is an exposure of folly and vanity and self-love that has been equaled only by Swift. Lord, how I hated the book! How I ran with my wits sizzling to read Nietzsche again and fancy myself a superman! Yes, darling, I was one of the human gods, squatting with solemn certainty on my shoddy little throne. And Cabell very slyly took the throne from under me.

"And was I mad? Bless your soul, I could have killed him. Athene, I think I see another matter clearly. Humanity doesn't want to lose its sense of guilt and shame. Because a sense of guilt, you see, gives flavor to the experience, intensifies it, makes it more enviable. We're all detectives at heart: we love plotting. Besides, guilt is an aphrodisiac. The heart always beats faster if the experience is forbidden. I think that in our cunning way we devised Prohibition in order to make gin taste better. Honestly, I do. And I think

that long ago we hit upon the notion of sin and guilt to add
zest to sexual adventure.

"Does that sound quaint? Damn it, I tell you we haven't
even begun to probe to the sly and cunning plottings of the
unconscious mind. . . ."

X

●

VRIDAR'S publishers had made it possible for him to meet some literary celebrities but he was not at all sure that he wanted to meet them. "Artists," he said, "have never been able to tolerate one another. Most of them have sense enough not to try. They know they're a bunch of asses. And here I am, appointed to a Rosita Armstrong tea."

"Have you," asked Athene dryly, "read any of her books?"

"One. It was delicately suggested that I ought to read her books before sipping her tea." He laughed. "Isn't it funny? I hike out and get one of her novels and read it. I'll pretend I read it long ago. I don't like it but I'll pretend I do."

"You'll pretend nothing of the sort."

"Yes, I'll pretend nothing of the sort. But I ought to. Writers who get ahead are those who cultivate one another and the critics. They have patrons in strong places."

"You be yourself."

"I'll be as mum as the bottom of a teacup."

Rosita Armstrong was a woman who would weigh, Vridar imagined, about two hundred pounds. She was aggressive and outspoken and regarded herself, quite obviously, as one of the titans. Her husband was a small man who could have been cradled like a child on her lap. He deferred to her, his manner humble, his gaze patient and inquiring. When out of her great bosom she delivered a platitude, he looked at Vridar quickly, eagerly, as if expecting to see him put out of his wits. He waited, a little breathless, for Vridar's reply; and when it came he turned to his wife, serenely confident that she would demolish it. Vridar sipped a Spanish liqueur and restrained his smile.

Rosita talked of art, her pronouncements booming in the small room. Art, she said, was the civilized, and all else was barbarism. And while Vridar sank in his chair, trying to understand how any person could be foolish enough to think art more important than life, two critics came in. One of them was a slender spectacled man with a round owlish face; the other was an art critic, a Jew, and a close friend of Rosita: of her last novel he had declared that it began where Dostoievsky stopped. And now the critics and Rosita talked of art, and the husband and Vridar listened. They seemed to think that art was something like a garden that flowered and gave off fragrance and made the world sweet. They seemed to believe that human intelligence had perceived, unerringly and beyond all further question, that art was sane and reasonable and that life was a vulgar and very imperfect nightmare. They did not seem to realize, certainly, that art always had been and still was the most evasive of all escapes: defeated vanity building its empires in fancy; the frustrated ego scanning its pentameters and trying to give meaning to regret and loss. Persons who faced life and lived it cared nothing about art, at least in its stiff and formal patterns, and had no need of it.

And after half an hour of talk the art critic turned to Vridar.

"Mr. Hunter, you are spoken of as a realist. I have not," he added, graciously apologetic, "read your book—you have published only one? but I have seen reviews. What in your opinion is realism and what is romance?"

The spectacled critic murmured and fixed upon Vridar a dubious stare. In a review he had dismissed Vridar's novel with furious rhetoric and had concluded: "Mr. Hunter is very young and has much to learn. There may be a novelist in him but at present he is only a belated offshoot of Zola."

"Or perhaps," said the art critic, "you hadn't thought of the matter."

"I have thought of it a great deal."

"Well," said Rosita Armstrong, gently malicious, "you will perhaps settle the problem for us."

Vridar looked at her and at her husband, relating her malice to its source. The art critic smiled. And Vridar hesitated, wondering whether he should speak to the point or beg off. Their patronizing incredulity amused him. It annoyed him a little. He decided to speak.

"Are these two terms opposites in your mind?"

"Yes, of course. Aren't they in yours?"

"But the two terms are very loosely used today——"

"I had never suspected that," Rosita murmured.

"Realism for me," Vridar went on, "means an effort to see life and ourselves for what we are. I do not mean these so-called realistic novels which oppose, like the old moralities, good to evil, heroes and scoundrels. I mean as detached and impersonal a view of ourselves as we can manage with nothing glossed and nothing glorified. Such realism as that we have never had and don't have now and shall perhaps not have for a long time to come." He stopped. Rosita said softly:

"And now tell us what is romance."

"Romance," he said, annoyed by this woman's patronage, "is, I should say, and has always been, evasion and escape. We speak of elopements as romantic, or travel, as well as a lot of other things which are not romantic at all. We are inclined to call anything romantic which is not a part of our deadly routine of living. A wish to dramatize our lives is not romantic——"

"I don't yet understand," said Rosita a little impatiently, "what you *do* mean by romantic."

"I mean all the inventions that disguise ourselves and the world we live in. I mean our self-deceptions and evasions, and our pretending that we are what we are not. I mean the carloads of vicarious books that are gobbled up by a humanity too stupid or too timid to make their own lives meaningful. Would you like instances?"

"They might help," said Rosita Armstrong.

"Take democracy, then: it is a romantic and unattainable concept. We pretend we have democracy because we don't like to think of ourselves as greedy creatures cherishing inequalities and fighting for special privilege. Take religions —I mean chiefly belief in personal immortality: they have sprung largely from self-pity and self-love and an unwillingness to admit that the universe will move along nicely without our consciousness of it. Take the ideology at present imposed on human relationships. It is romantic because most of our ideals have no basis in fact, not even in a desire to have a fact exist. We don't love justice—except for ourselves. We don't love mercy—at least, nowhere do we employ it. We don't love peace—and only fools any longer pretend to——"

"Oh. Then what *do* we love?"

"Ourselves."

"You seem to be a very gloomy person."

"That is the romantic retort."

"There is," said the art critic, "a lot of truth in what you say. But don't you think the fact of our having such concepts as justice and mercy must mean that we feel them deeply enough to have conceived them?"

"I think we'd have to understand first why and from what we got such notions. I think we do have potential capacity in those directions. I also think that such notions have been evolved in the past by physical weaklings——"

"Perhaps because they were forced to think more?"

"For their own preservation, yes. I'm not arguing that we don't need justice. Probably we need nothing more. I'm merely saying that it's a romantic evasion to pretend that we now have it. Mooney is still in jail. If *we* love justice, what have *we* done to get him out?"

"Well, very little, I imagine."

"If I may be personal," said Vridar, "allow me to offer my book as an instance. It has been called brutal. It is the romantic tendency to call anything brutal that strips our pretenses away. I'd say the only real brutality is to be found in the way we persist in self-deceptions. We are brutalizing ourselves with evasions, not with attempts to find truth——"

The slender critic rose hastily.

"I'm sorry," he said, "but you'll have to excuse me. I have an appointment."

"It's time I was going, too," said the art critic. He came over to Vridar and extended his hand. "Drop around," he said, "and see me some time."

An hour later Vridar stretched in a chair and looked at Athene.

"Well, I guess I shouldn't have gone. They drew me into a damned silly discussion and I didn't want to talk. Why can't I learn that most human beings don't want to talk about anything when they open their mouths?"

"How did Bunner take what you said?" Bunner was the slender critic.

"I don't know. He marched out like a Cæsar on an expedition to slay Tom Thumb."

"He'll probably flay you after this."

"Darling, why don't you say what you mean? Why not say, You blundered? You should have been tactful, discreet."

"I didn't mean that."

"You did. You think I make enemies wherever I go."

"Well, you do."

"I don't try to. And why should I forever be trying to say only what people want to hear? Everywhere I go I find persons with emotional parapets thrown up around them. They're hiding. I refuse to hide. What I am, I am, and the whole cockeyed world may know it for all I care. To hell with this sickly oafish stuff about the sanctity of private lives. Our everlasting fuss about privacy shows that

we suspect how much privacy hides. What the world needs
is a great house-cleaning. Throw the ghosts out on their
erotic shanks. And protest, if you will, but I'm going to
write a novel about myself."

"I don't protest. I merely ask you to be sure."

"All I need is enough detachment, perspective, so I can
see the preposterous Vridar Hunter for what he has been.
Darling, there won't be any self-glorification in that
book——"

"No, oh no. You'll just try to make yourself out as the
most detestable person that ever lived."

"Nonsense. Nobody is detestable. Haven't I told you
that only those with too much self-love ever think so?
No, I'll be after the plain confounded truth. No putting
of ghosts to bed and writing of the peonies."

"I'd think about it a while longer."

"I've thought. Another year or two and I'll be ready."

"And what about your friends?"

"My friends? Well, perhaps it will sort out my friends
from my enemies."

"And Idaho? Will you dare go back there?"

"I certainly will."

"And the American public: do you realize what it will
do to a book like that?"

"I'm not so sure. I think the world is coming to the
point where it's tired of evasion. If not, another war will
fetch it there. Oh, I know: a few critics may sail out to
slay me: there are a lot of Vridars among critics. A few
librarians may fall out of their chairs. But if I do the job
right to the point, without ever saying, See what a splendid
fellow this ass is! Dear reader, I hope you love him as I
love him—no: I'll strip the puritan right to his bones and
give him naked to the world. And as my critic, do one
thing: watch me for any sign of self-glorification."

"I needn't, my dear. You'll go to extreme limits as usual

and the poor Vridar won't have a leg to stand on—not even
a puritan leg."

"You annoy me," Vridar said. "What you really want,
my dear, is another of these sweet autobiographical novels
of whose protagonist the readers can say, What a splendid
person! He's just like me! No: I'm a scientist of human
emotions and Vridar is the bug I'll be looking at."

"And I suppose you intend to tell all the truth about
the persons you've known?"

"No."

"Then you're going to compromise?"

"Their lives are their business, not mine."

"You mean you'll invent some characters?"

"A lot of them. But no author ever invents. He takes
a suggestion and then searches himself for the reason of it,
the probabilities, the development. He tries to build something that will live. All his characters are only aspects of
himself, with the emphasis shifting from trait to trait. . . .
Well, you think I'll be unwise?"

"I'm afraid I do."

"You have the only cynicism that is really cynical. Or
am I still too credulous? All books, my dear, are autobiographical for persons with sense enough to read. Even textbooks. A catalog of facts doesn't make an autobiography.
Neither does a self-glorifying confession. My protagonist
will be born with the appetites and impulses of all persons:
his environment will make a personality of him. How that
personality comes to be and what shapes it—that's the job.
It will be a very incomplete job: we understand too little
yet. I'll have to tell much that most persons don't like to
have told: that's because the most important forces in
shaping us are those which we try most to hide from and
deny. Oh, I know what a job it is."

Athene smiled. "And are you going to tell the truth
about me?"

"Why shouldn't I?"

"Then you'll have to show me as an awful fool when I met you."

"Both of us."

"And perhaps we are awful fools still."

"No doubt about it."

"Vridar, what are some of the things you'll say about me?"

"Oh, I'll say that feelings of inferiority make you talk too much in an effort to impress; and that, sensing your silliness, you talk all the harder. I'll say you've always been a bit afraid of public opinion. I'll say you'd rather have a baby than be Sappho. I'll say your worst vice is making excuses for yourself: that when caught in any blunder or stupidity, you sail in with all your might to try to justify yourself. I'll say——"

"And will there be nothing good to say about me?"

"Oh, my: there you go! I'll say you took that awful fool Vridar and led him to love as a passionate and over-whelming and clean experience. I'll say you were his sternest critic: that he was forever writing tasteless letters and you made him rewrite them. I'll say he got furious and blew off the roof but rewrote. I'll give you so much patience that readers—especially men, darling—will want to kick you out of the book. . . .

"Listen, you know this is to be an awfully funny tale? It will show a colossus of vanity set back on his heels, with his long snouty presumptions tweaked good and hard. It splits me open to think of it. Lord God, how the oaf will thresh through the pages! What tireless and invincible imbecility! Do you suppose anyone else will find it funny?"

"Those will who don't love themselves too much. You can't expect smug extroverts to understand it. You can't expect evasive introverts to like it."

"I know."

"It will be funny if you leave me out of it."

"That's a nice two-edged one. I'll make you a parcel-post package of all the virtues, addressed to heaven. What a monster you will be! After you enter, the book will smell sweet and readers will have someone to love."

"You'll put me in for what I was and am: a green little simpleton out of college, her eyes fairly popping with ideals, her ears listening for the great heavenly symphonies. You will say I wanted to stay and make the fight and I wanted to run away. You'll say that at first I did not like *her*, but after living with you a while and after seeing your family, I understood her problem and so learned to love her. You will say that I too have an ego as big as a house and want to write books and be famous—Lord! Put me in for just what I am and was: that will help to make the book funny."

He went over and drew her to him and they laughed.

XI

●

THERE were other celebrities whom Vridar met in New York. Yielding to his publisher's urging, he went to the office of a literary critic and sat on a hard chair and listened. John Adgate was very dark and very voluble. He liked to meet authors, he said. He liked to get at the bottom of them. Some of them, he admitted, were pretty difficult: as a group, writers were morbidly sensitive and taciturn. But he usually warmed them up. He usually had them smiling in a few minutes and talking their heads off.

And Vridar looked at Adgate and smiled and wondered about the man. Adgate had given his novel a long and favorable review and he was very friendly now. "Drop around at the apartment and see us sometime," he said. And one evening Vridar went. He found the apartment full of cats and dogs, and Mrs. Adgate in bed with a cat in her arms. The Adgates had no children. And now Adgate and his doll-faced wife talked of dogs and played with them, as if this room were a nursery, as if these beasts were their daughters and sons.

"Do you like dogs?" Adgate asked.

"Yes—but not as pets."

"What kind of pets do you like?"

"None."

Adgate looked at him, his face sobering. "A dog," he said, "is a man's best friend. There's loyalty in dogs. They never betray you." He stared at Vridar gravely. "Don't you think so?"

"In American life," Vridar said, "dogs are glorified too much. I think it's another symptom of our national adolescence." And he saw at once that he might as well have struck Adgate in his jaw. Mrs. Adgate rose to her pillows, exclaiming.

"What," asked Adgate coldly, "do you mean by that?"

Why the devil, Vridar wondered, had he come here! Mrs. Adgate looked as if she expected apologies and floral offerings and her husband looked as rigid as a man suffering a stroke.

"I mean only," Vridar said, "that persons who love dogs are persons, as I have observed them, who are cynical of human beings. I have friends who devote themselves to preposterous poodles of one sort and another——" He broke off: that was worse still. Mrs. Adgate was looking as if she would scream.

"Go on," said Adgate, fixing Vridar with an awful stare. "Say what you mean."

"I mean," Vridar went on quietly, "that persons who make a fuss about the loyalty and devotion of dogs are persons, as I have observed them, who find human beings unworthy of affection and esteem. They want loyalty and affection—well, we all do. But despising human beings and turning to the servile devotion of dogs seems to me to be pretty silly——"

"Do you mean to suggest," asked Adgate suddenly, "that I am cynical about human beings?"

"Aren't you?"

"I love dogs," he said stoutly.

"And I," said Vridar, "love humankind."

"Oh, you do! Allow me to doubt that. And do you find human beings lovable? They betray and deceive you. They lie. They stoop to all kinds of greed and mean little tricks. I don't see much charity and kindness and loyalty among them. Dogs give you affection and ask for nothing."

"But isn't that the point? Dogs are stupid serfs. They flatter our vanity. They leap to our commands and vanish without sulking when we are weary of them. You don't mean you like only such friendship as takes the relation of peon to master? Isn't it that we like to be small Napoleons among the beasts?"

"Not at all, not at all. Dogs are loyal: that's the whole point."

"Well, what I meant, of course, is that dog-lovers are persons who have been disillusioned in humanity."

"And haven't you?" asked Mrs. Adgate in her small tremulous voice.

"Once, yes. Very much so, in fact. But that means only that I was disillusioned in myself. I learned that before I could expect to find others worthy of esteem, I should first have to become such a person myself. Because cynicism is contempt for ourselves, not for others. I hope I do not sound crassly egotistic in saying that I no longer feel such contempt."

"And," said Adgate, looking at him, "you really respect the stupid greedy race you belong to?"

"It isn't all stupidity and greed."

"Some dogs," said Mrs. Adgate, "are more intelligent than most human beings. Aren't they, John?"

"Yes—and a hell of a lot more decent. They aren't hypocrites. They aren't damned fawning shysters. They aren't murderers and thieves and whores and—and bankers. . . ."

When Vridar told Athene of this evening she was distressed. "Wherever you go, my dear, you're everlastingly poking a scornful finger at sham. Why not let them talk? You don't have to take their masks away and jump at them."

"Oh well, why can't they talk without blowing off a lot of steam? Anyway, I'm tired of this sick glorification of dogs. Veblen was right. And I'm also tired of cynicism."

"You've no right to be intolerant there. No one was ever more cynical than you a few years ago."

"I know it. I once sat at the grave of a dog all night and wept in sniffling self-pity. But to hell with all that. The human animal is not an act of God but he's the most magnificent beast on the planet today. If I can't love my own kind, I won't be a sick sentimentalist, leading a poodle down the avenues. When I seek affection, I won't go down on all fours to do it."

"But that isn't the point."

"Then what *is* the point?"

"This: Adgate gave your book a swell review. And you sail right into his home and outrage him."

"Athene darling, am I to be a hypocrite to get swell reviews? If an honest opinion is too much for him, then to hell with his reviews."

"Yes, you'll to hell yourself right out of authorship."

"All right. Then I'll milk cows."

"But that isn't it," said Athene impatiently. "You march around yanking down cathedrals. You——"

"They ought to be yanked down. We can never build a decent world until we get these totem poles out of the way."

"But you could be discreet. You'll run yourself out."

"I've never learned discretion. I think the world has too much of it now. Anyway, I like Adgate. His little world of pups and cats is his own business. But I also like ideas and frank hard discussion, and a literary critic, of all people, is one who ought to be seeing some things clearly." Vridar rose. "Damn it," he said. "Imagine a man so blind that he doesn't see into the psychology of dog-lovers."

"Well, again that's not the point. You'll never get any-where as an author as long as you sail out and whack human vanity with a mace and expect persons to like it."

"That's what I use to whack mine. Let others whack it: I don't care at all. The only lessons I've learned have come from the confusion and pain of having my vanity drubbed. And as for authorship, is it of any great importance if I never get anywhere? All critics are not like Adgate: God help writers if they were."

"I think it would be better if you saw no one at all."

"Imagine a novelist living like a monk! Well, darling, next time I'll keep my mouth shut."

"You'd better. I'll bet Adgate never reviews another of your books."

"You think so?"

"I do."

And Athene was right.

The next time Vridar visited a celebrity he kept his mouth shut. He went to the home of a famous American poet. William Randall Smith was an old man but he had a young wife, and it was the wife, smiling and gracious, who met him at the door. Vridar went in and looked across a large room. The poet was standing by a fireplace with his hands behind him. He did not turn. For half an hour while Mrs. Smith set the dinner on and chatted pleasantly, Smith ignored Vridar. It's all right, Vridar thought. He is a great man, shining in the sun, and I'm only an upstart, peeking over the horizon. But no: he is old, and he is weary of the enthusiasms of youth. . . .

When dinner was laid, Smith came over and was introduced. He did not offer his hand. He glanced at Vridar and grunted and sat to eat. He opened a bottle of medicated wine and like a man whose thirst was extreme he drank. And then for several minutes he ate in silence. Suddenly he looked across at Vridar and fixed him with weary eyes and began to talk. This man, Vridar now realized, had suffered, and in him was almost boundless sympathy for the oppressed and exploited of humankind. But this man's excoriation of capitalism, of political shysters, and of men, once liberals but now demagogues, seemed to Vridar pretty superficial and silly.

"Greed!" said Smith, and his eyes came to life. "A handful of men grinding other men into the earth. There's enough misery in this land to fill a thousand worlds. And

what do we have in Washington? A big moon-faced shyster
who is a messenger boy for the Morgans. . . ."

Mrs. Smith sat a little uneasily under the diatribe. She
was convinced, quite obviously, that her husband was a
great man but she did not share his great humanitarian
storms. And she asked of Vridar, "Are you by any chance
a communist?"

"No."

Smith turned on him a solemn and accusing stare.
"Every man," he said, "is a communist if he places human
happiness above human greed."

Vridar wanted to argue this matter but he remembered
Athene's injunction and kept his mouth shut. And Smith
now, as if discovering that he had no audience, retired into a
vast and gloomy silence. He opened another bottle of wine
and drank and then went to the fireplace and stood there,
an old and a very tragic man.

"Well, I did nobly," Vridar said to Athene. "Smith discovered I am not a communist and dropped me as if I had
burnt his hands. So I lose if I talk and I lose if I sit mum.
Next time I'm going to cut loose with hell and high water."

"You can talk without offending."

"No. I've never learned how to be both reasonable and
well bred."

Accepting another invitation he went to the home of
another novelist. Martha Jackson turned to the English
language, declaring it to be a very supple, a very marvelous,
instrument. This was too much for Vridar.

"I don't agree," he said.

"No? And why not?"

"I think all language is very obtuse. We have a great
deal to say of its richness and fluency. Perhaps that's because we exaggerate the value of everything that relates to
ourselves."

"You really don't think it's a flexible medium? Tell me why."

"What can we convey with it except the most obtuse thoughts and sensations? Take odors. What words do we have? We can say a thing is pleasant, pungent, aromatic, offensive: these are all genus words. How can we express the difference between the fragrance of heliotrope and lavender? lichen and fungus? We can't and authors never try to. How can we express anything subtle in regard to touch? We can say it is hard, soft, slippery, wet. Or taste? We can say it tastes of vanilla or curry or salt or some sort of bark. Or emotions? Who can get into words what he feels when he looks at a sunset? Don't we writers merely throw out suggestions and trust to luck? Do we ever achieve more than a skeleton on which there hangs an effect?"

"Well, perhaps we don't. I've been reading Jespersen. I suppose philologists write out of an excess of enthusiasm. They try to make of language something incomparable, quite as writers do of art. And here's another matter. Do you think writers think of what they want to say and then find the precise words to express it?"

"No. Do you?"

"I doubt it. I don't imagine any author ever writes that way. I don't. Do you?"

"Not at all. Among abstractions there are no precise words. I find combinations of words that fill up with ideas. If I like the ideas I use them. I mean that words come along and get filled up with meaning."

"That's the way it seems. But composition teachers say to find the precise word."

"I know it. It's easier to teach that way."

There was a long silence. Martha Jackson looked at a row of books, her eyes tired and meditative. At last she smiled and said:

"If a critic says nice things of your book, do you write him a note of thanks? Or is that in bad taste?"

"I imagine," said Vridar dryly, "it would be in bad taste."

"I meant, of course, only those critics who understand what you're trying to do. I asked the question because two years ago I wrote a note of thanks to two critics. Both of them ignored my next book."

"The hell they did."

"They certainly did. So I must have blundered."

Vridar felt deep sympathy for this woman. She was frail and very timid and she had no armor against scorn and rebuke. While looking at her he remembered another whom, legend declared, critics had driven to suicide.

"I wouldn't let the matter worry me," he said. "If those critics ignored you, it was because they have strong feelings of inferiority and doubt their judgments. Or perhaps they are thick-skinned and thought you were ingratiating."

"But I wasn't," she said. "I merely wanted to thank them."

"I know."

"You seem so serene and confident," she said, looking at him.

"I? Good Lord. I'm about as serene as a rabbit with a dog after it and about as confident as a knight in armor, stuck in the mud."

"Really? Is it just a mask?"

"Nothing but a mask."

"I like you," said Martha Jackson later, offering her hand. "Please come again."

"Well," said Athene, "how did you behave yourself tonight?"

"Oh, fairly. I jumped a time or two at another myth but I was almost well bred tonight. Darling, I met a very tragic and a very lonely woman. She broods over what critics say about her or refuse to say. And as I looked at her I wanted to take the critics and kick their pants all the way from Yonkers to the Battery."

"I've been reading her last book. She seems to be a very sweet and a very gentle person."

"She is. I love her. But there you have it!" he cried, and made a face. "She's timid and gentle and I love her! She makes me feel aggressive and strong. Lord, O Lord! How our vanity trips us up at every turn. An honest book? It's not possible today to imagine, even to imagine vaguely, what an honest book, a completely honest book, would be like."

XII

●

VRIDAR met other writers of one kind and another but most of them, it seemed to him, were masquerading within an attitude or a cult. But there was one who had looked deep into life. Robert Clark had just published his first novel: a sprawling chaos of a book, a cyclone of power and rhetoric: it gathered sham and flummery to its tide and heaped the dishonest gestures into mountainous distortions. In its huge and hungry way, it had taken from a score of novelists, and from Clark himself, the best and the worst and transmuted these into a personality and a vision of its own. But in spite of its self-pitying rhapsodies, its self-induced and drunken apostrophizing of empire and destiny, it was, in Vridar's opinion, one of the greatest novels that had come out of American life.

Vridar perceived at once that he and Clark had much in common: the same terror and distress in childhood, the same earnest credulity under their distrust and scorn, the same urgent need of loyalties and peace. That strange quality in Clark to which some deferred, and which some tried to father, was a shrewd and calculating disingenuousness. Words poured out of him and his manner of speaking was that of an untutored youth; but his eyes were awake and watchful and missed nothing, and often Vridar saw them darken with suspicion and hate. Yet most persons who knew Clark regarded him as an overgrown lad and never sensed the dark amusement or the pitying scorn with which he dismissed their patronage.

One afternoon Vridar went with Clark to his room. It was, like his book, an enormous and splendid chaos: manuscripts were piled on the floor, trunks were laid open, and letters and books and clothes were a carpet underfoot. Clark searched for a review of his novel, sent to him for approval. He pawed the mounds of stuff around him or loped from pile to pile. He found it and with boyish eagerness he read it: an effusive eulogy by a woman who no more understood the book than she understood why books were written.

"It's pretty swell, Vridar. Don't you think so? Too motherly and unctuous but it might sell some copies. You think so?" And with fresh eagerness he read again. "Nice of her to let me see it before it appears."

Before they left the room, Bob explored among cigarette stubs. He crushed a glowing one and went to the door; he stopped there, looking back. "Have I put all those stubs out?" He searched again. He came to Vridar, dubiously, wondering about fire. They went down the stairs. At the street door Bob stopped again. "I think I'd better go back. I want to be sure those stubs are all out. . . ."

They went down the street.

"Vridar, do you think my book will sell ten thousand copies? God, I hope it does. What? The critics have been swell. You see that column Haldon wrote? That was a peach of a send-off. . . ." On and on he talked, never waiting for an answer, never expecting one. His laugh was an enormous sob, strained, difficult, never coming to birth. He suffered most when he laughed. "Vridar, when I see how many books are published I say, What the hell do I amount to? One book in a million. I'm nobody. You're nobody. Look at the books in windows; thousands. But the stores give a prominent place to my book. Have you noticed? What? Great God, though, I hope my next book is better." And he ran a great hand through uncombed hair. "Authors are a crazy bunch, Vridar. You know it? We all want to be the only author alive. Isn't it true?"

"It's pretty close to the truth."

"What? Honest, you think my book will sell?"

"I think it ought to."

"My God, I hope it does. This is a grand experience,

having a book published. I could write a novel about that. Travis is a peach of a guy." Travis was one of Clark's publishers. "He's just like a father to me. You'll like him. Lord, I hope my book sells." And Bob stopped by another bookstore window and looked in. "See, I'm right out there in front. A swell jacket. What? Vridar, you say your publishers have rejected your next book?"

"Yes."

"Take it to Travis. He'll publish it. He's a peach of a guy. . . ."

"Bob Clark," Vridar said to Athene, "has enough power and drive for a dozen writers. If he'll only outgrow the wish of self-glorification; if he'll only learn that stupendous assumptions of zest, overwhelming apostrophes, and heaped and multiplied eulogiums, spring not from zest but are only hunger for it and a disguise of emotional emptiness or of a huge emotional conflict, then—but he can throw empires away and still be a kingdom."

"What do you think of Travis?"

"Oh, he gave me a glacial stare and murmured. And, Athene, do you realize what a racket authorship is? Look at these New York cliques who move within a snobbish and self-defensive integrity and tout one another to the skies; these asses who are paid to advertise themselves over the radio; these who run out and make friends of book dealers and so get their stuff pushed. It makes me almost ashamed to be a writer. An author, God damn it, ought to stay away from critics and let them be as disinterested as they can. Let a book stand on its legs if it has legs. But imagine: one of the most important reviews is sent to Bob for approval before it is published!"

"That isn't criticism."

"No; it's back-slapping: you tout my book and I'll tout yours. Darling, let's get a garden somewhere and be obscure and reasonble. Let's get out of this feverish racket that blows names into enormous reputations and leaves them to burst."

"I can see us doing that!"

"We ought to, my dear. If we were more civilized we would."

Travis did not read Vridar's manuscript, nor, so far as Robert Clark could learn, did anyone else. Vridar sent it to the office and it came back in four days. He took it to other publishers and all of them asked the one damning question: "Why don't the publishers of your first book want this?"

And feeling depressed he would walk the streets: down corridors of stone, through the impersonal throngs: squares and angles, corners and scarps and ledges; trestles and beams and shanks, bases and underprops; slabs and blocks and studs, girder and scaffold, rhomboid and pyramid, snag and tusk and spike. Mertyl had been right: this city was taking hold of him: its tunnels and gorges and smoke, its tall shadows of growth and decay. There was no wide curve of sky here, no lithograph of dawn, none of the landscapes and sculpturings of great spaces. Here were cats that howled all night; foghorns and screeching whistles and clanging cowbells; and a committee appointed to investigate the effects of noise. And Vridar wondered if the millions of poor here did not become insensible to everything but extremes.

After walking far into the north he entered a subway to return. At his side was a fat man, breathing angrily through his nose, his fat chin sitting upon his collar. His hands had huge dimples at the knuckles; his nails were black with dirt. Across the aisle a mother clutched a babe that slobbered between howls of wrath. Ahead sat a huge negress with a bosom that looked as if it had been built upon her. There were no happy faces here: only tired faces, going home to eat and sleep. Above them sea heroes at-tributed to Lucky Strikes the courage of lifeboat crews. In the seat ahead a man read a newspaper and Vridar saw that

Peggy Joyce was again in Monte Carlo.
Mexico was enjoying another civil war.
Pershing was prostrated with grief because Foch was dead.
Thirteen had died in Illinois of poisoned alcohol.
A shipbuilder had been made assistant secretary of navy.
Spring styles for women would run to pajamas. . . .

Upon leaving the subway he bought a paper and read as he walked. J. P. Morgan and Owen D. Young had dined in Paris. "The luncheon started with Ostend oysters, with Chablis 1921 as the beverage. Then came lobster l'Américaine, Pouilly 1919. A barbecue of venison was accompanied with Château Rothschild Bordeaux of 1881 vintage. The bird course was served with Clos de Vougeot 1921, and the salad, of fresh asparagus, with Château Karem 1910. Next came cheese, fruits and coffee, and finally the cognac Napoléon 1820. . . ." Tammany had also dined. "The menu was irreproachable: Lobster cocktail Orientale, okra créole, suprême of turbotin, lamb Colbert, chicken Virginienne, endive, génoise, glacé and demi-tasse. . . ." There had been a Kennel Club Show. "Come of all Celia, a tiny Brussels Griffon no larger than a house cat, was barking and snapping and pulling at Jeannot of All Celia. Chippy Again, a Pomeranian, was yipping at first-prize winner, rehalt Mollie of Ashburne. Lady Indo of Arr, a little Maltese, was sending piercing yips from her blue-satin-lined box, draped with blue velvet. . . ." On the same page was an advertisement of silk pajamas for poodles. On the next page was a plea for contributions to a milk fund for starving babes.

Vridar turned aside and went to the dingy little attic room where Telv Ethlec lived.

"Hello, Telv."

"Hello, Vridar. How's Hoover today?"

"I didn't vote for Hoover. I voted for Al Smith and if God will forgive me for that I can take care of my other crimes."

"He never will. Well, sit down. I want to talk. I want to know why you aren't a communist."

"Because it's the proletarian half-brother of fascism. Morgan and Marx with the same mother."

"Be serious for a little while. It's time you came along with us."

"It's time you stopped trying to find yourself in an ideal."

"No, be serious. We need men like you. You could write just the sort of satire that would slaughter the asses. Why don't you?"

"Because I don't see the asses as my enemies. My enemy is the barbarous society that produces them. Telv, why don't you become a realist?"

"What do you mean?"

"I mean that. We aren't ready for communism yet. We have to face a lot of facts first."

"What facts? What are you driving at?"

"This: all life is exploitation. The bird exploits the worm, the tiger the gazelle, the human being the tiger— endlessly. You miss everything but industrial exploitation. And another fact that my brother points out: in all of us there are two great basic urges: self-aggrandizement and self-immolation. The first lives within the small periphery of the individual. The second, which came second in evolution, is racial. Our struggle today is between those two. Our civilization is built upon the first and so it is that we have in all fields these tyrannical lords of empire. In sensitive and imaginative persons, Telv, excessive ambition —I mean selfishness, the hunger for personal privilege and power—is corrected and rebuked by the second, by a wish to make the individual strivings serve the race, the group.

But that second basic urge is much more superficial than the first—not in women but in men. Do you see? And today it is neurotic and bewildered and often fraudulent. It is of no use until it is understood and directed. You, I, communists, all crusaders, are persons whose egregious individualism has been rebuked; and we try to discover ourselves, our meaning, destiny, in a larger world of service— as a unit in a large social plan. And that is all very well. It is necessary if we are ever to be more than barbarians. But we're only children fighting in the dark until we understand the motives driving us.

"Now take exploitation. You communists are exploiters, too."

"I don't see how."

"Well, take writing. Anyone who exploits human credulity and so helps to prolong human delusion and misery is as much of an exploiter as the munitions baron. Isn't he?"

"Of course he is."

"All right. Well, that's all any writer does who hands out this romantic twaddle. Instead of helping to force humanity to rebel, he hands out the vicarious sop. The author of spurious romantic love stories for the unhappily married, spinsters, and all the rest of them, is just as vicious an exploiter as the man who builds an empire upon factory drudges. Humanity in the mass, Telv, is so stupid, bewildered, beaten down that it can be hoodwinked forever with vicarious fulfillments——"

"But we Marxists believe in revolution."

"Oh yes, to be sure. Yet there are communists who hike out to Hollywood and turn out romantic pap for the dollars. Clean your own house first, Telv. Get a realistic program and I'll go along with you. But not as long as you rave about bankers and preach a simple little ideology that is nothing but a corrective for your own monstrous egoism. Not as long as you divide humanity into good folk and bad folk and suppose that the exploited are any nobler than the robbers. Not, in short, as long as you preach plain stupid nonsense and refuse to understand what you're doing. Your journals are full of vicious attacks on some, simpering eulogies of others. Realists? Damn it, Telv, you don't know the alphabet of realism. And you don't want to know.

"Telv, look at your communist editors in this country. They even attack one another. And why? Because they really haven't corrected their excessive vanity: they merely think they have. Take your Marxist journals: they appeal to prejudice and hatred. Your cartoons of industrialists are horrible caricatures of brutality and greed. Very well: but the readers of your journals are just as greedy and brutal. Do you realize, Telv, that you communists are really giving a caricature of your own souls in what you write and draw?"

"Oh, the hell we are!"

"Or of the human soul, if you wish. I'll tell you: I'll write out my objections to communism—or the reasons why I'm not a communist."

"And I'll rip you up the back and down the front. I'll make such a monkey of your damned specious sophistries that you'll die of shame."

"Most likely you'll wave your hands and gesticulate."

"Well, I understand you now. You're a fascist."

"Oh, I'm a fascist? I hate fascism with everything in me. I'm a radical, Telv: not a schoolboy who throws the skeleton of Jesus away and tries to keep His self-glorifying nonsense. I throw the nonsense away with the skeleton. . . ."

Upon leaving Telv's room Vridar stopped to see Moses McGuire. These two persons, it seemed to him, were the X and Y of himself, long ago. Telv lived by his heart, Mac by his mind: the two, integrated, would be a titan among men.

"I'm feeling loose and unraveled tonight," Mac said. "When I tighten my mental processes, thoughts slip away like minnows from a clenched hand. And they're only minnows in an ocean of whales. But where are the whales? Did you know Choy Rolfe tried to kill herself?"

"Did she try very hard?"

"Reasonably hard. She jumped out a window but there was a roof below."

"And we grin. Today we don't know what is tragic and what isn't."

"Even Bors Emmet doesn't know. He whined all yesterday afternoon about Toulouse-Lautrec and I listened and thought of the cemetery of Abydos. Fabre's les mœurs des insectes and Mantegazza's physiologie de l'amour. Then Norman Mall blew in: l'étude historique sur les organes génitaux de la femme. There's a man I'd like to murder. While I hold a colloquy over the seventh commandment he makes a physiological excursion." Mac rose and paced the room. "Hunter, I wish I had an apartment instead of this kennel: a bedroom by Brancusi with wallpaper like gray spider webs and a carpet like an elephant's painted hide. A workroom by Bobritsky: a sun-parlor of tangles by Vasselevsky: stork-legs among a fungus of eyes, and pyramids of disease. A table of Australian black bean, torchères of snakewood. . . . Hunter, I ask again: what is wrong with me?"

"You read too much."

"I've thought and thought but I can't see that life is worth all the deference I pay to it. You've helped persons, Hunter. You put Shelley on her legs. You gave new life to John Elmen. Your students come to you, I'm told, and confess everything from their chins to their garters. Why don't you help me?" Mac fell to a chair. Vridar looked at him and was surprised: Mac was weeping. His suffering eyes were wide and wet. His mouth was white.

"Hunter, you've been through hell. I can see it in your eyes. How did you fight your way out?"

"By facing myself, Mac."

"Am I dodging?"

"I should say so."

"Well, tell me, blow by blow. I'll take it."

"You're much like what I used to be—an appalling egoist. And so you have an awful conflict in you—as I had."

"I know that. What is the conflict?"

"Between the self and the selfless. You're an animal, Mac, and you have hungers as old as life itself and you're trying to feed them with aphorisms. You might as well try to feed the tiger with the platitudes of Ed Howe. All your love-making you do in a library, bent over a book——"

"You think I should get a woman?"

"A dozen—if you feel you need that many. Get the shame out of you. Get out of you the notion that appetites are unworthy and degrading. Throw away the silly notion that there is sin in the world. The only sin is negativism. You live in a social order, of course: some of your hungers have to be disciplined, even restrained. It doesn't follow that they have to be disguised into assumptions that they are what they are not."

"Did you use to feel shame and self-loathing?"

"Did I! A bigger fraud never walked the earth. I was so good I was ashamed to blow my nose. Such a decent word as snot filled me with shudders."

"And how about the other words?—Mike called them the Anglo-Saxon potentates."

"They don't bother me now."

"The hell. Are you going to put them into your books?"

"In this country that is still ashamed of nakedness? Hardly. Mac, if I were dictator of the earth, I'd make the whole human race stand up at ten every morning and chant those words for half an hour. In a month or so they would be decent and friendly words. Then all the smirking smut would vanish down the sky. Then——"

"But you once said that human beings evolved notions of guilt to enhance sexual pleasure. You said guilt gives an intensity we don't feel in the absence of shame."

"Yes. Well, that's the only plausible origin of sin I've

been able to think of. But remember, too, that a sense of guilt defeats full realization. That's the trouble with D. H. Lawrence's people."

"Don't you feel any shame now about sex?"

"Very little. It's getting to be as natural for me as eating a macaroon or turning for a cocktail."

"And the four-letter word for defecation: doesn't that bother you?"

"No. I heard that word from the cradle up. It was a common expletive."

Mac bowed to his hands. Suddenly he looked up and said: "If I could find a woman like yours or Ferd's. But where? Not Choy, not Shelley, not Wanda. Where are they? These awful virgins!"

"Listen, Mac: don't get the notion now that your problem is sexual. That's where Freud runs off the track. Sex is only an aspect of it. Like me, you identified yourself too much with sex—and with notions of shame and guilt and physical inadequacy. All that led you, as it leads all such people, to abnormal self-love, self-pity, egoism. What you are trying to do now—what I was fighting blindly to do, what all such people must do to be decent—is to correct that abnormal preoccupation with self. The truth, really, is that you're sick of idolizing yourself. My brother would put it this way: the auto-corrective process has thrown you into violent conflict; and now you want to keep the small precious world of yourself that you've built up—and you want to destroy it. What you want to do—what you should do, I think—is to discover yourself in terms of a larger circumference; recognize that, in a social order, any ego fixated on itself and narrowly pursuing its own morbidly egoistic interests is a distortion. More than that: it is racially, biologically, off the track. That's the problem."

"Is that what you've been doing?"

"As I see it. I was once an egocentric little world of my own and I had a terrific conflict because, deep within me, I wanted to rebuke that excessive egoism. Tragedy forced me to face the issue. Since then, I've grown steadily to love myself less and to discover myself in terms of a large human fellowship. But don't swing to the other extreme. Don't try to become the godfather to all human misery and fancy yourself as another Moses. When narrow self-preoccupied egoism is corrected, it often swings to another extreme just as absurd; confuses its motives; hides behind assumptions of unselfishness. Such are your rabid reformers, your fanatics of utopias and millenniums. Telv is an instance there. The egoism in that case, Mac, is just as blind and lost and a hell of a lot more dangerous. There are persons in asylums who fancy themselves responsible for all the ills of earth. There you have it. They got so sick of their egoism that, to correct it, to rebuke their colossal assumptions of personal importance and worth, they stepped forth to take the blame for everything. Or some kill themselves—and that is the most devastating rebuke of all to egoistic pretensions. And some, feeling themselves drawn out of their small kingdoms of self-love, kill themselves to save what is left—to preserve in death, you see, their little integrity of self. I once belonged to that group. I wanted to kill myself because I didn't want to lose my identity in the larger identity of human fellowship—or possibly, too, as a protest against so much self-love. Perhaps both were working in me.

"Mac, it is a nice problem, a nice balance, and none of us achieve it quite as we should. But we can try, and it's a mighty interesting fight. Only those are wholly sane who do achieve that proper balance between the self and the selfless, the individual and his race."

Mac stood up. "How long did it take you?"

"Hold on now," Vridar said. "I'm not flattering myself that I've come to that nice balance. I say only that I've come a long way. I'm not done yet by any means."

"Well, thanks. I'm going to face myself with my back

to a wall. If you can lick your training, Hunter, I can lick mine."

"You might go talk with my brother. He can help you along."

"I will. Hunter, I've a job ahead of me. I'm going to do it."

XIII

●

IT WAS true that more and more frequently persons came to Vridar for advice. Some, turned upon themselves in loathing, came to bait him and pull his leg. But even for these he had patience and sympathy. "And why not? Their wish to humiliate others springs from contempt for themselves. Most of them are repressed homosexuals. If they want to try to feel better with themselves by abusing me, that's all right."

"You're a strange person," Athene said. "When I met you, you had patience for nothing. Now you have patience for everything."

"Oh, hell no. I'm still plenty intolerant. Now and then I return blow for blow. A fellow came in yesterday. He sat and fixed me with an insolent grin and said, So you come from the West where men are men. And I retorted, You're in the wrong office. The mental clinic is next door. Little by little that grin faded as if it had been peeled off. Next time that young fellow will lay all his cards on the table. . . ."

And some girls came to Vridar, as they went to other instructors, because they sought, unwittingly, to be seduced. These girls Vridar dismissed. One of them came again and told of her lover: a big stupid oaf who wooed quickly and turned to sleep. "I hate him," this girl said, and her eyes were shadowed and stealthy. Vridar murmured with vague sympathy and listened; and at last he asked:

"Then why don't you leave him?"

"I can't. He threatens to kill me."

"Well, what are you looking for? Some giant who will go out and beat him up?"

"That would tickle me to death," she said.

This girl did not come to Vridar again. She went next

to one of his colleagues: a big handsome fellow with eyes as stealthy as her own. A month later Vridar saw them drinking muscatel in an underground den.

But most of those who came to Vridar were earnest and bedeviled persons who were very unhappy. And they had reasons. To these Vridar gave all the patience and wisdom he had. "Five years ago," he said to Athene, "I was as scathing an instructor as ever faced a class. And now, damn my hide, I'm almost a benevolent godfather. I'll be blessing babies next. . . ."

There was Albert Goldstein: handsome in a fatuous way and superbly at ease. He was betrothed to a girl who was worrying him to death. She was wealthy. She had a hundred thousand dollars in her own name and she would inherit that much more on the day of her wedding.

"But I walked in on her the other night. She didn't expect me to call. And there she was right on the sofa— well," he said, and lit a cigarette.

"And who was the man?"

"Her own brother. You know, she's in the same class with me. Can you guess who she is?"

"I haven't the faintest idea."

"Sarah Opwitz."

Vridar looked at Albert and thought of Sarah: a dour chunk of a girl who slumped down in her chair and sulked.

"But should I marry her? I hate to lose all that money."

"What are you looking for in marriage?"

"Money. But I want children, too. Do you think she'll make a good mother?"

"Hardly."

"And would she behave herself? That's what worries me. I don't want to find another guy in the bedroom every time I come home. On the other hand," said Albert quietly, "I'd be financially fixed. I could have a mistress, of course. But I want children."

"How long has she been carrying on with her brother?"

"I don't know. A long time."

"Well, if you want children I'd not risk it."

"But all that money. I'd hate to lose all that money. . . ."

There was Wright Monnahan. He stood two inches above six feet, was broad and deep and had a strong handsome face. When he came to see Vridar he was ill at ease and kept picking at his nails. He looked at his hands while he talked. This was his story:

He was the only child of a wealthy doctor in Ohio. His parents wanted him to be a great man but he was weary of school and felt impelled to throw ambition to the winds. Back home he had been betrothed to a girl who had deceived him. Then he came East to forget and to find other women.

"But they all sicken me. They all smoke and drink and neck."

"I suppose you'd like to find a splendid woman like your mother."

He looked up quickly. "Yes," he said.

"Was she an old-fashioned girl?"

"I suppose you'd call her that."

"Do you ever smoke or drink?"

"No."

"Why don't you?"

"They don't appeal to me."

"Does your father smoke and drink?"

"Yes."

"Does he drink a great deal?"

"Well, yes, he does."

"And your mother doesn't approve smoking and drinking." Vridar leaned back and lit a cigarette. "Have one?"

"No, thank you."

"You're intelligent. Your problem is not at all serious. Do you want the truth all at once?"

"Yes."

"All right: you've been spoiled. The only child usually is. You've been your mother's darling and clean noble son. Most likely you were once the pride of your boy-scout unit. You don't like your father. He disgusts you. Your love for your mother is the kind that is often called incestuous. That's a superficial way of putting it. It's enough to say that you have made an ideal of her, you have glorified her, and now you want to find a woman like her. Your attitude toward both your parents is unwholesome and very stupid. Your desire to run away from school is nothing but a desire to run away from your problem.

"Now this is what I think you should do. Realize first that there are thousands of young men like you from Maine to San Francisco. Realize that your neurosis is one that Americans deeply cherish and glorify over the radio and in tons of cheap fiction. Realize that you are another victim of that American neurotic glorification of womanhood. Stay in school. Seek girls, and I mean girls as unlike your mother as you can find. If you want to do a good job of it in the shortest time, find you a clean sensible girl and become her lover. But avoid neurotic girls. Avoid girls who talk of ideals and platonic relationships and beauty. And never go back home until you have licked your problem."

Monnahan looked up and his gaze now was steady. "You think that is what I should do?"

"There can be no doubt of it."

"All right," he said, "I'll try."

Two months later he came to Vridar's office again. He did not stare at his hands now.

"Well," he said, smiling, "I found a girl. She's a swell kid." He shrugged. "She's not a bit like my mother," he said.

"That's fine. And how's school?"

"It's all right. I'm sticking."

"Good. You're on your legs now. Stay there."

"I want to thank you," Monnahan said, and offered his hand.

"That's all right. I went through the same thing myself."

And there was Esther Ohrback. She spread deprecating palms and her eyelids fluttered.

"I'm in a mess," she said. "Will you help me?"

"If I can. But why come to me?"

"Oh—— Well, you've suffered, haven't you? I think you have. Anyway, you're the person I wanted to come to."

"All right. Let's have the story."

"It will amaze you."

"Nothing human beings do any longer amazes me."

"Darn it!" said Esther, coloring. "I'm embarrassed now."

"Take a book and look at pictures. Here's Lynd Ward."

"No. I want to get it over with." And this was her story:

When only a small girl she had been ill and her father had slept with her as nurse. She was about nine then. He had taken her in his arms and slept and she had felt comforted and at peace. "I think I had a cold," she said. And then she had been ill a second time, a third, and her father had acted as nurse. He had lain with an arm around her: that was all. She became ill so frequently that her father got the habit of sleeping with her and her mother slept in another room. "But I was never really ill," she said. "I pretended."

"And does he sleep with you now?"

"No."

"You wouldn't lie about it? Lies will get you nowhere." She rose to her feet as if to flee. She looked down at him, holding her breath, and blood dyed her face. "Sit down. . . . And now let's be sensible about this. These situations are not uncommon. Does your father only sleep with you?"

"What do you mean?"

"Does he kiss you? . . . Does he?"

"Yes, a good-night kiss."

"Does he still lie with his arm around you?"

"He wants to."

"And do you let him?"

"No. . . . Well, just once in a while."

"Do you like to have him sleep with you?"

"I—well, I don't know. I used to. Not now."

"And what is your mother's attitude?"

"Oh, she looks funny. I guess——"

"And now what did you come to ask me?"

"A lot of things. I've read psychology——"

"I wouldn't. It will only confuse you."

"Well, it's this: my father says he will never let me marry." She spoke so earnestly that Vridar was startled.

"Did you see in the paper last week the account of a father who slew his daughter the day before her wedding?"

"Yes, I saw it."

"Well, there is only one thing you can do. You must leave your home and never go back to it. Have you any friends you can stay with?"

"He would find me."

"Yes, he would. Have you friends in any other city?"

"No."

"Have you money?"

"I could get some."

"Get it. Leave at once. Never go back."

"You think I should?"

"It's the only decent thing you can do. And write and let me know how you get along."

Six months passed before Vridar heard from Esther Ohrback. She was in Chicago. "This is to thank you," her letter said. "I'm a student here and I'm getting along all right. You will keep all this a secret, I know. . . ."

There was John Rodman. He came one night to Vridar's apartment, a terror-stricken man with sweat running from his face. "I'm going insane!" he cried; and Vridar remembered that hour, long ago, when he burst in on Dr. Gunn with the same cry. He looked at Athene and she left the room. But he learned nothing of John Rodman in this evening: he could only try to hush the man's awful terror and give him strength and calm. He went out and walked with him, talking all the while. He went with Rodman to his home and when Rodman's wife came, frightened, to the door, Vridar said, "He's all right now. He's coming to see me tomorrow."

Rodman came again and again and still Vridar learned nothing of the truth. This man was more hopelessly lost than anyone who had come to Vridar before. At Vridar's request he fetched dreams but they were so dark and cunning in their symbolism that weeks passed before Vridar found a clue. In a dream Rodman had been riding a trolley across one of Brooklyn's bridges and the bridge fell.

"Who was with you?"

"No one."

For several minutes Vridar talked of other matters. Then he said quietly: "When you were riding the trolley, you say a girl was with you. What was her name?"

"I don't know."

"She was sitting in the seat with you?"

"I don't know."

"Have you read this?" asked Vridar, taking a book from his desk. And for five minutes he talked of this book: a story by Ellen Glasgow of stupid pieties in the South. And then: "You say you were riding with a girl who sat in the seat with you. How old was she?"

"How old? I don't remember. . . ."

"How many sisters do you have?"

"Four."

"Older or younger?"

"Much older."

"Before you go to sleep tonight, say to yourself, Tonight I'm going to dream of my childhood, of my sisters. Dream of them. Keep that thought in your mind as you fall asleep. . . ."

Other weeks passed and still this haunted and terrified man dodged at every point. Vridar learned that he was riding the trolley with the daughter of his landlady, a girl of six.

"And you don't recall the name of the sister younger than yourself?"

"I had no sister younger than myself."

"Of course. Well, tonight you will dream of her. . . ." Vridar gave association tests and at every allusion to sex Rodman balked. *Disgusting,* he said, was the only word that came to his mind. And two weeks later: "And what was the name of this younger sister?"

"I can't remember her name."

"The name of your landlady's daughter is Bernice, you say. Tonight you will dream of all the girls you have known named Bernice or Bertha or Blanche or Beryl or Eunice. . . ." And for another two weeks, Vridar talked round and round this forgotten sister, bringing her slowly to Rodman's memory. Six months from the day when Rodman first came to him he said: "Rodman, you are being very ridiculous. When you were twelve your sister Beatrice was six. You tried to be intimate with her. I say you tried because that is all that lads really do. Then your sense of guilt and shame became so extreme that you actually forgot you had such a sister. For sixteen years you have punished yourself for this trivial matter in your childhood. You never once stopped to reflect that if the men of this country were to be hanged for such petty little philanderings in their youth, we'd have to hang nine tenths of them.

"Now your job is to get these silly notions out of you. What you did is nothing to be ashamed of. It's past and dead. Forget it. Stand on your feet and slug the world black in the face. Everywhere I go I see persons who are driving

themselves crazy with just such nonsense as haunted you.
As a matter of fact, it was just such unimportant matters
that almost put me in a padded cell years ago."

"You?" asked Rodman, astonished.

"Yes, I. So shake out of it. If you don't, next time I
see you I'll laugh until I fall out of my chair."

Rodman grinned. It was his first grin since Vridar had
known him.

"I feel a lot better," he said.

And these were a few of the many who came to Vridar,
seeking his help. Only rarely was one so lost as Rodman: the
most difficult cases, with few exceptions, he sent to his
brother. And he wondered endlessly at the emotional distortions which human beings had got themselves into and
which they glorified and cherished.

"Did you see," he asked Athene, "that review the other
day of Hemingway? The critic says Hemingway is off the
track now because he writes of the abnormal. Gertrude
Stein, he says, has given the final and crushing answer to
such nonsense: she detests the abnormal because it is too
obvious. Her detestation of herself must be mountainous.
And the critic revealed himself completely in what he said.
As a matter of fact, there is little to write about today
except the abnormal. Even these authors of sweet fables
write of it because nothing is really any more abnormal than
chastity and piety and cant.

"And I see clearly now another monstrous sham. I mean
all this unintelligible writing we have today. It's another
method of escape from self. It's the most cunning and
devious method that has ever been hit upon. It's *the*
twentieth-century method and how it flourishes! It is
catharsis, bleeding internally."

"I've been thinking, my dear, that you spend too much
time with these unhappy persons. You haven't done any
writing for three months."

"I know it. But how can I better use my time?"

"But don't give them all your time."

"How could I write with that man Rodman going mad? And listen: Ferd and I have decided the four of us should go to Europe this summer. You know what I want to do?"

"Drink Scotch whisky or see the Frenchwomen."

"Nothing so worthy. I want to ride a bicycle all over Europe. Would you like that?"

"I think it would be great fun."

"What I really want to do is to see a lot of prejudices different from my own. Then maybe I can tell how stupid mine are. Would that be fun, too?"

"That would be the nicest fun of all."

XIV

●

WE HAVE been sailing for four days out of sight of land and I am still trying to realize that the world is mostly water and that all of us live on islands. I look at a perfectly round sea and a perfectly round sky; smell of the salt and sea and the infinite centuries of time; and love it. For this tiny world afloat is timeless and the sun is a meaningless pilgrim and all this is a part of my ancient and buried life. And as I pace the decks, looking, breathing, and feeling the deep and ageless joy of mere being, I am troubled by the presence that haunted Wordsworth. Obscure recognitions swarm into the moment and overwhelm my senses until a journey becomes the lovely symbol of all human hungers and dreams. I look at this great rolling body of water, blue like the sky with time and with all that the world has forgotten, and make futile little attempts to understand how long I lived before I was born and what a magnificent heritage looks out of my eyes. For four days I have heard the sound of a rolling sea; have felt the ocean moving through my sleep and dreams; and am lost now in the wonder which takes us to its heart when intelligence looks back across the ageless record of emotion. If I were not a person of restraint, I should fling my arms to the zenith and burst forth into rhapsodic apostrophes to the boundless unknown. I should take my clothes off and stand in this spray of salt and wind and ancientness and look across two millions of years to the moment when the first man rose to his feet. . . .

I am sitting in a London hotel, remembering the last few days. I am remembering how the drab and rockbound coast of Galway rebuked, for a moment, all the green legends of Ireland; and how in Liverpool Ferd and I were accosted by nine harlots within two blocks, and how the policemen stood apart and grinned; and how Athene and Millicent wanted to go to the Lake Country—and I too; and how Ferd said, "I suppose you want to sit where Wordsworth sat. If you could find the spot where he wrote a violet by a mossy stone. My God, if you could only find that stone!" I am remembering that my traditions are more English than American: I spent several years in study of English literature: the background of Shakspere or Wordsworth or Keats is a part of my blood; but Poe, Hawthorne, and Emerson have for me no physical anchorage, and in memory are adrift upon the American landscape. I could go to the Lake Country and feel I had once lived there; I could go to New England and be a stranger. . . .

The journey through English countryside from Liverpool to Stratford is a memorable experience. In lush growth and magnificent trees, in acres of field and hedgerow, thatched and asleep, this country is somewhat like Illinois or Iowa in June. But there is a difference. Mary Borden declares that England's greatness has come from the passionate sense and feel and smell of its people for its lazy climate; that the United States, stripped of fog, lit brilliantly from sky to sky, encourages ceaseless racing upon the hours. In consequence, she thinks, we produce more abundantly than any other nation skyscrapers and religious maniacs, psychiatrists and drunkards and patent medicines, neurotics and tabloids and fads and cults. What we need, it seems to her, is a rainstorm that will last for months; a great fog that will smother our lunacy, paralyze our agents of noise and speed. But her thesis seems to me to smack of that condescension which foreigners give us by the carload.

It is true that the mood of this country is remote from the nervous and the flamboyant. It has been chastened and tempered by centuries of habit. Here is an analogue Mary Borden might have used: in the United States sage often grows eight feet tall but a man can seize and uproot one of these giants of the desert. In England the dandelion grows in abundance and its roots resist everything but an ax. Say that American cities are like the sage, these hamlets like the dandelion. But this analogy is trite and rather meaningless: it is the sort of thing that haunted Henry James and many another expatriate.

On our ride south I lay back and tried to realize the centuries that are England's; its enchanted ancientness, its heritage that has flattened out into this delta of quiet. My own background has been great mountains and prairies; frenzied towns; and all the gaudy imbecility of getting up and ahead in the world. In me—I imagine in every American—there is something of Babbitt, something of Uncle Henry in *The Woodcutter's House*. I have the backdrop against which these stand in meaning. I am aware that my cultural heritage has been lean and superficial, but if it had not been, I should probably have been hopelessly lost. Because it was superficial I was able to fight my way out of it.

I am not writing here as a patriot in defense of his country. That the land of my birth employs and cherishes the most monstrous shams in the western hemisphere, I admit. Too much of its education is myopic commentaries on trivial details. Adolescent still, it has little sense of humor, and the little it has runs to surface grotesqueries and smut. Irony it has no taste for: Cabell and Robert Nathan should have been born in France. Its art runs to the superficial modes of cinema and tabloid. Its social consciousness has an unclean conviction of social inferiority and so it falls over itself in vulgar welcome of such unimportant noddies as the Prince of Wales. It defers to all manner of dead and decaying royalties; spawns all sorts of adolescent cults; and declares its profound vulgarity in its perjured testimonials to all sorts of gadgets. Before long, I imagine, the President or the President's wife will be recommending an encyclopedia or a toothpaste. My country is overrun with asylums and jails, and many of its leaders are suffering from paranoia. It responds to demagogues with half a million letters and telegrams. Its national academy of arts and letters is the jest of everyone who understands the source of Mark Twain's lewdness, or why Howells declared in all seriousness that his wife was the greatest woman who ever lived. Even honesty is now regarded with a derisive smirk by many who are emotionally ashamed of emotion.

But to wail of America as a land of lunatics and boors and of England as a land of philosophy and culture is merely

to wail. The matter is more than one of fog and sunshine.
And as I make these notes I remember with shame the
American abuse of Dreiser, but I recall, too, the abuse
heaped by London upon Ibsen and Zola. Among the Langs
and Lillys and Steads and Saintsburys there was only one
Havelock Ellis and such men belong to no country and to
no age. I remember that Zola's English publisher, an old and
sick man, was thrown into jail and driven to his death; and
Belgravia's statement that "Evil, be thou my God" was Zola's
motto. On the contrary, that is England's motto and is the
motto of my own land, and in this, their terrible fear of joy,
they are and have always been alike.

We have been in London two weeks and I find the English most polite and most incurious. A policeman here will
walk a block to direct you; in New York City he might
knock you down. The bus driver on our way here drove for
miles, and patiently, behind a man on a bicycle. In my country the fellow would have been run down and knocked into
a ditch. Quietness here; frenzy in my homeland: what explains the difference?

I think it is largely the difference between growth and
decay. Our racial heritage is not, as I used to think, a
pastoral one: our spiritual milieu has been and still is the
jungle. We Americans have recreated it in our cities and
we have endowed them with all that we unconsciously remember of millions of years. That is why New York City
takes hold of you: you come to love its noise and stink and
confusion. And if its clamor is making, as some declare,
neurotics of its inhabitants, I think it awakens, and excites
to action, and leaves a man nothing to do but to climb a
tower or walk the streets. It's as if a monkey, listening to
the infernal din of the jungle, were tied by its tail to a tree
and unable to move.

And in England, on the other hand, there are traditions
of culture brought to their last impotence and left to rot in
the fog. England was great in only one period: when Eliza-
beth ruled and fornicated and nationalism was a new and
impetuous force, then adventurers sailed to the ends of earth
and art caught the spirit. Those who remained at home,

XV

●

DOVER I shall remember as the place where we saw six vulgar Americans drunk; Ostend as an enchanted loveliness in a dark night; and Belgium as the country which we left in haste. There descended upon us in Belgium that obsequious horde which preys on tourists, its attitude one of servility and contempt. Though we used all our cunning we found ourselves fleeced at every turn. "It's no wonder," Ferd said, "that internationalism is only a dream that Woodrow Wilson had at Princeton."

We have been in Paris two weeks. I am sitting in a shabby little hotel in Rue Git-le-Cœur. We eat in the most out-of-the-way cafés we can find and the food is always excellent, even though among the loaves of bread as long as Lindbergh's legs there often sits a cat, or the loaves sometimes fall to the floor. Only twice have Ferd and I yielded to the cultured impulses of our wives. We went to the Louvre but in an hour I was overwhelmed: pacing down these corridors as most persons do is absurd: you might as well try to read the five-foot shelf while eating a macaroon. So I gave up and sat before the Mona Lisa.

We also went into the depressing darkness of Notre-Dame and the sick mysticism of the place gave me a headache. The persons offering coins to the damned in purgatory made me feel as if I were watching a flogging. I went into a full sensuous afternoon and felt better. But our wives are culture-bent: the Institut Pasteur, Balzac's house in Rue Raynouard, Hugo's in Place des Vosges, the Sorbonne—they run around like two children. I have no wish to see: the human imagination builds infinitely beyond human achievement: I was disappointed in Yellowstone Park, Niagara Falls, New York City's skyline, the Avenue des Champs-Elysées. I want never to see Atlantis, the Hebrides, heaven or hell. . . .

I came to Europe to learn how the people live and feel and Ferd and I have just been exploring the dives. He has tremendous zest for freaks: a Russian-whiskered bohemian staggering with a cocotte from Shanghai, or a painted imitation apache breaking a tenth-rate Kiki across his knee, or anyone looking with solemn stupidity out of a posture. We followed one evening a group of students into La Source where they stole all the drinks in sight; thence to D'Harcourt where they turned the tables over; then to La Rotonde and Le Dôme. This, we take it, is a French student's notion of uninhibited living. Ferd hunts for a person with a real macabre air or a pose nourished in unpremeditated distortion. He finds none and he grieves. In Le Jockey the dances are supposed to be wild, the old French songs full of smut: the performance is about like that in a cheap Harlem cabaret. We went to Le Moulin Rouge which advertises "pretty women in as few garments as possible": the theatrical silliness bored us. We went to Le Cabaret de l'Enfer where damned souls do their infernal rounds: now and then an American screamed, a bridegroom clutched his bride: that was all. In Les Folies-Bergère I spent most of my time studying the faces around me. In one scene a woman, almost naked, assumed a statuesque pose and a man, amorously out of his wits, knelt to her; kissed her thighs, ran his tongue up her body to her breasts, and employed, I inferred from the American faces around me, a manner of lovemaking that was strange and exciting. When this show started, not a man in the gallery had his arm around a woman; when the erotic fanfare was done, there were arms around women everywhere. When the lights came on I found no gaze that would meet mine: girls looked flushed and guilty and the men looked as if they had been thinking very naughty thoughts. I shook with inner giggles and reflected that possibly my countrymen ought to be forced to read of the life and loves of Frank Harris. The solemnly erotic distress of some of these young men, the breathless guilty ecstasy of the girls, do make more credible the ease with which Frankie put his naughty hands under dresses. . . .

I came to Paris with a lot of illusions in my head. I came here believing that love in Paris is franker and more unashamed than in the United States. It may be, but the with peasants along the way. France I remember in two visions: the one in perspective with my sense of smell laid aside: then it is a gorgeous loveliness of poppies and quaint hamlets, picturesque dwellings and rolling hills. But only the fields and flowers can stand a close scrutiny: the hamlets have an awful stink about them, and France itself, from one point of view, is a sewer and a cemetery. Countless millions have died and been buried in this land, and the rain washes the old and decaying graves under the watersheds. Tiring of French beer, and unable to afford the water purified and sold in bottles, we ventured to drink of that served in carafes and for two days in La Charité (how we love that name!) we almost died. We sat with our agonizing belly-aches and reflected on the irony of this lovely land, fertilized by God knows how many forgotten graveyards, watered by the foul streams with their cargoes of dysentery. . . .

Some of my prejudices and habits have suffered thorough rebuke. Take food: I was trained to eat certain items and to regard them as clean. Over here I've been eating all sorts of cheese and I got along all right until I bit into a maggot that writhed against my tongue. Then I began to think of foods and to summarize myself in another respect as a preju-diced ass. I am a bundle of habits, and in smug self-love I have been looking with amused pity at habits different from my own. Until recently: now I reflect that maggots, for all I know, may be a tasty dish: it is absurd for me to gag at them and smack over tongue and brains. Frenchmen drink this cheap wine with bugs in it; and now so do I. In St. Symphorien we were served minnows fried whole and I didn't want to eat their eyes. Now I eat bread that dirty cats have slept on. I eat meat, sauced and incomparable, that has lain all day in a warm room under a swarm of flies. I sniff the rotten stink of cheese and wink at Ferd. The French don't seem to mind flies any more than we mind the seeds in an apple and we wonder how many we have eaten. Once we balked: they lay in a sickly stew as if it were dotted with raisins: our training in the matter of flies has been too thorough and this habit we decided to keep for a while and so went hungry to bed. . . .

We are getting a good lesson in the difficulties of internationalism. Wealthy Americans, we understand little by little, own all the highways of Europe: twice they ran us down and knocked us into a ditch. All native travelers give us the right of way. Possibly Europe figures that the highways ought to be sufficient pay for the war debts.

Keats was right: the mirth of Provence was certainly sunburnt when we went through: a barren rocky country blazing with sunlight, dwarfed cedar, defenseless sunscalded towns. The French Riviera is lovely but not to my taste: habit again, doubtless: but it is too much of one tone: orange and lemon and olive trees, cunning pale villas high or low by the sea, a magnificent coastline, a pitiless sun overhead. Every city has the same hard and glittering beauty; but what lovely names, after the Oshkoshes and Chicagos and Pittsburghs of my own land: St. Raphaël, Boulouris and Miramar and Théoule, La Napoule and Anthéor and Juan-les-Pins. I am sitting now in a flower-burgeoned house in Menton: certain famous persons, now dead, have called this little city the loveliest spot on earth. It may be but I like shadow and depth in background. Its turquoise sea is lovely, but so are all the bays along here: the gulf of La Napoule, Nice's Bay of Angels, the sheltered perfection of Villefranche-sur-Mer. But all these, all the towns and bays and hills, have the hard glittering loveliness of jewels. The Mediterranean at our feet looks, when no breeze is moving, like blue glass, and I have a notion that the persons who live here are brittle. I expect to hear the tinkling of chandelier pendants, or to learn that the flowers are made of gold-leaf, or to smell steel- and rock-shavings when I breathe. I'm an ass, Ferd says, and he soaks himself with voluptuous abandon in sunshine and vermouth or stuffs his belly with ripe juicy figs. But I want to feel the pull of muscles. I want German beer and a rolling landscape and an open road.

ing at the pocket into which I had thrust the watch and I called him dolt and blockhead, snoop and fool and lout, taking deep pleasure in the knowledge that he did not understand me at all. But he backed away, his astonishment growing, and I followed him, pretending that I was enraged; and I poured upon his head all the abuse I could think of. I showed him my passport and pointed triumphantly at Stimson's face and then abused him again. "Y a-t-il longtemps que vous en souffrez? Vous êtes trop amiable but I can't waste any more time. To hell with you, you blockhead!" Then I leapt to my wheel and cycled furiously; but after a moment, reflecting that he might pursue, I stopped and shook my fist at him. I gesticulated wildly. "Avez-vous fini? All right, then: good-by!" Again and again I looked back, and for as long as I could see him, he stood in the road and stared after me. . . .

As we cycled through Switzerland I kept thinking that one seldom reads of this tiny kingdom in the headlines: it is too peaceable to make news. Among all these nations, with their imperialistic aims and brawls and intrigues, it minds its own business; and I shall ride out of it with the ironic thought that I do not understand Switzerland at all.

XVI

●

A THENE is photographing the Rhine and I am left to
catch up again with my notes. We have spent two
weeks in Germany and I am still overwhelmed: having a lot
of German in me, I had expected to feel at home there, but
I forgot the war. The hatred of Americans has amazed us.
On our first day we entered from Bâle and at midnight we
were still seeking a place to sleep. From one Gasthof and
another we were turned away. At last, dispirited and exhausted, we entered a small place and a girl served us beer
and we asked if we could get a room and she said yes; but
when the mother came, a woman who hadn't smiled since
1914, she learned that we were Americans and would not
talk with us at all. There was a long argument between
mother and daughter and it was decided to let us stay, but
the mother vanished at once and we did not see her again.

We left this place without breakfast and traveled with
the low mountains of the Black Forest on our right, with
poppies and morning glories along the road. At noon we
passed a man in a wagon who had lost a part of his cargo
and I overtook him to tell of his loss: he scowled at me and
asked if I was an American. A little later, while we were
eating lunch under a tree, he came back and asked where his
property was. I went and showed it to him and he dug into
his pocket for a coin. "Nein," I said. "Sie haben mich
falsch verstanden. . . . Nein, nein, was liegt daran? Es ist
nicht der Rede wert." He was offering me the equivalent
of half a cent and he was looking at me with hatred and
memories in his eyes.

Five times in the second day we asked for a room and
were dismissed. In the sixth venture I found a large man
with haunted eyes. To my question in German he retorted
in English and turned to a group of men and winked. Oh
yes, he said with a sinister wink, he had rooms; and then
ignored me. But I persisted and when midnight came we
were drinking great steins of beer with him. He had been

captured in the war and had spent two years as a prisoner in England. "A hell of a war," I said. "A war for the big guys." He didn't understand what I meant by big guys and I clasped hands before me to suggest an enormous belly. He grinned. His father, his two brothers, and all his uncles had been slain. He was still so bitter after twelve years' that we could not make him laugh but we did make him smile, and on the next morning he gave us a hearty handclasp and stood in the road to watch us disappear.

Our experiences in the other nights were repetitions of these two. The climax of bitterness, the most hostile unwelcome, came to us west of Bad Dürkheim. We had been turned away from nine places and as we rode along, despairing of finding a room, I spoke the simple and necessary questions in German, trying to correct my accent; and I succeeded well enough to fool the daughter in the next inn we approached. But the mother came in and she was not to be fooled. She said she had no rooms and I said her daughter declared she had. Seeing that she would not yield, I decided to lie: I said we were Germans, born in America, but that our fathers had been born in Germany; and, watching her, I saw that I had struck a vulnerable spot. Her next question staggered me. On which side in the war had our fathers fought? I explained to her that our fathers had no choice in the matter and she saw the logic of that but she wanted us to go. She withdrew to a wall and looked at us. I turned to the daughter: it was silly, I said, to be so unfriendly because of a stupid war now twelve years dead. The daughter said her father and all her brothers had been killed. Then the daughter and mother drew aside and talked and suddenly the mother asked me our name. 'Hunter,' I said. She asked me to write it and I did and she came over and looked at it. She asked her daughter if Hunter was a German name and then she wanted to see our passport. After staring at it she wanted to know in what part of Germany my father had been born. I saw a map of Germany on a wall and I went over to it and saw Coblenz. "Coblenz," I said, pointing to it. "Coblenz?" she asked. "Ja. Coblenz, es liegt mit viel daran. Gott lasse ihm seinen Willen." This last statement, that God let my father have his choice of birthplace, I expected to please her. It did. She said we could have a room.

But our attempts to soften what war had done to her were of no use. She gave us a cold supper and her manner said that she had gone as far toward friendliness as it was possible for her to go. I told her thousands of Americans had been killed, too, and that the mothers of these had been saddened by loss. She retorted that millions of Germans had been killed and I had no answer to that.

On the next morning we rose early and were flabbergasted to find our door locked. We were prisoners of war. I dare say Germany had been full of stories of American soldiers who raped German girls. We waited patiently and an hour later we heard steps in the hallway and a key softly turned. And as I write this there are stories of the friendliness of Germany for my own land. Of course it is friendly in those places which American tourists endow with their patronage. But we have looked under all that to the most intense and tragic bitterness I have ever seen. It is not easy to hope that Woodrow Wilson rests in peace. . . .

It is appropriate, I think, that we should have ridden out of Germany and across the desolation that is Lorraine. I shall never forget the sudden and overwhelming emotion I felt when, after leaving Metz, we came to the first barbed-wire entanglements. They beat me down. I looked at the trenches, the wire, the crosses in the fields of oats—all a record of that other war in which Germany was triumphant. I tried to understand this record of blood and death: I can get hold of nothing but a sense of something brooding and darkened, of something passing into a great body of legend wherein the truth will never be told. It was not until we reached Douaumont that we realized how deeply quiet everything now is on the western front. Rain fell during our journey through this wasteland. We climbed to France's ironically magnificent monument to the murdered and stared a long while at the Tranchée des Baïonnettes where men were entombed alive at the moment of charge, with their bayonets thrust up like a row of pickets. We stood here in shell-gutted land, under a dismal wet sky, trying to realize not only that four hundred thousand men had been slain here, but also that only eighty thousand complete bodies had been recovered. They were digging for bones all around us. Imagine such indifference to life, and such patient care to seek out and preserve the skeletons! Those who donate ten francs to this resurrection of bones "will receive an artistic parchment, designed by Georges Scott and bearing Marshal Pétain's autograph." Where are the smug simpletons who say the human race is civilized? Take Thiaumont: it was lost on June 23d, retaken on the 24th, lost during that night, retaken by the French on the 29th, lost on the 30th; and between then and July 4th it changed hands again four times. "It is soaked," says a French guide which we carry, "with the glory of France." How lovely! We made a long journey in rain to see the American cemetery of Romagne-sous-Montfaucon. Near the infamous Mort-Homme we read on a monument this nonsense:

> *Qui que tu sois, Français qui passe, salue*
> *bien bas ceux qui sont morts ici pour toi*

Then we stood here in rain, looking back over the awful desolation of a land that has been soaked with human blood.

On our way out we paused to see the Rheims Cathedral; and while looking at it I remembered the rage of some American editors when the Germans almost shot this building into pieces. It seems quaintly silly that anyone should howl about the shooting of a building and approve the shooting of twelve millions of men. A lot of the saints on this cathedral got their heads shot off, a matter which I found quite thoroughly to my taste. But they are rebuilding now and I have no doubt this cathedral will be ready for the next war between Germany and France.

Athene had wanted to see Versailles and I was now in a mood to learn what sort of a cabin the animal Louis had built for himself. The Palais du Roi proved to be a fittingly ironic

climax to the devastation around Verdun. When we came
to this extravagant blunder I had my sleeves rolled up and
we were both coatless. The guard looked at us with withering disdain: to imagine we could enter, coatless, into the
decaying haunt of a long-ago dead mountebank. So we returned for our coats and when I gave the tickets I dropped
them, as if unwittingly, so the prig would have to stoop;
and when he stooped, his face red and angry, I wanted to
kick him. And inside, while looking at paintings that com-
memorated one slaughter and another, I asked Athene if she
did not find it a little strange that all of America's *great*
presidents were *war* presidents.

Athene had also wanted to see the Bois de Boulogne and
on our way to Paris we rode through it. It is very lovely
and we stopped here to read: in Menton I had bought for
sixty francs *Lady Chatterley's Lover* with Lawrence's excellent preface. Here in the Bois we read to one another. It
is a sincere story and in some respects an important one. All
his life Lawrence struggled to write one book, and from the
groping *Sons and Lovers* to this last effort, he made an ago-
nizingly slow pilgrimage to an idea, a vision, which he never
emotionally came to. Only intellectually did he achieve it.
He understood what we must all understand: that we can
never be reasonable as long as the mind is ashamed of the
body, the body afraid of the mind. He says that "words
which shock so much at first don't shock at all after a
while" and he asks if that is because the mind is depraved
by habit. He concludes that words merely shocked the eye,
not the mind; and "people without minds may go on being
shocked, but they don't matter." They do matter. And to
say that the eye, not the mind, is shocked is to say, it seems
to me, nothing at all. He must be trying to point out why
persons who listen with relish to obscene tales go wailing
to legislators when they see them in print. I doubt that
Lawrence ever understood why we have erotic legends: they
compensate those who delight in them for the sexual raptures which they are ashamed to take.

We are today, he says, "evolved and cultured far be-

yond the taboos which are inherent in our culture." That
statement is, in my opinion, absolute silliness: we are not
evolved beyond the taboos inherent in our culture and that
is exactly our trouble. He goes on: "Probably to the Crusaders mere words were potent and evocative to a degree
we can't realize. The evocative power of the so-called
obscene words must have been very dangerous to the dim-
minded, obscure, violent natures of the Middle Ages, and
perhaps are still too strong for slow-minded, half-evolved
lower natures of today." What foggy thinking! What
patronizing summary of thousands of sensitive intelligent
persons: half-evolved? Yes, and so are all of us. "In the
past, man was too weak-minded, or crude-minded, to con-
template his own physical functions without getting all
messed up with physical reactions that overpowered him. It
is no longer so." Indeed! If Lawrence had read in ethnology
he would have learned that the *lower natures* do not get
messed up: the messing up has come with what it pleases us
to call higher culture. "There has been so much action in
the past, especially sexual action, a wearying repetition over
and over, without a corresponding thought, a corresponding
realization. . . . When people act in sex, nowadays they are
half the time acting up. . . . Mentally, we lag behind in
our sexual thoughts, in a dimness, a lurking, grovelling fear
which belongs to our raw, somewhat bestial ancestors." My
God: why couldn't Lawrence get the self-pity out of himself
and come to the vision? Why must he flee into the cant
about somewhat bestial ancestors? The fear is not the same:
with our ancestors it was fear of the physical world; with
us it is fear of joy because of a monstrous notion that we
are depraved and a silly conviction that we ought to be
punished. We seek pleasure in guilty excursions and then
return to the estime de soi-même of our pieties. But I like
the furious eloquence of his last paragraph: "So, between the
stock old puritan who is likely to fall into sexual indecency
in advanced age, and the smart jazzy person of the young
world, who says: 'We can do anything. If we can think a
thing we can do it'—and then the low uncultured person with
a dirty mind, who looks for dirt—this book has hardly a

space to turn in. But to them all I say the same: Keep your
perversions if you like them—your perversion of puritanism,
your perversion of smart licentiousness, your perversion of
a dirty mind. But I stick to my book and my position: life
is only bearable when the mind and the body are in harmony,
and there is a natural balance between them, and each has a
natural respect for the other." That is a summary of the
morass in which I spent twenty years. He uses Lady Chatterley herself as an example of this shamed impotence:
". . . do what she might, her spirit seemed to look on from
the top of her head. . . . Yes, this was love, this ridiculous
bouncing of the buttocks. . . After all, the moderns were
right when they felt contempt for the performance; for it
was a performance. It was quite true, as some poets said,
that the God who created man must have had a sinister
sense of humor, creating him a reasonable being, yet forcing
him to take this ridiculous posture. . . . Even a Maupas-
sant found it a humiliating anticlimax. Men despised the
intercourse act, and yet did it."

Such was my plight once. But did Lawrence realize that
persons despise the act because they are sick with self love?
Did he understand that all this cant about bestial ancestors,
about subhuman and inhuman and unhuman and animal-like,
grows out of that preposterous self-love? To suppose that
we can achieve harmony between the body and the mind,
and achieve it within those traditions that have made dis-
harmony inevitable, is, in my opinion, to be self-deceived.
Malinowsky has pointed out, I remember, that among our
bestial ancestors of British New Guinea, " 'Unnatural vice,'
on which we need to impose heavy penalties, has no place
except as a subject for contemptuous amusement." We who
have "grown beyond the taboos inherent in our culture"
now fill asylums with "unnatural vice" and can no longer
even approximately guess its extent. As a matter of fact,
we of the *higher natures* are now writing books in its defense and demanding for it everywhere that tolerance within
which in a few parts of the world it now rests secure. We
get nowhere by supposing that in morality we are superior
to "savages": we have taken a vast part of their ignorance

and superstition and have cherished it and glorified it and built it into cults. It is precisely those taboos inherent in our culture, and our desperate attempts to pretend that we have outgrown them, that are leading us daily farther into stupidity and evasion. They have become so familiar disguised as virtues, and in every field we have gone to such pains to cherish and excuse them, that they are no longer recognizable for what they are. And there, in my opinion, lies our modern problem.

We embarked at Cherbourg. I am sitting on deck now, making notes; looking back to Europe and remembering; trying to see what its lesson for me has been. It has given me a larger horizon and a more certain faith but it has also left me to ponder the imminence of another great war. I belong to a race that has in its leadership enough intelligence and more than enough courage but it has never learned fellowship. And the pity of it! For each of us has, as Robinson says, a darkening hill to climb. How much less difficult the darkening hill would be if we could unite in a community of fellowship and reach out in the gloom now and then to touch hands. But that we have never learned to do. . . .

XVII

●

THE months abroad sharpened Vridar's interest in the
political and economic affairs of the world. He had now
given six years to relentless searching of human motives, and
he believed he had arrived at a philosophy of life which his
intelligence could accept. Humanity, it seemed to him, had
both the courage and the faith to civilize itself, but he did
not think that civilization could be achieved within most
of its present cultures and traditions. These were betray-
ing it to brutality and greed and waste. Trying to build a
social order within them was like trying to reform a psychopathic criminal. Humanism or fascism, the philosophic
realisms or the refuge of the Church, or even communism
itself, he regarded as superficial evasions of the central
problem.

He often talked of the matter with Telv. Telv was a
profoundly unhappy person who dreamed of a utopian order
wherein peace and a classless society would make everything
wholesome and sweet. His credulity, his furious faith, and
his flight from self into what he called a cellular development within the group, were once Vridar's own. With mad
impatience he evaded all knowledge of himself and declared
such knowledge to be unimportant. He said:

"You're a Marxist. You admit that."

"Yes, I'm a Marxist."

"Then you're a communist too."

"No, I'm not a communist."

"Oh, in God's name! You mean you breathe but you
don't breathe. You live but you're dead. What kind of
damned quibbling is this?"

One evening Telv came to Vridar's apartment. He was
distressed. He asked for a drink and Vridar poured for him
a glass of gin.

"I'm thirty," Telv said, "and unmarried. But all these women around me are narcists that Aldous Huxley has turned loose from his mind. The sexual act for them is a dismal and obscene irrelevance." He ran a hand through his mop of black hair. "I can talk to you," he said. "You're too stupid to be a communist but you do have a heart. This is what I want to know: why aren't you? There are thousands of men like you today. They have brains and hearts and they know the capitalist order is rotten. But they won't come over to communism. What is wrong with the cowards?"

Vridar listened patiently and meditated on the hunger and loss in Telv's eyes. "Do you," he asked, "want me to speak frankly?"

"I do."

"All right. Telv, you're the sort of fool I used to be. You come here to talk of women and sidetrack into communism. Deep in your heart you want a sweet old-fashioned girl. Tons of sentimental mush have been written about the country girl. The Maud Mullers, raking the new-mown hay! Wordsworth's highland maidens! And on the covers of magazines, all the innocent-eyed creatures, standing by sheaves of corn or with their tresses flying in a wind or with a lot of lilies in their arms!"

"You're cynical," said Telv.

"Cynical? All right. But I no longer have Anglo-Saxon notions about women. I've outgrown the cult of the virgin. I don't get into a monastic fever about chastity. Chastity, Telv, is the silliest vice among the virtues and you should have learned that. Yet it is what you seek. These women around you—Choy, Mae, Shelley—have had lovers. But like the oaf I used to be you want a virgin. Your sickly notion of pure women! Do you know why men demand chastity?"

"Keep it to yourself! I'm sick of hearing all life explained in terms of emotional leprosy!"

"You're sick, Telv: that's it. Get down to earth. And,

like it or not, I'm going to tell you why most men demand
chastity. It's because of reverence for mothers: adolescence;
male vanity—and all that adds to fear of themselves as
lovers. This country is full of men who never grow up. As
they enter middle age they become more and more effeminate in manner, habits, thoughts. I was once on my way to
all that. I almost wrecked my life over just such sentimentality as you and this country are full of. Why don't you
grow up? I mean why don't you get out of the nursery?

"Well, find you a virgin. But don't go to the country
for her. Go to bedlam. A lot of them are there."

Telv got his hat and went to the door but he came back.
"Where's your gin?" he said. "I want another drink."

"No, sit down."

"I come over in trouble and you throw at me the cheap
retort that I want a virgin. Do you see all life in terms of
sex?"

"You must, or you wouldn't howl when it is mentioned.
The thing that makes a person furious is the thing he is
trying to ignore. . . . Sit down."

"And listen to more abuse?"

"You asked for frankness. Now you're in love with
Shelley but you've learned that she has had lovers. I repeat
that you're just the sort of fool I used to be. And——"

"Oh, to hell with all that!"

"—and you're a communist——"

"Damn your cheap arguments! You swallow all this
bourgeois blather about neurotic Marxists! There are no
communists in all these asylums that fill this confounded
country."

"I've never said all communists are like you."

"Well, to hell with women and sex. Are you going to
tell me why you're not a communist or aren't you?"

"Perhaps I'd better write it down."

"You said you'd do that a year ago."

"I hadn't thought my way through it then."

Telv went to the door and looked back. "How soon?"

"Right away."

Vridar spent the better part of a week writing his letter to Telv. "It seems," he said to Athene, "that I'm not writing to Telv at all. I'm writing to the self-pitying and evasive part of me that is now dying. I am writing to X. . . ."

This is his letter:

DEAR TELV:

Before I give you the reasons why I am not a communist, I want to make a few preliminary statements. I believe with you that all religion which rests upon the thesis of personal immortality must be destroyed. As the Church stands today there can be no doubt of it as a colossus of special privilege; but it exploits less, I think, in its relation to capital than it does in the pomp and ceremony, in the ministering to the cheapest aspects of human vanity, and in the perpetuation of delusions which help to keep us in emotional serfdom. That Christianity has made no worthwhile contribution to human welfare I should be inclined to doubt; but that it is now as vulgarly fixed in inflexible and empty ritual as that more ancient form which has crucified India, seems to me must be obvious to anyone who has the courage to think about it. Religion—that effort to give to ourselves a small but invincible significance and to find that significance spiritually satisfying—has always passed collectively into ritual and theology and has lost in consequence everything about it that was once alive and unique.

You and I agree that in a social order no human being has a right, because of the fortuitous accident of inheritance or aggressiveness or intelligence, to amass and control property and so make of it an instrument of power over his fellows. That the resources of this earth should be held in common and exploited for the comfort and growth of the entire group seems to me must be admitted by all save the most greedy. I agree that everything which contributes to

the collective human welfare ought to be socialized. I agree
that exploitation summarizes better than any other word
the object of the Marxist attack and that it ought to be the
object of attack of everyone civilized enough to understand
why group welfare must transcend personal privilege. I agree
that the great mass of humankind is exploited and does live
in a condition of slavery. Peons do spend their wretched
lives for barely enough to eat and an unsanitary place to
sleep; and those who profit from their labor do wallow, as
Peacock long ago declared, in all the redundancies of luxury
that can be wrung from their privation and toil; and their
elected leaders do, with few exceptions, ignore them and
fight for their own greedy ends. This is a condition which
must invite the sympathy of every person with enough
imagination to reach beyond the privileged boundaries of his
own life.

Now what I have said, as well as much more that I could
say of the same nature, adds to this: you and I find our
present order rotten to its core and dying of its own sickness and vulgar excess. I am a socialist, like you, and much
of the Marxian analysis I accept. Marx was too like one of
the blind men pondering the elephant: what he got his hands
on he saw pretty clearly but much of the beast he was unaware of. I am not a communist because the program is too
incomplete and too premature; too dangerous because of its
ignorance; and too likely to be only another huge betrayal
of human credulity and hope. Now economic exploitation,
the only kind you admit and the kind against which you
direct all your energy, is nothing but the more obvious
aspect of an exploitation which is very deep and evasive.
You attack the obvious enemy and it would be quite as
sensible to abuse a man for being drunk and to ignore or be
ignorant of the cause of his drunkenness. Your economic
proposals, in short, seem to me to be quite as superficial as
the reasons given by sociologists for divorce. Until we have
destroyed those false traditions which have betrayed us to
excesses of cruelty and greed, and until we have developed
a new tradition, economic exploitation in your communist
state will be replaced by other forms; and it is in your re-

fusal to see such an inevitability that I find you superficial and evasive. You assume that a body of Marxist leaders are at present civilized enough to achieve disinterested conduct and an integrity of leadership, but there is nothing in history or in the world today to support that assumption. It is the implications of your own capacity for self-discipline that I cannot accept: I need only look at all the petty little envies and feuds and bickering within the communist party in my own land. You fall into that wishful thinking which is to be found everywhere when the matter at hand touches intimately on what human beings do not wish to admit. And as an instance of your superficial thinking, let me take the causes which you give for war.

Now war *is* caused in part by the greed of munitions-makers, by struggle for markets, by the necessity for expansion in such countries as Japan and Italy, by rulers who get into a jam and run a nation into war in an attempt to save their faces, and by sexual neurosis. But none of these is the chief cause and all of them together do not in my opinion add to very much. The real cause of war is to be found in two facts: first, men are animals, let the æsthetes howl as they will, and their most avid hunger next to sexual appetite is for conflict. Publishers know this, even if pacifists don't. The second fact is this: nearly all of us today live cabined and monotonous lives, undramatic and stultifying: in consequence we are driven to vicarious fulfillments: watching football and prize fights, reading blood-and-thunder fiction, looking at pageants and parades, reading about feuds or gossiping about our more violent neighbors. In consequence, too, we have (not alone for this but, I am sure, to a large extent) invented the myths of good and evil, and so oppose the two in practically all our civilized patterns. Your constant talk about revolution and action is related to all this, and the full truth of the relationship might make you turn uneasily in your chair. One of the big appeals of your program is the fact that it promises dramatic action; and after you have established the world in your communal state, with armaments destroyed and peace assured, you tell me that men, to escape neurosis, will fulfill their need of action in sublimation and art. You say, "After we have thrown off our economic chains, neurosis and mal-adjustments will disappear." You say that neurosis is caused by economic serfdom. To that every psychologist in the world would say nonsense. You have pointed out to me Havelock Ellis' statement that the earliest men did not wage war: of course they didn't, but they weren't neurotic, either. Of course they didn't, but they weren't set down in such deadly and stultifying lives as we lead today. I do not argue that men want to slay one another: they do not. Nor is it true that any nation really hates another nation, or that Germany hates this country today: the Germans hate the lives they have been forced into and they regard us as an agency in that degradation. No: but it is true that men— at least those not effeminate—demand action and cannot live lives free of neurosis without it; and the motive here, the frustrated wish, is the chief thing that leads them to lynchings, third degrees, concentration camps, and to the other brutalities that afflict us. When you combine this frustrated hunger with sexual neurosis you have produced the human brute.

Now it is true, of course, that among the more intelli-gent and sensitive we do have some discipline. But it is also true that the number of men sufficiently disciplined to refrain from war under the most stirring "provocation" is very small, and particularly if the war is disguised as noble endeavor: I saw that in 1917 when college professors all around me showed humanity to be the dressed-up savage that it is. Some of these men were economically independent but all of them were bored. And I want to point out a curious thing: the vicarious urge today is so strong that if most critics read, let us say, a novel in which the hero is not glorified enough so they can identify themselves with him and in self-love fulfill his destiny, they are annoyed. They abuse him, and most likely they abuse the author, too. This is not so if the "hero" belongs to poor white trash of the kind that critics patronizingly summarize as subhuman; but it is true if the protagonist is a person much like them-selves who becomes "detestable" by revealing those traits

which the critics themselves are trying to deny. That is
self-love for you at its neurotic extreme. Now I am not
defending war: I shall never take part in another; but I am
saying that we shall never achieve peace until we achieve
within a peaceful order enough latitude for vigorous fulfillment of our hungers. Those hungers you communists are
for the moment taking care of: you have a crusade, a program of action. Those hungers will be taken care of in the
communist state, you tell me, by the sublimations which we
call art: I can say only that I am not fool enough to accept
a thesis which all of life denies. Art is neurotic and has
always been; and in your refusal to see so obvious a fact you
again declare yourself to be looking at nothing but the elephant's tail.

It seems reasonable to suppose that peace is a desirable
thing, but that in the present age it is not we declare with
all the cunning which we employ to circumvent it; and deep
in our hearts we recognize that war—by which I mean not
so much the murder as the frenzied and united enthusiasm
for delusion and escape—offers to us the only wholesale
catharsis. Oh, peace is all right, my friend, for certain pacifist authors who get their action vicariously by writing dramatic stories—as I do. Peace is all right for certain well-to-
do pacifists who can travel over the earth and with change
of scene keep themselves from going to pot. Peace is all
right for those *fighting* in its name. But for the great mass
of humanity, roped to the monotony of a job, it is not all
right and will never be, in Russia or anywhere else. I come
now to what I think is the heart of the matter and I urge
you to lay aside your prejudices and approach what I say
next with all the detachment you have.

A long time ago, when our ancestors were savages and
becoming conscious of themselves, they were beset by fear
and by notions of having sinned; and in consequence of
these notions they established a host of compensatory concepts. These concepts have grown and have become our
traditions. Today, therefore, we are trained to believe that
as human beings we love justice and mercy and tolerance
and peace, that we are conscionable and know right from

wrong, that we believe in brotherhood and love our fellow
men. The teaching of these concepts and our assumption
of them as virtues have been easy because they disguise and
hide, as they were intended to, our savage impulses. Upon
such concepts rest our ideologies, including yours, and our
institutions; yet all these concepts are either false or at
present unattainable ideals. For any person who has risen
above wishful thinking their falseness or their distance beyond us is supported by recorded history and by every
newspaper in the world. It is supported by the fact that
you communists in your journals appeal not to intelligence
but to prejudice and hatred. We are all of us betrayed at
almost every turn by sickly refinements of compensatory
concepts. Now try to imagine what we should be like today
and what our civilization would be like if in the far distant
past we had not begun our civilized pilgrimage with, on the
one hand, a conviction of our depravity, and, on the other,
an earnest compensation toward false ideals. In that case we
should have admitted, long ago, our animalism, our selfishness and ferocity and greed; and, frankly aware of these,
making no pious attempt to hide them, and not driven into
evasions by shame, we would probably have built a social
order within which our emotions could have been disciplined
and directed. But many of these emotions we have persistently denied and still deny; we have disguised them; and
today we are betrayed by our pretenses in nearly everything
that we do. Take an instance: so determined are we to
deny our animalism, yet so active is it in our unconscious
minds, that we commonly speak of murderers and rapists
as fiends, and imply, of course, that they are abnormal monsters among us. We miss the fact that often they are more
normal than we, and we reveal in ourselves the same impulses by the fury with which we condemn them. Lynching may be, and doubtless often is, an attempt to wreak
punishment on one of his kind for that very animalism which
the lyncher feels in himself and which, by lynching another,
he rebukes: most of our evasions do now reach to such hideous extremes.

Now in all these ancient compensatory notions which

for no good reason flatter us we have been trying for centuries to make ourselves secure. With all the cunning of which we are masters we have interpreted reality to mean that consciousness of ourselves which is most pleasing to our self-love. The most tragic consequence of all this is the fact that we have brutalized ourselves with evasion and self-deception and have in the name of civilization invented innumerable cruelties for which anciently we had, surely, no taste. The appalling implication in that I hope you will not overlook. And in all the centuries behind us there has been very little realism and we have very little now in our attitudes toward ourselves: we have had and we still have only less egregious degrees of romantic evasion. Our next job is to try to adapt ourselves to the world instead of trying to adapt the world to our self-pitying notions of it. That we must if the race is to survive seems to me unanswerable.

If you understand the point of view I have sketched briefly, you must understand why I regard communism as both incomplete and premature. You should understand, too, why communism in the world today can be, in my opinion, only another shibboleth and romantic crusade. The Russian experiment began in a frenzy of idealism and high purpose, and in such beginnings corruption has never in any vitiating degree been possible. But until we have a sustaining tradition, there must come, as there has always come, an end of the high purpose; exploitation in new and more disguised forms; and all over again the dismal process of rationalizing and trying to make acceptable to conscience the sordid results of a premature undertaking. In what until recently have been the three great "democratic" nations, there has been just such a process: an empire founded on principles of equality and freedom that has year by year repudiated its original program and tried to justify its multiplied evasions. I cannot, in other words, swallow the terrific nonsense of benevolent dictators in a world in which knowledge of ourselves is resisted even in the highest reaches of intelligence; and that your Marxist leaders have too little self-knowledge for wise leadership is declared to me by the fact that they see all problems as economic. Your assumption here, that you Marxists are sufficiently sympathetic and disinterested to place collective welfare above your personal ambitions, is not only an assumption that no realist at this stage of human development is fool enough to accept, but is also an assumption which is denied by the jealousies and feuds within the party itself. The fact that a dictatorship is necessary to sustain your program predicts for me its eventual failure. And I see other predictions. I see a strong tendency to make of Marxism your bible, and of Marx and Lenin and Stalin your gods. You are already becoming inflexible within an ideology. Any new doctrine, once established in autocratic power, fights to consolidate its position rather than to advance beyond it. You are now interested not in perceiving that the Marxian analysis is very incomplete: on the contrary you are giving to your whole doctrine and program that inflexibility which must be its death.

And I hear you asking impatiently what my program is. I propose first to destroy with education, and from the top downward, all the ancient delusions and taboos and self-glorifying ideals inherent in our culture. That will mean almost the complete destruction of our culture itself. It will mean, too, a destruction of your self-pity and all your romantic nonsense about yourself as a good fellow who has the welfare of his race at heart. For our next social and political frontier must be as frank and full a realization of what we are as we are capable of: then we can build, knowing what we have to build with. Then we can see, and see within the limits of our utter selfishness, that the fullest growth and happiness of each individual do depend on the growth and happiness of the group. But your contempt for such realization is declared by your everlasting insistence that the psychological approach must be social and not individual. Social psychology will never mean anything until we understand the separate, even if related, units that make it. You have said to me very solemnly that lynching is an aspect of the class struggle, and if such a statement does not declare your evasive ignorance, then what in heaven's name can? If I were to give you the reasons why you are a communist they would only madden you: let me, then, make an example of myself and explain to you why I am a radical. To do that I must be very personal.

My life in its unhappiness and stupidities has been more extreme, perhaps, than most lives, but not unlike them in essentials. At the age of sixteen I was a socialist: I was so bent on evading all knowledge of myself that I swung to those ideals which in theory most completely dispossess human beings of their animalism. That on my part was self-pity. Sensitive adolescents when frustrated in love or made to feel socially inferior usually flee to an idealism which will allow them to remain in their self-esteem. This in large measure is the history of art and social reform. I do not say that this flight from self may not produce worth-while results; I do say that idealism may be dangerous and may lead to incalculable distortion, including bedlams and jails; and that in the majority of cases it always will until we understand its compensatory nature and what it springs from.

Seven years ago, having been betrayed by those ideals common to most of us, I resolved to understand myself. Against exploration of self there are boundaries which we have neither the sensitivity nor the intelligence to cross. But I have learned, and without shame I admit, that I am a completely selfish and vain and greedy animal; that my love of justice and mercy and peace is, when these do not touch me intimately, only love of those as they touch me when I project myself into circumstances not my own. I know (and this is of greatest importance) that the more I have forced myself to admit what I am, the deeper in consequence has become my sense of human fellowship. Formerly such sympathy lay at a superficial and self-pitying level; now it is down to earth where we are all just one remove from barbarism.

I am a radical not because I care or have any power to care what the world will be like after I am dead; or if I do care it is only because I project my personality into that world and hope that in some fashion it will live after my body is dust: but such vanity as that is no longer very strong within me. I am not even a radical because I per-

ceive that I was born into a stupid world that ordained for
me thirty years of anguish. I can give you only one logical
reason: I am a radical because it is my heritage to need foes
and something to fight and because I see in struggle the
only way in which I can grow and express myself. I get
awfully tired, therefore, of your statement that you are a
radical because of your sympathy for the oppressed. You
have such sympathy, and so have I and many, but it is only
because we project ourselves into their conditions. Our
sympathy, then, is not for the oppressed but for ourselves:
you communists say you like realism: there you have it and
it makes you furious. Now this need of foes, of struggle, is
imperative and right, and to deny it or repress it is to invite
distortion. But human beings are not my enemy nor yours:
our enemy is those evasive traditions which are the enemy
of every one of us, no matter what his class or his economic
level. And some of these traditions, such as your romantic
notion of your own invulnerable integrity, are precisely
those ideals which you communist leaders profess. You profess them because you are incurable egoists in love with
yourselves.

My program, then, is a combination of what we find to
be true in Marxism and Freudianism—and I mean not only
Marx and Freud, who perhaps were off the track in several
fundamental respects, but also those who have come after
them, and will still come, to explore the directions which
they announced. These two men, both Jews, and among
the greatest of the moderns, have pointed the way out of
centuries of self-deception: the one has given us, within
loose outlines, the social structure which we must come to,
and the other has suggested the foundation upon which it
must rest. The thought of these two, corrected and har-
monized and developed further, will fetch the revolution
that must come. Marxism alone cannot be successful because it has no tradition to make integrity of leadership
mandatory. We must have thorough exploration first, and
then a tradition leading to, and finally resting upon, the in-
violable responsibility of leadership; and that ideal must
displace, in all fields of endeavor, the symbols of office and

property and social distinction. It is not a tradition that can be achieved briefly under dictatorship: it is one that will take centuries to build. I know your impatience: I am impatient, too; but there is no use to build a new social order until we have a foundation to put it on: haste will only lead to another betrayal, and to a more complete cynicism than we have now. And in that revolution when it comes—and it must come if science does not abdicate to mysticism—there will be no self-glorifying group like yours, extolling the more stupid even though more unfortunate part of humanity and heaping abuse upon the other part. Such a revolution must work *within* the facts of human selfishness and greed, recognizing that these are our strength: they will be disciplined, but not because of a conviction of depravity, not because of shame, not through suppressive legislation: no, but because we shall have been trained to understand human motives and to recognize evasions and sham the moment they appear and to rebuke or control and redirect such excesses of vanity as cannot be allowed within the collective order. A tradition that will support and make mandatory such an integrity of leadership may be a long time in coming or may never come.

But I believe it will. Am I overrating the intelligence and courage of humankind? A cynical humanity will doubtless say so. Nevertheless, that is the only kind of program I can give my heart to and the only kind my intelligence can approve. It is a program that places enormous demands upon us but I think that we shall eventually have for it both the courage and the faith. Most likely we shall have first another terrible war; the steady development of Russia into the most autocratic and capitalistic of nations; and then increasing weariness with all the elaborate ritual of self-deception—and then complete chaos, or a humanity stepping out of evasions to face itself.

In friendship always,
VRIDAR HUNTER.

PART FOUR

SEPTEMBER, 1901

His struggle might have been less intense and bitter, it might not have been violently insane, as in time it came to be, if two facts in his life had been different. One of these was his father, that powerful and silent man who never knew fear and had for it only contempt. The other was this wild and unpitying outpost that was to be his home.

I

VRIDAR resigned his position here and returned with Athene to his homeland. He was unhappy in leaving this college where he had taught: his chairman had been sympathetic and generous, and his colleagues with few exceptions were the most alert group of persons he had ever seen in a university. But out in Idaho were his sons and his parents. His father was fighting cancer, and his mother, now abandoned by children who had remained with her too long, was tragic with loneliness. "They gave their lives to us," he said. "It's time I did something for them. . . ."

It had been years since he had seen the Bridwell place, the river, the desolate Antelope country: his fear of life, of death, was no longer with him, but the sunken bowl of his home had remained, implacable and waiting. Out of memory had come the sight and smell of it when he cycled across Europe, or when, standing in a tall building in Manhattan, he looked at the Jersey hills. And when he came to the benchland and looked down, he expected to feel as in former returns the nightmare of his youth. Everything was unchanged here: the river flung like an arm around the bottomlands, the marshes and hillsides, the peaks. There was the thicket where in many a time he had knelt in anguish and prayed to God; there the field where Jed Bridwell had stuffed his throat with earth; there the corral where he had fainted under the reek and stench of a branding iron. But there was no sense of desolation now: his early years were so remote, so strangely unreal that they did not seem to have been his at all.

"It's queer," he said to Athene. "When I faced myself I was facing this country, too. There is no terror now. In fact," he said, trying to understand the difference, "I think I shall love it."

His sons, Lincoln and Keats, sprang from the house to

look at him, their eyes sober with doubts. Vridar gathered them to his arms.

"You rascals. Don't you know your dad?"

"We haven't had much chance," Lincoln said.

"Well, you're going to have."

Joe and Prudence now came from the house. "It's Vridar!" Prudence cried and her voice was wild. Joe's gray eyes filled with pleasure. Vridar took Prudence in his arms and looked at her: in her wrinkled face, only her eyes, steady and blue, seemed a part of what he remembered. He turned to his father: this man, once so invincible in health and strength, now looked shrunken and old. His face was a great blotch of cancerous sores. They entered a gloomy old house smelling of age and Vridar looked at the shabby walls.

"How long you intend to visit?" his mother asked.

"Oh, a year anyway."

"A year! Honest, Son?"

"Honest to John."

"I'll have to stir up a big dinner," she said.

Vridar stood by the door, reflecting on the tragedy of parents who build their lives into the lives of their children and are abandoned at last to silence. In her letters to him Prudence had often wished herself dead. "I have nothing to live for. I gave my life to my children and they are gone and I want to sleep. . . ." But Joe had said he would live to be a hundred: the more he sank under illness, the more determined he became never to die.

"Dad, what are you doing for those cancers?"

Joe raised a hand and prodded his nose. The largest sore on his face was eating into the bone of his nose and an ugly sickness lay almost the length of the bridge.

"I'm all right," Joe said.

"If Mertyl and I will get a great surgeon——"

"I don't want no surgeon."

"No, you'll just sit around and let that eat your nose off."

"I don't need a nose," he said.

Vridar smiled. The same negative father, fencing his life around with obstinate whims. He was putting sheep-dip on them now, Joe said. He had tried creosote and lye and carbolic acid. He had another idea: he was convinced he could destroy these wounds with nitric acid.

"Do you want to kill yourself?"

"Well, I figger nitric acid is the thing. Sheep-dip, it ain't strong enough. . . ."

When the dinner was eaten, Vridar went to the yard with his sons.

"Come on, you big husky scoundrels, and see if you'n throw your old man down."

Keats hopped around, grinning and eager. "Come on!" he yelled to his brother. "Let's make him pop!" But Lincoln was dubious.

"We'd probably kill him," he said. "He's just a college teacher."

Keats hunched forward and spit on his palms. He leapt to battle and got a headlock on Vridar and grunted and twisted; and Lincoln, after a long stare of pity and doubt, came to his aid. Vridar allowed himself to be thrown and lay on the earth muttering.

"You've broken my arm," he said. He made a face and groaned as if dying. "You've killed your father. . . ."

They stepped back and looked at him. "He's pretend-un," Keats said, but Lincoln said imperiously, "Wait, I think we hurt him. He's only a college teacher, I tell you. He never works." Vridar looked up at them, his face agonized.

"You've thrown a scholar down and killed him."

"You're no scholar," said Lincoln. "'You're a writer. But why don't you write books that will make money?"

"Let's pile on him," said Keats, hopping around like a monkey.

"No," said Lincoln, with the aloof pity of twelve years. "He never works. I tell you he's soft."

"What sons I have!" said Vridar, affecting extreme anguish. "I come to visit you and you lay me out."

Keats knelt and stared at him. "If you're hurt," he said, "I'll doctor you." He entered the house and returned with a bottle of iodine and an armful of rags. He took Vridar's shirts off, and Lincoln, amused and skeptical, stood back and watched. "Where you hurt?" Keats asked, and winked at his brother.

"This arm. . . . Don't do that!"

Keats poured iodine over Vridar's arm. He bandaged it and wrapped it with binder twine.

"What are you doing here!" Prudence cried, coming to the door.

"He got in our way," said Keats, "and we hurt him."

"It's your letters," Prudence said. "What letters you write them! What crazy ideas! You made them laugh every week until they were sick."

"I want them to laugh," Vridar said. "I never laughed when I was a child."

"He's a writer," Lincoln said. "If his books was like his letters, then he'd make some money, I think."

In this night Vridar and Athene talked for a long while as they lay in bed. His parents, she said, were tragic.

"I suppose. Aren't most parents when they get old? But my mother has a will of iron: she'll die standing."

"Your father is the more tragic one."

"Those cancers?"

"No. I thought you said he was a stolid German. I thought you said he was brutal."

"He used to be. Well, it was all a big bluff. I never understood him until recently. He was brutal, my dear, because he was starved for love. Your brutal man nearly always is. My dad has always been a lonely person, more Celt than German: a poet in his way; a pagan. It was puritanism that made him brutal."

"You used to be brutal."

"Yes—and for the same reason."

"You couldn't cut a chicken's head off but you could have destroyed the whole human race."

"Because I wanted to love it and couldn't."

"You're a strange combination of your parents. You have your mother's will and speed and versatility. You have your father's tendency to reverie. The poet in you comes from your dad."

"I've known that a long while."

"And your scorn of conventional life."

"Yes, I know."

"Your ruthlessness comes from your mother."

"Yes. Well, my father never was ruthless. I didn't understand him. All during my childhood he scared me to death. How silly it was. Because he was denied tenderness he blustered around like a titan of ill-will. I guess I hated him. But I have a great affection for him now."

"So have I. Anyone must have who understands him."

"He was always very vulgar—not lewd but vulgar. His vulgarity was his way of protesting against my mother's puritanism."

"Of course."

"And he made a thorough job of it. The more she rebuked him, the more he belched and sneezed. I can hear her still: Joe, I'd be ashamed around my children! And Joe, his eyes darkening, would sit in silence, and his next belch would be twice as loud and long."

"Your mother has never understood him."

"Never. For her he has always been a complete enigma. If she had given him tenderness she could have shaped him to her will. But she gave him none and so he brutalized animals—a weird sexual sadist; or he deliberately outraged her with his unprintable doings. And I, his son, was driven to terror at sight of him. It was all very pathetic."

"He is not brutal now."

"No. Now he would sit up all night to nurse a sick animal. And now he wants to live to be a hundred because he knows he has missed so much. It is terrible in this life, my dear, to have missed passionate sexual love. It is more terrible to be old and to realize you missed it."

They were silent for a long moment. Then Athene said:

"But your mother was not to blame. She was shaped to the puritan tradition. With education she would have outgrown her shame of sex. She may have a will of iron but she is very resilient and she is not now what she was when I first met her."

"True. As she grows older she grows more liberal and flexible."

"She knows she made mistakes. She has told me so."

"I blame my parents for none of my unhappiness. I blame no one. And why should I regret it? Without it, I should most likely now be a fatuous mediocrity."

"That's the irony, my dear. No one ever comes to sympathy and tolerance without suffering. . . . And tell me: what have you meant by saying you were not paternal?"

"Protest again. I've never wanted my children to be imitations of myself. I hate that. I don't want them to grow up with much affection for anyone."

"But you did love them."

"Yes—but I wanted to give them their freedom."

"You haven't answered me."

"Well, damn it, I was too self-centered. On top of that I swung to another extreme. I'm bored by parents who talk of their children. I'll wait to see what I've sired. They may turn out to be imbeciles."

"Now you're ridiculous."

"No, a realist. They may be a couple of Babbitts: I don't know. Anyway, I'll never pretend they're more than they are."

"They're two very fine boys."

"Yes? You have the woman's attitude. My dear, if you

were to have an imbecile how you would excuse the beast!
You'd remember you once dropped it on its face; or gave
it an overdose of fig broth; or saw a half-wit the day before
it was born. Lord, how you would fly into the face of
reason!"

"You're silly."

"Would you love an imbecile?"

"You can't control mother love."

"If I had an imbecile I'd kick myself. That's more
vanity: all right, but I'd sneak off and hide. . . . You
want a child yet?"

"Not yet."

"It's a hell of a civilization to bring one to. Well, if you
ever have a child and it's a son, be decent: none of these
mother-and-son sweetheart relationships in my household."

"And if it's a daughter?"

"I won't live around her. No daughter of mine will ever
go hunting over the earth for a husband like her dad. Now
take my sons: they have no great affection for me or for
anyone: that is as it should be. Let them grow up and make
their friendships and their love after they're grown: then
they'll be decent."

"But you?"

"I'll get along. I do love them and I'd die for them but
they never need know that. . . ."

Vridar fell asleep, thinking of his sons, wondering if he
could help them to avoid the blunders and agonies that had
been his. Lincoln was like his mother: the same smile, the
same eyes, different only in color, and the same abstracted
look, half-amused and half-alarmed. He had all her mannerisms that Vridar had known and loved. Keats was like his
mother in no respect. He was headstrong and reckless and
extreme. "Just like you," Athene said. How much do I
love my sons? Vridar asked himself; and he fell asleep and
dreamed.

He was high in the Italian Alps, looking down. To the

south of him, across the landscape of Italy, were two great armies, fighting with bayonets and gas. He could see the fog of gas and the dying and the dead. He went down the mountain, looking for his sons, knowing they were fighting there; and he found them, both lying with dead faces in the sun. At their side was a dagger and Vridar took it and climbed the Alps until he came to a small plateau. Here were Mussolini and his staff and the industrial baronage of Europe. They were drinking wine or jesting, or peering through glasses at the troops below. Vridar looked at this short man with heavy jaws, and eyes that dreamed of the Cæsars. Then he approached him, hiding the dagger in his shirt; and with one quick plunge he put it through Mussolini's heart and saw the point of it sticking out of his back. Officers came toward him, yelling with fury, and he folded his arms and waited. "This man," he said, "has murdered my sons. What you do to me makes no difference. . . ." Then he awoke in a sweat and could not rest in peace until he had gone quietly to the bed of his sons to learn if they were asleep and well.

II

●

THE quietness of this country Vridar found a little strange. He loved the earth here, not with that reverence which apostrophizes it as the great mother; not because it seemed to be rugged and eternal, his own life fretful and brief; but because in his conscious mind it was the scaffold and structure of meaning, sweet of smell and lovely and ancient of sound and touch. The nights were hushed and deep, as if centuries of time and silence had been piled upon them, and the days moved serenely from morning to dusk. He often looked back to that great melodramatic city, lying between two rivers: the raw and unshaped stuff of an empire, without poise and peace. There his days and nights had been full of horns and sirens and hand-organs, cats and vendors and trains. Here there was almost no sound at all. A reservoir had quieted the journey of the river; and cats, turned free here by valley fishermen, had eaten all the birds. A part of him was in all hours back in that tumultuous and tortured city which he had left. The Rousseaus were perhaps not so much courage on a new horizon as they were flight from a life too complex and inscrutable for their taste. Persons everywhere sought the simple and eternal things and struggled meanwhile with a social organism so intricate that they could no longer see its outline and form. In this baffling paradox, it seemed to him, lay the chief reason for fascism and dictators, and for that neurosis which for all save the most evasive had come to be the most obvious characteristic of a bewildered world. But retiring to a quiet spot to think, and, as one writer declared, to catch up with the world, was perhaps another subterfuge. Meditation in a quiet place, with the world shut away, ran into hypnosis: Thoreau by Walden was abandoned to the moment of his withdrawal and never lived beyond it. And Vridar had not been here many weeks before it seemed to him that he was a solitary passenger who had left a train and now stood aside, watching it vanish into distance and the future.

"We must get papers and magazines," he said. "I can almost feel the rush of time out there. Things are moving swiftly and the world is now living many years in one. Don't you feel as if you'd left an ocean liner to drift in a rowboat?"

"Yes, that's about the way I feel."

"We're in an eddy now. No wonder the country doesn't understand the city. It lives always in what is past and dead. . . ."

In nearly every evening they sat under trees and watched the sun go down. The western sky was a gorgeous extravagance of color, with long flaming reefs, and great crags burgeoning up into purple towers. Vridar's father would come out and look at the sky and rub nitric acid on his wounds. A faint smoke would rise from the acid on his flesh. And while watching this man, patient and gentle now, and fighting against cancer and death, Vridar would marvel at the courage of humankind. His race might run in cycles of growth and decay and leave dead kingdoms behind it and continue to be for a long while its own most implacable enemy; but only absolute extinction could stop its desperate pilgrimage to that eventual hour when intelligence and yearning would meet in the moment and be one.

"Athene, what is beauty?"

"Does anyone know?"

"I think it is nothing but that which enhances our sense of well-being. Beauty is anything which we regard as friendly to our will-to-live. But today it exists on a pretty low level. The sunset there: how many millions of lines have been addressed to it? But the beauty of a person who understands fellowship and who sees that exploitation cannot live within it—is not that kind of more worth to us?"

"Hooey!" said Lincoln.

"Well now, young man: what *is* beauty?"

"A pretty girl."

"That settles it. And is a pretty girl more beautiful than that sunset?"

"Sure. And I bet you think so, too."

"At your age I did. As we grow older we turn to sunsets."

Lincoln gave the sunset a long and dubious scrutiny. "I never will," he said.

"He thinks," said his brother, grinning, "that a girl is pretty if she has black eyes. That's because he has blue eyes."

"Hooey!" Lincoln said.

Vridar looked at his younger son. "You have a mind," he said. "I hope you keep on using it."

"He has a mind," said Keats. "He combs the hair on it every morning."

"Bright boy," said Lincoln. "Very bright boy."

"Sure," said Keats. "My dad is a college teacher."

Lincoln turned his dubious stare on Vridar. "There's lots of college teachers," he said. "That don't mean a thing."

Vridar spent many hours playing with his sons or talking with them. Lincoln was approaching puberty and Vridar rode with him one day over the hills. He talked to him in a quiet and casual way of mating and birth, using the four-letter words, once so full of shame for him. "Those words, my son, are clean words. You will hear men use them as if they were nasty words but it is the men who are nasty, not the words. Pity such persons but don't imitate them. And when you have questions to ask, come to me. I'll always tell you the truth if I know it."

Lincoln looked across the hills, strangely, in the way of his mother. "You mean I'm to ask you anything I want to?"

"Anything."

"Thanks," he said. He smiled. "I've got lots of questions to ask."

And Vridar learned that Prudence had told his younger son he would go mad or sores would break out all over him. He learned that Keats already felt degraded and guilty. He took him off to gather wild berries and talked and jested with him; and said at last:

"This habit you have, Keats, is pretty silly, isn't it?" Keats looked at him and his face reddened with shame. "What your grandmother has told you is not true. It will do nothing of the kind. In fact, you big shyster, it's so silly that it's not even important. That is it, Keats: just plain silly. That's why I wonder about you: a young fellow of your age, with a sense of humor, making wisecracks at your brother, yet doing what little babes do in their cradle. I've been wondering why you don't laugh at yourself. That stumps me. But one of these days I expect to hear you whooping around in great style: then I'll know you've found out how silly you've been. Yes, one of these days I'll bet I hear you bursting with giggles. Lord, a humorous fellow like you can't go on forever kidding himself. . . ." And quickly Vridar changed the subject, talking now of his son's prowess as a swimmer, of his wit, giving him confidence and respect. And in the weeks that followed, Vridar watched him closely; jested and wrestled with him; won his confidence and faith. And one day:

"What in the world were you guffawing at the other night?"

"Did you hear me?"

"Did I! You almost shook me out of bed. Were you laughing at yourself?"

"Sure. Why not?"

"Listen, I know a swell place to fish. How about a mess of trout for dinner?"

"And yet," Vridar said to Athene, "I don't know what is best. Most parents know exactly how a child should be taught. If children are normal lusty animals, unself-conscious, they grow up to be pretty smug and fatuous and superficial. The Tom Sawyers make good Babbitts and that is all. If they are made self-conscious, if they get notions of sin and shame, then they are driven to achievement to prove themselves worthy. Then they become poets and philosophers and social leaders. So who the hell knows what is best?"

Vridar was now writing the novel about himself. In his mind he built scenes again and again before trying to write them to the page; and often he laughed. Hearing him laugh, his mother would look at him.

"Son, what are you laughing at?"

"Myself."

"Yourself! Do you think you're funny?"

"Very. I'm one of the funniest men who ever lived. Mater, I'm writing a book about myself."

"Is that anything to laugh at?"

"I think so. In its way it will be a very funny book."

"I'd say it would be a very tragic book."

"No. It's high comedy."

"Is that why you laugh in bed?"

"Most likely."

"Your son," Athene said, "is a big clown."

"He never used to be," said Prudence. "He was always a very serious boy."

"Wasn't I, though! I breathed sermons when I talked."

"You were a very unusual child. I'm not so sure about you now."

"I was a very remarkable fool. Eighteen years ago I made a promise. I said I would learn to laugh and be glad."

"But you never will, Son."

"Oh, I've learned to laugh at myself: that's the only kind of laughter that has much meaning in it. As for being glad —well, trees swept by fire don't grow foliage again. Anyway, why should I be glad? In the world right now, what is there to be so glad about?"

"There's pain in your laugh," Prudence said.

"Yes, but I manage some pretty lusty cackles."

"For years now," Athene said, "your son has mimicked himself. He is very funny sometimes."

"And you're writing a book about yourself. Son, why are you doing that?"

"Because I think it should be written. Anyway, it's going to be a kind of prelude to a big project I want to do. And what an ambitious project! I blush to think of my presumption. And just now, when you interrupted him, my hero was talking about ideals because he's afraid to love."

"He should talk of ideals."

"He does—even enough to satisfy you. He was saying, 'I believe in equality and justice and the glory of woman-hood.' Or some such stuff as that. He believes in equality because he doesn't feel strong enough for competition. Especially in love," Vridar said, making a face. "The poor fool is in love with a girl and has never kissed her. So he says, 'The world is given to corruption, and scoundrels sit in the temples, and petty shysters traffic in the affairs of God. Honesty is an outcast from the souls of men.' He makes pretty speeches. What he says is true, of course, but he doesn't know why he is everlastingly saying it. And then he thinks of the girl and groans and blows his nose. Oh, he is a splendid fellow in a brutal world. Listen to him. He says, 'We have sold the heritage of our sons to the money changers, and our integrity into the political pawnshops. Jesus, as our greatest poet says, still hangs on the cross, and Judas goes up and down the land kissing the babies and collecting the votes.' He's something to listen to when he gets steamed up."

"He sounds all right to me," Prudence said. "Son, what has happened to you? Don't you believe in virtue any more?"

"Mater, you're a very funny person. You've worn yourself out trying to love every person in the world. You're tired. Why don't you rest awhile?"

Prudence laughed. She turned to Athene. "It's true," she said. "Sometimes I think I'm plumb full of the devil. It scares me, the way I feel. And then sometimes I do love everyone."

"Sure. When you love yourself, then you love the world. When you're in disgust with yourself, then you want to sail out and murder people."

"I don't think that's true."

"The world doesn't either, Mater. But that's the way of it."

"Is this that new psychology Mertyl writes about?"

"I don't know. All the psychology I know I've dug out of myself. And now I want to tell you more about this splendid fool who talks about ideals. When a child he gets a naughty little habit that gives people the jitters to think about. He runs to a tree and hides and prays. He says, 'O God, our father, please look down on me, kneeling here in sin, and make me worthy. Give me strength to be pure and noble——' "

"And you laugh at that!"

"No, Mater, I'll never be able to laugh at what we do to children. That poor little wretch, kneeling there under a bush, covered with sweat, pouring out his heart to God! No: I'll fight all my life against what we do to children. But later, after he's a man——"

"But why," asked Athene, "laugh at the man and not at the child?"

"Damn it, is there nothing to laugh at? When this oaf——"

"But he isn't an oaf."

"When this simpleton, this imbecile, this knothead——"

"You're being stupid."

"Isn't it funny when he says, 'Shelley, my dear, talked

of these matters, too, when he met in the graveyard with Mary. But he was a great idealist and duty called him and he went.' Isn't that laughable?"

"Of course not."

"And you laugh at such things!" cried Prudence, frowning at him.

"Damn it, you women bore me. I tell you this fellow is absurd."

"So are we all in our time of growth. Why laugh at him? You must neither laugh nor pity. You must present him for just what he was."

"You think so?"

"If you laugh at human pain and folly, you'll be more absurd than your protagonist."

"But I think the book is a comedy."

"And haven't you said that there is neither comedy nor tragedy in life? Those, you said, are only two points of view, two distortions. You've said it is distortion to make either the point of view and approach in a novel. To make great fun of your protagonist would be as stupid as to glorify him—as most persons do when they write of themselves. In fact, Vridar, making fun would be just an oblique form of self-glorification."

Vridar looked at her. "Athene, when you really try to think, you do a fair job of it. Well, you win. I stand rebuked."

●

III

A S FALL approached, Vridar went with Athene and his
sons into Burns Canyon to cut timber for a house.
They broke fir and cedar boughs and laid them by the
stream, and upon the piles they made their beds. In the
forenoons Vridar sat under a fir with his typewriter and
wrote chapters of his early life and in the afternoons he
swung an ax. His hunger for news of the world was like
his early morning hunger for a cigarette. And while sitting
by a campfire in the long cool evenings, smelling of burning
cedar, of forest and stream, he wondered if this great nation,
founded on principles of liberty and freedom, was yet re-
cruiting greed and privilege into a fascist state. With what
pity and amazement, he reflected, historians a thousand
years hence would look back on his age: its emotional distortions, its intellectual serfdom, its institutions of privilege
and greed. They might think of it as the age of asylums and
psychiatrists, cynics and despair; or the age in which intelligence, abdicating its leadership of the unintelligent and the
underprivileged, fought desperately to keep its symbols of
power and superstition; or the age in which a triumphant
intellectual barbarism established under dictators, for the
last time in history, its vulgar excess of hypocrisy and pomp.
They might write of it:

In the second decade of centuries after the legendary
birth of the legendary character whom it called the Son
of God, the western world integrated loose and nomadic
bands into national units. Solidarity in these it achieved
with patriotic manias, the superstition of racial superiority,
and ruthless economic exploitation of what was then called
the proletariat. Behind national frontiers, fortified and de-
fended with all the ingenuity and cunning of barbarism,
the intellectual minorities established themselves in oligar-

chies of special privilege, and brought to the defense of this privilege both their gods and their art. But privileged barbarism, running to its degenerate excesses, was inevitable within a social system in which vanity was undisciplined and in which the symbols of power and distinction were nearly always as literal as pageants. More amazing for us today is the fact that intelligence everywhere deferred to these symbols, as more anciently humanity had deferred to totem poles, and failed completely to recognize or to fulfill its obligation of leadership.

It was this failure that led in the twentieth century to that violent and world-wide conflict between two political ideologies. One of these, called fascism, was an attempt on the part of most of the intelligent minority to make itself secure within the special privileges it had achieved by repudiating its leadership of the ignorant and unintelligent mass. The other, inspired by the idealism of Marx, was an attempt to destroy national frontiers and to establish a world-wide hegemony in which intelligence would again assume leadership and show the way to a classless order. In the vicious resentment with which Marxism was fought, and in the fact that fascism for the moment won and remained in power, we can measure the intellectual cowardice and confusion of the time. And when the second eventually came into control, and also abdicated, after a while, to personal ambition and greed, it declared to a deluded and self-pitying humanity that before it could establish a social order that would endure it must first face itself in emotional education. Marxism, without such education, proved to be only another evasive detour to that political corruption which dispossessed the order it replaced. . . .

So Vridar's thought would run while swinging an ax during the long afternoons. Often he would pause and wipe sweat from his brow and talk with Athene.

"Think of all the scope and madness of what is happening out there in the world in any one moment. Right now, for instance: thousands of slaves are working in factories for barely enough to eat. If we are to be born and to spend our lives for just enough to keep us toiling, then life is not worth it. But there's the point: rebellion springs from imagination and imagination is an intellectual faculty. Or it springs from utter starvation. So social growth, when all is said and done, will probably have to wait on the very slow development of intelligence among the exploited."

"The rich," Athene said, "are no happier than the poor."

"Of course not. The happiest persons I've known are among stupid farmers I've seen. They may not have a dollar to their names. But they haven't any imagination either. And the unhappiest are sensitive persons whose imagination has allowed them to think of ambitions which they can never achieve. Imagination can be a damned deadly enemy: it leads us to expect more from life than life can give. Take us: we're entering the middle years. What can we reasonably expect?"

"Not a great deal. High blood pressure, bad teeth."

"A bald head."

"Fat around my hips."

"Vanity rebuked. But, seriously, what do you expect?"

"Little. What do you?"

"Not much. I used to want great fame but the utter oblivion of death makes that look silly. Or money: money doesn't buy what I want. The worth-while pleasures are close to the earth and are not trademarked."

"We women have always known that."

"And some of us men learn it. A cigarette, a cocktail, a good meal, a sound sleep. Sexual embrace with passion and without tricks. The pull of muscles when I swing this ax. A purging sweat, a bath, a good book. A good talk with a person who can really think above the level of his prejudices. Darling, what is the world doing out there now?"

"Loving and lying and plotting."

"Hoover and Roosevelt are flattering prejudices to get votes."

"And the Prince of Wales won't marry."

"MacDonald has sold labor to the Tories. France is wondering who her next allies will be."

"Mussolini is thumping his chest and looking fierce. He wants more land for his Italian madonnas."

"For their kids. He's an incredible hunk of stupidity. And bankers are wondering if human credulity has reached its limit."

"And some editor right now is rejecting the poem I sent out."

"And other editors are hungrily reading a sex-story and then rejecting it. Good Lord!"

"Oh, well. A lot of wives are wondering why their husbands are called out of town so often."

"And every man thinks he's the greatest lover in the world."

"And every woman, when she looks at another wife, wonders why the man married her."

"The husband probably wonders, too. Mooney is still in jail."

"And does Rockefeller still give dimes?"

"Nickels during the depression. College presidents with another season about to open are dressing up the old platitudes. Down South a Negro is lynched."

"And the crooners croon. Women are still titillated by something that sounds like a child moaning."

"An engineer, a doctor, an aviator, a swimmer are in one photograph, swearing that Camels don't bother their nerves."

"On the next page a society matron says Chesterfields satisfy."

"On the next an opera singer says Old Golds protect her throat."

"On the next a doctor says an amazing discovery has been made in regard to yeast."

"On the next a bride and bridegroom have discovered Ex-lax."

"Professor Palmer of the University of Chicago says it is

all right to sell a two-thousand-dollar car for three thousand. The other thousand is subjective value."

"And Dr. Laird of Colgate says cornflakes induce six per cent more sleep."

"And Dr. Bogen of the University of Cincinnati says to smoke a cigarette only halfway down."

"And Professor Hart of a theological seminary says Jesus discouraged demands for justice.'"

"And Professor Bogert of Columbia says delicate perfumes are very important in helping to sell a high-priced automobile."

"Oh, well: Johns Hopkins has a Fleischmann fellowship."

"And Princeton has a Du Pont de Nemours fellowship."

"And the University of Chicago has a Corn Industries fellowship."

"And Ellsworth Vines recommends Camels but tells the boy scouts he doesn't smoke."

"Ginger Rogers uses Lux."

"Claudette Colbert eats bread three times a day."

"Mrs. Victor du Pont III uses Pond's."

"And Mrs. Reginald Vanderbilt, too."

"And Mrs. Howard Chandler Christy uses Cutex."

"And Mrs. Franklin Roosevelt sells a testimonial for furniture."

"And then, my dear: 'With what pride he remembers that he did all that love could do, gave to love the best to be given, insured it against time and oblivion.' Down below: Argonaut Grave Vaults."

"But civilization is a glorious thing."

"In Yale."

"Oh, in New York City."

"In Chicago."

"In Antelope."

"Around the world and back again. Darling," Vridar said, "we are at too low a level. There is more than prostitution. We don't see far enough. Let's climb."

They entered the north and climbed to a high peak and looked around them; they could now see a great pile of mountains and canyons on all sides, with far blue valleys beyond.

"And how far do we see now?"

"Much farther. Clear beyond radio and perjury."

"Beyond the lynching."

"Beyond Pond's cream."

"Back of us and ahead. Let's look to the rear first: back there, down that dark corridor of innumerable centuries: to the steaming fog, the heat, the rolling molten mass out of chaos: and then, something beginning to stir, a force, an awakening—far back there, infinitely farther than records go: in that slow crawl of a beginning: a coming into life but not yet into meaning: something obscurely reaching this way and up and beyond: the faintest outline of a notion, a wish—and then, after the hundreds of millions of years of patience, of blind dark effort: life now building on death and going a little, an immeasurable little, beyond the level of the last death: a vague intimation that grows: a slight but imperishable part of every record now, transmitted, carried to the next level—and far ahead, against that black backdrop of the future, something like a candle in the sky. What an infinite record of agony and blood! What worlds buried in the birth of a world!

"But out of that chrysalis of fog and heat and brutal stupidity, consciousness is slowly coming into form and meaning: the dim soul of an incalculable background of time and death—and the thing that swam and then crawled now walks; lives and dies and lives through eons; and now goes upright through the jungle: there, the first terrible image of man, the savage, the beast: that dim, that groping, realization against the meaningless eternities: your ancestor and mine—upright at last, looking out of that tiny dark kingdom of its mind—that lone record, that summary, all that has been won from the uncounted ages of struggle, of courage, of death. And then——

"Fear now comes to that dim consciousness, is the dark god of that savage breast: fear had always been but this is more awful: it invents superstitions to make it less terrible to bear: gods now come, and devils; confusions and persecutions and spiritual manias, taboos and totems, black religious awakenings: torture in the name of right, murder in the name of good. But, darling, what a tremendous picture there, back in that jungle: that magnificent figure emerging from that long pilgrimage, beginning in the ancient cradle of the sea: your ancestor and mine, long long ago, now building a fire, now kneeling with its savage face turned upward in prayer: splendid vision of the forward march, the undefeatable hope: something that has come out of darkness and into the sun: unreasoning, groping, blundering, murdering, but directed somehow by an intuitive force within: call it god: it does not matter, for it has come down those millions of years: an impulse as imperishable as the tides and as eternal as the path it travels: our heritage, to respect, to love, to look back upon with awe.

"And now see: with what patient and tireless effort, with what pain and confusion, it comes slowly forward, striving to make beauty its kingdom, to record its dreams in art. But see too how it comes, bringing the whole infinite past with it: its mind a record, darkly and deeply buried, of all that has been: in its heart all that is primitive, back to the farthest reach: its kingdoms now wrought in its image, its weird and savage monuments to its weird and savage gods; but always pushing forward and upward, building its empires of confusion, struggling to forget. And what a pity! Darling, what a pity that it should try to forget, should want to forget, that exodus out of darkness toward the sun! As long as we live, let us hold all that in memory, our anchor and discipline and strength.

"And now, around us everywhere, a mighty race of

beings, only recently delivered from that dim dead eternity of time: with a little love in their hearts, a little wish for fellowship and peace: but under it all the savage, the power, the primitive and undisciplined force trying to come into its kingdom; but lost still, with only the faintest of light; shrouded still in all the mists and superstitions, all the fears and cunning and false ideals; and remembering, too, but darkly, and trying to deny memory: lost now and bewildered, and piling confusion upon confusion, meanness upon meanness: not needing more courage, for of courage they have more than enough: needing a sharp recognition of how they have come to be, and from what, and of how much of what they have been still lives within them; needing not denial of the animal, but pride in its magnificent pilgrimage: needing humility and understanding in this, another supreme crisis: needing to know, above all, that in the vast reaches behind them they have abandoned old kingdoms to enter new ones, always moving forward, never content; seeking always a new and better frontier; and needing to know that they are burying themselves now under what they have outlived and outworn. . . .

"And ahead of them? Who dares guess. Another great war; and perhaps still another; and then, weary of dodging, weary of evading the manner in which the dark and ancient still guides and moves them, perhaps they will turn, a humanity meeting itself face to face in its greatest crisis. Or is that long struggle to rest at last within the orbit of an evasive and self-pitying consciousness, dissipate itself in empty patterns, return to the dark? Is there to be only silence and graveyards after those millions of years of effort? I like to believe that somewhere, sometime, this great race of ours, this savage and animal kingdom with its splendid heritage, will travel by one star and one meaning: an enthusiasm for emotional honesty as its mode of life, its standard of men. When and if that time comes—and it is my belief——"

"—and my belief."

"—that it will come—then what a civilized empire humanity will build! But now, remembering out of what we have come, and looking out to that low level of the present, with its graft and perjury and greed, what can one do, darling, except to bow his head in shame and grief? . . .

"And yet, in single instances I read faith in the group. If we learn to perceive how our heritage directs us; if, rising above cynicism, we know that despair is traitorous and stupid; if, with our self-pity rebuked, we learn to love life simply and fully, with neither self-contempt nor self-glorification; and if the time comes when, unafraid of truth, we learn that it is our only friend—that, my dear, is the vision we've been fighting for. When we look back upon that long lone way of darkness, upon that magnificent heritage and birthright of our race, then we feel the humility, the awe, the pride in which is to be found our noble and mighty strength. In all that lies our certain knowledge that no villain need be. Out of all that, once we sense it deeply, will come a splendid fellowship, and fellowship when it comes will be enough. . . ."